DREAMLAND COURT

Dreamland Court

Paperback ISBN 978-1-947951-48-8
eBook ISBN 978-1-947951-49-5

Portions of *DREAMLAND COURT* have previously been published in THE CHICAGO REVIEW; ZYZZVA; BEZOAR; THE POETRY PROJECT, ATTABOY; and BLUE PRESS.

Printed in the United States of America.

Published by
City Point Press
PO Box 2063
Westport CT 06880
(203) 571-0781
www.citypointpress.com

Books by Dale Herd

Early Morning Wind
Diamonds
Wild Cherries
Empty Pockets: ***New and Selected Stories***

DREAMLAND COURT

A novel by **Dale Herd**

The characters and events portrayed in this book are fictitious. Any similarities to real persons, living or dead, is purely coincidental and not intended by the author.

IN GRATITUDE
Wynston Jones, Barry Hall, Dick Spray, Robert Creeley, Bobby Louise Hawkins, Lewis MacAdams, Larry Fagin, Ed Dorn, Tom Raworth, Fielding Dawson, Louis Warsh, Geno Conahan, Frank Holmes, Richard Gates, Michael Lally, Marjan Peters, Sara Houston Culver, Jim Hartz, Neal Brown, Barbara Wright, Gordon Craig, William Petersen and Penelope Milford for their contribution to the work.

A SPECIAL THANKS TO
Stephen Emerson for his superb editorial skills; Oscar Aguirre, Mary Ann Abramowitz, Ted Pearson, and Kevin Opstedal for their careful textual reading of the manuscript; Michael Wolfe for his always helpful advice and unwavering support. The book would not have come into existence without the imaginative thought and graphic skill of Hans van der Kooi. And to David Wilk who had the courage to publish the work.

This work is dedicated to the memory of

DONALD ALLEN
and
RICHARD FAYE HERD, JR.

TABLE OF CONTENTS

Chapter

Chapter

“She can look up as long as you can look down,
'cause she’s a truckin’ little woman, don’t you know...”

– Big Bill Broonzy
“Trucking Little Woman”

“She’ll do me, she’ll do you,
She’s got that kind of lovin’...”

– Irving Mills & Cliff Friend
“Lovesick Blues”
as performed by Hank Williams

DREAMLAND COURT

BLUE SHEET: DALTON, JOHN RANDOLPH

HT: 6' 3–1/2 WT: 236 SEX: M HAIR: BRN EYES: BLU

DOB: 08-06-59 CAL: RO44240296

COMMENTS

3rd incarceration in past 3 years. Knows routines, regulations. Approved for general population, exercise yards. Seems pleased, happy with self. Asked how he's been getting along, stated: "Can't complain; in or out, it's been a good time to sort out a lot of stuff, either through correspondence with friends and family, including wife, mother-in-law, and children, or by reading, ignored during my last go at civilian life." Said the main problem, not only for himself, but for others, was duration of hot water during shower time, that it was obvious the central water heater was clogged with rust as when you first turned the taps on the water poured out brown before running clean, and then the heat only lasted, at best, a couple of minutes. Asked for psychiatric counseling, enrollment forms for a preveterinary studies correspondence course from U. C. Davis. Both approved, pending initial 90-day review. Shower complaint has been forwarded to the Maintenance Dept. Request for Work Furlough Program backed by confirmation from owner of Bump & Shine Auto Body in Ventura, Ca. Address, phone number on file.

BOOK ONE **FALL**

JACKIE

I came, he came, it came, we both came, everything came, the whole car came, the whole car was surrounded by our come and I was so happy and so glad to be part of this boy who had given me this, it seemed to come from some kind of magic between us, it never mattered where we were, or what position we were in, it happened each time, every time, each time all the time, and I was always ready, so ready if I kicked my panties off, kicked them high enough, they'd stick to the ceiling they'd be so wet, and then I was pregnant and I think really happy about it, but mostly felt sick all the time so I really wasn't happy about anything, I really wasn't, but it was really nice to have it out of my belly, though, and in my arms. I had two labors, two, one kind of easy, the second really hard, it went really hard into my hips and my back, my kidneys, and lower back, and I didn't like it, not one bit, and decided if I was going to have it, to really have it, you know, so I just went right down into it and went to work. This went on and on for the longest time, but what happened next was just fantastic, it really was. John had just gotten to the hospital. They let him in to see me, see, and he walked in and I said, 'Hi,' and he said, 'HI,' and that was the next push and it crowned, that's when it crowned. We both wanted a boy, I wanted a boy, but when we saw her, she was this perfectly blue, all blue, blue little baby girl, she looked just like a little old man, my heart just melted...

CHAPTER 1

BACK ON THE VENTURA FREEWAY

JOHNNY

I'd just got off the Hound there, the main terminal, right, 'n I'm walking out the big glass doors 'n there's this cop I know. 'Dalton,' he says, 'now what the hell are you doing?' 'Doing,' I say, 'whatta you mean? I'm just getting off the bus.' 'No, Dalton,' he says, 'not the bus. See that car over there?' 'What car?' I go. 'N he points to some car parked across the street. 'That car,' he says, 'that blue one there; now that car is hot and I'm gonna have to run you in.' 'Hell, Brownie,' I say, 'I'm just getting outa the can so why would I do a jackass thing like that?'

Well, I'm a little slow, see, real fuckin' slow, 'cause he's already been yakking into his collar mike calling a Black 'n White, an' I'm standing there twisting around with my thumb up my ass watching it roll up, rollers flashing, sirens chirping, doors opening, the whole fuckin' bit, right? But I finally get it together, I mean you got to, right? So's, 'Hey, Brownie,' I go, 'how would it be if I just turned around and got back on that Oxnard-Ventura bus right now?' 'Why sure, Dalton;' he goes, 'you do that; that'd be just the ticket...'

JACKIE

What would you do? Say your old man was gone and you found yourself with someone new. And say, without you meaning to, something good happened, something really, really good, and you really couldn't break it off, even though your old man was still your old man; what about that?

JOHNNY

Do you remember you telling me I'd made your heart so glad by giving you the most beautiful gift a man could give a woman, our beautiful baby girl, Dawnie Gwen? I love you, Jackie. I'll always love you. I want to grow old with you. You will always be beautiful to me. Can you tell me everything there is about you all over again, but slowly, ever so slowly, so very slowly so that it takes a very, very long time with your sweet smile and thoughtful ways spreading joy on me, looking me in the eye, telling me what I need to hear, making me more than I am. You know I've always said when you meet the right person you know it. I've always known it. I can still see the light in your eyes. Is it still there? Just a *little? A little little?*

TERI

John said that? Shit! She's got bruises all over her! Really! She's had to go doctoring from that, and even he couldn't believe it, the doctor, right, and wants her to press charges. Yeah, charges! Sure! On John, 'cause he shows up just outa the blue, like no one even knew he was getting out, 'n he's so ripped! I mean *like* ripped! Like new heights in the history of human fuckuppedness, 'kay? Like he doesn't have no clothes on! All's he's got is his underpants, swear to God! And her, she doesn't even care what's happened! He's thrown-up all over the back of the car, broke into it and spent the night there. Left the door open so the battery's run down and it won't start in the morning. 'So he's back;' she says, 'big fucking deal.' Well, hey, you've got to give her credit, she knows the guy, but what's she doing? I mean, so what if she seems clear about some things 'cause, shit, she'll do anything with anybody, know what I mean? I think Welfare's gonna get her kids, man, is what I think. Every time I go over there it's the same thing – the kids are out in the living room, the bedroom door's closed, the kids are tearing the living room apart, and she'll come out yelling, 'You fucking kids!' I tell her, 'Hey, Girl, what do you expect? They're just getting even with you. Spend more time with them and stop doing that crap you won't have to be yelling at them all the time.' I mean if I knew Welfare was gonna take my kids I'd go nuts. I really would. I really love kids. I love her kids. I'm always taking Dawnie over to Mom's on nights off and letting her sleep with me. She's a real cuddler, just hugs and hugs me. She's just so, so sweet, she really is, but like the other night I was over there, Jac's with this new guy we've just met, I'm out on the couch sitting with Dawnie watching cartoons 'n Little John's gone over t' Mom's, an' Jac comes out, sayin', 'Ter, you know where the Vaseline is?' 'Me?' I say. 'How the hell would I know where the Vaseline is?' 'Well,' she says, 'Car wants to, 'n it would be easier with Vas an' I'm gonna.' Well, you shoulda heard the yells. She was yelling her ass off in there. Then he comes out, right, and just splits, and she's in there calling for me. Now no way am I gonna go in there. So she starts begging me to, 'n I take Dawnie into the kitchen and get her some Kool-Aid and then go into the bedroom and Jac says, 'Look, I'm bleeding,' 'n shows me, an' I about pass out! She was really bleeding all over her butt and was crying and smiling, too, and then them kids, like Little John? The other night he got in bed with me and just started hunching. 'John-John,' I said, 'what're you doing?' 'What Mommy does,' he says. Can you believe it? Man, I don't know. I'm getting real worried about her. I don't know what she's doing. I just hope she doesn't go under 'cause she could, man, she really could, like with this Carson creep? He's always gaming on her, then doubling back 'n wanting her ass, which she always goes for, too, which is just like ol' John, too, if you ask me. The both of them, all that nice and polite stuff until you get to know them, know what I mean?

CARSON

Slow-like, you know, like really, really taking her time. So lying there, there wasn't no hurry, and she was rubbing my neck, my shoulders, my back, and I guess she was done 'cause she wasn't moving, and I looked at her over my shoulder-like, and she was sitting back on her knees looking at me, just looking, you know, and she just sat like that for some time, and it felt right, too, you know, like, uh, she was jus' seeing what was there, 'cause later, man, later, we're, uh, we're really into it, and there's this kinda break where she's up on her hands and knees, like not together, you know, 'cause we're shifting positions so's we're not touching, an' I just sit back and look at her, and we're looking at each other, her at me back over her shoulder and, man, I see it, that's when I see it, that she's just as wild as me, that she'll just get into it as far as me, and that just blows me away, it does, 'cause I'll go all the way, and looking at her I see there'll be some places she'll go first, she'll take me into, 'cause I can see that, too, man, I can, I see that in her right fucking there, and like, Jesus, I can't wait!

JACKIE

You want I should tell you? Do you? 'Cause I can't even think of going back is why. 'Cause I can't. 'Cause the only reason you go back to a person is for comfort, 'cause you know that person, 'cause maybe you don't seem to do too well without that person, 'cause maybe, well, who knows? Maybe you are right. Maybe I will...

EDDIE

Hey! Wow, man! Your timing's just unbelievable! This is just fuckin' great! Wow, put 'er there, Bro! Gimme five! This is so unbelievable! I mean I just now got over a big, big fuckin' problem 'n then here you are! Yeah! Jesus! Goddamn! Gimme a hug! Remember this ol' Jimmy? How long I been at this cocksucker, more 'n a year, right? Two years? Yeah, well, what did it, I finally put a new starter button in. Just broke down and did it. Tore the old bastard out and put in a new four-wire button. Somethin' I shoulda done a long time ago. Haven't even tried it yet, but I can just feel it. The whole frickin' attitude of the truck's just changed, know what I mean? No fuckin' around; just mainline it, right? That's how to do it. Let's go inside. I wanna get this grease off my hands. I've got some hand cleaner in there. Damn, Bro, it's just great to see you, man! No shit! Well, hey, of course you can. Why the hell not? Maybe Luis, or even that ol' San Pedro crew. A few of them assholes are still gunnin' the drill...

JACKIE

Huh-uh, no way, I told him if he wanted to see the kids Mom had 'em and how come he was so hot to see them anyways 'cause he never wrote them or nothing. Yeah, over there. 'Well,' he said, he knew they sure were growing up and that was making him real sad 'cause he wasn't around much to see it, 'n what else was more important anyways? He sure bet Dawnie was a regular young lady by now, and he sure wanted to see that. Plus, 'cause

CARSON

So's, so, Big-J,' I says, 'what makes you think anything's been going down at all?' "Cause I know her, you stupid butt-hole,' he says, 'n then just looks me off, you know, like this, like turns to the side with his goddamn hand in his goddamn pocket like he's carrying, right? Like he's got a goddamn piece in there, and I fuckin'-A know the fucker's just got off the bus, no way he's got a piece in there. He's got a taped-up cardboard box under his arm that flat out marks him, man, like straight outa the slam, right? So's I laugh. That's right. I jus' laugh. 'N he stands there, his eyes getting bigger and bigger, 'n I know he's getting ready to come right on to it, so's I say, 'Hey, John, man, it's summertime, man; can't get pissed off in the summertime. Time to kick back, have a few brews, smoke a little zip. Things'll change. Can't get burned off 'bout some old shit that went down last spring, man; no point in getting all twisted off about that. All that shit's long gone, man!' And what's he do? Nothing! Just stares! 'So's,' I says, 'pull it. You got it so's you could pull it, didn't you? So do it!' But he didn't, see. It was a nothing; a goddamn slide. He ain't gonna do dick. If he was, that's when he would a' done it…

I was glad to see him! Yeah, that's right. 'Cause I was, that's why. I'm not gonna lie about it. 'Cause I'm not…

JACKIE

You wanna see a haze come over my eyes? Do you? 'Cause women always get sleepy-eyed around men they're sexually attracted to. 'Cause men do, too. They always get that same look in their eyes when they're making love to you. They do. Even you. *Definitely* you! You do, too! Look at me, Car. Com'on, I wanna see your eyes. Come on, now. Stop that sulking! You are, too! Oh yes, you are. You *definitely* are...

JACKIE

I have never met one person whose sex life is in apple pie order. Some say theirs is but they are not to be trusted. If one person could be found with a harmonious sex life, I felt if I could find that person I could begin to find out what is really going on. My goal has always been to be completely human, to do everything humans do...

JOHNNY

Well, that's probably true 'cause Eddie doesn't have any fucking friends – all's he's got is his dope. So when he starts asking about Carson, 'n what's my take on that, I think 'What's this?' 'Cause Eddie knows I won't start wolfin' on a guy jus' 'cause I don't like him. Now that's how most people are, right, but not me – so when Eddie starts in about some old bro of his, 'n how he grew up with the guy 'n how he always stood up for the guy, an' always tried to help him, and how this guy just turned around and fucked him, 'n then wants to know if Carson's, 'Well, do you trust him?' I say, 'Meaning how?' 'Business,' he says, 'when it comes to business?' Well, beautiful, right? He's just wolfed on his friend, setting it up so's I'll feel free to do one of mine, right? So I say, 'Sure,' which dodges the game. So he goes, 'Well, let's go back some. How'd you get to be friends with this Carson geek anyways?' 'Well,' I say, 'I didn't. He came up and wanted to be friends with me.' 'Okay,' Eds goes, 'look, things have changed some. I used to be a not-give-a-fuck kinda guy, which I still am, but,' he says, 'basically,' he says, 'I'm pretty conservative now, I still give, but I could give more.' 'Sure,' I go, 'that's copacetic with me,' deciding now is not the time to bring up what's owed me from before, like on the Ramon deal, for one, or on the Luis deal for another, 'n instead we make this new arrangement, a nickel on everything I do, 'n I'm back in business, and then the fucker starts telling me all about this pain he's been having in his chest, which has made him cut way back on all coke 'cept for some righteous pink flake that's been around. 'The pains are like little, tiny burns,' he says, 'or bites, like little, tiny animal bites or burns in the heart.' *'Tiny li'l animal bites*

JACKIE

No, from a fall, okay? Mai Tai's, then Old Fashioneds. A stupid tree root under the sidewalk. It'd buckled the concrete up and I tripped on the edge. 'Cause I left the car and walked on home. In the dark. From the Ban-Dar. No more stupid DUI's, right? Huh-uh, the Chevy is not here. It's not. Ter took it. This damn thing

in the heart?' I say. 'Well, Eds,' I go, 'maybe you should think about quittin' entirely, okay?'

JOHNNY

So when I finally go over there Jac says, 'Of course I remember that. Remember Dawnie, how she would say, 'Oh-e, Oh-e, Oh-e,' over an' over when she was happy? She was two years old then. 'Oh-e, Daddy!' 'Member that? When we lived by the Fair Grounds and you were working over at Anderson's Auto wrecking? You liked it down there? And we had that old blue Ford pickup you wrecked?'

JOHNNY

Jeez, Earle, still fat as ever, huh? Maybe you oughta go back to work toting them mail sacks again, ha, ha. Jus' funnin' ya, Boss. Can I borrow the wagon? You still got it, or 'd you sell it? If them freeze plugs are still out I'll get 'em fixed. Won't cost you nothin' neither, 'kay? Mom got the keys? Where is she, in the house? Don't tell her I'm here. Lemme go in and surprise her, okay? How many new cats she got in there now?

was like a baby watermelon. I'd cracked the patella. It still really hurts. Don't touch it! No, John, don't! *No!* The car is not here. I already said that! *'Go out dancing?'* Hey, I can't even *walk* yet, let alone think 'bout going out dancing!

JACKIE

You're tripping! You're totally tripping! I did not tell you to come back here! I did not! Don't give me that shit! Just go back to Irene's! I just wanna get some sleep, okay? Are you listening to me? No! Absolutely not! I did not! Who told you that? If you're gonna get sick over what you *think* I've done, you're just gonna have to get sick somewheres else! No! No! Absolutely not! There is absolutely nothing at all like that! There is no – *What! What!* Oh, for Christ sakes, John!

JOHNNY

Hand me that rubber hammer there - the big one. You heard anything about this Carson guy? Doin' with 'ol Eddie now? Yeah, little white dude; yeah, the skinny fucker, wears that big 'ol fat silver crucifix like he's in tight with the Jesus? That's the one. Got a pair 'a brothers walled up in Soledad, right? Lifers, both of 'em. Uh-huh, 'n the blue cowboy boots, right? No, nothing bad 'bout him. Jus' curious if you heard anything ...You wanna know why that weld din't hold? Overheating and dirty steel. You gotta feather that heat. Grab the Bondo tub there, 'n hold on. I'll just bust the lid off. Have to get the chisel in the slot there, see, 'n then whack the fuck outa it. Still a bunch of paste in it - more 'n enough for this, 'n then that other quarter panel on that Grand Prix. Here we go...Hold on now, 'kay?.. *JESUS!...CHRIST! OH, FUCK! Did that drive into your arm? Goddamn, Bro! Sorry 'bout that! That must hurt like a bitch!* Putting plastic lock-rings 'round these tubs is really, *really* friggin' stupid! I'd like to run into the fucker who invented 'em - drive a fuckin' chisel into *his* arm, right? You better get a rag on that. That thing's dripping like a bitch. Good thing that tub was plastic, 'n not metal, has some soft to it...

JACKIE

When I was a kid I felt the only behavior that was mine was bad behavior, my mother took credit for good behavior, but bad behavior was my behavior. Now I was usually good, but regarded my life as a sort of prison term and that when I got out of school or married or eighteen I would start my own life. I didn't nurse Dawnie. I wanted to nurse. I really did. But sometimes you can't, even if you want to, not if you're nervous. There's a reflex mechanism in your head that won't release it. I thought she was taking it. I would feel she was, but she wasn't. I felt I was squirting it out but she wasn't getting it. So I had to give her the bottle, which made Johnny mad. He said having a breast in your mouth was one of the best things in life and he wanted only the best things for his daughter and that ice cream was just a substitute for breast milk and that's why vanilla ice cream was everybody's favorite, people that had been breast-fed, that is, that people that hadn't been breast-fed had to have all those fancy ones like Cherry Jubilee or Mint Chip or Rocky Road, which were never satisfactory.

CHAPTER 2

EAST THOMPSON BLVD.

IRENE

Well, let's see. There's Gun-Gun and Leo-Peo and Margarette an' then there's Pepsi 'n Lejo, Frosty 'n Pucksters, and Skip. How many is that? Eight? Nine? That should be nine. You know, it's just awful when one of them goes. The only thought you have is go get another one, you know, one just like it, so's the others don't get lonely, but, well, there you are again. Did I say Skipper? I did, didn't I? I said Skip. And Pansy June? So there's her, 'n Rags, 'n Solly. The last two are both boy cats, they come from the same litter, real little wild cats, too. An' John? 'Well,' I said to him, 'I just called Bob Wheeler and asked if you'd really been released with no probation,' and he said, 'Not likely.' So then John says, 'Who're you gonna believe, a goddamn P.O. or your own son? Would you just give me the gall-darn keys, please?' And I said, 'Honey, now I know you think your wife's driving you crazy, but if you're feeling crazy it's because *you're* doing things that are making *you* crazy.' I told him, I said, 'That's just the way it is. That's the way it was with your dad, 'n that's the way it is for you, too. So if you really want to do something about it the first thing you need to do is to just stay away from her until you get yourself together.' Now that's exactly what I told him.

JACKIE

See these two straws, and this one, this little one here in the middle? Now that one's me, uh-huh, 'cause I've got two guys loving me, uh-huh, two, 'n they're both sayin', *'I love you,'* the both of 'em. So what can I tell you? 'Cause I love the both of 'em, uh-huh, I do. Now take this big one here? This one's my old man, see; he just got out so he's gotta be on good behavior, 'n he'll say anything to me, absolutely anything, 'n this other one here, this candy-striped one...?

JOHNNY

Baby, Baby, I know you've been with other people, but I don't believe it, that you truly have. I know you know what I mean. I just don't want you to keep on going with anyone. If I was home you wouldn't have to do that. I'm willing to let bygones be bygones. You aren't doing you or the kids or me any good by keeping me away. I'm sorry for what I've done. I don't know what you mean when you say there are *'strange energies'* around me. Now I am really sorry, but I don't want left-overs either. I don't want you saying, 'Come home,' because you're not making it off right with someone else, and I do know who it is. You know I do, no matter what kind of B. S. you've been trying to hand me. And you know me, how I am, how I never say anything and just let things go on like I'm not payin' attention but my time comes, it comes, 'n then the fangs go in, and it's, *Adios, Motherfucker!* But for now, forget that! I know I've done a lot of shit to you. I've got a lot to talk about, 'n a lot to do. And you know what I mean. Why I told you to tell me who you were with is not that I care. No. Don't get me wrong. I do care but not who it is – just that I'd always rather have you telling me the truth, and you know I've always been like that. The same way we used to lie in bed and just talk, Sweetheart – you know what

JACKIE

I didn't wanna hear that! I wanted things to be wonderful between us! I didn't want him getting sick! I told him, I said, 'All's you're doing is using this as an excuse so's you can go on out 'n get even more fucked-up; why even bother with an excuse? Just go on 'n do it!' Then he says, 'Are you kicking me out?' 'I sure am,' I said, 'n he grabbed at me and was saying, 'No, no,' all's he wanted was for me to be happy! 'Like hell,' I said, 'all's you want is for *you* to be happy!' Yeah, an' that's when he pulled this stupid gun. One second he's jumped back an's sitting down staring at me 'n biting his cuticles, the next he's got me down on the couch with this stupid little gun pointed at my stomach and he's firing! Twice, man! Two times!

I mean. It's just come down on me what I'm trying say is I just can't wait any longer. I don't wanna be turning over to any other woman. I wanna be turning over to you! But if not by Monday, then don't! I mean it! Now I'm going down south for a few days to be working on a few things and to be giving you time, but by Monday I'll be there! At the door! I can just taste you, and you know what I mean. I don't care who you've gone with. They can't do for you like I can. You know I have the real thing for you. You know you need it. If I hurt you, then that's me. If you hurt me, then that's you. But you know what it can be – like it was. I'll be coming back on Monday, like I said, but no matter what, there won't be no fighting nor leaving, not if you say. I can take what you say to me. Can you take what I say to you?

JOHNNY
Harms might call. No need to lie. Jus' tell him I've gone home sick, okay? That I'll be back on Monday. I'll be seeing some people. Yeah, limping around on one leg. Fucked up her knee, or somethin'. Tell him to come in then, see for himself he wants to. Shit, Luis, if they got it I'll get it. I already told you the stupid amount. Hey, Right here! Look here! Look at these! These are frickin' powder burns! Yeah, powder burns! You see these? You bet they hurt! Yeah, they were blanks, see, but them damn things really do hurt, lemme tell ya! It took me damn near all night just to get back to myself. I had just one thought, you know, I thought, *'This is it, this is the big one! The son of a bitch has finally gone and killed me!'*

JOANN
Dear Di, this is so crazy but at Cheryl's party there was this older guy who told me to go get him a beer and called me Pee Wee and said I reminded him of being back in Junior High and going into the girl's locker room when he wasn't supposed to and seeing a girl like me. I told him I was in High School and I hated Phys-Ed, which I do, so he never would have seen me in there! I hate school, period! He asked me to go down to Seal Beach with him! God! God! God!

tell him you'll sign the damn sheet and mail it in then. No, no, Jac was cool, for real. Oh, yeah, 'ol Miss Magic Body - that's her, all right, Yeah, I'm lucky. You betcha. Hand me the slidehammer there. You got a new pad for the dent puller? No, no, the pneumatic one, that one there. 'Cause I'm dead broke. They don't give you no mustering out pay, do they? It's not the goddamn Army, an' right now I'm broker than a dead dog's dick. Like I said, I get some, you got some, 'kay? I'll see what they got down there. That's where I'll have to go. They're ol' school Canos, jus' like you. They'll have it. No; no, Luis, let's leave Eddie out of it. I'll do this, okay? You don't know him like I do. 'Cause I've known him all my life. He's all right, he's cool, but I'll do it. Either I'll do it, or I'll turn you on to some other peeps, like righteous ones, 'kay? Listen, the P.O.'s name is Harms. That's who 'll be callin'. Yeah, right; Harms, Bill Harms. A mean little fuck. Jus' tell him I've gone home sick, the flu...

JACKIE

Even if it's someone you've known for ages, if you're new to them in a romantic way, it takes some kinda time before you even think about telling them your fears inside, right, and I guess with Car, when I saw he was actually listening, really listening, you know, which was, wow, you know, I mean that I was even thinking about risking my weaknesses. Well, so then I had to start thinking about him. I mean, Jesus, 'n so what if he wasn't my physical type of dreamboat? I mean the man was getting to me.

CARSON

Hey, don't let me influence you! Why don't you girls chew two sticks a' gum at the same time? You ever tried that? Like one Doublemint, one Spearmint? Think about it. Sure. Hey, *"Foolin' Around And Fallin' In*

JOANN

That is not a transvestite! I know what a transvestite is. How can you say that about someone? Com' on, John, don't get that way. You can not! I know you already. I do. Oh, yeah? I don't care how much older you are!

Love," man. Hey, where'd you get those great fuckin' shoes? I love those shoes! I love thin, tiny orange straps. It makes your ankles look hot! Yeah, hot! Like in locked together around my neck, ha, ha! People love to sing in bars. All by themselves. They get, look at him, the little bald guy, all by hisself, right? Yeah, him. See what I mean? What's he singing? *"Help Me Make It Through The Night?"* Ha! That's it...

I knew you before I knew you. Don't tell me you know how to watch people. Take it back. You can't even watch a whole TV show! Ha, ha, ha, ha. Sure I can. Who found the motel, you big dummy? So there! Can we go back to the L. B. Pier again Or *"Freddy Versus Jason?"* Cheryl saw it with Anthony and got so scared she threw up. Anthony had to keep telling her it was just a movie, and she threw up anyways.

TERI

Dance? You mean like bump butts with you? Ha, ha. Sure. No...gimme your hand...

JACKIE

If I put a quarter in your mouth will you dedicate a song to me? He sang, *"You Are So Beautiful To Me."* Shit, Hon, grab my bag! Let's us go! Then on to Eddie's where we was supposed to meet and then he doesn't show and was I pissed? Then he shows! Man, I stayed pissed! Ter was digging on it, too! Did we have a time? Hon, you wouldn't believe! Kick out the jams! The both of us! He took the both of us on! Little Ter-Ter, too, the Kaa-Kaa girl! Just flat-ass, plain, out n out in hcat, man! What else can I say? That I fall in love with motherfuckers? So what's your problem?

CARSON

You know what I'd like t' do, what I'd really like t' do? Run barefoot across a big ol' field of bare titties, all different kinds of 'em, big ones, little ones, round ones, hard ones, soft ones, pointy ones, feelin' 'em all squishy under my toes, 'n every time I'd stumble I could fall 'n jus' bury my face in 'em, wigglin' it back-'n-forth, goin', 'Umm,' like this... 'Um-um-um-um... um-um-um', ha,ha...

JOHNNY

Pop me another soldier there, will ya, Pee Wee? What's your favorite color? Like what you got there on your little toenails. What color is that? 'Cherry Pie Red?' Can you pull that up? Not all the way. Yeah, jus' like that. Yeah. Them 're so pretty, like li'l sweet baby cakes pretty...

TERI

The choice came down and it wasn't her, it was me, 'cause Car said I was getting the best of him, yeah, 'n he liked it, but then she offered him to me, too like, 'Do it, take him, he's yours,' like there was an ocean between us, see, 'n if I didn't take him they would drift away from me forever, so it wasn't like I was ripping on her, no matter what she thinks, 'cause if he's really the one for you, you don't give the man away no matter how hard you're partying at the time...

CARSON

Isn't that a trip? I mean the first time I did coke: Hey, Bang, Bang, I open the door. It's this Mex friend I've got, and he says, 'Hey, Bro, I can't make it to the party, but here's a little blow for you,' an' this knife blade comes up with a little white on it, right, a li'l white dust? I snoot that, the blade goes down, 'n comes back up. I snoot that, too, 'n just immediately get the burn in the back of my throat, 'n go, 'Man-oh-man-oh-man, I can't deal with this shit at all!' I've got my speed in there, right, all ready to go, I can deal with that, but this shit? Man, my tongue and the back of my throat's gone all numb! So's I walk back in and sit down in my chair, an' all I can think is I gotta get offa this stuff, man, I gotta. 'Cause speed was nothing, right? 'Cause you could mellow it out with weed, smooth it out with some weed, but I didn't have no kinda trip going with coke at all! None! Isn't that a bitch?

TERI

'Don't you *bratty* me!' That's what we'd say when we were kids, that's what we called it, *brattying* each other. 'N that's what Car wanted us to do, stick our fingers in each other, 'n some other stuff, too, gross kinda stuff. He kept after it, too, but I wouldn't, like no way, but her, man, she was all for it, don't think she wasn't...

JOANN
Could you please maybe with sugar on top not call me Pee Wee, but something more cuddly, like Baby, or Panda, maybe?

BUD

Even when I was a little baby my mother never liked to hold me, she would never rock me. Now I don't know why that is and I don't want to know. All I know is I spent more time over at my Aunt Flo's house than I did at my own. Now in high school I loved a girl. She was my true love, a brown-eyed blonde. I've longed for her all my life. We were in love and then your granddad moved us away and I couldn't see her. I wrote her for a time, and then I met your mother. Now she was just as pretty as anyone could be, and I didn't know bad about her. She loved me, see, and then you was born and Jill was and it all went by with you growing up and Jill growing up and then your Mom and me had our troubles and I finally got my chance to go back and see my real girl. She'd married a guy, and then another guy and had two girls of her own and it hadn't worked out for her neither, see, and seeing her, the damnedest thing was getting that same old feeling in the gut, that same old sudden sinking twist in the gut that I'd always got whenever I saw her, and then driving back home I stopped off to see Flo, and talking with her, I was looking at her, see, and suddenly realized it'd been her all the time, it was her, Flo, Flo was my first brown-eyed blonde, see, the one who'd loved me as a little boy, my first real love, and then I knew where my strongest feeling for anyone came from, that my first girl had been my Flo for me, and why had I ever let her go? Something I regret to this day. So what I'm saying to you, if you ever find one you really love, don't, for Christ sakes, ever let her go 'cause it don't come around like that but once in your whole goddamned miserable life.

CHAPTER 3

SIMI VALLEY AUTO WRECKING

JOHNNY

One of the best times I ever had, one of the very best, and this is something even my own people don't understand, was like when I broke into this wrecking yard. Now I knew there was this big German Shepherd in there, see, a great big German Shepherd. I'd seen him, see, and I had me a baseball bat, a sawed-off baseball bat. Now I was really hoping he wouldn't see me, a big junkyard Shepherd, right, you know what those damn things are like, but as soon as I dropped in I knew I would, I could sense it, and it was dark as hell in there, too, 'n I didn't know where the fuck he was, you know what I mean? I mean I was barely moving. I mean I was so uptight that when I did move, like take the first little step away from the fence, the next thing was I'd jumped 'cause I couldn't even tell it was me that was moving, now that's how tight, and I'd taken me about three of them little jumps, just about three, man, when I heard him! Man, I couldn't believe it! It was just incredible! Really incredible! The son of a bitch was *whimpering*! That's right, just *whimpering*! He was lying way off hid under some junker somewhere in the far corner of the yard just *whimpering*! Now that really got me off! Now that was really a good time!

JACKIE

I walked into the Ban-Dar 'cause I knew Car was drinking in there and I walked right by him. I didn't even look at him and went on into the Ladies and when I came out he turned around and said, 'Well?' '*Well?*' I said. 'Is that all you got to say? You know what your problem is? Your problem is your ego's bigger than your cock.' Well, you shoulda heard the people laugh, and he laughed as loud as anyone. That's when he got up and followed me down the hall, out past all the stacks of empties. That place always reminds me of Dad, doesn't it? The smell of it? Anyways, so I says to him, I said, 'So when you're married you can't fool around, can you, but if you're separated? If you're separated it's, "Let's get it on, right?" Is that how you see it?' 'N he goes, 'Well, I hear you've got a vibrator, too.' Right, 'a *vibrator.*' 'N I said, 'Now where'd you hear that? Now maybe if I was a rug muncher, a carpet scrubber, I'd have even more fun, right? A scrubber, man, but I'm not.' Then I ask if he's ever seen two chicks together on one vibrator, ha, ha, ha. 'N he goes, 'Oh yeah? Are you for real?'

JOHNNY

Hell, no, that's total bullshit, total fuckin' bullshit, 'n that's all the fuck this is, just more a' the same. He's got no use for the woman. If he's after Jac, that's just to get me. He's just playing her, see. That's just the way the punk thinks. 'Cause even if he was to get somewheres he couldn't keep her, see, 'cause it's not about her, it's just about him, 'n seeing how many women he can get, that he can get more women than me. He hasn't got no babies out there. He doesn't know what a woman's all about. 'N all I can say is I now have every confidence in the universe because she'll finally see right through that B.S. because it ultimately doesn't matter what one does 'cause there's a real lesson in everything you do, even if you don't know it at the time!

JOANN

Now I didn't say anything. There was nothing to say. I just smiled and he put his arms underneath me, pulled back the covers 'n we got into bed. It was so sweet; so, so sweet. God, it was sweet. 'Do that again,' I said. 'Make that feeling come back again and again...'

JOHNNY

Coming back from Long Beach Jo asks me this question. She asks if I was to be reborn and had a choice, would I want to come back as a man or a woman? I tell her as a man. 'I knew you'd say that,' she says, 'n kisses me, then says, 'Thank you, Honey.' Now that was great, 'cause up till then I hadn't even thought of her as a person to get involved with, you know. So I guess that's how that happened. And she was not seventeen, like she said, but sixteen, or maybe even fifteen. 'N I liked it. An' looking at her sitting over there with the wind blowing her tight little curly hair, 'n her tight little red shorts, 'n her red-tipped, little tippy toes up on the dash?

JACKIE

I fight it, I do, but the minute I saw him I knew we were gonna be involved. There was all this energy between us. I wanted to scratch his eyes out. I knew the kind of dude he was, that he would hurt me if I let him, but that was the kind of dude I wanted. Hey, I still watch the streets. He's still out there scratching in the streets. I still look at the scratch in the streets. And he knows it, too. He knows it, and he knows me. He knows he's not gonna mold me how he wants me. Not this time. Not this man. And that's why he loves me. He does. He sees the kind of woman I am. He loves me and he hates me, 'cause I play all his dirty little games with him and I don't give in. I won't give in. And I love him, too, but hate is stronger than love 'cause hate thinks. I said to him, I told him, I said, 'I know you're gonna try 'n hurt me; you've got no choice 'cause I'm stronger than you.' 'Cause he's a man, see; he won't take no back talk from no one. He can't believe it, that I talk back to him. He can't stand it, which I gotta say I love, to see him get all bent outa shape like that; it drives him crazy...

JOHNNY

Our first real time to party down together, 'n I got a taste, bad Mexican brown. All I did was puke. Saw myself for the miserable puke dog I was. Made the deal anyways, sixteen Franklins for every pound. Called Eddie from the motel and told him they agreed. Kept thinking about Mom saying I shouldn't be talking about taking Dawnie away from Jac, that it scared her. It was all I could do to get Jo to go over to the corner mercado to get me some Alka-Seltzer 'n raw garlic for my hangover, 'n she says, 'Look, it's not like I'm trying to get into your business, but I thought you said you wasn't into dope no more.' I said, 'This isn't dope; it's money.' Then on the way out to do the delivery, I said, 'You're right, Jo, this's fucked.' 'Cause I'd just told myself I've got to stop thinking an' let things happen on their own 'cause I'm really starting to super dig on Jo now, 'n right then I get this feeling of Jackie being there, like watching us, you know, an' I started to get real upset 'n couldn't even talk about nothing, and Jo said, 'I'm glad you see that.'

JOHNNY

Just like Eddie said; right on the dot: six o'clock sharp. Cool dressers in the old veterano homie style: creased slacks, white dress shirts with the collar button buttoned, greased-back hair, two with hairnets. Snorted the shit off the washer lid. Probably took a hit of Tide, ha, ha, which'd get anybody sick.

JACKIE

Car fulfilled me! Loved it! SEX with all the flashing lights! 'Are you a big strong man?' I said. 'You're the best,' I said, 'and the lewdest! You've ruined me! God, you're a fantasy come true!' He suggested we should be engaged! 'I'm not even divorced,' I said. 'You know that!' But he didn't care. He's so mature. He really knows me, knows what I want to hear, because he really does understand my feelings, that what happened wasn't anything, just all the coke an' stuff, that it was me he kept feeling himself pulled to. I told him how sad I was, and he said a true relationship wasn't based on the bedrock of sorrow that everyone has, that he was always unhappy inside, too, but always tried to do something about it and not let it get the best of him. Said everytime he found out he was unhappy he knew he was wrong, 'n not to try and put the blame somewhere else, that it was up to him to change things so that it went away, that happiness was first of all based on good friendship, and that it was even more important to him that we were deep and good friends first, and that there didn't even have to be sex between us...

JOHNNY

Some Coors and a coupla them canned Club Margaritas, okay? What else? No, make it three of 'em; yeah, three of 'em.

JOHNNY

Oh, my God, Jackie, my crisis with you has passed in the most unbelievable way! I wish I had words to tell you. All I can say is it was the most profound moment of my life. Can you understand? I know just coming back here, full of hope 'n that, that I thought it would be real easy without realizing things must've happened to you, too, while I was away doing my bit. I wasn't being very realistic, was I? I hope you can understand me, what I'm saying. I now feel that all the trouble we've had in the past was coming from me. I don't wanna say what's happened to me. All's I'll say is I was down on my knees in some lavanderia in a puddle of puke. All's I'll say is I said to myself, "What the fuck are you doing? What the hell have you been telling yourself every night for the past three and a half months and every morning an' every day all day? Haven't you learned nothing?" All I'll say is I now know what I'm doing. I mean this, and about time. The main thing I wanna say is I now have a clear understanding of who I am and where I'm going. I know you, too, and how, deep down, you really are. And Dawnie and I will do right together, and in time, with time, John-John, too. Know that. I am now clear about us having other children and feel it is time to have them. I genuinely have a plan for all our growth and happiness. It genuinely doesn't make any difference whether you sleep or have slept or will sleep with someone else or not. I imagined myself in your situation and saw I would've done the same. Again, I'm a different person than I was when you last saw me. I keep saying that, don't I? Well, it's true. So I do say it. I'm just not as uptight as I was

JACKIE

I sure wish you'd get here. I told Ter if someone doesn't come over here P.D.Q. and rip my panties off I don't know what I'm gonna do, ha, ha, ha...

JOANN

Now I can't get upset by your being truthful. I love the truth. Do you remember me telling you more definite things I love before. That's a stance for men who don't live in this world. And I do know what's been going down, but if you decide to keep on Car, or whatever, okay, that's up to you. I won't bug you again unless you say. And don't worry about me. Just do what you have to do. But it goes without saying, for both yours and mine and the kids' sake, that you'll say what I'm hoping you'll say.

are bracelets and necklaces and Pandas? Do you remember me telling you in a friend I would want him or her to be trustworthy, loving and caring? Do you remember I told you, 'Yes, there is someone I trust as much as myself – Cheryl Beth, and she gained my trust by keeping my deepest secret a secret and never told anyone?' I also told you one thing you don't have to worry about is hurting my feelings. If my feelings are hurt I will usually hide it and forgive and forget. And if I don't, I'm usually sorry afterward. You haven't told me much about yourself and I want to know more, like where you really live, and how old you really are? And I never actually look for a friend. I always just sort of bump into them and we become good friends. And I dislike a person who lies, and to get accepted by a friend I would just act like myself, and if he or she doesn't like it we shouldn't have been friends to begin with. I feel with you we can be friends, or even more than friends...

JOHNNY

'We're the people who're here to help other people party, Bro.' That's what they said, and this Bernardo fuck, he's screaming, 'I'll throw your ass outa here; I'll throw you right in the face with a fuckin' razorblade, motherfucker! Screaming like a fag with lighter fluid litup his highway, 'n it's like I'm back in the can, you know, doing kitchen work, an' some black dude walks by 'n says, 'Ooops!' An' your stomach turns 'cause that's what they say just before they shank you, see: 'Ooops!' So that's what's happening here, 'n my stomach's slidin' down to my ass, then these four other

JACKIE

Jesus, John! You've gotta be kidding! Like I don't have

dudes come in in them hooded sweatshirts with them drawstrings pulled tight, so's all you see are eyeballs 'n mustaches, each of 'em carrying these pistol-gripped sawed-offs. Now how am I gonna call Eds, 'n tell him I got taken down by six pug-ugly jungle bunnies outa Eastside Long Beach somewhere that knew exactly when I'd be pulling up 'n parking at this fuckin' Beaner's digs? 'N I'm lookin' at this Nardo fuck then, thinking, *You rotten pendejo!* Knowing he's totally in on it, the whole thing's a frickin' bag job from the get-go, 'n Shotgun Number One pushes me down on the floor, then puts a pillow over the back of my head, 'n now I'm thinking, *This is gonna be bad, real bad; please, please, please, dear God, lemme outa this one, please dear God!* An' Jo's out in the car honking on the goddamn horn, thinking I'm taking too long!

any mind of my own? Well, I don't care what you heard! No, I don't! No! 'Cause half of its so's you can get yourself excited! The hell I don't! You don't hear what other people are saying! You don't! You only hear what you want to hear! I've lived with you, for God's sakes! 'Cause it excites you is why! You've always been like that. What should I tell you, that I was spitting on his cock, for Christ's sakes, or that I had it in my mouth? Is that what you wanna hear?

KAREN WONG, AFDC

Her husband, John R. Dalton, 29, Mrs. Dalton states, is back in town, but with no current address, although Mr. Dalton's parole officer would, in all likelihood, have such an address if one exists. At this time, Mrs. Dalton, further states, there exists no possibility of a reconciliation unless Mr. Dalton is willing to settle down in a steady job, either here in town near her family or over in Arizona out of the smog. Mr. Dalton, when she does see him, is usually stoned, or 'high,' as she puts it, but will tell her his feelings inside when he is, how he really feels about things, a change from his past behavior, which, in her words: 'He never did other times unless he was mad about something, like finding the lid of the salad dressing left off, for instance; you could get food poisoning that way,' adding that not that she herself didn't know what to do, stating as a child she had always watched what her mother had done, but had had rheumatic fever then and was always babied, and guessed she naturally expected the same from him, to be babied, that is, which was, she continued, one of the things Mr. Dalton always said he was mad about when he said anything at all.

CHAPTER 4

DRIFTWOOD LANE

JOANN

Dear Di, seeing this new guy whose looks are soooo fine!!!! Yum!! He's an older guy, but likes me!! Said I was pretty and told me my face was like a flower. Other mushy stuff, but I liked it. We went to Long Beach! My first time! I told Mom Cheryl and me were going to her Grandma's house for the weekend and she let me go! I couldn't believe it! I called her from the road and told her we were swimming and eating out, which was true, I just didn't say where. I don't like lying, though, it makes me feel bad. We stayed in a big motel that had a pool with Jacuzzi and ice machines which was just great and went out on the old pier and bought a picture of a PANDA standing on his head and a little red heart painted on his chest. Then one out on Ball Road by the racetrack in Los Alamitos which he called Death Motel because he said he almost died there once doing some business and also he got sick after he was gone all afternoon but everything else was good. He's very different from everyone else I know and won't tell me anything about himself. He said he was in jail once and has friends that have killed people. And won't tell me how old he is. Says he won't tell me until he knows I'm crazy about him, but I think around 22. He's a man and I like that. He's probably too old for me, but said he's never met anyone like me. He spent a lot of money on me. He said he thought I was the kind of person he thought he could really love. He said, "Not just be in love with, but LOVE!!!"

CARSON

Here, here, I'm gonna take this hit, man,'n when I give it to you I wanna see if you get the same rush off it I get. Here, oh yeah, wow, they're wild chicks, man. I told them, I said, 'Yeah, you're my kind of people.' Listen, I was so fucked-up, I took, I took about five different kinds of reds, man, five. I couldn't even stand I was so fucked-up! Fuck it, you know I had a good time, man.

In Long Beach people don't get as high as they do up here. They don't. And they'll pay more, too. Hey, straighten me out 'n I'll be a rock star, man! A major motherfuckin' rock star! Yeah, yes! That's what she said, 'Get a band, practice, sing in that voice. That guy's voice makes me cream!' Meaning *my* voice! That's it, a singer! A Jagger, or a George Michael, or someone older, man, like a Joe Cocker, someone dirty-voiced like that, right? What was it you said? 'You can't even get a hard-on, man?' Yeah. Wow! Hey, that's true. I'll cop to it! No shit. I couldn't even stand up, let alone get my dick up! Ha, ha, ha. I couldn't! Had both these cuties in my arms, too. A chick sandwich, man, ha, ha. Yeah. Yeah! You bet'cha! That's what it was.

JACKIE

Listen, Car, I know I said 'I love you' and I know 'I love you' is such a simple thing to say to sum up so many emotions it hardly touches on what's really happening. I just wish there weren't all these other problems right now, but if we want to, there's nothing that can't be overcome. I just want everything right out front, and if you care about me as much as I think you do I hope you'll accept my feelings, and if not, well, at least once in my life I'll know what it is like to be totally ready to give myself completely, as well as be ready to accept another person's love, perfections, and faults.

JOHNNY

Another time I was there with my lawyer, this little stiffass bitch from the Public Defender's Office, 'n she says, 'Well, you've got to go through the process and I'll bail you out at the other end.' Now I know they're gonna clean me down, do the DDT number, give me the fuckin' jumpsuit, 'n all that, so I get my hand in my pocket and cup these caps, these're four humungous ups, right? Like industrial strength motherfuckers for shipyard welders 'n truckers, right? And I know I can't throw them anywhere, so while this one turkey is questioning me before we go downstairs, I fake a yawn 'n pop 'em in. Christ, I'm buzzin' around in there like a fly with a wire up his A-hole before the fuckin' P.D. gets me out 'n drives me home. Now she knows something's wrong, an' asks me. I tell her it's nothing, jus' nervous tension 'n hassle. 'N then she asks me if I can score her any toot, okay? If I can she'll make it clear to the court that these outstanding traffic warrants are my old lady's, 'n not mine. Now that was a real mistake, saying no to that bitch!

TERI

Well, I can't help it if I'm as attractive as Jac, or even more attractive, as well as not having kids, which most guys don't want anything to do with. She forgets that. She always blames me, like I want things like this to happen, that some of her men really do come on to me…

CARSON

Down, yeah, your tongue there, yeah, the clit, her clit. Yeah, yes, now lower, yeah, 'n there, right there, 'n slower, yes, slow... oh, Christ... that's...so... *oh… fuck… fuck…* 'n up here! Here! Here! Here! Up... *oh, oh... oh...*

JOHNNY

Let me tell you something. No way have I ever walked out on a woman I was serious about. The only time I ever did was a big misrepresentation, and I had no choice with her telling me if I didn't get off my ass and get a real job she was gonna totally kick me out of the house an' that kinda shit. Now I didn't mind that, 'cause she's right about that, but she called me out in front of a buncha people, see, a big, big mistake, 'cause I was gone, just like that. And it hurt me, too. It did. I was cryin' when I left. I said, 'Goodbye,' walked out the door, hung my shirts all in a row on a wire strung 'cross the back, then took myself a nice long drive back in the mountains. Took a coupla downs, just drivin' around all night mellowing out, then about six in the morning coming back into town I hit onto the highway where there was this kinda on-ramp, off-ramp trip

JACKIE

Then I hate him and hate her and despise them and how they are and I think about her and want to tear the jealousy out of her, then think, *What are you doing? Don't you have better things to do? Like just to stay home and get high and have a good time without thinking about fixing anybody else's fucked-up bullshit?*

going on, I don't know, they were doing all this reconstruction on the road there after the flood, 'member, when all them houses and house trailers 'n cars got swept away, and there wasn't no sign? So anyways, somehow I didn't make the turn, 'n did this sorta bumpin', bunny-hop-skidding kinda thing. 'N blam! Right into this power pole. Sheered the sucker right off, the whole top half dangling down from the wires, 'n did one of them engine-coming-back-in-your lap numbers, just totaled that fucker, twenty-four hundred bucks worth. Broke a fingernail getting out 'n that was all. There was this big rig stopped, 'cause of the power lines down on the ground, an' some guy watching me lose it lost it and went off the embankment and rolled three times, which I never even saw. That's what the cops told me when they came 'n I was just as calm as could be, too. Just this amazing fucking scene, right? So at the station I called Jac and said, 'I got in a wreck and the pickup's totaled.' An' you know what she said? She goes, 'You wrecked my truck?' That's it! That's all. Nothing like, 'Are you hurt? Are you okay?' Just, 'You wrecked my truck?!' I hung up on her. I told that to the cop, too, what she said. I said to him, 'It's goodbye to that bitch!'

JACKIE

John, John, okay, okay, I did not ask you to come over here! That is not being a gentleman at all! It is not! Will you listen to me? Will you? Five minutes? Two minutes? Hey, fuckin' calm down! No, I am not! You're all hyped-up yourself. You can't even laugh, can you? No. I always thought you could. Now it's no sense of humor. No, I mean, hey, what can I say that's right? You're going peacefully, right? Now listen, all I want is…NO! *You came back!* What the hell did you come back for? Don't lay that shit on me! I'm not gonna listen to that! I'm calling the cops! The hell I won't! I sure as hell will! I will, too! I'll call a twenty-four hour watch…!

JOHNNY

Number one: don't be paranoid – just flow with the now. Number two: don't wish for things. Wishing means you are not this, not that – which is all a weakness. Everything I am right now is all I need to be.

Talked with Jac-Jac again. Said I had little choice in what we were doing because we were one person for all time, for all forever. Told her she'd get a new truck, plus a real wedding ring like she'd always wanted, that Eddie'd see me to a stake and could start a great weed business of our own renting a big house with rooms for the kids, including big double garage to seal, insulate, and hang grow lights. Each harvest 'd yield fifty pounds minimum, and would get a regular job, too. Didn't go over so well. Said I was always making promises like that, and, realistically, how could I take care of her, or the kids, when I wasn't even doing such a good job taking care of myself? That got me to laugh, her talking so soft like that. 'Listen,' I said, 'you know when you first get out you've got it in your head you're gonna be so damn good to people, there's so many things you gotta make make up for, so maybe I'm just trying too hard 'cause maybe other people, they just can't see it, they think it's all too weird, the way I'm coming on, that I'm loving them so much, so they like drive me away. You ever thought of that?' Which made some headway. 'Cause she said, 'Maybe.' Then I told her I'd rather die than live without her. She didn't say nothing, then said, 'That's because I sleep like a flower.' I said, 'Yeah, like a night flower that opens up in the dark.' To me, see, that's what happens. Like when under the covers she rubs her foot on my leg, you know, the arch of her foot, 'n we're rockin' back 'n forth without me really trying nothing, 'n she begins to begin things, you know. Shit! Now I don't know if that's how it is for other people, but afterwards, you know, like say in the morning when I gotta

JACKIE

Children are not strange to me. Until you have them you don't understand what is really going on in life. Of course you worry that something will happen, that someone or something will try to take them from you. This is a feeling you always have, a feeling that comes up in your mind all on its own, a feeling you'll have all the rest of your life.

TERI

...plus John's got a new girl he's not telling anyone about, 'cause

go out 'n do what I gotta do, well, it don't matter one great big goddamn what's out there to deal with, you understand, 'cause it *all* can be dealt with...

we saw them, even though Jac's saying he's still begging her to let him come back, which I know she won't do even if he's got no place else to go, an' plus I know John, too, he's done this number before, like when I saw that girl, she looks like she's barely even a teenager yet, if you can believe that! An' what's he gonna do, crash at her mom's house if Jac doesn't take him back? Yeah, an' this one's got some real big boobs, too, not like that other one that was so skinny. 'Member her? What was her name? Angie something? She always had that dirty hair? How'd you describe her: 'Doughnut knees 'n piglet toes?'

CARSON

Jac's just a total trip, man, just totally. She's got a whole 'nother type a' nervous system than anyone else walking. That's why her tolerance is so high. She can do more coke than anyone, man, I mean *anyone*, even more 'n me, 'n I'm a coke whore, man, I mean I can do it, then when John came in, and sat down with us and scarfed up that last bunch his fuckin' nose started jetting all that blood out and he hit his head on the glass and we got him over to Eddie's and put ice cubes up his nose, 'n then two ludes, and let him an' Jackie talk it out. Now we ain't seen him since. I mean it's obvious, Bro, he was already on somethin'. Like Fog City, right? Angel Dust? Like his eyeballs was popped?

JACKIE

Oh, man-o-man, wow, I am really fucked-up! I am *so, so* fucked-up! Don't judge me that I get like this, okay? I mean I am, but, hey, I really am, so don't, okay? Yes, I'd put the man over the child. I would. Did you hear me? Did you just hear what I said to you, Car? Hey, I would. I said I'd put the man over the child, you son of a bitch! Yes, you are! Listen to me! Don't look at me like

JOHNNY

Controlling one's temper is very important, and not changing one's philosophy to please other people. I'm also finding out I don't care about the fact that other people always say they know where they're going when they really don't. So what? That's just people. If my wife wants some other other asshole, fine, I can handle it. No fucking way will she stay with it. I know what she does. I'll get my chance. I always do. Just saddle up! Drop your cocks 'n grab your socks! Move your men out! Pedal to the metal! Break on through to the other side!

that! Goddamn! How come you're so goddamn cute? Isn't he just so cute? He is! He is *so, so* cute, right? Look, his face is turning red! It is! It really is! Red... ha, ha, ha, ha...

JACKIE

I really can't tell you about the time I had this past weekend, Mr. C. C. It's been a long time since I've been romantically around someone on the same level as myself. You do brag about being on a higher level. That's why I said 'around.' I hardly know the first real thing about you to tell the truth, but I feel I can trust you and that you'll always be honest with me. Let's not even mention Sunday after Johnny left, if it's all right with you. I had things on my mind that had nothing to do with you and me. And, I must admit I was very nervous, a state I seem to find myself in a lot around you. What I wanted to say was let's not try to define our relationship, but just let it be. Words sometimes complicate things, don't you think? In any case I really like you, Mr. C. C. I like you a lot, but to what extent this will grow I can't say, but I will say this – I have a need for you in my life and needs are things that can't be denied. Now it would appear a bit frightening to a twenty-six year old woman to have a twenty-three year old man come along and blow her cool, but not for me. First of all, I don't really have a cool, I'm just me. And I'm not making fun of your name, ha, ha! And second, you make me forget your age and mine. This is, or could be, the love that knows no limits, not age or space or time. Even so, Mr. C. C., it may take me

BUD

I'll tell *you* something! You know ol' Mick Delaney, that

old head-knocker? He came in here one night, set down right there at the end of the bar next to this ol' gal and her old man, 'n said, 'You know, I think a little change is good for a person; whatta you think?' And the gal, she says, 'That sounds reasonable.' 'N Mick says, 'Well, I'm available, but the problem is, finding out when you're available.' 'Well, just telephone sometime,' she tells him, a big blonde with these great big cans, see. Well, he did, and she made a fool outa him. Cost him thirteen thousand to get rid of her. Then she went down to Costa Mesa and took some other poor son of a bitch for a house – married him, got the house he had, got it in her name, then left him and went back to the first husband she had sitting right here in this bar when she met ol' Mick. So who knows how long it takes, or what they'll do? Like I say, if Jac's the one, hang on in there, she'll get back to you…

a while to let my guard down, understand? And now I must elaborate on your sweet, love – provoking poem. Your poem is an invitation, and I accept the invitation...

JACKIE

Now from what I've seen around here, all these girls, they just go ahead and have kids 'cause they don't nurse. If you nurse you've got eight, nine, ten months of natural birth control. These girls here use these damn baby formulas that you buy in those little pink or yellow cans. Their titties dry up an' zing, they're pregnant again. Now they don't plan ahead, see. Now I nursed Dawnie and I nursed John-John, too, and if there was another I'd do the same. 'Cause I like nursing. You might say I love it. And I don't see what's wrong with that. And I'd like to receive a message, too, a clear, loving message from someone as I don't like playing games, or game playing either. My social worker said that, and it's a good point, too, that you've got to plan ahead in every phase of life, 'specially if there's a new man coming around in it.

JOHNNY

You can't be loving them so much that they hafta drive you away. This time I knew that, I'd thought about that, this time

I knew if I went to Jac I'd have to play it sharp, 'n not say shit like, 'I'd rather die than live without you; I really mean that.' So, of course, whatta you think after, 'Baby,' was the first thing outa my mouth? You got that right: 'I'd rather die than... blah, blah, blah!' 'N she said, 'You don't know that.' Well, that gave me a break. I caught myself, I composed myself, I didn't say nothing more, just left, 'n drove down to Big Taco and had a couple of fried pork skins 'n chiles...

JOHNNY

Talked with JoAnn about it. Told her I can't go in with some bullshit story about some fucked-up bunnies ripping me off, and she said, 'Well, so? That's what happened, isn't it? Just go tell Eddie the truth. People like hearing the truth. Everyone always lies to him, don't they? Aren't they always trying to scam him outa his stuff? He'll like you for it. Isn't that right, Baby...'

JOANN

Met Johnny's Dad, who was this real old dude with dyed black hair and oily wrap-around dark glasses telling me I had a foxy figure which was YUK! They had to talk private and Johnny seemed to get all mad about something, but wouldn't say what. His Dad kept sneaking these looks over his glasses at me, like at my bod, 'n things...

CHERYL BETH

You kidding me? I actually think your nose looks really good! When was the last time you cut your hair? In the eighth grade, right? Oh, my God! Didn't that big muffin take you into Gensler Lee's last week? What've you got to worry about? 'Cause we were walking by and saw the two of you in there, okay? They were pulling all the security bars down and taking all the watches and rings out of the windows an' putting them in trays. That older woman was. You were in the back by that big framed wedding photo, the black and white one above the counter. At the bridal ring counter, right? The one with those white gold bridal sets? I knew it was you! And he's hard to miss, too, okay, and you had those white sneakers on, with him looking like he was trying to pocket something. No, no! Ha, ha! Did he let you pick out something? Oh, my God, Jo, even if the stone is tiny you can get a halo put around it. Lots of li'l baby diamonds to make it look bigger. Getting the right setting is everything! You don't want something that looks like a pile of broken glass. That was so good that he could share the experience with you. You guys looked really in love. No, I'm not kidding. I'm not. Even Anthony said so. He even said he was jealous of how you guys looked, which sorta hurt my feelings, too, okay?

MILLY

First of all, thanks for the extra money. It's not the amount, it's the thought that counts. I'll use it to get John-John more Pampers and a new pair of little shoes. Where'd you get it? Not from Johnny, did you? I thought you said he wasn't on his feet yet since getting out of jail. Well, here I am now in the hospital. Will have emergency surgery in the morning, 7:30 A.M. Remember all the trouble and pain, lack of sex urges? Well, it was a tumor in the vaginal channel up near the end and was causing all these problems. So tomorrow a hysterectomy and tumor removed and all the stuff that makes babies and hopefully no more periods. Did you see on TV about that sickness tampons are causing in young girls? They had that trouble with it a few years back, I recall, and thought they got it fixed, and now here it is back again. My friend Sandy is a nurse here. The room is 608 and tell Teri Ann, too. This is why I wasn't home yesterday to babysit while you went to Welfare. It all came so suddenly. Dr. Melcher just put me in the hospital right away. He seemed pretty upset so I'm upset, too. Not the best frame of mind to be facing surgery in, I know. I want you to get a job of your own. That's where I made my big mistake. I always thought all I had to do was party and get some man to take care of me and now look at me. Things are a mess...

CHAPTER 5

DOS CAMINOS AVE.

JACKIE

On the other hand I didn't want anyone saying I didn't love my husband good enough. I told him, I said, 'If you're so stupid as to think you can go back to work with Eddie again, just like nothing ever happened, 'n get yourself knifed by another goddamn Mexican again, or shot, or killed, who cares, go ahead and do it, but if you do, not only can you not come around here to see your own natural children but you can't even see them like over to Mom's, or Ter's, or even anywhere else, like even on neutral ground somewheres, or even to talk to them on the phone.' You bet that's what I told him. Then that fucking Eddie? I mean that guy just tripped my trigger…!

JOHNNY

Yeah, jus' standing there justifying like a motherfucker! Said he hoped I wasn't out on the warpath, but just accept what he was saying 'cause he didn't want any mistakes made over something that didn't mean squat. Yeah, that's what he said! That's *exactly* what he said! The fuck it wasn't! And that you were screwy, too. Like *mental*, or something…

JACKIE

And then Car says, here's what he says, he goes, 'I love fucking you.' Now that doesn't sound so bad, does it, but that wasn't how he said it. The tone of it wasn't, 'I love *loving* you,' see. It was, 'I love f*ucking* you,' see. That's how he said it, 'n that's just someone screwing, right? I mean he coulda been watching me doing someone else and got off just as much. So I said, 'You know what? I'm not into that kinda space at all. I mean, how about a little feeling here, know what I'm saying?' And what'd he say? Says, 'You know what? I think that's fucking nuts, okay?'

CARSON

Man, I'll second that. She's like off the charts. I tell her I love fucking her. She says how about telling me something with some feeling in it. I go, 'Jesus Christ, I just did.' She says, 'You said you love fucking.' I said, 'I do, but with you.' She says, 'Listen, that's just, well, I need something with some great *big* feeling in it.' I go, 'Jesus H. Christ on a broken crutch, what the hell do you think I'm saying?' 'N she says, 'Okay, that's better. But you still haven't said it, have you?'

JOHNNY

...then Li'l Paul comes up an' says he hears I'm back gigging for the Hook and wants to know if I can get him about half a pound of diamonds. Yeah, diamonds. So we go over to Eddie's and Carson's there. Now I tell Carson – he's in the den there – but he won't talk no business, see, he can't even look at this guy, 'cause he's all jacked-up that I'm gonna bust his chops, do some revenge bullshit on him. I tell him, 'Look, Car, that's just personal stuff, but this guy could be business; I'm gonna let personal stuff get in the way of business?' Then this Li'l Paul fucker jumps in with he's got about six or seven Franklins to give for the half a pound, which I can't believe, 'n even Car says, 'We're outa here, okay?' So I say, 'Hold on a sec,' 'n I say to this Paul fucker, 'Well, you're about seven large short, but you're not thinking about half a stone, right, you're thinking about grams, right? You want about half a dozen grams?' 'Yeah,' Li'l Paul says. 'Yeah; grams. But first I wanna test it.' Like *unbelievable,* right? So Car waits 'n I go out to the garage to get the Clorox, 'n to tell Eddie, who's working on his truck. And Eds goes, 'Is this guy for real? What the hell are you doing?' 'N I say, 'Let's just do it for the laughs, okay?' So's I get the Clorox 'n Eddie says, 'I gotta see this,' and goes back inside with me, and this Li'l Paul fuck says, 'Hey, I've got a dude in Colombia that's bringing me in a half a stone for just a grand.' 'Yeah?' Eddie says. 'Yeah,' Li'l Paul says, 'so's I thought I'd let you know; maybe help you guys out a little.' 'N I look at Eds, and me and him just laugh – we can't help it. There is no way that anyone is gonna sell anyone half a pound for anything less than at *least* seven or eight large, 'n Eddie says, 'I see you know a lot about coke, man.' Now I don't look up 'cause I'm too busy choking back a laugh – what I'm doing is tapping out a couple of bumps, laying out two for Li'l Paul – he's decided he doesn't need to run the Clorox test now – so what he does, he toots one up, then sets back, pinching off his other nostril, sucking it all in, 'n says, 'Well, 'I'm afraid this isn't it,' then dives back down for the other pile. 'Well,' Car says, 'everyone else is buying it.' 'No,' Li'l Paul says, 'not this bunk.' Now you know ol' Eddie, this's first cabin coke; it hasn't been stepped on at all, an' Eds, he just flips, an' Li'l Paul, he looks around, 'n says, 'Hey, no hard feelings, okay? Let me pay for those, right?' 'Well, how about on the house,' Eddie says, 'and you just leave.' 'N Li'l Paul says – meaning Eddie – 'Who the fuck is this guy?' asking Car, see, thinking Car's the Hook, right? 'N suddenly Eddie's got his big chrome-plated Bulldog right to the top of Li'l Paul's shiny bald head. That thing's a big fucking Forty-Four Mag, right? 'N Li'l Paul, he splits so friggin' fast we almost don't see him go. What happens, he's carrying his cash inside his boot so he's bent over pulling out his wallet 'n ol' Eds puts the muzzle right to the top a' the fucker's shaved skull 'n clicks back the hammer. So now Eds, thinking Car brought the guy over, says, 'What the fuck, Car?!' 'N Car, the dumb shit, looks at me like really, really pissed, 'n I can't help it, I crack up...

JOANN

Dear Di, yesterday was the most horrible day of my life. Went with Johnny over to his best friend's house and got scared to death. All these real creepy guys were there and Johnny got into a fight with a really scrawny, skinny one with a sorta acne-scarred Keith Richard's kind of face, then chased up the street after me when I ran away but asked me to get a place with him. I told him if you really do have a wife and several kids like your friend said, you have to give your money to them and walked away and he didn't come after me and I wrote a note and put it on his windshield. I wrote you may not read this or you may not find it or you might hate me for writing but since I already think you don't care that much about me anyway I don't stand to lose too much but feel I have to tell you because I love you and I have to try and be honest with you, even though you haven't been honest with me like about already being married and things like that, and if people can't be honest with each other then what is there between them and it should best be forgotten but I am writing this anyway because of what we have. I hope you understand and don't get all mad about it. I wonder if he read it or even found it? Sometimes people just drive off and the paper blows away. Or maybe since he's a liar he didn't want to face the truth. Like the last time Cheryl's big sister Elsie saw her husband was at the Texaco gas station on Thompson filling up his gas tank because he didn't want to face the truth. I don't think anything like that will happen to me but Cheryl says going out with an older guy is bad enough but going out with some older married guy and a married guy who has kids is just crazy. She couldn't believe it when I told her some of the things we were doing. Said she going to try to get Anthony to say things like that. Said they were already doing some of the same things me and Johnny were doing, so I wasn't to think I was so hot. Also she was very jealous when I told her, which made me feel real good. She said Elsie, her big sister, was still upset about her husband.

JOHNNY

So, call 'em, Eddie. Nardo. That's the fucker's name. Bernardo Suarez! He'll tell you. That's the dude's number there. It was like this, man. Me, I wasn't talking for once, but just listening, listening 'n figurin' out how much to ask for, an' while Nardo's rapping I'm thinking, 'Well, maybe it's too much, I've asked too much here,' but I'm chilled back, 'n not saying nothing, an' when he finishes and says what he'll give? Man, it's higher than what we were gonna ask for in the first place! So, great, right? 'N now I'm getting off on that, on finally learning to keep my big lip zipped, 'n that's when these other mother-jumpers show, like four of 'em! Like, you know the sound of a shotgun being cocked, a pump automatic, one of them sawed-off, gray-green ones that has that black electrician's tape wound around the handle – that fuckin' hollow,

JACKIE

Call it my nasty side, or one of my other sides, whatever, like steel-on-steel click that echoes right in-ta your nutbag?

EDDIE

John, John, man, you know something? D' you know the smartest animal? Turns out it's the crow. Totally true. They pick up walnuts 'n walk out in the road and drop 'em. Then they go back on the side and wait until a car comes by and breaks them open. Then walk back out to eat. So, see, I'm the crow here, Johnny Boy, 'cause the truth is you're real good at stories; you really are. They're real complete, right, just like a walnut is, right, but once they're cracked open? The problem then is the smell test. Yeah, the request for the smell test, and this nut don't pass. It don't smell right, 'kay? You gonna say anything? Jus' act like you didn't hear me? So tell me; where were you yesterday? I mean, for real?

we're all made up of a bundle of different sides like the nice one, the crazy one, the loving one, the party one, and like that. And with Eddie? Like I told him, I said, 'Eddie, you know better than to help John out! You do! Just don't do it! Help someone else out! Give your helping hand to someone else, man!' He knew what getting back into the trades would do to John. Eddie's not stupid. He's seen it all before. And what'd he do? Just laughs, says Johnny's already been fronted and's claiming he's been ripped by some black dudes, some hooded-up 'Sambo dudes,' he called 'em. 'Eddie,' I said, 'for Christ's sakes, John's already on close-watch probation, you know that! He can't afford no kinda slip-ups at all. Not ever. Not even one.' Now that was my reasonable side, my sweet 'n good side, see. And Eddie, he goes, 'Hey, Jac, it's all karma, Baby, you know that. John keeps his karma straight, his karma will keep him straight.' And now look at things. Where the hell is Johnny now? Karma, my ass! Then Eddie says, you know what he says? 'You know what the problem is, Jac? *You* are the problem, not John! Who do you think he's running this scam for?' Unfuckingbelievable!

JOHNNY

Goddamn, but if she didn't see Eddie's truck and just plow

right into it. She drives by once, see, an' then here she comes again, but this time going for it, cracks right into the front door panel 'n takes off. Now Eddie don't see it, see; he's ordering more pancakes, and me, I had Jo's head pushed down under the table so's Jac wouldn't see her 'cause that's what I thought she was coming back around for, see, to check things out. Man, was Jo pissed! She came up spitting 'n slapping, yelling, 'n all that! Got a lotta moxie, that's for sure. 'N Eddie, man, he didn't know what the fuck was happenin', just that someone crunched into his truck, which got a huge big laugh outa me! This was at the I-Hop, okay?

JOANN

Johnny, my dear sweet love, my joy in the morning, my happiness during the day, my soon-to-be-ecstasy-in-the-night. I want you to pick me up this weekend, as soon as possible, Puppy, Big Puppy, my heart is aching, my lips are thirsty, come on, Mister Painkiller, Doctor Feelgood, come lay some loving on me – your own home remedy. We're going somewhere different, doing something different, my best friend and her boyfriend have got her Grandma's house up in Pismo Beach for the for the weekend and Mom says I can go! So don't delay! Don't doubt! We can't start without the Star Attraction: YOU!!! Are you really getting your fender fixed? And why does it take three days, and you can't see me during them?

JOHNNY

Always hammer it down. Like with Little Jo? The first time I came in her? At the exact same moment I came, 'You're mine!' I said. 'Know that!'

CHAPTER 6

EAST FRONT STREET

CARSON

I hope you remember what I can do with it. I eat McDonald's, but think pussy. Too bad you can't give head over the phone, ha, ha. I'm so stone exhausted that I'm falling out, but I'm sober now, Baby, and thinking of you. I hope you made it home okay and I really want you to think about splitting for a while. I can't see any reason why we shouldn't. I know a couple of places that'd tickle the shit outa you again, like 'member that town with the Madonna Inn that had that big pink sign and the honeymoon suite with the big round bed with the pink fuzzy spread and the heart-shaped Jacuzzi on the tile ledge next to it and how that little pretty thing of yours opened itself for me, you lying back there, holding your legs open in both your fists, 'member that? 'N I'm strong to the finish because I eat my spinach, ha, ha, ha. Think about it. I've got the big bucks for it. What I've got right now could all be gone tomorrow. I wanna do it. Don't you wanna do it? I know I really wanna do it. And just remember, this isn't only about partying down while you still can...

JACKIE

I was afraid to groan, to make any noise, 'cause what if he knew I was turned on first, 'cause what if he wasn't?

JACKIE

Then I listened to my own voice on the phone and thought, 'Listen to that, I certainly don't ever talk to anyone else in such a sexy way 'cause I certainly don't talk to Johnny like that.' And poor Johnny, calling here about how he always used to get excited watching me walk off into the bathroom afterward, and get all hot and bothered all over again just from looking at me which makes me feel real bad 'cause I know he thinks I'm doing this just to hurt him, which I'm not, which is the dirtiest trick, that I'm really doing it 'cause I might really, really be in love, that when I try to tell him it's not him, but more likely me being caught up in something that's larger than me, he won't hear it, not even when I spell it out. Not that he cares at all about me; what would really be best. Well, you have to ask yourself what good are these thoughts doing you? Like with Dad – Mom put in all those years, then Dad never said a word, just went off and left her. And that's the best way, too. Just stick the knife in and twist it, 'cause then it's done. 'Cause she didn't have the faintest idea he was thinking anything like that so she wasn't unhappy until she had to be, right? And why should I make two men unhappy, 'stead of just one? Wouldn't that be better?

JOHNNY

'Cause then I kept myself from slapping the Bejesus outa her 'cause she just got pissed that I went over and opened the refrigerator like, 'You can't open the refrigerator, man; you don't live here no more!' Or some weird kinda shit like that! I mean I had given my word I would never be hitting people again and I kept it. I really did, even in the face of certain provoking events that I'm not even gonna mention. And then the next thing was, it was like I just didn't care if we were together or not, 'n I guess how it really stopped was her, not me. She said, 'You really want to hurt me, don't you.' And for some reason that did it. It stopped me. It did. I said, 'You're not in love with him.' 'N she said, 'Oh, yes I am! 'N he's the only man that's ever made me, too!' Now that wasn't true. I didn't buy that. I said, 'Ah, fuck, you're just a chick and chicks can be seduced, so don't make out like it's the romance of the century!' She does that to me all the time, let's me get so close, then tells me she wants to be with someone else, sees if she can get me pissed, see. It always excites the shit outa her if she can get me pissed. I don't know, I don't know, but I see I'm getting more patient. I just didn't take the bait. Or

JOANN

John was very upset and very mean until I suggested a back rub which we did. We talked about my problems dealing with Mom and Grandma. He

like death. Take death. I see it for exactly what it is. Like them Paras coming in to get me. I saw them looking at me. They were standing over me looking down at me but I wasn't there. I was up on the ceiling watching them talking down to me and me talking up to them. I wasn't really there, see, 'n what they did didn't matter. Then I was in the hospital knowing now, for sure, consciousness goes on to exist, but, hey, maybe not! Maybe you can only leave your body as long as it's still alive! Ha, ha! Hard to say, you know, and only one way to find out. One of the Paras said it was cosmic to see someone dead, and then to bring them back to life. 'Wrong, you Peckerheads,' I said, 'I was never dead!'

asked me if I liked taking showers with people. He asked if he could borrow twenty dollars. He said maybe he'd buy some beer. I said I don't feel like getting high or loaded or drinking. He said it wasn't drinking, it was just having an adult beverage, that no matter how much beer he drank he never got drunk like an an alcoholic, like his Dad for one.

CARSON

Justify?! Justify?! Hey, fuck you, man! No one's trying to justify nothin'! I told you! Right up front I told you! When a dude tells me he's done with a chick I believe him! You did, man! You told me yourself, man! The hell you didn't, John! You did! The day you got sentencing you told me! The hell you didn't! The day you got on the bus you said it, *'The bitch and I are done, man!'* That's exactly what *the* fuck you said! 'N I can prove it, too, man…

JACKIE

Well, he says no, he didn't, but he went white, you know. I'd seen him do it before, see, and these people hadn't and just panicked and called the Paras and took the works and the shit and tossed it, all of it. Well, when the Paras got there they figured it out and revived him, and then in the hospital you know what he did? Tried to have me go over there and find his junk, which I wouldn't. And do you think he was glad they had called and got him saved? No, he was mad because he thought they'd copped his stuff! Said he was gonna kill 'em! 'Johnny,' I said, 'that's really stupid, you know that? You know what you're doing? You're committing murder is what you're doing and I don't mean with junk. You're killing the good parts in yourself, and what's more, you know it, too; that's what's so damn ugly.' Well, he started crying then. He'll say he didn't but he did. Sure, he did. Because he'd already said he had the money for us, is why. I had to go there. When he called I said, 'I'm not going to any goddamn hospital to see you over something you did to yourself as stupid as that!' I said, 'My own mother is in that hospital and I won't go to see her 'cause it won't do any good.' I said, 'It must be some kinda epidemic!' I said unless he came up with some kind of child support, at least four or eight hundred bucks for starters, at the very least that, he could forget about calling here again. I knew he had it because Eddie said he did, plus he'd already given me some, but I don't know where he got the smack. Eds doesn't deal smack. I told John this was was the absolute, final straw. 'No, come get the money,' he says. I lied for him in the hospital, saying he's had these concussions, that he gets these seizures. His P.O. didn't even check on him. Well, he's at work today. Well, for some car painting guy over in Saticoy. As long as he's working I'll think about it. Maybe that's stupid, but I guess that must mean something.

JOHNNY

All's I wanted was for her to say, 'I'm sorry, Baby. I didn't mean to hurt you. I'm glad you're back. Lemme put my arms around you...'

CARSON

Yeah, doesn't she look like she's stoned? She always does. You're absolutely right. Hey, she's my buddy, man. Anybody says shit 'bout her I'll kick their ass, man. I'll kick their motherfuckin' ass, whether I can do it or not!

CARSON

Now the hot one over there, tha' little one, she was ponying her ass off, she was definitely out there, was how I was thinking, first time I ever saw the two of them at the Palomino Club, they both was dancing together then. Now this is something that goes way back, like right after I first met all them people, Johnny, Eddie, Teri, Jackie. 'N Jac 'n John was tight then, before he got popped off for wrecking into all those cars in the Ban-Dar parking lot that time 'cause he was pissed off at her or something, when I'd first moved up here. So this time I'm watching Ter dance, 'n Jac says, 'You've always liked that, huh? 'N I go, 'Your little sister?' 'Yeah,' she says, 'I've seen you watching her.' Now I don't say nothing, and she goes, 'Hey, I can handle your weirdness if you can handle mine.' Then the next second, 'cause I don't say nothing, I'm thinking about it, see, she starts in at me, like really pissed, saying, 'I see that really gets you off, doesn't it.' And then walks out! Man, I'm not even sure what she's saying, right? She's the one that had the idea that I had the idea, which I did, ha, ha, so's I had to go on outside an' run her down. So then she wouldn't talk to me, so I says, 'You know you love me; you know that.' 'N she unlocks the car, lets me in, then pushes me right out again. Then changes her mind, tells me to get back in, takes me back to her place, an' we get down, 'n she's mad about it all over again, and kicks me out!

JACKIE

When he got busted for that joint he had in his coat pocket, you remember that? Right after he left here, the night I fell asleep in front of the TV, and didn't know whether I had my robe on or not, and I think maybe Carson was already there like on the couch, or something, and Johnny just walked in and just started getting rowdy on me? I had to shut it off! I did kick him out! Well, that's when he starts thinking he wants to kill a cop. I've heard him say it, things like that before, so that's no surprise, so what he does, swear to God, is holdup Bell's Liquor and deliberately takes too long. He does. So when the cops come he takes the clerk and runs him out the back into the alley. The cops'll shoot the first guy out the door, see, that's the way he's thinking. But there's no one there. So he goes on out alone, and he had that gun, too, and he could see them, the cops, way out in the street, and he starts running toward them and was gonna fire at them, but stumbles or something, I guess, and falls, and the stupid gun goes off and the bullet, it ricochets off the alley and a wall and comes back and hits him here, up here, right near the hip! So I guess he's lying there on the ground and sees the cops running at him, they hadn't even seen him until they heard the shot, they were all watching the front, I guess, but he doesn't have the gun, it's skidded away, an' he can't get up, so he goes for that little twenty-two he's got in his boot, but he passes out before he can get it! Isn't that incredible? That was his one big moment, right? He deliberately takes too long so he can have this one big fantasy moment and then he passes out! I mean when I heard the news that a liquor store was held up and one man was shot I knew it was him! I just knew it! I didn't feel my mind go into least bit of doubt. And then the really incredible part is, they take him to the E.R. at Saint John's, 'cause he's shot, and the gun – the one that went off – I guess it skidded into a storm drain or something and disappeared, so when he comes to in Emergency he asks what happened, and tells them he was shot at by a guy that came running out a doorway and he didn't even know he'd been hit and was it true? It must be 'cause he hurts, his hip burns! And then the liquor store guys give a description that doesn't fit Johnny, which he doesn't know, but he sees they aren't going for him for that, the cops aren't, see, 'cause in going through his coat they find that joint, and that's what they bust him for! Now that's what I mean by lucky! That's just how lucky he is! I've always been blown out by his luck! Some people are just like that. Oh, the twenty-two? He tapes it under a gurney. It was in his boot, see, and when they started treating him they cut his pants off over his hip to get at the wound, they didn't take his pants or boots off. See what I mean about lucky? So when they leave him alone for a minute he tears some of the tape off the wound and uses it to hide the gun!

CARSON

'Mommy likes you, she wants you to come back and see her. She's sorry about being so mean.' That's what her kid said. She coached her, I know she did. First she says what her name is. 'I'm Dawnie,' she says. Then says how far along in school she is. Then, 'Come see Mommy; you better come!' Eight years old, man, and already she's running a hustle. Now this is right after the first time we've gotten down, Jac 'n me. So now I'm talkin': 'Meet me at the Stardust,' I say. Like no way am I gonna be on her turf, not till we get some clear understanding laid down. Hey, you gotta believe! Like no way am I gonna rub Big J.'s nose in it. I hope to Christ he never knows! Yeah, I know how he does. Yeah, and forget it. Making the dude feel bad is just not my style okay? So, anyways, the motel, right? She says she'll get rid of her kids if I want that. That's what she says. She'll leave them with her mother – now this's before we even get down – she'll leave her kids, she knows I'll really like her, she can see everything that's ahead, she knows how it's all gonna work out, it's all gonna be just wonderful, that's how it's all gonna be, then says she'd like to have another kid, like one of mine, maybe. 'Well,' she says, 'not one of yours, maybe, but, if the right person came along?' Yeah, *'the right person.'* Sure. You bet. 'Cause you know what I thought? If she'd do that to them, go off and leave her own kids, why wouldn't she do that to one of mine? 'Look,' I told her, 'calm down; don't be so damn desperate; things are all right the way they are. You don't have to give up your kids.' So you know what she said? 'No one leaves me,' she says, 'I always leave them.' 'Well, great,' I say, 'you do that; there's the door and that round thing there, there about halfway down, that's the doorknob.' Which starts it, right? And now we're down and going at it and she can't get her nut! I mean, no way! Nothing works! 'So, look,' I say, 'are you on the pill?' 'The pill?' she says. 'Well, maybe I am, and maybe I'm not.' 'That's it,' I say, 'that's why you're so uptight. I mean you sure weren't the last time. You sure got off the last time.' 'Well, sure,' she says, 'cause that was with a stranger, you can always get off with a stranger, now you're not a stranger!'

BUD

Nope, he's always been like that. 'One a' these days, Bub,' I says to him, I told him, 'you're gonna get your ass knocked clear up to your shoulders.' Shit, I've got the diabetes, the emphysema, the chronic heart disorder to deal with, the two leaky heart valves 'n all that shit, but that's nothing compared to the worry. It's the goddamn worry that's killing me. 'Cause if he'd just quit fucking around 'n start playing on the square. Well, he won't. 'Cause you tell a kid something and don't follow through on it, you break something that never comes around again. The day his mother kicked me out I told her it'd come back on her. Her whole damn family's like that. They did it to her as a kid, and she did it to him. 'Cause he don't trust nobody, see. He'll tell you he does, but he doesn't. 'Cause she quit on him right from the get-go, and he quits on himself. Right from the get-go! All she could say was, 'It's dead, I tell ya; it's already dead!' 'N she wouldn't push, see, not one lick. 'You wanna die, goddamn you,' I told her, 'You just go ahead 'n die, but don't you quit!' Well, she quit, and I hadda go out there, grab me another doc, 'n have the poor little shit cut right out. Put him in an incubator. Cost me a goddamn bundle, too. I've seen it all, Kiddo; you can take it from me. I've been fucked by experts, and big ol' bright eyes thinks he can slip one by me, coming over here wanting two hundred bucks. 'What's that for, Jackie and the kids? Bullshit,' I told him, 'I know what it's for. You ain't foolin' me. That oughta take care of you and your problem for about two days,' is what I said. 'You show me a paycheck, an' then we'll talk some money for your kids.' You know, I raised the dumb bastard and he thinks I don't know what he's thinking! And her, Irene! All that pious and holy talk now! She was hell on wheels, Buster. She could tell you the length 'n width of every cock in this town, hard or soft, an' now every other word outa her mouth is, *'Jesus'* this, 'n *'Jesus'* that. Been born again, see. Thinks that's gonna do her some good.

CHAPTER 7

SOUTH VICTORIA AVE.

JOHNNY

'Let's be frank,' I say. 'What is it?' So I get back she's real excited about me being out, she hopes it stays that way, but not if I keep pushing at her all the time. 'Okay,' I said, 'n she finally said, 'Maybe,' 'n we finally got down to it, but, well, it wasn't much, so I left. No shouting, no yelling, nothin' like that 'cause I wanted her to see I could just split, she couldn't get my ass. An' then that joint! Fuck, man, with this bullshit rookie cop butting in with, 'We know who you are, Dalton, you're the biggest dealer in Ventura County.' 'Dealer?' I says. 'Dealer of what?' 'Of weed,' he goes, 'you asshole!' Now that's when I stood up, 'n I could barely stand, too, my goddamn hip hurt so bad. 'Listen, you little turd,' I said, 'I'm not any kind of fuckin' dealer, you got that? And even if I was, you're way outa line calling me anything. 'N right now, man, right this fuckin' second, you're so goddamn close to getting it, it ain't even funny. You better get your ass outa here and bring in someone who's a bit more rational!' I was *ready,* see. Now his goddamn arm went back. It was there. It was comin'. Then this other cop, the one that knows me, goes, 'Hey, Dennis, chill out,' to this asshole, 'n pulls him out and they leave me for a minute. Now that is one lucky fucker! He doesn't even know, know how fuckin' lucky! 'Cause as soon as they left I got my little piece outa my boot, they hadn't even undressed me yet. I mean I was standing there bleeding right on the fuckin' floor with my little over-n-under in my hand jus' waiting for that cocksucker. Now I don't know if I would a' done it, pulled the

JOANN

You got any more blow? You big fibber! You do, too! You don't? You liar! You are! Can we get some beer? How come you're pulling your lip back up over your teeth then? See? That's what people do when they lie. Like my mom, for one. Yeah, she does. You want to?

trigger, but I'll tell you this, I wasn't thinking I wouldn't....

I'll pay. I don't believe a woman shouldn't pay. I do too have some money. My mom gave it to me. Com'on, Honey. You aren't mad I called you Honey, are you? 'Cause you look mad, is why. Hey, no! No! Keep you hands to yourself! Keep your hands, ha, ha, ha....

JOHNNY

My P.O. said if it really wasn't my coat, and only a goddamn roach anyways, okay, he'd back me in this one. And what really pissed him off was the deputies making all the decisions, that the Sheriff's Department thought they were the entire force of law, 'specially the new Undersheriff, that when you'd ask them to pick someone up, when it was really necessary to, they treated it like it was a big favor and not that you was part of the team, which I thought was right 'cause when you look at it you can see he's got a pretty tough job without the necessary forces to back hisself up. I can understand that.

JOANN

That night when you told me about Jackie was precious to me. I felt you open up to me, telling me how she hurt you, and the next thing I knew was you telling me you kind of liked me, that you really hadn't taken a good look at things before, and that now you were, and then I started to be feeling some kind of deep feeling and started thinking how sweet it would be to be a couple with you. Deep down I always felt it would work out, like when I saw you that first time at the party when you told me I was too young and to get lost, remember? That all you wanted to do was dance, and we'd better leave it at just that? Well, I've been sorta happy lately. What do you think that's from?

JOHNNY

Little guys always wanna fight me, see. Like, *'Hey, you big son of a bitch,'* right? You know what I'm saying? So if I kick ass I'm an asshole; if I back down I'm a punk. Like that happened the other day, and this guy used to be a friend, too. So's all I could do is sit there 'n look at the guy 'n eat shit, or something like that...

JOHNNY

Dad thought Jo was really pretty, a mini Marilyn Monroe, or like a cute, big-titted Madonna. Said all Cesarean babies were pretty, told me I was a C-section, said I came out like a little lamb, butt down, arms and legs up in a jackknife. Jo said she wasn't Cesarean but natural childbirth. Dad said, 'A Hippy.' Jo said, 'No,' her mother was Christian. Dad said he was getting pretty sick again. He wasn't sleeping with Marge anymore, but out on the couch, that he didn't want her waking up some morning with him dead next to her, and Jo wanted to know how I got my finger smashed. Told her when that guy shot at me, and I fell...

JOHNNY

I'm a pretty determined person, which is something a lot of people seem to forget, 'cause if there's something I want I'll go after it, no one has to come after me, 'n no one better try to stop me neither, 'cause even if they was to kill me I still wouldn't

IRENE

Now I've read the Bible, Honey. You can't question someone's right to be the way they are. You might think something's wrong, that you know better how they should be, but if God made people a certain way, then there's a reason for it, and that's the end of it, okay...

JACKIE

You think those people deal with Eddie 'cause he's not both smart and dead honest? You can't pull that jailhouse shit on them! Hey, I know you, John! Just like you did the last time! Hey, I don't wanna hear it. Eddie knows you kept the money. Of course, he does!

TERI

I'd brought the kids back from the hospital after seeing their Grams. Jac wasn't home, 'n hadn't been answering her phone, so I drove over to that Lily chick's house and there she was. 'Your kids are out in the car,' I told her. I musta said it a coupla times, an' this Lily bitch, comes out of the bedroom with just a bra on, no panties or nothing, just her ugly black bush showing and Car right

stop, 'cause even then it'd take me several minutes just to realize it, that I was dead, and I'd keep on going just long enough to get over 'cause of the sheer disgust with having to quit…

behind her. He didn't even look at me, which I could care less about. They were drunk or loaded, or both, but Jac wasn't. I mean that's what I thought, which was real strange. Then Jac said, 'It's so nice to see you,' she says. Well, she was loaded 'cause when people talk to you like that, like you're not even there, they're loaded. So I'm looking at her, just figuring this out, and this Lily bitch says, 'Take that little whore-bag outa here.' 'Fine, lady,' I say, 'that's exactly what I want.' But Jackie ignores me, just locks eyes with the bitch. So I look at Car, but he's not saying nothing, just flops down on a chair and starts watching the TV. 'Jackie,' I say, 'let's get out of here,' but nothing, no response, she's not moving, 'cause it's a real stare-down going on, which they hold onto for a real long time, neither one backing off. Now I don't know who's winning, but finally Lily looks over to Car, right, like: 'Are you gonna do something?' Well, Car doesn't do nothing, just keeps on with the TV, so I guess she loses for real, and next Lily's back in the bedroom, slamming the door. Okay, great; but no, Jac doesn't move, just turns 'n stares at me, her eyes all dead looking inside. I tell her to come on home, that we'll treat her nice, really, really nice, that the kids really want to see her, that we'll get stoned together, 'n take some long walks together 'n talk some of our bullshit out including some things I really want her to know that I feel bad about, and, all of a sudden, like her eyes come into focus on me, and she says, 'Are those my new green parachute pants you're wearing?'

CARSON

The dude's lost all his self-respect. He wants to fight, see, but he can't. He can't, 'cause he's lost his balls… He's all like this: 'Blah, blah, blah…'

MILLY

Hello, Sweetie, how are you? I wish I knew. I just woke up and have to tell you the dream I had last night that I really believe was a message from God. It may sound crazy, but somehow I believe it's true. I never do dream about Johnny, but last night I dreamt he was with a group of police officers and we could see them all taking care of little children and grownups who seemed to be walking down the street. The children seemed to be barefooted and the grownups seemed to be helping them walk in the right places. Do you remember Sandy, my nurse friend? She was there, and with some others that seemed to be like you and Teri Ann, I'm not sure about that, but Johnny definitely was, and he came up behind us and put his arms around us, assuring us that everyone was doing just fine, that you two would be getting back together. Now this message came to me through this dream. Remember that I told you I was having all these terrible nightmares? Well, this wasn't a nightmare and to me a message. That nice caseworker came to see me and she talked about you, Honey, and she was very definite that Dawnie and L. J. would have a good foster home if it is necessary until I get myself straightened out. I'm trying very hard, Sweetie, and I felt she was very sincere. Even if you and John should get back together and things prevent the two of you from having them with you right away, I'm sure she would arrange it so you could see them and talk to them as often as you want to be sure in your mind they both are all right. Also, Teri said you told her you hadn't eaten in two days. That worries me so much. You can't be well if you don't eat. Someone told me if you're not hungry you should at least eat cottage cheese and drink milk, the calcium is good for nerves. So that's what I'm trying to do here. You try it, too, okay? Think about getting back together with Johnny, will you, Sweetie? He did come to see me here with such sincerity in his heart that I truly believe he has earned the chance. Have you

JOHNNY

You know what? Jac does have two kids, but only one of them is mine. You think I don't know that?

CARSON

Well, hell, go back with him then. 'Cause how'd that change anything anyways? We'd always be tight 'n right, right? An' be seein' each other...

thought about going to church? I know that sometimes ministers and pastors help people with family and personal and thought problems that they have. Sandy asked me if I'd like her pastor to help with my personal problems. I told her yes and she is seeing him today and hopefully he will visit. Maybe this is the answer for us all. Johnny said Irene has been going to church and wanted him to go, too. My fingers are crossed for all of us. At least I'm going to try. Maybe you can try, too. Ter said John-John and Dawnie were fine. That makes me feel so much better. About getting a job. I know you've worked hard and I know you're tired, raising two children by yourself is not easy, but even your baby sister works, and if she loses a job, well, by the evening of the same day she has another one lined up. I also want to say the excitement of having a new man in your life will only last for a little while. I know what I'm saying here, believe you me...

CARSON

I say, 'No rubbers at all.' She says, 'Right; you don't use nothing, neither do I – no diaphragm, no foams, no jellies, no pills!' 'Hell,' I say, 'you don't wear galoshes in the shower, do you?' 'I mean it,' she says. 'Well,' I tell her, 'I'm not into buying no abortions neither.' Then she laughs, see, 'n says, 'It'll take more of a man than you to get me pregnant, no matter how many times I do you!' Well, you gotta love her, right? *'How many times I do you?'* That kinda sass?

JOANN

Johnny, are you really going to marry me? I'm not trying to be funny. When you left you said, 'Take damn good care of yourself for you're all we've got.' Johnny, who is "We?" Now that you've said you weren't going to see your wife I feel a little better. If I could be with you everything would be good. I need you more and more just like every day I love you more and more. And

JOHNNY

Hey, if she's on the loose then I'm on the loose! That's always been my thinking, but this time I finally dummied up. I wasn't goin' 'round telling people how much I loved her, 'n leaving flowers at the apartment, 'n notes sayin' how much I cared, roses, carnations, tulips, tiger lilies, all that shit. I only told her Mom how much I loved her, an' my kids, an' her, too, which had us both in tears. It was just terrible, and made me feel like a real shithead…

even though you may be mad at me I do love you. It's getting harder and harder to live here. Mom is driving me up the wall. I bought a new light aqua blue peacock type original soft summer breeze mini and charged it on her card. I'm going to have to tell her, I guess. Anyway, it's buy now, cry later. As much as she loves clothes she should understand, especially since I'm in love. Tonight I'm going to the tent meeting. It's a tent revival meeting, and Cheryl is supposed to go, but I don't think she will. She keeps saying she doesn't have hang-ups about different churches but I don't think so. This is my second time asking her to go to a different church and each time she doesn't and doesn't have a good excuse either. I told her if she came with me tonight it would help me with Mom for the weekend so I hope she comes. The meeting last night was real good. The minister made some real good points. He said Satan was not going to meet you with a punch but with a kiss and a hug. Neat to hear the truth. About my hair, it's only blond in front but still dark in the back. Everyone likes it, but I don't know if you will. Cheryl says it makes me look Latina and hot. Remember those hot-looking ones we saw in Long Beach? The ones in MacArthur Park, and them on Fifteenth Street? The Latina that was rubbing her hand on her boyfriend's bare chest and how he stood there liking it? The one in front of the liquor store? She had those real big gold hoop earrings? She kept wagging her tongue in and out at him? He had his hand on her you know what?

JOHNNY

You think a guy like Carson cares? What the fuck does he care about? Remember them dabs of shoe polish? When we put them on them plastic sheets 'n sold them as hits of acid? Now whose idea do you think that was, for Christ's sakes? An' don't tell me

JACKIE

Car would do Ter while I would do Eddie, we all four would watch each other. I say, that's just business either. That's not business! That's a *quality!* The guy's got no *quality!*

'Is that what you want? 'Well,' Car says, 'do you?' 'Well, no,' I say, 'but I'm not afraid of it neither.' 'Oh, yeah?' he says, and so we do, and then, in spite of myself, I find myself kinda thinking about Eddie again, 'n agree to meet up with him when we can be alone, but Car, overhearing me, blows up, saying, 'Oh, no! Oh, no! How the hell can you? What the hell kind of person are you? This is it! I'm through! I've got no respect for you! I've lost all respect for you! I'm leaving!' 'Well, good,' I tell him, 'go, but it isn't my fault; you can't put the blame on me, that, after all, whose idea had the whole thing been in the first place, and besides, how was I to know that Eddie'd be so nice?' 'Oh, no, oh, no," he starts screaming, 'a thousand times no! I'm not leaving! I'm never leaving! This's something we'll work out if it takes us the rest of our lives!' 'So, okay;' I say, 'so, great! So later that night, long after Eddie's split and Ter's asleep, I wake up, and Car's not there, and I go into the living room an' catch him and Ter going at it on the floor and toss 'em both out.

JOHNNY

I told her, I said, 'Look, if I'm not the person you want, okay; I'll be hurt, I'll get angry, I might even act like I don't give a shit, but listen, when the both of us have finally licked our wounds and can really be with other people again, when that finally happens, I'll be your friend, your only true friend, and I really, really mean it.'

JACKIE

So I listen, I do, I really try to. I tell him, 'Sure, John, but look what you do.' So then he says he'd die for me, if it comes to that. So now I'm thinking, Whatta my really doing? This guy really does love me and he is starting to change. I can see it in the way he looks at people. Like he's starting

JOHNNY

Now every five minutes Luis gets up and goes in the can. I can't figure out what he's doing so's I go in. Blood's soaked in wet, red curves on his shoulder an' down his T-shirt, the needle an' plastic syringe dangling outa his neck. 'Taking my life in my hands, Bro, but I'm not supposed to die,' using a new hype every five minutes. 'My vet gives 'em to me.' Wiping off his neck, trashcan's fulla puffy wads of bloody tissues, firing hisself up every five minutes, 'n offering me, 'Want me to do you? I'll do it!' 'Cause no way, 'cause the next thing would be me all geeked up, trying to make T. J. long gone with Eddie's eighteen hundred, plus my four hundred, burning that up, 'cause now this other ol' banger, Zito Ramos, comes in, and him and Luis settle on two large and give it to me. 'Take it, my man,' Luis says. So I agree to give them the bindle. Go out to the car and bring it back in 'cause I'm thinking now give Eddie back the eighteen, get your own money, then everything works out. 'N start treating Jo better 'cause she is there for you, an' fuck Jackie, maybe take Dawnie and Jo and move up to San Luis Obispo or Santa Cruz and get something going, maybe even start my own gloss shop, get into some rad paint work. All custom stuff. Hell, why not? I can do it. Or furniture, or lawn mower sales 'n repair.

to enjoy people, 'n not trying to impress 'em...

JACKIE

Johnny got John-John and Dawnie from Ter, and took them in the car, saying he was going to get them ice cream. Then he drove them so fast going around the corners that when the car would tip and start to slide he'd get them screaming and shrieking and he'd just do it again at the next corner, and they just screamed 'n screamed 'n completely loved it an' he said, 'Don't tell your mom,' and made them promise, 'cause if they told, he wouldn't take them for any more rides. That's why they want to see him. He didn't buy them ice cream. If he did I don't know where he got the money for it. He took all the money I had in my purse before he left here and when he came back he was broke and I told him, I said, 'Don't you dare look in

JOHNNY

There's Car's sleek El Camino sitting out front of the apartment building, just asking for it, with that new, baked on bronze 'n cream hi-tech paint job 'n the four new Goodyear Eagles, 'n Moon spun-aluminum wheel covers. He's got a lotta coin in that rig. Those tires are designed for a Corvette! 'N look at that slick assed, cocky fucker! Eddie must be givin' him all the cakes. Fire would fix that shit up in a second! 'N no god-dam back seat. You can't even hook up a child's seat in there! What the *fuck* is she thinking? *'N fuck me stupid! A twisted–up strip of towel down into the gas tank 'n a Mini-Bic, right? 'N, what the fuck else...?*

my purse, there's no reason for you to be looking in my purse,' and he said, 'We're still married, aren't we?'

JACKIE
Just drive off! There's nothing he can do!

WILL HARMS
Personal inventory, review of family circumstances: Parolee Dalton Co-operative; meeting weekly check-in schedule in timely fashion as of current date. Father, mother, though divorced, both cooperative. Employment schedule met. No unusual problems at this juncture. See recorded interview tape for recent contact with father, a part-time oilfield worker currently on work-related disability, very forthright about what is wrong with his son and what can be done to: "...straighten him and his whole stupid f...k..d-up situation out..." as he put it. Seems very sincere, actively working in support of son's rehabilitation, having secured the initial employment for Parolee Dalton at Bump & Shine Auto Body. Spot visit at shop found Mr. Dalton at work. Vouched for by Mr. Jose Marquez, owner. Mr. Dalton currently deemed compliant. Low risk of recidivism. No adverse action to be taken at this point in time. Parole requirements met. Discharge recommended.

Signed...
Will Harms
William E. Harms
State Parole Agent

MILLY

No, Missy, I'm talking about the whole cookie. Remember when you were a baby if I took a cookie and broke it in half and tried to give it to you, you wouldn't take it? It had to be the whole cookie? You'd cry unless I gave you a whole big one. And that's all that Johnny wants from you, too. Now I do love Johnny, and I understand him, which is something neither you nor Teri Ann do. Neither one of you girls understands the first darn thing about men. In my time if you didn't learn about a man you didn't have no chance at anything what so ever. Don't you shake your head at me! I know what that look means, Missy! Don't think I don't!

CHAPTER 8

WEST RAMONA ST.

JACKIE

Yeah, 'cause he grabbed the keys and was going out the door. There wasn't any weather-stripping on it and 'cause I slammed it so fast it caught his hand and clipped the top of his finger off. I felt pretty shitty about it, I really did, but when he came back he more than made up for it – he tossed me through the door. They were picking wood outa my back for a week. And that's not the first time something like that's happened neither. I should be on total disability, too, you know, not just Aid For Dependent Children. There's no way I can do any kind of work now, let alone be looking for work.

JOHNNY

My basic problem with myself has always been in thinking I could make it alone in life. I now know that isn't so. I was very clear about this with Jac. I told her over and over that being alone was only selfishness and nothing else. I also said I'd made a big, big decision. I told her I no longer had to have her and I meant it. I said she could just go her own way if she had to. I didn't want nothing from her.

JOANN

Johnny, you tell me, no, you haven't seen her, and I know you have and then you expect me to behave as if what you say is true. After what you said last night I guess you don't really care for me anymore but why are you going back to her? I guess that's where you've been, isn't it, and not at your grandma's like you said. Maybe this is the way it has to be, but the only reason I went to see Eddie was to see where you were and he said he didn't know. You say you love me and me alone but look at the way you're acting. Hey, believe me. And I do love you and just you alone. I was only over to Cheryl's after I left Eddie's because I couldn't be with you when I wanted to. You told me to stop bugging you and

I did. Then you get all mad at me. Well, love is not being mad at someone all the time, no matter what you say. Love is being with someone and loving them because they love you and you alone. Don't tell this to anyone because this is our personal business. Loving you always, your Panda

JOHNNY

'Okay,' I said, 'I'm miserable, you're miserable, maybe we should be separated like this. Maybe we should be divorced. You're young enough, there'll always be someone out there that'll wanna fuck you, even when Carson gets sick of you, 'cause there's a whole lotta pussy out there just waitin' for me, okay? 'Now that's exactly what I told her. 'Hold me,' she said. So I did. I gave her a wonderful hug.

TERI

'Take him back then, I don't give a damn. It's you I care about, certainly not him. Besides, I don't even like him. Just the idea of him drinking beer for breakfast makes me sick, okay?' I told her all that, and what'd she say? Said she couldn't even fit into any of her clothes right now, she was just too popcorned out to even care! Can you believe it? She wouldn't even acknowledge me, see, that he'd been with me. Uh-huh. She really *is* rotten, an' she believes she's normal, too.

CARSON

Now it's later, see. I'm on my back there, 'n I've woke up with this giant boner, 'n of course they're both asleep, right? So first it's Ter, I look at her, but she's on her side snoring, so's I turn to Jac, an' her eyes open, she's awake, man, an' puts her fingers to her lips, shushing me, then licks her fingers, 'n, hey, you can guess the rest, but also says, 'John's been asking about us,' so I say, 'What's to ask? How many times we been down now? Three? Four? Gimme a break, okay? I don't wanna hear nothing more about the guy.'

JACKIE

Now the funny thing is, is I'm missing Johnny, even though he's around and such a bastard at times, like always exaggerating to make himself look good when in fact he looks the worst I've ever seen him, and is completely desperate to talk to me. Then Car calls to say how it's going with Ter, who is also such a liar, but try as I might I didn't get jealous. This was right after Car left here, luckily missing John. We'd smoked some dope, listened to some Stones, took our clothes off, touched a lot, and fell asleep. That was just awesome and made me feel as if it was really all worthwhile, really good feelings, and consequently good sex and all was right with the world. Then when we woke up I got up to make dinner and came back and found him asleep. I laid down next to him for a second, and he jumped up, all wild-eyed. I asked if he was hungry and he jumped on me, grabbing me, and began grinding. I took off my T-shirt and started going down on him. After about twenty minutes of this and four gags, tears streaming from eyes and nose running, I screamed, 'What do you want?' He tore off my pants, ripping buttons off, and shoved himself deep inside me. The next was crazy, him walking me around like a wheelbarrow. I also came once with him inside and his finger in my ass, which was great. We also did me on top, doggies, various others up to and also finally trying to put it in my ass. I'm sorry now I didn't let it happen. In truth, though, penetration was accomplished for about an inch inch or so, and now my ass hurts like hell. Talking about all this is making me horny. Then when he finally came, he jumped up, put on pants, said, 'Let's eat,' and stopped talking to me. No matter what I said he wouldn't say a thing, just ate and left. Cute, huh? Then he calls me up and tells me he's down with Teri. 'Fine,' I tell him, 'hop to it.' Fun little Carson Cool games, right? I couldn't even get upset because it was all so obvious. So I've decided to hell with him and he knows it, too, but sex, though, is very confusing because it's not like any sex I've ever had, not even with John. It's very animalistic.

I told him the way he came was weird, that he never made any noise, that I couldn't even tell when he *did* come. He said that was his style, that a smooth even come was the kind he liked best, that that kind of come produced a smooth even kid, one that'd be easy for us to live with...

I both love it and I hate it. It's how pimps get a hold on their ho's. The least I can say is it's certainly more interesting than any before because of the cruelty in it. But I'm stronger now than I was before, and can handle the ups and downs more. Also, I'm starting to love him, an' want much more from him, and no more games. His don't work on me, and mine don't work on him. Sometimes I feel like crying, but can't really decide who to cry for. I wonder what is going on inside him? What makes him so scared to be really close to someone? Why does he think he always has to have the upper hand? He doesn't need to. Why doesn't he trust me? I'm a nice person.

CARSON

We're down now, an' I say, 'You know, what about a bambino here?' Pulling myself out, see, but Jac grabs me. 'Ah, com'ere,' she says, 'don't worry about it – it'll take care of itself.'

JOHNNY

Now that's where I've seen a lot of guys go wrong. 'Not me,' they'll say, 'I don't need no old lady running my scene.' Now assholes like that, they've lost their purpose inside, 'cause what good is it sittin' around doing blow 'n talkin' nonstop about yourself 'n all your bullshit? For what? So in two days the whole ounce 'll be gone, and you'll be riding out one ass-kicker of a headache. An' when you think about it, do you know one fuckhead that's gone all the way to the edge, teetered there, and come back? Can you name one? So I see I'm getting wiser, that I've learned something, 'cause where's the fun anymore, know what I mean?

JOANN

I'm really sorry I got mad! What's more I'm just waiting for you to blow my mind, give me a natural high, take me to higher ground, and find total commitment with me! Cheryl says I'm right and you know it, too! Johnny, I needs to be with you! I loves ya!!!

TERI

Well, maybe I wanted to see if I could get him is why. You

just don't let him know you like him, that's the thing. I told him, I said, 'It's simple, man, like I don't feel safe enough with you, with putting myself in your hands.'

JOHNNY

I said, 'I'll buy you a condo.' Jac says, 'You'll buy me a condo? You don't know anything about the Southern California real estate market of today. How much money do you have anyway?' 'N I said, 'How much does a guy need?'

JACKIE

No, John, absolutely not! He has not! The only reason he hasn't been around is not because of you, it's because of *us*! Yeah, *us!* 'Cause he doesn't want to break us up as a family! Yeah, that's what he said, and I think that's nice and an unusual thing to say! 'Cause he didn't think it'd be fair to the kids, that kids need a dad; they need their own dad, their real dad…

JOHNNY

I thought I might as well have some fun outa this. So I got a pound of hamburger. I drove over to Arnie's and got some Telazol he'd scored. I had one of them huge canvas mailbags Earle'd left in the wagon, plus some rope. I tossed the burger over the fence and smoked a joint. When I went in the yard Bucky was already staggering around. He's a monster huge Dobie, see, so I'd really packed the Telazol in. I smoked another J, 'n then went 'n petted him. Then I got him up off his side, bagged him, then roped the bag shut and took it up the steps and laid him in the doorway. I cut some holes in the bag so's

JACKIE

Then Car said some other kinda stuff, some more real personal-like stuff, and, well, like, 'Oh-oh,' he goes, 'I don't know if I can control myself.' 'Oh, well' I said, 'maybe you shouldn't; maybe you can't.' So what else can I say? Say that for ten or twenty minutes this morning I was able to pretend my sore titties were really premenstrual, and my period is really on the way? I don't know whether to be completely depressed or totally happy...

he could breathe. I went back out in the alley, 'n had just about finished stuffing the rag down Car's gas tank just before I was gonna torch it, when Bucky started barking and Car's asshole buddy Larry started coming outside yelling. I hadn't put enough dust in the damn burger, see! What a fuckin' dog! Looks like a tanker truck, man, I swear! So's I walked down the alley, lighting another Lucky, listening to all the commotion, 'n thought, Hell, to actually worry about anything is bad. It's either get upset about about everything and get yourself crazy, or don't get upset 'n let it pass, but *most* of all quit getting sucked into other people's games...

JOANN

Dear Johnny, I am spoiled. I always want my own way. I want to stop, I can't stop, can't even do a simple thing like that. I remember everything you said. You said you would leave Jackie. I feel really uncomfortable. I want to change us so bad. I won't even be able to kill myself. I want to stop with us so bad. Your Mother called my Mother and warned her that the first time you got out of jail and had that trouble with Jackie, you told another girl you would divorce Jackie and marry her, and you didn't, and that girl gave your Mother a heads up about that, and now your Mother called my Mother and gave her heads up about your promises, how you don't keep them, and I just don't believe it, and need you to tell me it me it isn't true, just like I told my Mom it wasn't. I told her it didn't matter because that was before you met me, once you met me I knew you were going to marry me because I saw the look of love in your eyes when you said so and the eyes don't lie so I need to hear you say it again so I can look in your eyes and see it again and then I'll really know...

CARSON

Now most dudes are broke, if they're in the trades they are, 'cause they're party animals first, right, I mean up your nose 'n down to your toes, you don't need no ball 'n chain, an' mos' bitches think that's how you think. But me, huh-uh, they just know better with me, so even if I get two bitches pregnant but can't pick one, 'n just let 'em duke it out – or not – 'cause that's not a bad way to handle it 'cause maybe they'll both stick, like with two sisters? If they know you can handle it? Wouldn't that be a blast? Like some a' the Mormons do? I've got a cousin, lives over in Utah. She knows people like that, that they dig it...

CHAPTER 9

SEARS ROEBUCK, SOUTH MILLS RD.

JOHNNY

Saw Larry B. in Sears and said, 'How was Bucky; was he okay?' So Larry, the little shit, says, 'What do you mean?' And I say, 'I heard he was sick.''N Larry says, 'He was for a while but he's all right now.' Then he goes, 'How'd you know about that?' 'N I go, 'Ask your asshole buddy Carson about it, okay?' 'You're gonna get it one a' these days, Dalton,' he says. 'N I go, 'That'd be just peachy, Bennett; this is as good a place as any.' That's how all them coat racks got knocked down. It was nuts. He tore into me like some coked-up rabbit. It was wild.

Ter was there with him, her 'n some crazy-eyed black bitch, too; the one that's been hanging with Car, okay? What's her face? You know her. Yeah, you do. I didn't hurt Bennett none neither. Ask Ter about it. She saw the whole thing. Check it out. She was laughing her ass off...

JOANN

What I'm trying to say is what if we got married like we planned? The first time you got mad at me I'd be dead because you would try to kill me because when you touch me something tells me what is he going to do to me or is he going to get mad? I start thinking you don't tell me anything except what you want and don't show other people that you really care for me. I can't even talk to anyone without you saying I'm trying to go out with them like when I was talking to that Robert guy over at Cheryl's. You make me think all the time I am wrong when all the time it's you that is wrong like not coming here when I know you are here and not in Oxnard like you said. The only time you want to see me you you get all mad at me or want me to be second best or criticize me or have hot sex with me. Please don't get mad at me 'cause I'm telling you what's on my mind. Please tell me the things you like and dislike that I said or did or anything. Please be truthful with me. What are you so mad about anyway? My Mom has been on my back all morning about my attitude and things. She's driving me crazy! And to have you mad at me, too; it just isn't fair!

JOHNNY

'Everybody's sick of your act!' he goes. Yeah, my 'act!' Can you believe that shit? Yeah, Bennett. Little fuckin' Larry Bennett! That little fuckhead! What a total asswipe...

JOHNNY

Saw Eddie and gave him his bread. Said Carson was doing pretty good for him now, been given a little more responsibility and was handling it well. 'Whatever,' I said. What I did next was sorta inspired. I mean I never planned it or nothing. Went back into Eddie's, 'n got into his jock bag stashed behind the duffels, eyeballed out about two, two 'n a half ounces of blow, re-sealed 'n re-rolled the Zippie, dropped it back in, then took some of Jackie's Shalimar, 'n sprayed it on the jock bag, then just a little touch on some a' the coats that was hanging there in the closet, and decided to get a sixer, maybe some Dos Equis or Coronas, somethin' Mex, 'cause I'd been thinking a' headin' down that way...

TERI

No, no, John, she does not want you back! She only thinks she does 'cause Car is dumping on her. You go back she'll just dump on you...

TERI

No, Jac, no, none, these're such little lines; that's only enough to get you jittery! I mean, com'on...

JOHNNY

I was in there getting a blanket for sleeping in the car, for Christ's sakes! 'N a pillow, too, 'cause everything in that whole damn car is covered in cat 'n dog fur! I copped John-John

JACKIE

'Eddie's not stupid, John. "Black guys?" I told you he wasn't gonna believe you, that he'd make you pay.' That's what I told him. So what's he do? Just dumped a baby blanket too. It's out in the car. I'll go get it. It's a god-damn flannel, okay?

a pile out, snorted a cone out of it, and sat there laughing like a jerk. And now he's out selling lines. Yeah, frickin' lines. Goin' around in bars trying to sell 'em for five bucks a line. 'N mostly getting eighty-sixed, too. 'John,' I said, 'don't you know about lines no more. If a person buys some-thing for five bucks, they buy buzz now.' And him, he goes, 'Coke is still coke, Jac-Jac, you know that. I'll do all right.'

JOHNNY

So I actually get to work on time 'n I'm sanding down on this big block IROC-Z an' this other fucker, Pedro R., he comes in and tells me I gotta go up to the office. He walks over there with me 'n tells me Jose wants to lay me off 'cause I haven't been getting the work out fast enough, they've hired a more experienced paint-er. I say, 'You had to walk me all the way over here to tell me that?' So I left all bummed out, pissed, and god-damned depressed. I called the P. O. He said, 'Calm down and go get something to eat, 'n call me back in five.' So I go get a pizza with sausage and meatballs and then call him back. They say call again in twenty minutes. I do, an' now he's gone for the day an' now I'm really pissed and get in the wagon to take off, but the goddamn radiator hose blows. 'Cause I've spent all my coin at Sears I don't have the eight bucks for a new cocksucker so I tie a rag around it, but now the valves start clacking, the fucker's just too hot, 'n I shut it off. So, of course, everything fucking blows. I get out. There's all this steaming hot water pouring down around the right front tire. Now that's when I start thinking. I'm lying there on the ground, look-ing up into the greasy blackness of the engine compartment and I smell oil burning, which means the head's probably cracked or the bearings are scorched, and there's all this rusty water's sizzling down, dripping off the exhaust mani-folds, 'n I see I've got to change.

TERI

That's not true. I know what Dad told her. 'I'm sick 'n tired of all your stupid phone calls 'n stupid church talk and not paying attention to your own

I mean it's just obvious. 'John,' I say, 'you dumb son of a bitch, God damn you, you've got to quit looking for the goddamn shortcut!'

family.' That's what he told her. And who told me that? *Mom herself.* Yeah, *Mom!* She told me herself! *Carson!?* Why the hell are you bringing *that* up...?

JOHNNY

Not knowing where my wife was, thinking maybe I hadn't said the right things, 'n like that, I drove back home but no one was there. Then to Eddie's, then Jo's, then back to Jac's. Going in through my daughter's window, the place was a fuckin' mess. No one there this time either. I went back to Eddie's and gave him some cash, 'n drove over to Cheryl's. Now I'm sitting in there, having a few brews, trying to read this letter my mother-in-law sent me I'd picked up at Mom's, I'm re-reading it actually, which is sorta hard 'cause it's a teenage party happening, an' all a' sudden there's all these cops running in, which just wigs me out, 'n I'm running into the kitchen, throwing all this kitchen shit at 'em: pots, pans, knives, forks, spoons, then I bolt into the head an' they're yelling, 'Watch it! Watch it! The son of a bitch's crazy!' Shit like that, 'n they grab me an' get the cuffs on me. I break a goddamn chokehold, see, 'cause now I'm mad, see, an' dive through the front picture window an' crash out on the lawn, the wind's knocked outa me, they're still yelling their macho cop shit, right, an' CLANK, I'm in the can with all the winos. You know how that goes. So I'm sitting in there and a guy comes in with my yellow sheet. I grab it: "Resisting Arrest, using Abusive Language, Disturbing the Peace, Assaulting an Officer." 'They catch you on the concrete?' this one wino says.

JOANN

Dear Di, Johnny came by this afternoon and we almost got caught! He went out the window and Mom came in and said, 'What's that smell?' I almost died! He told me he loved me and wanted me forever. I said, 'Prove it.' He said he would tattoo my name on his neck. I said, 'JoAnn?' No,' he said, 'PANDA! Can you believe it?!!!

'No, you fuckin' retard,' I say, 'they did not catch me on the concrete,' meaning, No, I was not drunk 'n puked out on the goddamn sidewalk like the rest a' you diddly-fucks, so, 'So okay, Dudes,' I say, 'all right; where's the Bull Durham; roll out that seed!' Then a few minutes later: 'Dalton, bag and baggage, get your hoofs on, you're outa here!' Out? What the fuck? 'Some friends of yours have gone bail,' this guy says. 'Friends, man? I ain't got fuckin' friend one, Jack, but, hey, you know, all right! Now listen up,' I say to the winos, 'I'll see all you diddly-fucks later!' 'N I'm already outa there, tippy-toeing around all the puke an' these sorry shit-bags, and, man, there's my sweet li'l Anda Panda Babes standing outside the gate, and I'm so glad and so happy to see her, and then we're outside and going down the steps, and we hear, 'Halt, there's been a mistake!' *'Halt?!'* Motherfucker! So's I turn around. 'What mistake?' I say. And there's this red-faced, pot-bellied, grey-headed son of a bitch sayin', 'For Christ's sakes, Dalton, you're on Close Watch Probation, you know that! You're not eligible for bail!' So's I say, 'Hell, Paddy, I know you're a good Christian man, so hows about a little Christian charity here, okay? 'N I look at Jo, see, so he can see what I see, an' say, ''N let 'em come after me in a few days, know what I mean?' 'N Jo's hanging on to my arm real tight, which I also want him to see...

JOHNNY

Well, son of a bitch, Rube! Man, I thought you'd be out cruisin' up 'n down them Whittier Boulevard bricks by now! Wha' happened? Slice somebody's squawk box open again, ha, ha? Gimme five, Bro! Hey, High Five! Low Five! Chile Relleno Five! Ha, ha, ha! Jesus, it's hot in here! Whatta they got the thermo set to? Naw, I'm marked for second floor, man, but let's do it. Don't make no never mind to me, man. You still carryin' the weight in here, right? Still up on top three, right? Mustard *and* mayo, Bro; let's do it. Still the big ol' choke collar, right? So here's what I got comin' for you: six cans a' Bumble Bee, six cartons a' Camels, a dozen packs of Oreos, giant size party packs, Bro, an' pens. Yeah, Camels and pens, plain ol' Bic pens, all black ones, an' a pack a' different colored pencils, like twenty-four of 'em, all different colors. You still drawing them big ol' brown babes 'n lowridin' Riviera's 'n SS Impalas on them pillowcases and handkerchiefs, right? They letting you use any paper yet? Yeah, GM's, man, they got that X-frame that lets you mount the hydraulics, right? No shit. Why'n't you draw some of 'em flipped upside over? Showin' the chromed-out hydraulics 'n wishbones mounted on them reinforced frames all sandblasted 'n painted that satiny, velvet black. Bounce on down on-ta the whole nitty-gritty, the what of what's underneath all that happy shit?

BOOK TWO **WINTER**

GRAMS

I've made up some Pecan Pie I'm going to wrap and put in a box and mail you. Do you remember how you used to yell, 'Pecans, Pecans Pie, Lama?' I sure do hope you are all right. I am praying for you every day. I worry a lot about you, honey, and I want you to write your old Lama, she gets lonely when she don't hear how you are. Do you remember your "Big Rock?" I bet you don't, but the day Jill was born I had to give you the "Big Rock" to get you to sleep, and when Irene's pains started she grabbed you up and set in the rocker and tried to rock you to sleep. It was about seven, and you was used to being rocked to sleep nearer midnight, and sometimes I used the "Big Rock." You was so surprised that she was rocking you. Your eyes kept getting bigger and bigger. Finally she threw you in the corner and went to the hospital. You always was such a sweet baby and loved to get in your Lama's lap. I hope you still like pecans.

CHAPTER 10

SALINAS VALLEY STATE PRISON

JOHNNY

They put me in this cell with this fuckin' spade, man, and bad? He was bad, man, real bad. He was in for Murder One, Murder in the First, man, and he was outraged, just pissed off about me, that I was in for dope! And that's what it was, he was pissed off about dope! Now I couldn't handle his hassle at all. 'Look,' I said, 'just do what you've gotta do, I just don't give a shit.' Well, he hit me! And was he fast? Man, he was so fuckin' fast! He was fast with both hands. His hands were a fan, man! I had a black face! I was a nigger for a month! My face was swollen out to here! I couldn't handle him at all! I just fuckin' panicked! I grabbed, you know what I did? I grabbed the pipe under the sink and ripped it out! I mean I ripped it out with my bare hands and brained that sucker! I split his fuckin' skull! Blood! There was blood all over everything! He was still lying there in the morning! I couldn't even see! My eyes were swollen shut! I was up in the bunk still shakin' when they came in and got him.

CARSON

Smiley eyes creamy blue, teeth white, tap, tap, tips of lashes mascara sticky black, kisses soft, not like Jac's biting into lips bloody, but little sisterly kisses, peck, soft, peck, shy, nail polish, chipped blue, stubby li'l fingers, so light, tapping my lips, sayin', 'No, no, no, but, oh maybe, maybe, but just maybe once only 'n only just once, 'n don't look, 'kay, 'n don't tell Jac, 'kay?'

RUBEN

Big John's been comin' down hard. Tha's the word. He's been in solitary and shittin' on the floor, then smearin' it on the walls. He also beens throwin' it at the Screws. They threw him in 'cause he wus eatin' light bulbs so's he could gets in the hospital again, least that wha' he says...

EDDIE

Now I know I ain't said nothing about this, Car, but you banging Ter is one thing, but banging Jac *and* Ter, well, that only means you're gonna lose both of 'em, and that's probably all right, but what you won't lose is Big John coming after your ass. Now that's an actual hard fact. I know him and you don't. Now you can nod your pointy little head at me like you're actually listening, but I know you're not hearing me; you're sitting there thinking, 'Like so what? I can handle him.' Well, no, you can't; 'n right now you're sticking your head into a bowl filled with a whole kind of whoop ass you got no frickin' clue about...

JOHNNY

Where's that at? I swear to Christ, if you'da seen all these supposedly good hombres around here when I had my li'l incident you'da cried! All the punks did was stand around with their punk mouths open! It was too mean! See them hogs! Shit! It's sick! I've been in lockup now for three days for supposedly downing some black dude or something, but everything is still everything, they're really uptight at the freedom you and I possess, freedom they can never have. I wish to express the confidence in the cosmos that contains our freedom 'cause the time is coming, it's coming, and either we'll all get it on and get it over, or possibly join our brothers in the search for a joyful life away from all these shit-filled hate-holes with their mind control bullshit and all the filth it breeds...

JOANN

Hi Tiger, if you don't quit going around smacking folks you are in big trouble! Got it, Johnny? You should have better control over yourself, you big dummy! Now about your so-called wife, no problem! She is too concerned about a certain Mr. Carson Cool for me to worry. Don't ask me how I know because I just do. I'm only worried about when you come back. Will she like you then? It is said she doesn't, but you aren't here to prove her right or wrong. And please don't call Cheryl a little kid. And I didn't mean to hint about her ring. Smile! But a ring from my man would be nice. Cheryl and I talk about weddings, gowns, bridesmaids, colors, honeymoons, cars, houses, kids, goldfish, and many other things. Her wedding gown will be light blue or aqua or turquoise. We talk about our men, and to me you are better than anyone else's man. I'm glad you feel we shan't have any problems. Keep thinking about our future for it shall soon be our present. I give you my word and promise I'll wait. We'll do even better than our promises when you come back. I thought you'd be happy about Cheryl. All she talks about is Anthony. I know how she feels. I read everything I can when it comes to marriage, babies, how to give birth, homes, money management, anything that will help us later. I know how to pick out apartments and fill out credit applications. I'm reading myself crazy, but it's for a good cause – US!! And I know if we leave my family – and yours – we will be happy! I want a Hope Chest, too, for things we will need like sheets, towels, pillowcases, table cloths. You better behave yourself or you won't be able to come back, Johnny. Johnny, I'm not gonna put up with you going around hitting folks. Johnny, try and find out and see when you can be back for good, Baby, and then I know I'll be happy and please, now that you can, call me soon.

JACKIE

Same old story, isn't it. Once they've got you either they don't want you or they don't trust you. It's always one or the other, and even if you're new to it you know better. You do, like with Car and me? When we first got started? He couldn't match me, see. He couldn't. He had me in the kitchen, looking in my eyes, his face to mine, like really, really looking, him pinning me back against the wall, my arms pinned back against the wall, me looking back at him, the both of us looking, like really, really looking, he was and I was, the both of us, just taking it higher and higher, me getting very excited behind it, very, very excited, my mouth getting shaky, my eyes getting shaky, tears coming to my eyes, his eyes going with me, my whole body starting to go, there was farther to go, our eyes weren't even eyes anymore, we weren't even looking into each other's eyes anymore, and he broke, he did, he put his hand on me and said, 'Hey, take it easy.' That's what he said. He couldn't keep it going, see. He couldn't. He couldn't match me. 'Hey, take it easy!' Now maybe he didn't want to, but I think he couldn't. And that's when I knew, see, Now I don't know what he thought, but it musta scared him, 'n you can't trust when you're scared... so... so... I mean, there it is...

CARSON

You ever been with two at a time, at the *same* time, like sisters, say, both of 'em really wet, but then you can tell one of 'em really hates the other, even if she's doesn't say so, 'n then one of 'em, the one that does the hating, shows up the next day with like this little fuzzy baby kitten and says she needs you to have it, that either you take it and keep it or she'll have to take it to the pound where they'll put it to sleep, 'n whatta you wanta do?

TERI

Jac really shook us up. We didn't know what to think. We thought she was off with Car, but, no, it was Jamal, this black guy we know. 'Where've I been?' she says. 'You won't believe, but I've been balling.' 'Balling,' I said, 'for three days? I thought Jamal was a fag.' 'A fag?' she says. 'Well, Sweetie, that's certainly one fag you'd love to know.' First she calls from Santa Paula, she's in a motel. 'A bed bug motel,' she says, and tells us to take all her clothes out of the closet and burn them, then for me to go to hell. Then calls again, she's not in Santa Paula but over in Fillmore, and then calls again, she's not in there, but right down the street in the Vagabond Ventura where she's been all along, room number 11, 'n asks me if I'll come 'n give her some change for the Coke machine 'cause she wants a cold Coke, and not a word about scaring us all to death. So of course Mom and me was really upset but Dawnie got on the phone an' told her, 'I hate everything about you,' told her to never come back, then hung up and got on our case, called me 'a skunky stink,' and Mom 'a bitch!' Isn't that a riot? 'A *skunky stink*?' Boy, was she mad!

JOHNNY

Naw, just figure when them C.O.'s rat-pack you, jus' grab one and take him with you. It's either that or curl up on the floor and cover your head 'n balls and let 'em take their shots. Them kicks and slugs on the back don't hurt you none. It's the head and balls you gotta watch. Now if there's just two, I love that. I'd rather there was two, 'cause with two one is gonna lead, an' the other'll hold back some. Now that's usually what happens, so's you just tear into the first dude, 'n mop up with the weaker one.

JACKIE

You talk about going all the way? All the way for you is when you finally get to shoot your wad off! That's all the farther all the way is for you! Yeah, that's right. You heard me. You can just sit there and look at me like that all you want 'cause I know you've got nothin' real to say. I am not talkin' mean to you! Because you like it. You think I don't know that? You think I don't know you?

TERI

Something's bothering her, that's for sure. Every day it's you can't get her up, sleeps all day, then has to have coffee and smoke cigarettes an' have her horoscopes read to her before she'll even talk. I mean she won't talk. You asked about my love life. I don't think I can be more than a friend to anyone, though there is someone new. Well, not really new, but sort of a surprise. Sort of. Anyway, not someone I'm really serious about. Please write to her again and encourage her to get off her ass and come to work with me at the club. Who knows, maybe the both of us can influence her mind. I don't know what else she needs as she's pissed off at me and doesn't want me talking to her about anything personal so I guess it's money she needs most so if you can get some, send it along, Boy. Well, maybe you could call her, too, or something....

JACKIE

I'm not gonna lie. If people ask a question they're gonna get an answer. If they don't wanna know, don't ask. I don't deny a thing, but only want to point out after you got busted the last time it was you that said, 'Go ahead 'n go out, I want you to.' Then Car shows up, right, on *your* recommendation! And's nice to me. So... I didn't plan on nothing with him, and, as it's worked out, I've learned the truth in time. He's selfish, jealous, a lowlife and a creep, and doesn't really care about other people's feelings...

JOHNNY

Yeah, Jackie, I got your letter which is some surprise, to say the least, and sick as I am about everything now that the pain has been burned away by the cold reality of my present situation I want to ask you a few things I've hesitated to ask but considering I didn't get to see you for a whole week before I got busted again I've got nothing to lose. I've been pissed off about a lot of things before and was always ready to let it be circumstances or something I didn't understand or maybe it's my fault or whatever weak fucking reason I could swallow without throwing up on myself. Well, wrong! What it is, is this – YOU'VE TREATED ME LIKE SHIT! THAT'S IT! WHAT ELSE IS THERE TO SAY? I don't really understand your trip but it's FUCKED and SO ARE YOU!! Where were you when I got back? Where was my little wife? WE BOTH KNOW WHERE! And at a time when a guy coming out needs all the support he can get so he can get his head on straight about what's important. There's a guy in here that's got a saying: BIG WOMAN, BIG CUNT – LITTLE WOMAN, ALL CUNT!!! YOU FIGURE OUT YOUR PLACE IN THAT ONE! Now I wasn't out to hurt you and you know it. All I ever wanted to do was talk and I don't mean the talking we did. God, I just wanted to see you so bad, I really did. And look what I got. I also know your side of it, but my present reality has made one thing very clear: I WILL TAKE NO SHIT FROM NO ONE, INCLUDING YOU!!! Also, I'm worried about you. Just what the fuck do you think you're doing? Right now there are just two things on my mind – me getting outa here, one, and, two – YOU GETTING YOUR ACT TOGETHER! I wish things were different but they aren't, and right now I don't give a rat's ass what either one of us does so long as one of us does something right, and for me – WHAT THAT IS, IS NEVER HAVING SHIT TO DO WITH YOU EVER AGAIN!!!

JACKIE

After what you've said to me I've now decided to not only continue being truthful but to be completely honest and open with you. Either things will work out on the basis of honesty or they won't work out at all. There's no need for you to threaten me. I received a reply from Adult Authority today. It was from a man named Harms. He said there was no way he could know what will happen but he appreciates my concern. I wrote another letter today explaining the money you owe Work-Furlough. And that I would pay it as soon as I can and asked him to explain the situation to the Board if it's necessary. He did say he didn't think you would be in very long. I said you would get the money to them as you had been working right up to the arrest, that you had some saved, but until you paid up the back child support first they would have to wait. I did send $25, so that leaves you owing $105 on the advance they gave you. Is that right? How come you never said you had money from them anyway? I want to say one thing about my seeing Carson. Look who took another girl, did you not? And as soon as you got out! And how many times have you done this? I'm glad you're finally getting hip about like who's to blame, but wonder if you really are. You say you've disappointed yourself in how you've dealt with me, then say I can't control myself. I guess it really doesn't matter what I say to you. On my side I suppose that being alone the past two Christmas's doesn't count, or the fact that both my birthdays were forgotten, or that J. J.'s and Dawnie's were. I didn't mean to surprise you about Carson. You always knew there was a little thing between us, but it was never nothing, and now that Teri has opened her trap about the latest B.S. just cause she's nasty I guess there isn't any way you'll listen to what I have to say. I'm sorry you prefer your own conclusions without knowing the facts. Just ask yourself this – do you love us or not? How many women would put up with what I've put up with and still want you back? Remember when you said you were going to put a hardon through my heart? How I thought that was funny? Well, I don't think that's so funny now. I've tried for too many years to let you see I loved you, but you've always been more interested in making your so-called friends think you're hot shit instead of making me think it. I mean admitting you love someone and acting to prove it when the other person admits it and acts it at the same time instead of saying you do only when I've pulled away from you. I don't know what will happen when you get out this next time. Sometimes I think about you, but all you do is think the worst. I don't know why but I've put the picture of you with the fish back up on the wall, the one when we were at Tahoe and stayed in King's Beach at those old cabins, remember? When we rented that rowboat and went fishing and caught that baby trout, then came back and watched the Wizard of Oz with Dawnie on the bed and I made buttermilk pancakes for supper because Dawnie felt sorry for the fish and made you let it go?

CHERYL BETH

No, no, that was with Angie, the one with the silver bullet tats on her ankles. She was a quiet one. She actually OD'd on cookies, chocolate chip cookies. She ate two whole boxes without drinking any milk and had a diabetes attack or something. John told her he'd give her a baby, too. Yeah, when she was sixteen, just like you. My mom knew her mom. The one who cut herself, remember? No, *not* her mom! *Angie!* Remember all those red slices up her arms that time and those bruises up under her eyes? That's what she did. Did that to herself, and then went out and got herself beat up. All over Johnny. Speaking of bullets: what else did he say? That he'd get you a big Airstream? One of those that are shaped like a fat chrome bullet. Those are pretty cool. They have a shower and stove and everything in them. John's got a pickup truck, too, doesn't he? Or he used to. He had it when he was with Angie. You can hook an Airstream up to one and go anywhere. Maybe Anthony will get us one. We could both have our babies and hook our trailers up side by side at a trailer park anywhere we wanted and our babies can play together. Wouldn't that be neat?

MILLY

Dear Johnny, what a nice surprise to get your card with the lovely message. I'm feeling much better since home but have had a rough five days, feel like I'm still cut into with the stitches pulling every time I move. Teri and her new boyfriend have been here almost every night. She babies him so much it ends up with me doing the cooking and dishes and picking up after them, been lots better if alone. Dr. said rest at least three hours a day and I'm lucky if I get one. I know Teri and her boyfriend will blow up. They get boozed-up, plus there's some sort of trouble with Jackie. If I say anything they just tell me to shut up. Wednesday they started in on beer at 3 in the afternoon and after dinner Ter and Jac and this Carson person sat in the living room smoking that marijuana stuff. The room was so thick with smoke I couldn't breathe. I went in the kitchen and started to clean up and Teri told Dawnie to help and of course Jackie got all snotty and jumped on Teri, telling her to butt out. Then Dawnie, bless her heart, told her Ter is right, and for her, Jackie, to go to bed, but she wouldn't, just kept on yelling and drinking and crying. I just went in the backroom with the kids and Ter came in and said not to get upset and pay no attention to Jackie, so then Jackie comes in and starts in on me, how I'm driving everyone nuts because I'm sick and can't do for myself, as well as for everyone else. Anyway, this Carson person went and sat in his car for an hour or so, hoping they'd all cool off. I don't know what Jackie was so mad about. I finally asked her to leave. Then when she finally did, she went outside and this Carson person was already gone so she got mad all over again and now no one has seen her for three days. My healing is going slow so it's been a little rough. I hope this is your mother's address. Call me if you know anything about Jackie. It may be you'll have to come get the kids and take them down there if that's where you are. How long has it been since your mother's seen them anyway?

BUD

Just like you, Bub, I never took no shit from no one, and always thought I wasn't whenever I grabbed my hat. A stiff middle finger to the world was my attitude, which seems to be yours, too, but don't ruin your chances by thinking you can avoid the choices you've already made because you can't. Marge has pulled out on me over this drinking business, and I've been taking a hard look at things. I know I didn't treat you good as a kid. All I can say is I didn't know no better. I did what I thought was the best thing. I know now I never should've bought you out of any of your troubles. Maybe when you're my age you'll understand what I'm trying to say. And not think your old man was such a prick.

JOANN

My Grandma asked me what I was going to do. Johnny, do you think we can live off what you can make? Can you really get a good job considering you have been in jail? I've been thinking about getting married since Monday when I found the letter you wrote in my Grandma's cabinet. When I found it, it told me she has the other one too because I have not got it. Johnny, please call and talk to me about what is going on, Honey. Sometimes I wonder if I am going to be any good for you. Maybe you don't want to get married. I think I really do and then I think we should wait. I need to know you really do want me. I'm scared to stay alone. Remember how sometimes I would start panting? Well, it's my heart. It starts to beat fast like it will bust. And I almost blacked out the last two times, the first time right in front of Mom and the last time alone, and now I can't help but think I might die and how hard some people might take it. I had a strange dream, too. I was walking by this 7-Eleven and there was this Chicano guy and blond girl and she was saying, 'Don't do it,' to him. He was holding his hand up over her head and he did it anyway, poured that stuff out over her. There was this little can in his hand, one of those little canned cocktails like you like, and as soon as he did that, poured it all over her, she disappeared and reappeared in the air over him and fire came out her vagina. She was naked, see, a bright green fire. And then these little cretins came out, too, and I was really scared, and finally a little Frankenstein, which was really funny because I laughed and woke myself up. It still scares me, though. What do you think it means? You know what a cretin is, don't you? A cretin is something that is deformed like with a big forehead and bulging eyes. I have some other NEWS! to tell you, but won't tell you until I'm sure. I don't know when that'll be, but I hope you'll like IT! I don't know that you will, but I bet you will !!!!

JOHNNY

I guess I do do a lot of mental masturbation, a lot of mental jacking off, and just don't get anywhere 'cause, well, I guess I just don't give a fuck. People will tell you you can't run away from life. Well, fuck that, man, I think you can. People are always telling me all kinds of shit. There ain't nothing about myself I haven't heard in one form or another from different people anyway. And another thing, sometimes you're supposed to have a certain attitude toward things, right? Well, if I get stoned, righteously stoned, that clears away all the confusion around a problem so I can see things for what they are and not get hung up in bad attitudes. The secret of drugs is to be a user, not an abuser. Now most people can't do that, but I can, and believe me, I know what I'm talking about when you know the people I know.

CHAPTER 11

SAINT BONAVENTURE HIGH SCHOOL

JOHNNY

One of the things I like is standing in the library, and things like that, watching the birds out in the yard. Some of the cons feed them. The same ones come every day and there's a beat-up one that comes when you whistle. He's an old blue jay we call Rocket cause he's the fastest to get to the bread. Rube calls him Corredor, which means Speedo, and when I told him about taking the two ounces outa Eddie's closet and said, 'That's what I got busted with,' he goes, 'So tha' wus yus beeg crime spree?' So then I told him about getting ripped off by them bunnies down in Long Beach, then holding up the liquor store and shooting myself in the thigh, and he started calling me Earp, after Wyatt Earp, the fastest gun in the West, and I tell him he's got a pretty good sense of humor for a Greaser, then I says, 'Well, if you wanna know what else? I almost torched a dude's car 'n bagged his dog, too, ha, ha, ha,' and he says, 'You knows wha' your problema es, Ese'? You problema es yus ain't has no good sex since God wus a li'l child,' which for sure is certainly true. Sometimes I get a hardon that's so big I can't even think. All the blood's drained offa my brain 'n gone you know where…

JOANN

If your ears start burning you'll know it's because Cheryl and me are talking about you. What made you decide to? I mean if necessary you would get a vasectomy? Don't you think it could do something to you? After the children we want come, could you then? I was sitting here watching a program on VAS and thought I'd ask you. Wouldn't you feel better knowing you could have a kid whenever you want? P.S. I found the stuff you said was under the backseat of the car and decided to flush it down the toilet. Now don't get mad. P.P.S. I got my Edible Undies! They sent me Hot Cherry, though, instead of Peppermint.

JOHNNY

Well, you could call it acting out, 'n stuff like that, if you wanna, but most people think I'm totally behind it. They think, here's what they think, they think I don't know that's not really me. See what I'm saying? That even if it looks like I've crossed over, hey, what I'm doing is having a big laugh behind it. Now that's what burns the shit outa me. No one sees that. None of you people do. You all wanna make me out like I'm some kinda big time O.G. gangbanger or hardened street numb-nuts criminal type A-hole or something...

JOANN

Every day now I have to see my despised, upsetting, disgusting, pimple-faced, bowlegged, liver-lipped, chisel-necked old boyfriend come to pick Cheryl Beth up from school. You didn't know Anthony was my old boyfriend, did you. He comes to her class and walks her to the car. Then they drive off. And I sit by and watch. Then I remember when my wonderful man would take me to and from school and then I get lumps in my throat, close my eyes, and pray the Lord will bring you back to me. But he doesn't, so what the hey. We're still friends, even though he doesn't cooperate, ha ha. I can't wait to see you, feel your arms around me, kiss your sugar lips and feel the heat of your beautiful big body against mine. Just thinking of all the times we made such sweet sweetness warms me all over. Just the thought of those times alone makes me yours and yours alone. No one else can do for me what you can and make me feel.

JOHNNY

Time to hang up this letter, Panda. There's an inspection in here in a coupla minutes, the old spread-em with a finger-wave to see if we've keestered anything, so I gotta go. What I want you to know, though, is you were so hot to touch when we touched it'll be a fuckin' miracle if I last another week without touching you again so be sure 'n get your beautiful little butt back here on Sunday again. And don't let your Mom hassle you too much, but remember she's got her good points, too, and loves you in her own kinda way and don't bother trying to make me jealous by hinting about any little punks trying to talk to you or walk you home or other schoolgirl type B.S. because I don't get jealous so it won't work on me like it does on them when you tell them about me.

ANTHONY

Fuck, no, Jo. I think your boyfriend's really cool. I do. Six Black 'n Whites, plus two squads of cops, or twelve freakin' cops all to take down just one old dude? Yeah! I know he's a great big fucker, but still! That's a lot of people for just one old guy. When I got popped that once, all's I got was one prowler an' one ol' fuckin' fatso cop, okay? No, *two* cops. Yeah, *two*. Fatso, plus that one chick cop that sometimes hangs around the school trying to act like she's some kinda lady undercover TV cop, know what I mean? You've seen her in the hall, always popping into the girl's bathroom, right? Tryin' to see who's selling weed? The one with the Rasta weave? Keisha? Wasn't you talking to her the other day 'bout something? Yeah, her... Keisha, the little bug-eyed one with the big ol' bubble butt? Yeah, her...what were you telling her?

JOHNNY

No, sir, I do not want to be here at all and will co-operate in any way I can, short of being a snitch, to relieve the County and the State of the burden of my support. Yes, the burden of my support. 'N, no, I am not mad at anyone. Not at all! If you wanna talk about law and order I'll talk about it. In here there is no law and order. Only over there, that C.O. with the thirty-eight on his hip, that thirty-eight there... that's the only law and order. Other than that there is none. I understand that. And I certainly understand if I'm going to live without law and order, either here or on the outside where there is law and order, people're gonna put me in a place where there really is no law and order, which they've already done.

TERI

Well, probably when I said, 'I guess we're together now,' and then he said – you know what he said? 'We'll see,' he says. Now I meant it, that maybe we *were* together. But right then, right after I said it, I knew I shouldn't a' said it like that, with the *'I guess'* starting it out so's it sounded like I was hesitating, like maybe I didn't really want to be with him, and all that, you see what I mean? Like maybe he had something more to prove to me. So, of course, he backs off, 'n nothing I could do about it, it was too late or, maybe not even that, maybe he just didn't want to really be together at all and was just keeping it open? So there you go. No matter how it went down it didn't go down right, so you won, Jac, all right? I lost, okay, but for myself? Who really cares? I don't even like the guy.

JOHNNY

You did what? Jesus Christ, Jo, I don't believe it! *All of it? All of it?* We were gonna go to Mexico on that! I told you that! The hell I didn't! 'Member me telling you about the beaches 'n bars there? I sure as hell did! 'T.J.?' That's Tijuana, okay? Don't you know that? It's on the border, Panda, the Mexican border! T.J., and no, you don't have to be eighteen to go there...

CARSON

So when Jac finally calls me, 'It's money,' she says. Now she wouldn't ask, she says, but I did say she could ask, didn't I? Not that she really has to, but maybe if I had some extra? 'Extra,' I tell her. 'What extra? We spent all the extra on takeout in the motel last week, in case you've forgotten.' 'Yeah?' she goes. 'Well, how 'bout this week?' 'N says, 'Go fuck yourself,' 'n hangs up, then calls back. 'It's not money,' she says, 'it's something else; there's something else that needs thinking about.' 'Like what?' 'Wouldn't you like to know,' she says, 'n hangs up again...

JACKIE

This is really ridiculous. Like the other night I was upset and had my head down on the bar and was crying so Car would approach

’n say, ‘What’s wrong, Babes?’ But he didn’t, right, ’n was making me feel like my cunt’d turned black or something, you know, that no one wanted it. So then this other guy comes over, this real beat-down, old alcoholic guy, an’ says, ‘Now, Jackie, don’t cry, you’re so beautiful, you’ve got nothing to cry about. Please don’t cry, Jackie!’ Well, shit, let me tell you I stopped crying like immediately. Here I’d gone down into this poor old beat-down person act, and what’d I get but a poor old beat-down person to come pick me up.

TERI

No, no, no, ’cause I really don’t give a damn about getting the better of you! I don’t! My only concern is you believing what Car says and not what I say. Because he can’t be something he isn’t, because I did *not* go behind your back! *I didn’t!* And if I did it wasn’t like I knew I was. Hey, you approved it! You certainly did. The hell if you didn’t! He’s such a son of a bitch! And I just left right then. No! I did not! For Christ’s sakes, Jac, he followed me all the way home. I don’t know what he expected. He said he thought he was in love. He did say that! No! That’s what he said. It was really stupid. I am not cheap, okay? Get your mouth offa that. Don’t even go there. I mean I might’ve got carried away, okay, just for that one little tacky moment, okay, but that’s all... well, just take that shit up with him then, okay?

JACKIE

John, John, I know that’s true, and it really does hurt when I remember certain things, things I said I’d never let happen. It seems as if everyone else I know is happy, or can be happy. Having confronted my behavior myself, and not just from what you’ve said to me – and I must admit your last letter shook me up – having to go through that with such intensity for the past month, with me being more defensive, more uptight, more a nervous wreck just waiting to happen and still not being accepted by anyone, well, I have finally released it all. I don’t know what else to tell you except I’m no longer in that ugly place, have mellowed out and am now flowing with all that is around me, even Teri Ann and me have got our heads together, even over some perverted weirdnesses. Nothing much else is going on. Do you think we're just supposed to be with certain people for a certain time and have to find that out before we know where we really belong? Am I wrong? Why is it so hard for men to accept love? Why can't they give what they feel and not just try and see how many women they can nail?

JOHNNY

It did, Jac, it really did, your letter just hit home. I am so sick of this sorrow. My words are not me. I've always looked to run away from things, afraid I would run out on you, afraid you would run out on me. My feelings are pushed beyond what is real. My thoughts rebound inside my head and become more real than any reality I know. The best thing to do is to keep smiling, keep calm, show no weakness. Thinking of you with just half a mind keeps me calm. I'm so sorry for getting crazy. I'm scared, Flower, really scared. I'm so close to getting away from this fucking mess, this stench and decay, that I feel it in my soul something is gonna happen, something bad that will fuck me up for a long time to come, something so bad that'll forever make it impossible to ever come home again where all I want is to live, to love, and in return be loved. I guess that's too much to ask. Too much to ask! Isn't that a trip! Shit! I'm tired, Baby, really tired. I need rest, I need love. I get up each morning surrounded by hate, I lay down each night sunk by it. I feel as if any minute my mind will collapse. I feel a need to be close to you, closer than I've ever been. Well, I just have to press on, press on, damn it, press on! But no matter what happens, I've had you, and I wouldn't trade nothing for that, not even the getting out of here...

MS. KAREN WONG, AFDC

We have reviewed the information you gave us about your circumstances separate from those of your husband and family and find that: You are not eligible for Aid To Families With Dependent Children for Aug. because: Refusal to comply with requirements. The laws and/or regulations which require this action are: Title

22, Section 50496, Failure to provide essential information. This action does not affect your application for the current period. If you have any questions about this action, or if there are additional facts about your circumstances which you have not reported to us, please write or telephone. We will answer your questions or make an appointment to see you in person…

JACKIE

That's not all. I feel like I'm gonna drown in overdue bills. It's so bad I don't even look in the mailbox anymore. There's just too many ways to get upset without having no money being one of them and I've pretty well decided I'm gonna have to do something about it. Now who has your Mom's wagon? She says she doesn't, that you promised to return it after you got settled and maybe it's stashed at the paint shop? She thought I had it. She also said Earle was pissed off about it and was gonna charge you with car theft.

JOANN

Yes, I did do like you said. Cheryl drove me. Your Mom is very nice. I also met Earle. That's how he spells it, doesn't he, with an E on the end? He doesn't talk much. Plus he smells. She gave me a Bible to bring you. Cheryl is pregnant by Anthony but doesn't like his personality and neither do I, he has accused me of some pretty mean stuff, like turning him into the police for selling some joints or something and she's waiting for them to have a fight so she can break up. I looked it up in my little book from my pills and it says it depends on the person how long it takes to get pregnant after using the pill. I haven't started my period yet. I know you're thinking I'm pregnant and you're right. But just for you I'm hoping I'm not. But if I am, will you still want it? Johnny, I want to know. Johnny, will you let me order a ring now? I have some money left from what Grandma gave me for a car and now that I have yours I feel like some of the money belongs to you. The size of the diamond doesn't matter anymore but I want a fairly nice one in white gold like my good and best-running watch. Last night I was so mad at Mom I didn't know what to do. I felt like running away and never coming back except for her funeral but didn't have the energy so I baked a coconut fudge cake which tasted really good. I wish you were here so we could move to Seal Beach. Last night I dreamt I lost the baby. I guess I had him and I put him in the mailbox and somehow forgot where he was and when I remembered I ran out and opened the lid and he was in there all covered with ants! He was still alive though and I got him out. I'm also daydreaming a a lot, too. Like a few minutes ago I daydreamed we were married and had an apartment and neat car like a buff Mustang convertible and good paying job. I'm willing to work also. I still think I was right to get rid of that packet of stuff. And Cheryl says so, too. She says Mexico is too scary a place to live and you couldn't get work there anyway since you are 100 percent American and would miss the USA and don't really speak any Spanish and really would be going there to get more drugs. And I do know Tijuana is in Mexico. Everyone knows that. And that stuff wouldn't go down in the bowl and I had to lift it out and poke my nail scissors in it and the dust powdered up in the air and think I breathed some of it before I could flush it all away. It was awful and really lucky my Grandma didn't come come in and catch me. I want you to talk to Anthony when you get back and tell him to stop saying all these big lies about me. I know he will listen to you as he really respects you and told me so.

RUBEN

Hey, Ese', roll me 'nother one a' them Buglers, hokay?

JOANN

I'm sorry I made you so mad, but why aren't you calling me? I miss you yelling at me on the phone. I want to be with you more than ever but I can't say what I did was wrong. I miss talking to you. I want to make sure there is nothing coming between us, Mr. Panda. I'm thinking about getting a gold star tattooed on my ankle, on my right ankle, not too big a one, but maybe a little gold and red and blue outlined one right around my ankle. Would you like it? I bet you would. If you say no, I won't do it...

JACKIE
I could go see Eddie like you said, but if I ever did that you'd know I was way beyond the point of trying to get it together. Also, his place was ripped just before you got busted, an' for some messed-up reason he's been putting it around that I know about it. I don't know about it. Is there anything about it that you know?

JOHNNY
It would take a pretty damn good doctor to figure all this shit out, so maybe that's what I'm gonna do, start crapping around with the main squeezer here. You should see the guy. I bet his mommy had to hold his tinkle for him every time he had to wee-wee. He's got more tics 'n a clock, plus he's always trying to bum smokes offa you. He's trying to quit, see, but he doesn't have no willpower in his deal. 'Look,' I told him, 'that cigarette didn't leap up to your mouth all on its own, did it? It didn't place itself between your lips, pick up the lighter, and light itself, did it? You picked it up, you put it between your lips, you held it in there, then lit the sucker, right? So you don't pick it up, you don't hold it in there, 'n you don't light it, right?' Now I gotta say he liked that. So maybe I'm making some headway here, okay? Kinda like grinding the metal down past the base coat before you get the sprayer hooked up. You gotta strip all the Bondo, rust, 'n caked-up filler off before you can work the paint job, right?

MS. KAREN WONG, AFDC

Dawn Dalton, age 8, born five months after Mrs. Dalton's marriage when Mrs. Dalton, age 26, was eighteen years old, is considered to be a normal child in spite of throwing frequent tantrums, the situation complicated by the presence of an unemployed non-related Caucasian male sometimes visiting in the home as Mrs. Dalton (whose husband is absent), usually tired when returning home after seeking work, is forced to divide her attentions. Not only does the little girl shriek, scream and cry if frustrated in her wants until sending her to her room, shared with Mrs. Dalton's other child, John Dalton Jr., age 3, is the only solution, but lovemaking, Mrs. Dalton states, is nearly always an unsatisfactory experience stemming from a sense of guilt about her current life situation. Mrs. Dalton also states she is working hard at setting her priorities straight, including communicating with her daughter better by taking time out to listen to her daughter's words, showing her she does listen to her, and does understand and respect her feelings. Further states, at this time there is no adult male living in the home.

CHAPTER 12
EAST VENTURA BASIN, VINTAGE PETROLEUM

JOHNNY

Guess what I heard out in the yard today? 'You know what the three most dangerous things in the world are? A spade with a gun, a spic with a knife, and a Greek with sneakers on!' Ha, ha, ha. Now I'm sorry to hear Eddie's accused you of something as stupid as ripping him off, he should know you better than that. I know how you feel about working for him, but just tell him to give you some samples, then sell them if you have to. Tell him some Bros here know his whole scene. Some heavy Bros. If he says he won't do it for you, tell him I'm gonna find out about it. If you have to go that far. Don't say I told you this. Just see what he does. A guy got tossed off the second tier here this morning. Split his head from the top of his scalp to the back of his neck. The dumb son of a bitch just stood there looking at me, blood pouring down his face. 'Dude,' I said, 'you don't know it, but you better get your ass over to the infirmary muy pronto 'cause you're dying.' He was just standing there all steamed-up, looking to kill someone, you know. Now that's a guy to stay away from. Too damn stupid for his own good.

JACKIE

No, 'cause I'm a lot stronger than that. Really a lot stronger, and I will not fall back into drugs and drug life all of which, well, as for Eddie, he's only into controlling other people, he could care less about anything else. I told him, 'No, I did not take your goddamn blow!' As soon as he makes a bunch more money he'll forget all about it. The only way I'd go to him now, I'd consider it because of the money situation 'cause Ter is spending it as fast as she makes it. And right now we have none. So I figure if I turn over, say, maybe an ounce or two, we can make this month's rent. But thinking about it, I think maybe our chances are better in Reno. It's just let's see how the money goes. A person can always fall back, but I don't want to. You know when you smoke gram after gram, when you smoke five or six grams in a night you know you've got a problem. Like a gram in a half-hour? Now I've learned something, a big, big something. There was a night here with Ter, and I got her zoned-up, which wasn't any big deal to me 'cause I don't get half as high as she does, my tolerance is just so much higher than hers, but, anyways, she zoned half of what I did, and got so fried and weirded out, like yelling at me about things that weren't even close to being true, and things that were just so nasty that I looked at her and thought, 'Man, it's doing the same thing to me, but I don't see it, you know, I just don't see it,' and, you know, that's when I pretty well decided that was the end of it for me. Now I've had to disassociate myself completely. And that means with all the people, too, including both Ter and Eddie 'n whoever else, which isn't so hard, you know, because as soon as they see you're not into it they stop coming around. Now I could go back over there to Ed's, say, and sure, I could have maybe a hit or two, but what's really gonna freak them out is me telling them, 'No, I don't want any, I don't need it, thanks a lot, but right now I'm just happy being me, okay?'

RUBEN

Look, Ese', yus burns a vato like your man Edwardo there, Ese', yus bet your ass he'll catch yus on the rebound, man. He's a vato, Ese', now hain't he? Now he's a smart vato, too, so it be nothin' violent. He's not that kinda vato. He's too smarts for that, but no one gets him, right? To use violence on yus, that's to admit yus gots him, right? Yeah? Well, like going after you leetle Amigita, for one – tha' leetle hoodrat that's been climbin' all over yus in the Day Room. Wha' her name, HoAnna, right? HoAnn? Well, think abouts it, Ese'. Like maybe by getting her together with someone else, Ese'. Yus ever think of that? Yus think tha' can't be done?

CARSON

Some ladies are like that. They'll do anything with anybody. They can't help it. And it's a good thing to find out, too. People'll say there's a real nice person in there, you know, inside of them, but maybe not. An' maybe there's a reason why not. You know, like maybe no one takes them seriously, you know. Or they've been fucked over, 'cause maybe their brain is too small or their ass's too big, right? So maybe that's why so many of them are out there getting stoned. There's a lot of 'em like that out there, lots of time on their hands, out there just looking for what to do. It makes for good business. And, hey, you know how hard it is to start out from nothing? You know, like when you're taking a bike up over a hill, just gunning it, and going on up there, riding like your balls are on fire, 'n you hit the fuckin' crest and then you've gone airborne and don't even know what's on the other side, an' it's jus frickin': *'Ahh-hhhhhhhhhhh!?'* Well, it's like that for them, too. They don't know what's gonna happen. So they just go for it. But listen, you know what my religion is? It's jus' plain ol' fucking, man; plain pure 'n simple. That's where it's at. You can ask any of my ladies. They all know they can have it any time they want it. All they gotta do is ask. And with this older chick I know? Why I keep going back to her? I guess 'cause she's like some kinda sexual genius. Like I might go there a couple of weeks from now, or maybe next week, or maybe even tomorrow 'cause she's, well, she just dangles you, man, I mean like holding a palm out, wiggling her fingers toward herself to call you in, then, as you get close, putting up her other palm in front of her face to stop you. I mean like I might even sort a' be in love with this one, see. Now my policy has always been to get respect, give respect. And if I don't get it? Hell, I can shout just as loud as the next guy 'n kick ass just as hard. But her, she don't even try to get respect. She don't give a fuck what kinda bullshit you're trying to run, so you *gotta* respect her. She *makes* you respect her. Hell, I might even truck on up to Nevada, you know, where she is now. Reno, right? Just talking about it makes me think about it, you know, getting my little ol' Johnson on outa here…

JOHNNY

I've been thinking real hard about all this crap, Jac, and the doc here says he always knows who the psychos are, the first ones to jump up, shake your hand and give you a smile. He says guys who're trying to help themselves are the guys who keep back to themselves cause they're working on their problems themselves. Now that makes sense, and that's why I haven't been writing you that much. I haven't had that much to say that makes sense. So what I do want to say is this – I think we should be good to each other, kind to each other, loving to each other. That's the way I want to be living my life with you. I now think that's the only way to live life. I think we both want to be good and loving, even when we aren't. That is my thinking. Now the problem is making that thinking come true. Do you think something like that is possible between the two of us?

JOANN

Dearest Love, I'd like to bring it to your attention that I've been having tidings in the pit of my stomach. I wish you hadn't said you felt I was pregnant. I've been scared ever since. I wish you would tell me why you think so. It really does bother me. I'm scared to have a baby. What if I died or got sick or it died? Oh, Boy, it's gonna hurt, too! You can ask Cheryl! I'm glad you called. What's going on? I was so happy to hear your voice I think I feel a little better. I wish you were here right now so I could kiss your sugar lips but I wish you were not because you're there to get yourself straightened out and to make things better for us. I hope you're not mad at me for some of the things I said before. Like I said, I don't want to be lonely, I'd rather be loved and needed and depended on, Honey, that's all I ask.

BUD

Three days, John Boy, then the fourth day woke up with blood all over hell – chin, neck, pillow, sheets. Scared to get up, but made it to the sink and damn near filled it. Musta thrown up near a pint or more. Didn't know what it was. Was just as weak as a kitten. All

I could think was cancer of the lung. I made it out to the couch and lay there. Marge was already up, getting ready to go to work. Told her I was sick and not to go into the bedroom but she musta thought I was dogging it cause she never said I'll take you to the hospital and left for work. The R.V. was still outside, but I knew I was too lightheaded to drive, but had to do something so I got up and walked to the hospital. They gave me a shot of something, plus a little white cup of pink fluid to drink, and sent me home. Pneumonia is what they said. This left lung collapsed on me. I musta slept the next couple of days out. I don't remember nothing there. Then was still coughing out blood, but only little flecks and Sunday was finally able to smoke a whole cigarette and Monday smoked three. Then was checked out again, Doc said he wanted to check for cancer. I haven't gone back to hear the results. For right now I'd rather not know. They found I've got some good-sized gallstones to come out, but otherwise I'm all right but haven't got my usual energy back so I've laid off trying to work for a spell and no more drinking.

JACKIE

Women's libber? *Me?* Are you kidding me? Hell, no, I'm no women's libber, but I believe in rights, all right, I believe in *heart rights, equal heart-to-heart rights!* I mean no more give and give, I want give and get! I'm sick of this give, give, give. I've had it with give, give, give. Like with this last man? Now he *is* a man and takes what he wants, he's not afraid of that, but then he never keeps anything either, which isn't so strong when you think about it. In fact I know it isn't. What is strong is the sex, though. The sex is outa this world, you gotta say that. He'll turn you on in a whole bunch of ways, 'n have you thinking how incredible it all can be, then snap your head around by saying things like he really does understand your need for your own life and a chance to be by yourself in your search for self-independence, good shit like which means, when you think about it, that he's leaving, right, and you're supposed to be all happy and cheering while he's sliding on out the door. Yeah, ha, ha, the backdoor, and then talking about it with my sis, she says it's all my own fault, I'm letting him walk all over me. 'Well,' I say, 'I'm in love.' *'In love?'* 'Well, love is fucked,' she says, 'love is just one person loving 'n the other person just taking that love, that's what love is.' And I say, 'It isn't; it's two people trying with each other.' 'Well,' she says, 'try a little harder; try telling him to take a hike. Tell him you and John are gonna get back together. Tell him, 'Hey, you've had your shot.' Tell him, 'Hey, I hear what you say, 'n I see what you do.' So I did. Face to face, too. Didn't back off an inch. Which was just great. Like he couldn't even believe it, you know. So who knows? And I've gotta say I'm feeling pretty good lately, I like the way things feel. Like even with John. Seems he's getting his head on pretty straight lately, he's said some pretty sincere things lately. Of course, no one writes love letters like prison love letters, I know that, but this time no one's gonna help him out except himself and I think he sees it. Hey, I don't rule it out. When he's thirty-six he should be coming around! Yeah, maybe thirty-six! Hey, we've been going along in spurts since I was sixteen. First him, then me, then him again. See what I mean? Now alls I need is a Tampax and a ride outa town, right? Ha, ha, ha, ha...

IRENE

Gunner isn't with us anymore and Earle isn't over the loss yet. That's one reason I thought a different house would help. Frosty had to be taken to the Vet's because he developed cystitis just like Pepsi had. Frosty wasn't as sick but was peeing pure blood. He's better now, but neither one of the cats can have dry food anymore. Seems it contains too much ash content for their kidneys. Lejo, though, is still the same little weak-eyes lover she's always been and there is a new addition. When we moved here the new yard had a very skinny boy kitten in it. We vowed not to feed it but Pucksters and Pepsi shared their meals with it so now there is Angel Baby who is just like his name. He is a little white and gray-striped tabby. It is really funny to see Lejo try to make up to it. She still doesn't know that cats and dogs don't mix. Poor Angel Baby, he gets all sorts of unwanted attention. Actually Pucksters and the new addition are the better friends of the four. Frosty is back to his old self of chasing certain cats around the neighborhood. When we first brought him here he wouldn't come out of the back porch for two weeks. He hid himself on one of the lower shelves and the only way he would was if I'd coax him with food and then only if he was hungry. Lejo decided under my bed was the only place she felt safe in. She stayed there a week, never leaving the bed except to stay glued to my leg and foot if I was home which I have been. Pepsi was her usual peppy cat self and adapted right away. She investigated the yard, the back porch, the house, and seemed right at home, something I'm not yet. I gave the large aquarium to the man who lived on Pine St. behind us. He promised to take good care of it and the fish and Hamburger went, too. It was really sort of sad but I knew I couldn't move them this far and expect them to live and they had such a hard life before, I felt they deserved the chance. He and his daughter moved them and came back to tell me all went well. Since the man and girl were so happy to receive them I felt better. I do wonder how they are doing, especially Hamburger and Little Tiger Barb and Three Spot. The pretty blue one didn't survive the long haul, though. I just wish there was something I could tell you that would sink in and make you a productive citizen again. I don't have the talent or I'd make the effort. You are the only one in the family that is carrying on the family name and are making a mess of the opportunity. I know that sounds harsh, but what you are doing to yourself is more harsh. When a child is born with all the breaks you had it does seem rather hopeless when he determines to ruin himself and all those he knows for the sake of what I will never know. And by breaks I mean things like having a healthy body and mind, the very essentials of being a person with no problems attached, such as not being able to walk, talk, see or hear, or having some part of your body retarded from birth. You started out with a clean slate and as soon as you were old enough to be responsible for it you proceeded to muddy it. Oh, almost forgot to tell you that the State sent you a letter here to find out your thoughts about the Work-Release Program. Are you getting out on the Work-

Release? They actually wrote twice since we last saw you! Also, you got a letter asking you for jury duty. Seems this world is pretty big after all and the officials of government just don't get together on some things. I'm sure you're not eligible for jury duty, not even in the future. Earle says that I will need my car back real soon, and for you to think about it. He's not a mean man, Johnny, no matter what you think, and says we'll be up to see you in a few weeks if that's what you want. I gave the girl a little Bible to give you. Did you get it? She certainly was nice with good manners for so young a girl. She wanted to know the kinds of food you liked. Isn't her mother Martha McKinnon? Although I don't know what her last name is now. It certainly could be something else. I knew Martha back when she was sorting strawberries out at Lorca's in Oxnard. She was always a wild thing. I'd heard she finally married a guy after having an abortion in high school but that was years ago. You know I've never been real fond of Jackie and know how she's treated you. Just like my own mother always said Bud wasn't good enough for me, I suppose, and maybe she was right, but I never broke the law over it, and even when we had our fights neither did he. Because I believe in the law because we are all brothers and sisters and the law is there to show us that we're all bound together. Smarter people than us have made the law, Johnny. A person with no kind of rules is not the kind of person other people look up to. People look up to a person who knows the rights of others. You must stop this fighting and drugging and getting mad, Johnny. You are not a kid anymore. That that marriage is over with is the best news I've heard in a long time. When you marry a person you should marry them for life, and not be with a person who is going to run around on you with every Tom, Dick and Harry who comes along. I hope you have enough sense to stay away from her, no matter what she says, and you better help those kids before you get yourself all tied up again with this young, pretty girl. They are your kids. I remember the last time when you got out and said you were so grateful that me and Earle were so wonderful to you when you was in trouble that if your kids was ever to get into real trouble you would sure want to give them the same help you got, so what are you doing? They need your help now, not later...

JOHNNY

Ah, it's all a buncha shit. I'd asked my wife to hit me, see. She'd said even on our wedding day I didn't understand her so how could I understand her now. I said, 'What's to understand? I know exactly what I've done, so take it all out on me now and we'll be even. Go ahead an' hit me.' I wasn't mad at her or nothing, no matter what she says. We was drinking some brews 'n I said, 'And what the hell does understanding you on our wedding day mean anyways? You let me put the goddamn ring on your finger, didn't you? You weren't complaining about nothing then, were you?'

GRAMS

God loves all his children. You may think he doesn't. You may think because you believe Irene is stupid that she's not in the center of God's mind, that she can be hurt and it doesn't matter. Or because Eddie is a criminal drug dealer you can mess him over. Or because Jackie messed around on Harold Bowers with you when you first started seeing her and that she told you she only loves you, that Harold is a person that doesn't matter, but you're wrong. You and her hurt Harold, and God will hurt you and her. You hurt Irene, and God will hurt you. You hurt your friend Eddie, and you will get hurt. You think I'm some crazy old woman, but I'm not. You are not the only person in the center of God's concern. Everyone is, John. Everyone. And you better learn this or you will continue being hurt and hurting others over and over again until you are dead. Do you recall Jackie and Harold was going together when you broke them up? I'm not saying it was all your fault as you was just a boy and didn't know no better, but that was the start of all your troubles. And look what happened to Harold. He married that Delaney girl and has two daughters and a job at Getty Oil and goes to night school three nights a week and plays softball on a team that drinks beer together the way that drinking beer was invented for and has such a good time and are in first place in the league. You might think about that…

RUBEN

...not me, man, if a woman slides someones else I don't wanna slides her. Sliding in on someones else's juice? No way, Homes, faithless love don't interest mes one damn bit. Thes' es a tough ol' world, Ese'. Yus don't wanna wakes up one morning and think yus've wasted your life, Homes. Too many mens 'er doin' that, chasing their tails 'cause some bitch es breakin' theys balls 'n they don't even know why they're doing what they're doin'. Now mes, whatsever I's had to do to get over, that's wha' I's done. If there's no feria, if tha's wha' people needs, then I's goes out and gets mine. If it's mota, I goes out 'n gets mota. If yus gots something out there that's gonna make it for yus, do it, but do it for yus, understands, 'n quit thes' goddamn li'l stories 'bout thes' stupid bitches. Tha' one yus cryin' over now, you think she's even thinkin''bout yus? Es yus even in a place wheres yus can helps her? Then what the hell's she needs yus for? I don't care how many chiquillos she's give yus. Es all a' bunch of shit. I don't care if yus wus the big Hesus Christo hisself sittin' there, I'd be tellin' yus the same peche' thing, hokay? *Chiquillos* es *kids,* man, *nino*s. Yeah? So jus' go break the bitch's arm then...

JOHNNY

What people really mean when they say they're trying to get themselves together is they're trying to get themselves together with the one they love – WHICH IS YOU. I don't know what else to say. Tell Dawnie I miss her sweet little hands on my face, her sweet, sweet little hands, and Daddy sends her a bazillion kisses and tell John-John to think of his Daddy once in a while and that when I get back we're all going to the County Fair and ride all the rides, even the one that looks like a giant yellow chili and spins around upside down while it circles around and around on the big arm, the one you got sick on. Does he use that little blue flannel blankee I got for him? Tell him I got in a beef right after I got it, but I remembered to keep it and make certain that he got it.

GRAMS

Things are a mess, Honey. Your Dad and Marge are split again. And what to do about him, he's gone off the deep end, not only sick, but acting crazy again. He doesn't know I'm writing this. I want to send you some money but he takes care of my checkbook. Did he give you any of the money he said he was going to? I'll make sure he does if that will help. I'm so upset I can't write but hope you can read it. I don't have much but am sending thirty dollars. Maybe you can call him and have him visit if he starts feeling better. Hate to upset you but you and Jill and him are all I have. Don't mention this to anyone and write back what you think or you can call collect. Something else happened. I had a dream and saw your mom and dad in a rowboat and she held an umbrella over his head, like she was protecting him as he rowed. Sometimes it takes a very long time for people to work things out, so maybe you could call her and tell her...

JOHNNY

I was rearrested and held in the County Jail and taken to the State Hospital where I was found incompetent to stand trial on Cases #367112-367113. I was kept in the hospital for over a month and finally taken back to court, only to be put off. They told me if I would remain in hospital another month all charges would be dropped. I was returned to the hospital and was taking thirty (30) days when I filed Writ #1, so I could go back and stand trial on these charges. I also filed Writ #2 because they were keeping me in seclusion without bedding. During the day they expected me to sit on a straight back chair for over twelve (12) hours a day locked in a 17' x 10' seclusion room for trying to hit the Posse Captain and the rest of the scum Posse Members when they tried to strip my clothes off. I was kept down in seclusion for five (5) days and after that put back in numerous times. I was given meds without my consent, held down on a steel bench in a different seclusion room and given a shot of Thorazine. This happened four (4) times. Six or seven other patients held me while an attendant shot me up. Also during this time I was trying to get my case back to court. Writ #3 was never sent because the Third Judicial Court acted on Writ #2. I was returned to court and after a two (2) week wait in jail was taken to court and had Case #367112 reduced to a 1st Class Misdemeanor which carries a maximum of one (1) year in jail, or prison, and a $500.00 fine. I was given a six month stay of sentence and sent back to the hospital. Then when I went to court again I was given a second six month stay of sentence on Case #367113. Or at least this is what I was told by the Deputy Public Defender. When I went to see the Judge he told me he hadn't sentenced me to another six months. What I would like to know is what is going on? Why am I back in the hospital when I'm supposed to be back in jail?

JACKIE

Before Welfare I seldom enjoyed life, but felt I had opportunities and didn't feel excluded from living in the same way that being on AFDC makes me feel. I lived in a twenty dollar a day room (kitchen and bath) working at two lousy jobs (tandem) but was satisfied with the way I was raising my daughter (my son wasn't born until after my husband returned) and with my right to enjoy her. I felt no guilt but was sorry over the things I was unable to provide for her, but felt I was smarter than other women in similar situations. I felt I had more success and was satisfied and proud of myself as a mother and a person. The only problems I had were financial and sex in that I was not sleeping with anyone because I had limited amounts of time and money and I chose not to sleep with the sort of person I could attract. With my husband again in confinement I will be reduced once again to staying in such circumstances, but with the additional burden now of a second child. Unless my husband is released this will necessitate our family remaining on AFDC, a situation both of us would like to change (as with a second child I am having a hard time finding work) for the reasons given above. As to the presence of a non-related man in the home – the person seen was only a friend for a short time who was sleeping on the couch while out of work himself and currently is not on the premises nor has been in some time. There is no man in my home whatsoever at this time nor in the future.

CHAPTER 13
STARDUST MOTEL

JACKIE

You wanna see some pictures? Sexy pictures? Do you? Maybe alcoholic is what, all right? Or ex-alcoholic. Whatta you think of that? 'Cause I like it, is why. Whatta you think? You have to think of the glow, right? You think of the glow. People put it down but forget the glow. You believe that? It's the only time I'm happy. Well, not really, more *maybe* happy, not like happy-happy, like halfway happy, okay? My little boy doesn't understand that. He doesn't. He's just a little guy. He's never hurt anyone in his life. He doesn't know anything about sitting around in a Welfare office. Huh-uh. No way. Or my little girl neither. Yeah, 'n she's real pretty, too. Well, sure, 'cause it's, 'pretty momma, pretty baby,' right? 'N she'll be a pretty momma, too, but I've got some good years left, some real good years, but I need a pretty man. And I'd like another baby girl, too, or maybe another little boy, but I can't find anyone to knock me up. And what are you, jus' another card table cowboy? Yeah, *a card table cowboy!* You got anything else? 'Cause that's why I'm here, man. I'm not gonna bullshit you about it. Those are the *facts*, man. I wouldn't be here if they weren't. If I didn't have my *facts* straight. *The facts of life, man.* That's *what* facts. And to *dance.* People don't think it's an art, but it is. Look at her! Isn't she the worst? And she thinks she's the greatest, too. You have to know what to say and how to say it. Well, I've got a speech all ready for her, believe you me, 'n she's gonna hear it, too. You understand what I'm saying? Isn't she a scream? Tries to get by on personality, see. Puts her hands on her hips and shakes 'em. Thinks that's dancing. You can't blame her. That's just the way she is. What else can she do? Can't do anything else. Not really her fault. If all I had was that cowlike mattress of an ass I'd shake it, too, you dig? See what I mean? Isn't that a riot? Here, look at these. This one here. You think that's me? Or this one? Before

I did my hair? Well, look again. Just another bleach bottle blonde then, right? Right, 'n this one? Yeah, that's me...it certainly is... Hey, don't bend 'em...

CARSON

Plus her laugh. She has this real ballsy laugh. She really laughs a lot. I really like chicks that laugh. Hey, I'm friends with the guy. I am. I'm not out to fuck him. Frankly, John's beautiful people, you know. I mean as a friend he's okay, he mostly does what he says he's gonna do, but I never saw a guy so crazy over a chick. Never. Remember when he got popped offa that liquor store deal? Remember that? When he shot himself? You know just before that happened he was over at my place flapping around like an eagle? Flapping around like this? Running all around the room, his arms spread out like this, sayin' he just couldn't understand it, he couldn't, how could she do this to him, just flappin' his arms out like a pair a' wings 'n asking me about it? Like completely outa control, man, 'n I said, 'Look, man, all's I'm into is the fucking part, man; I got no interest *whatsoever* in the love part, you can have the love part...'

JOHNNY

Then they gave me drugs without my consent, including a 500 wallop of Thorazine with five or six attendants holding me down. A squeezer out there named Fullmer told me about the main squeezer in here and how to talk to him. With Thorazine, trying to talk is like having a dirty wool blanket stuffed in your mouth and wrapped around your head. Your jaws won't open, and if you have to piss it takes forever to get your pants untied. Fullmer was a solid guy and showed me how to gag the other meds back up, which SORTA helped in "my recovery," ha, ha. How are the kids? Don't believe any shit you might hear about me flipping out. I was was bouncing around the padded room, all right, 'n scratching my ass on the canvas, but I was never down for the count, and was always thinking of you...

JACKIE

I guess you know by now the phone company sent a notice to shut our service off. I still don't have the rent and don't know when I will have so I went back and saw Eddie like you said. He acted real surprised. He said the burn was done by someone who was either really lucky or else knew where to look, as nothing else in the house was broken into, and definitely thinks it was either me or someone I know, so that idea of yours is definitely out. I just got back from taking the kids to the beach and took a shower to get rid of all the salt and washed and set my hair and now I'm under the hairdryer. Not a blow dryer, but Mom's old hairdryer. If some miracle happens I'm going to get my hair triple bleached again or have Ter do it for free. The bad news is Welfare has been trying to cut off the money this month as they've found out through <u>someone</u> that <u>someone</u> has been living here. And I think I know who. And it's not true. The other news is that the manager searched the apartment while I was gone and found the swim trunks you took out of his wash. I got pretty ticked off and called him a no good sneaky bastard and some other things. He said get out within three days and then let him know my address and I can arrange to pay the rent a little at a time so that isn't so bad. Last night the Asst. Manager came by and turned me onto some weed. His name is Jamal and he's very nice. He really laid me back. He says I'm a soul sister and because I told him you were my old man he said you must be out of sight, too. Maybe you'll be able to meet him sometime as he's a real nice guy and very respectable. At any rate he respects me and has always been a gentleman around me. Also, he kept me from getting arrested. Those people we got the stereo from came with the Sheriff, either to get payment on the check or to put me in jail, and Jamal was here and made the check good for us and made the guy take all the stereo junk back including the cabinet and speakers and give me a release because we can't keep up the payments. The two pics of me in the bikini are here at the apartment. The guy behind me with his fingers up in the V is Jamal. Groovy? He and I went on an acid trip the night before last and it was very strange because I forgot all about the rent and

Welfare and Eddie and Ter and Mom and other hassles and really enjoyed myself. Someone put FAST CAR on by Tracy Chapman, and I got all hung up, it reminded me so much of you that I went off into my own little space and just created you right there with me. It was so real real and so groovy. It was just as if you were here and were grooving on Tracy, too. And even when the cut ended I was still in that space for about twenty minutes. Ah, Hon, it was so fine and you were so real. I think I've been acting pretty nutty lately and now realize how awful everything was for you when you returned and you did what anyone would've done. Well, maybe not just anyone. I'm not saying things were my fault either, but just that I was sorta spaced. A lot of time had passed. Just seeing you was like a sort of flipout. In truth that first night when I asked you not to stay and you came in and crashed in my bed and I got up and went out in the living room and watched the TV out there, it just seemed like all the old days all over again. It's really trashy watching TV by yourself, and I couldn't help it, thinking that, and what was gonna be any different, 'n all, your first day back, cause I'm not talking about other women here? And right now I mean your little girlfriends. Cause I think that's all right, as long as you tell them you're married to me, and don't get anyone pregnant (the one thing we both know you're good at, ha, ha) because I really didn't expect you to sit around waiting when I know what you must've had on your mind. You deserved all the fun you could have, as long as that was all it was, just fun. No, I'm thinking of how fucked-up you were, that you were just interested in getting fucked-up, and didn't realize the changes in me, which is a real lonely place for me to have to be in by myself. Anyway, I'm sure you've had time to think about this, and lots of other things...

JOHNNY

Hey, I've only been in two fights, not three. There are some barebackers in here, for sure, fags, fairies, jizz queens, whatever you wanna call 'em, but it's not like everyone thinks. This one hinge, in on an 806 (he raped some eight year old, then killed him – they've they've got him on hold before sending him over to Atascadero), came up to me and said, 'Shit on my dick, or blood on my blade,' but some bro said, 'Hey, man, no nigger's gonna fuck one of our brothers,' and that was that. Man, I don't let that crap get me. That stuff's nothing. What does get me is losin' my feelings. That's what is happening. That I'm getting so I don't feel for no one or nothing. And that's just the way it is. You can see it in the old guys. There are some pretty old guys in here, some who shouldn't even be here. They killed the wrong guy or it was an accident or fate is bad. You make one bad turn and you're nailed for three turns. I'm talking about fate, the fate of even letting these pricks know you exist. Once they do, it's fate. You become shit and that kills everything. There's this one amigo here named Ruben that I've been rapping with pretty good. He's been around and tells me a lot about business deals and like that. How he got here was getting fired from picking beets. He got fired and this foreman told him to get off the field. Rube was owed fourteen dollars and asked for it. The foreman kicked his ass. He was a big bastard, too, Rube said, about six-foot-seven, three hundred pounds. Just hauled off and coldcocked Rube, broke his nose, broke both his plates, split his lip wide open, you could peel it aside and see the gums, just put his ass in the dust. There were about fourteen or fifteen other cholos standing there watching, and Rube just got up and walked out to his car, got his pistol, and came back and shot the son of a bitch. Said he had him dead center between the eyes, had it there, then changed his mind and shot him in the belly. No one fucks with him in here. He's the real choke-collar, the jefito who runs the house. Everything passes through him, job assignments, smokes, snacks, pruno, dope. Rapping with him is good, unlike most of these hogs which is nothing, nada, no response, no juice, no hope, nothing but zip, zero, zilch inside. This place kills love. It kills hope. That's what it does and what they want it to do. All it takes is for you to make a mistake and they take your hope and throw it down and trample on it and you feel dead inside – dead, sick, worthless, and gone to hell, so what I'm trying to do is maintain, Babes, just maintain, and if you can maintain then I can maintain so neither one of us gets all fucked-up again like we was the last time. My problem the last time was the same as it's always been, not making my feelings clear to either you, or the kids, so of course you'd be looking somewheres else. I'm just beginning to realize that.

JOANN

Johnny, I know you are still pissed at me. And this Robert person said you called him to ask why his number was on the phone bill I sent you. I don't know why you are so mad, me and Robert are friends only. I don't get all mad, pissed off, upset, and angry when you are calling Jackie and them on the phone. Which I know you are, Johnny. Johnny, I am tired of this bullshit between you and her. Johnny, I believed you when you said that you and her weren't getting together. Well, I'm starting to believe it isn't true. Well, if you want her that bad maybe it's because you have no chance to get her. Is that it? I really believe you when you say you love me. Is it really true or are you just saying that to make me feel good or are you talking from the bottom of your heart? Are you and Jackie talking as friends and friends only, or is it for more serious things? Well, if you are going to be talking to her I guess I should stop writing you and taking your calls and stop having sex with you, especially in the Day Room, or by phone. I thought we were going to be together for real, but I guess my thinking was wrong. And I know you are calling her and not just finding out about your kids and if she is on drugs so you can get child custody like you said. You were on drugs yourself, so I don't know how that's really possible anyway.

JOHNNY

No, man! No way! I know that! You let a woman do that the next thing you know she'll be strapping a peg on and donkeying you yourself, ha, ha, ha! Or else be out tearing around looking for some other dude who'll do her wrong, right? I know that! Hey, no way would I let anyone peg me up the butt, male or female. Hey, you Gava motherfucker, lighten-up. I'll set your fuckin' mattress on fire! Oh? You think I won't? Oh, yeah? Watch this!

JOANN

Don't make me wait! I can't wait! I need to be with you! I want to be with you! I just got your letter today AND IT WAS SO FAB! I can't believe it!! Honey, I loves ya!!!! My Mom and Grandma just got back from Safeway. I have to go out and help them with the groceries. Take care and be sweet. Always thinking of YOU. P.S. SMELL THIS LETTER, Honey.

JACKIE

Anyways, Eddie gave Car this job scraping dust outa baggies an' said if I wanted I could do it, too. Said keep half for personal use or to sell or whatever. So I said, 'Listen, either trust me like to sell an ounce or two, or don't, but I'm not doin' any kinda shit work, all right?' Also, he's started this new business growing magic mushrooms, and has this big metal shed with beds of wood two by fours inside and wire bottoms filled with manure that gets covered with this white fungus stuff that turns into mushrooms, he says, and I guess Car's doing the shit work there, too, while Eds sits back 'n complains about all the money he's having to spend up front, even though the shroom business is supposed to be the coming thing and he's gonna be making even more money than ever. Now who wants to sit around listening to that?

TERI

Jackie, I am so pissed that you ate my Bar-B-Que ribs. I spent my last cent on them. I walked all the way down Thompson to get them. I looked forward to having them because I was starving and you ate them! I ate your chicken salad but you also ate that cottage cheese, the spice cake, and the apples I bought. I have no car to replenish those things. I don't mean to be petty. I try to share. I buy food constantly to offer you and the kids things, but shit! You got me up yesterday after no sleep and told me to clean up the 'Fucking mess!' Have I ever spoken to you like that? Ever? So I got up and cleaned right away and did the dishes for the millionth time. I feel like I've been cleaning for a week. Do you remember our talk about respect for each other? Are you blaming me for the money Carson owes you? The ribs aren't the end of the world. Maybe I'm over reacting but I wanted them and expected them to be there. It's a drag walking some place every time I want to eat, and right now I have no cash to replace what you eat. Will you bear that in mind in the future? And I did tell Car he had to pay you back and he said he would bring the money over tomorrow or you could meet him over at his place and get it then, and no, I will not be there!

CARSON

The thing about pussy for most guys? They just wanna get it, piss on it, 'n walk away, right? Right. But not me, 'cause I'm not out there just looking for the one that's got her tail in the air; I'm out there looking for the best one, okay? An' there's not one woman out there that I've ever been with that I didn't feel something for. I won't look 'em in the eye 'n say 'I love you' unless I do. And you know what? I find it a very easy thing to do. All's you gotta do is find that one little piece of feeling in there, 'n say it outa that. 'N there's always one little piece of feelin' in there, right? You'd have to be a real son of a bitch not to have that. An' sayin,' 'I love you' has a real nice feel to it, too, doesn't it? Don't you just love the sound of it? *'I love you.'* Isn't that great? It's just a great thing to say...

JOHNNY

Ah, shit, Panda, all that happened 'cause I'd used up all my luck, see, luck I had coming from before I met you, all bad luck. When I met you it was just starting to change to the good luck, which was you. The bad was from before, okay? As to dope being complete self-indulgence? Okay, you're right, I agree. But you'll never hear me say I won't go back to it. I will say I hope I never do. I've talked to this one yardie here who says using it is the same as using your lips. When you open your lips saliva comes out. Now that's a body fluid, same as blood, right? You open your mouth, a body fluid comes out, you put the food in. The same with a vein. You open a vein, a body fluid comes out, you put the food in.

So the whole thing is in how you see it. Now that last statement's the only thing he's got a full deck on – how you see it – but dope isn't, and never has been any problem for me. It's just there to do when there isn't anything else to do, another life trip experience I know about that gives me an edge over people that don't know. And the getting sick part isn't that bad. It's not like being drunk sick, where you're down on your hands and knees with your head in the can and you just wanna die. When you throw up on dope it comes up smooth, real smooth, like turning a faucet on, then off, but that's all. And you can still take care of business. The whole four weeks I was out I only got fucked up twice, and never when it counted. And here's something else to know: I've always been a guy who hates anyone telling me what to do, and whenever anyone or anything tries to take over my life I cut it off. Also, dope's just like speed, it ruins your teeth. Sucks all the minerals out and makes them brittle as shit. Remember when I was fighting those cops at Cheryl's? I lost two from a little tap, remember that, so now all's I got left are the good ones, ha, ha. Anyways, I guess this is my point – it's no problem for me. But I'll never put anyone down who uses. They each have their own reasons. And that's another thing about me, whatever I go into I go into until I know everything there is about it that I wanna know. Which is also my point – all I know about is for me, anyone else's trip I don't know for shit, okay, but for me right now things are definitely working out in a more positive direction in that, no, I am not using at all (and there's lots of it here, don't think there isn't), but them days are over, so in all truth what it comes down to is no more dope of any kind and maybe you flushing that bindle away was good and now includes that thinking by yours truly. What I'm sayin' is, I agree.

BUD

You don't remember this, you was a young squirt, but years ago when Irene and me broke up the first time, and she told you that's what was gonna happen, you came in the bedroom and hung on to me for a very long time and said, "I love you, Daddy." Well, Bub, that's meant a lot to me over the years.

CHAPTER 14

WEST MISSION AVE.

DAWNIE

Dear Daddy, I am very sorry you don't love us. We love you very much and miss you. I have been a bad girl lately. I cry very much of the time. Mommy does not know what to do with me because I am such a brat. Here is a small picture of me so you don't forget us. I love you, Daddy, and so does Mommy. Please meditate fine thoughts for the four of our souls. If you love us, Daddy, let us know because we can't pick up any love vibrations from your beautiful soul. If you don't love us, let us know that, too. We want you to be happy and if you can't come home and will be happier with a different person and not with me and Mommy and John-John please tell. Big kiss, Dawnie. P.S. Did you get me a blanket, too? Mommy said you didn't. How come John-John got one?

CARSON

Or it could be that one chick is just as good as the next, you know what I mean? Like cars, man; take cars. Like some guys'll say: 'That 409's boss, man; that Camaro's cherry;' or, 'I want a Porsche, man, a Turbo Porsche,' and then some other guy'll say, 'I don't give a shit; all I want is something that'll get me to where I'm going.' So Jackie, man; take Jackie. Now she'll more than get you to where you're going – you never know what the fuck's gonna happen! Like the time she told me to come on her face, which is great, right? 'Either come on my face or don't come at all, but definitely do not come *in* me, okay?' Ha, ha, ha. Which is why Eddie's always said she's too good for either John, or me. She probably *is* a Turbo Porsche, know what I mean?

JOHNNY

This is making it hard, Babes, but the greatest moment you can ever have out of all the great moments you do have is when you first and finally decide to just let 'er fly, an' if there's a kid out of it there's a kid, cause I certainly remember that moment with you locked onto me like the whole world was dyin' 'n this was for the last time ever, and when I first saw Dawnie I remembered exactly how that was and every time I see her I remember. You hear what I'm saying here? Well, the transfer back to jail was okay and that's a lot better cause all the fucking paperwork is flying now and I'm not in limbo anymore and the good news is that time spent in the bin counts. Some people I knew here and didn't like are also gone so that's good. The fuzzheads that are here leave me alone cause they think I'm crazy. I told this one guy if he touched my towel again I'd shit in his shoes. He didn't know what I was talking about. He'd never touched my towel. He'd been getting too nosey, see. He knew I'd been in the bin, so that was all it took. There was a guy out there at the bin that did that, shit in people's shoes. What he did was stand around all day at the drinking fountain putting water in his mouth, then spitting it out. Every time you'd cruise down the hall you'd see him doing it. He wouldn't swallow the water, see, cause he thought he'd fill up an' bust cause he thought he couldn't pee. And he couldn't. He couldn't cause he wouldn't drink any liquids! He'd eat, though, so they were giving him all these laxatives. That's why he had to shit all the time. I have no idea why he picked shoes as toilets. He was a pretty hard guy to talk to, ha, ha, ha. Then there's this other guy, he's just deaf, or just bugged, or something, 'n just keeps walking back and forth, never sleeps, see. This is about six in the morning. So they come in and grab him and say, 'Put him in the box!' There's a real narrow box here about five feet high by eight feet long, the insides coated with grit, sandpaperylike plaster, and in he goes, the poor fucker, you could hear him keep walking in there, scraping into the sides, getting hisself all cut and torn up. Well, I've been quite busy winding up my case and have found out it's legally finalized. The shrink recommended me for Work-Furlough again and that'll be good. They'll probably try to find me another car painting job, but if that happens this time I'll stick it out and pay off all debts, you can count on that. I heard some bad shit today. You remember Fredie Salsedo? The short dude that worked at the Midas shop? He was outa Saticoy? The guy with the black onyx ear studs? Well, somebody got him. Tried to make it look like an O.D. but they O.D.'d him four hours after he died, plus tore his lip off. So you know what they thought he did. They found him in some avocado grove on the front seat of his Firebird. The headlights were still on. Like this friend of mine said, 'There are other ways of taking care of a problem other than putting a plastic bag over a guy's head, then mutilating him.' Yeah, I wonder who'll get that bird? That is certainly one cherry machine. You asked about the car. Okay, a friend of mine has it. I guess it's time I told you. One of my little girlfriends, I guess you'd call it. She tried to get me out when I couldn't get hold of you. It was the least I could do. She's a very good person. And's very sweet, too.

CARSON

'Cause in a way I'm sorta envious of the guy, too, that a guy can care so much. In a funny sorta way it sorta puts a higher value on Jac, too, know what I mean? And, plus, man, plus, an' this is something I don't like to admit, I can't stand the idea of her going back to him either, know what I mean?

TERI

'Okay,' I told him, I said, 'listen, Car, you said you wanted to talk about other people's feelings, okay? Like my feelings, okay? 'Cause I really thought there was something special going on with you, but you telling Jac that I was a cold ass bitch who couldn't even get herself off was a really trashy thing to hear in itself, but I didn't think you'd be telling *her* about it, but I guess I was wrong. Yeah, dead wrong,' I said, 'cause you just screwed the pooch, man, you sure did, 'n I hope Jac wises the fuck up to you, too, 'cause you don't love her neither, man, no fuckin' way do you love her. There ain't no one in this world you love or care about but your own sorry ass.' That's what I told him. You just ask him...

JAMAL

Ter said I was a fag? Ha. That's a crackup, girlfriend. Now I wish I *was* a fag. Them fudgepackers gets laid alla the time, 'n never has ta' pay nothin' for it. 'N get off four or five times a night, right? Like Barry? Y'awl knows him. Where I got them strobes for the club? The li'l dude that's got Madonna tatted big 'long his forearm? Yeah, him; the Radio Shack dude. Real li'l flower of a guy. Now maybe that's the kinda boy you need, get your mind offa all the hassles, let your mind jus' focus on your dancing here. You ever think of that – jus' getting a friend, girlfriend, 'specially you…

JOANN

Hi, Handsome. I just bought myself a new diary and I call her Princess Di #2 as she is the 2nd Di and knows everything about myself. My Mom says send the money for the phone which is now up to $48. It costs too much for me to call and I can never get hold of you in there. I want to go out on you so bad but I can't bring myself to do it. Cheryl and I went out last night. I met this real fine dude named Leonard. He is a real nice person. But I have you and that's all I need right now. I hope you like the picture I sent you, Boy. My Mom took your car to L.A. today. She hasn't come back yet. She left the house at 10 and it's now 7:30. She was supposed to be home at supper. I've been wondering what you'll do when you find out I took "Pain-Killer" off the rear door. It came off with nail remover. It didn't take the paint off, so don't worry. I know this guy who does pinstriping so we can always have it put back. He's got real great hands, but he's real old so don't worry, ha, ha. Your stepdad said I could continue using it if I took the "Pain-Killer" off and got the engine fixed which was real nice of them and I think your mom likes me. Look, you Curlyheaded B……, you better write me and not just call if you know what's good for you. Johnny, when you get out and I turn 18, let's live together, not get married, but just live together, okay? Cause real soon we might have something needing us living together, okay?

Well, I can't think of anything else to say. Guess what? Cheryl and me had a fight and I told her to go to hell. Later, Kiss, Kiss, Kiss, Kiss, Kiss

JOHNNY

Telling me to get out of there wasn't when she got it. She knew I could handle that. When she said, 'All you are is a dope-dealing jerk,' is when she got it. She didn't say anything that wasn't true; it was just that she said it. And she was right. She wanted me to think about it, see. You gotta say things to people to get them to think about it, right? How else 'r you gonna do it? She knew what she was doing. She is a very smart person. I've always known that...

JACKIE

Both of them were kissing me, the both of them, kissing and kissing me, my legs, my thighs, sliding my dress up, pushing it up, holding it up, I had no panties on, 'n somehow I couldn't reach them, couldn't bend to reach them, an' they began fighting, hitting each other, their faces beginning to blur as they hit at each other, I couldn't recognize who they were, then one of them showed me a flower, a little white flower in a little wooden box, a sandalwood scented box, and kissed me on the lips, licking his tongue across my lips, across my tongue, then kissing my belly. And I looked and my belly was naked, the other man had vanished, was gone. Only one of them was left, and that's how I knew …

JOHNNY

You ever look at the walls in here? That kinda paint? You know what that's called? Mocha brown, Bro, 'n indigo blue. Like Mexican chocolate melting 'cross an evening T. J. sky, you ever seen that? Now I'm good with colors: Cabernet Red, Twilight Royal Pearl – that's a Cholo purple, man, a lowrider special. 'N I can mix anything you want: Acrylic Enamel Pearl, Silken Saturn Blue

Metallic, Centari Torch Red, or goin' more uptown: Chroma-base White under Red Pearl mixed in a clear topcoat – that'd be primo – but you know what my favorite all-time fave is? Primer, Bro, just plain fuckin' asphalt 'n concrete battleship gray primo primer. Not rust-orange, but plain ol' undercoat gray; so all's you see when you see me comin' is a gray blur on gray, you can't even be sure you've seen my ass, right, 'cause I'm flyin' right by onto the on-ramp, 'n *Whoosh*, I'm gone, like in, 'Whah the *fuck* was that…?'

MARGE

Your dad is not drinking today or the day before but had something Sunday night when we got back from seeing you. His latest quirk is to strongly defend his right to take Valium. This was after the doctor told him Valium was the beginning of the first slip and now after his past experiences with it he should know he can't mix the two. Also, as you saw, we have been arguing more than a lot. At the very least I've got to get away for six months. You know it's best. He needs to bottom out and you can't bottom out unless you are really alone, but it is awfully hard for me to take these steps. Contrary to what your grandmother told you I never left him, and won't, certainly not while he's sick...

JOHNNY

Now Jo really tripped Dad off. She's got a pretty good set, see, and it got to him. 'Big tits still running your life, huh,' he goes. So I go, 'Yeah, well, why should I be any different than you?' 'Same old shit;' he goes, 'never learn a goddamn thing,' plus some other things, plus disowning me. I called him a fucker, then Jo called him a perv, 'n he got so pissed he walked outa his own house with us still in there, so I ran out and he was getting in his van 'n yelled, 'Fine, you old fart, jus' take off then!' 'Well, fuck you!' he yelled. Man, it was just pitiful. So I ran down there. 'Ah, com'on,' I told him, 'we'll take that cup of coffee.' I mean I wasn't about to give in, but, fuck, you know, it was a good thing to do. It was his own house, you know. So we went back in…

JOANN

I keep having this dream where your wife comes in just as you and me are about to get it on and she says she wants you. You tell her to go away because you love me and she can't do anything for you. Then she pulls out a gun and shoots you. I get on the phone and call the cops while she's shooting and yelling and the cops are here in seconds and take her away and she's only hit you in the shoulder and we go to the hospital and fix you up and you tell me how much you love me and we kiss and I make love to you until you can't stand anymore and are completely satisfied. Do you know she is now going around with someone new and telling everybody he makes fabulous love? Cheryl's sister knows Jackie's sister from when they were in high school together and she found that out for me. But he's probably nothing next to the things you can do. As far as I'm concerned you are the best. Speaking of best, how is KING? Are you taking care of him? Is he getting fed enough (I hope not)? Is he kept warm at night (I hope not)? I'm very concerned. Even though he's big enough (HUGE) to take care of himself I still worry. You take care of my BABY. And take care of the rest of you, too. I guess one wouldn't be any good without the other. Do you know what I want? I want a beautiful baby girl, Gloria Olivia Dalton, or Barbara Olivia Dalton. Either way how do you like it? Her initials will either be G.O.D. or B.O.D.! Neat, huh?

JOHNNY

What I'd done I'd won this pool table, see, and was trying to get it on top a' the car and damn thing was crushing the roof in and these two cops pulled up. There was about five of us out there, we'd just heaved it up, and they thought we was stealing it, and the fuckin' barkeep, he hadda come out and say, 'No, no, man, the big motherfucker won it, won it on the fair and square.' Boy, did that get their ass. No, swear to Christ, man... ha, ha, ha...

MARGE

Well, his wild story this morning to try and play on my sympathy was saying he knew he loved me the first moment he saw me. He said you two were in the checkout at Payless when I was cashiering there and he told you that right off and it was you that followed me home and got my address as he was too shy for that. You must love your dad a whole lot to have done that for him. Would you write him and say about not mixing his drugs? Anything I say he takes as meddling. You looked very nice Sunday. Going out, he broke down, crying and all that, telling me Irene made a liar out of you when you were little by sending you out to get a haircut. You spent the money on something else and when you came home she wanted to know why you didn't get your hair cut and you said you had, and she drug you down to the barbershop and made you point out the man that cut it. He said he hadn't. After that Bud said you would never admit to anything. He was really wound up, saying a whole bunch of things about Irene and himself, that he felt real bad how things had turned out for you, so I know it tripped him up to see you behind that glass and wire mesh.

PSYCHOLOGICAL SUMMATION:

Results indicate asocial tendencies and likelihood of actions unwise and self-defeating. Data also indicates sexual predation syndrome overlying partial lack of adequate masculine identity. Inventory is that of an individual who is unconsciously asking for help for his disturbance. At this time, however, because of the severity of his disturbance, Mr. Dalton does not appear to experience psychic pain. When asked the facts of his situation replies: 'Well, that's the way it goes.' After thirty hours, however, subject was finally able to cry.

CHAPTER 15

THE BAN-DAR

JACKIE

I don't know for sure and I've decided to tell you straight out and right now I'm very emotional but have you thought about us having another baby? There was only that one time, but did we use anything? Even though it was pretty safe, I'm pretty certain we didn't. And about Carson, you know what an ego trip he's on, all humble when you talk to him, which is even more ego because I told him I didn't belong to him, I belonged to me, and wasn't going to be his ever. So he is completely out of the picture. Also, he's stopped working for Eddie to get a job either dealing blackjack on a cruise ship that has gambling off the Gulf Coast or in an Indian casino or selling inflatable bass fishing boats in Hollywood or some whacky bullshit like that. Oh, God, Johnny, sometimes I feel like I'll fall apart if we don't get this worked out. There is something else that is really bothering me. You know, I keep wondering were you really going to kill a cop? Wasn't that some big fantasy you had? You aren't really like that. What made you say if you had, it would've been both our faults? I don't like kidding like that. How much coke had you done? Was it that real speedy stuff that clogs up your nose? You can't do that stuff. It makes you crazy. I know it does me. Was that it? But I guess doing a cop would be better than one of us, or someone who was innocent, like the liquor store guy, or a gas station guy, or someone like that. Oh, I have to tell you what John-John did this morning. He watched Dawnie get me to write her letter for you and took off his shoe and said, 'Smell it,' then he saw this picture of some bunnies and went over and kissed it. Isn't that precious?

MARGE

Your Dad said ever since he was ten and his sister died in that fire life has not gone good for him. They were playing with matches and a window shade caught fire and he ran outside yelling, 'Fire! Fire!' and ran back in to get her but the heat drove him out. He said it was so hot his shirt started to melt. This is when he started crying. He gets this way all the time now. The firemen thought a bad connection in the stove. We got into a real argument over this. I said all this being sorry stuff was this damn Valium and drinking. I said I was going to leave him flat if he didn't quit. He said his quitting was causing the pain, that the body manufactures alcohol for itself and when you drink artificial alcohol the body doesn't need to manufacture its own and forgets how so when you go cold turkey after you've been drinking a long time your body has no alcohol in it, natural or artificial, to numb the pain and you start suffering. That's why the need for Valium and the "occasional drink." Now how are you going to deal with a mind that thinks like that? When I saw how good you looked, and how healthy, it scared me to pieces. My own health is not what it should be over this. Maybe whatever it is you're doing in there could be passed on to him. I used to run track in high school and know exercise is very important. I'll tell you, I still haven't learned what to say when he's on those damn Valiums. All he wants to do is lay on the couch and stare at the ceiling. He gets so sullen and mean I have to go around on tippy toes or he'll snap my head off. Well, I have to get ready for bed. It was real nice seeing you again and both your Dad and I are thinking of you...

JOANN

Johnny, are you calling Jackie after you call me? Or vice-versa? I got to thinking about what you said about dope. Sometimes when I hear what you say I just don't know what you're talking about. Dope IS complete self-indulgence! And talking with friends, they are of the same opinion. There just isn't any sharing. And I don't care what you say. And I don't want a doper judging me as uptight. I have made a decision to stop being a teenage baby and to grow up and drugs is where I start. Doing both blow and beer are just not right. And not right for children either. If you are P.G. it gets in their little systems and they don't even have a chance. I know I did some blow with you, but that was wrong and I'm sorry for it, and going back to Church has helped me to see the right way to be. Cheryl and Anthony have got a one-bedroom apartment together and asked me to move in with them. Johnny, do you really love me? I have to know. And, no, I haven't gotten myself inked because you told me not to, okay? Not even a tiny dot of a star, okay?

JACKIE

I woke up this morning with one of those summer colds and guess that's what I get for working topless, huh? Going Public, as they say, but sometimes we all have to do things we don't like to do. I can't say I dislike it, though. It's real good to be making some real money. I thought your little friend was very cute, I got to admit. I did ask her about the car, but she was scared to death, like I was going to bite her head off or something. Her little lips were all quivery. I called your Mom and she said definitely take the car. I'm real glad you're missing the kids. Even when they're not here for a few minutes I miss them like crazy. Someday I'll get used to working nights again. The job isn't as bad as people think. The policy is strictly HANDS OFF. Our friend Jamal is helping us find a new apt. He's got a lot of real estate and business experience and talked the manager into letting us stay another two weeks. The most horrible thing just happened to his family. His grandmother got her eyes blinded. She had a friend put eye drops in for her, but there was another bottle next to the eye drop bottle, and the friend took the wrong bottle and put drops of Crazy Glue in her eyes and blinded her. Then, guess what? Last week his mom went to get tested for snoring, or something, and had electrodes attached to her head while she slept. You won't believe this, but when they took the electrodes off they told her to take a shower but she didn't. She got in a hot tub and got steamed and put her head back because she got sleepy. Then the steam melted the glue they'd attached the electrodes with and it ran down onto her eyes and she didn't think anything about it and then rubbed her eyes and it got in there and now she's lost eyesight in her left eye and

75% in her right eye and it's not going to come back. Isn't that terrible? It made me feel really bad for him. I'm just not with it today and to have to go out and look for another place is just a drag. The world is full of Jelly-Butts and that's what I feel like. Life here is sleep, eat, work, once in a while get loaded. Once in a while, that's for sure. Ter says she's going to start taking court stenographer classes. Incidentally, what she says about Carson is not true. No way was I dumped.

JOHNNY

Now I certainly don't wanna know anything about that, but I'll tell you this: I've been doing a little thinking and I've now got it pretty straight that there isn't much point in getting mad about anything. Sometimes, you know, I just get sick and tired of being myself and it comes out on you. You don't deserve it. I just get pissed. I get you pissed. Then I can't take it back. I just can't. Like that the one time right after we *did* get it together? Remember how ugly I was. Well, I know that now. I see that. Well, I am not gonna do that anymore. And another thing, remember that night in Garden Grove when we got in that fight over that twenty dollars? You threw that beer on me? An' I got so mad I rammed all those cars in the parking lot? Well, pee-punkee-doo, Baby, that was me! If you remember Eddie was sitting behind us and I got him. I had a drink in my hand and knocked him down, then knocked him down again, and by then there were four of them that held me? I remember how fast Eddie came across that floor. Boy, he can get across a floor in a hurry. He's not smooth, but he's quick! He was real quick! But not quicker than me! What I thought it was, was you, see. He always wants the woman I have. I told him you weren't anybody's woman, and that shut him up. He didn't know what to do. You could see him start to think, ha, ha, ha. So, Carson is nothing to me either, I can handle him, too...

JAMAL

Now I'm jus' sayin' this as a friend. I don't care whats he's tellin' you. He's jus' after yus pussy, Lady. You gots a real witches' coochie down there, some real wicky shit, but asks yourself, is that all you gots? That don't play. Y'awl gots lots more 'n that, Lady Girl, so whys you doin' yourself so low, and things of that there nature?

JOHNNY

Considering what you told me, plus other info I have, I'm not feeling so good right now just coming back from chow and writing this. Cons putting butter on the floor so other cons coming in will slip on their ass. Certain dudes that can't even eat their food without spilling it all over the table. Dudes stealing packets of chicken noodle soup from each other. The bad thing is I'm starting to do stupid stuff like that myself. Smearing Ben Gay in a guy's underpants. Pouring water over a guy's toilet roll. Shit that could get me shanked. I've messed up so much, and all behind this acting crazy and dope, Jac. It's just not right, but don't let me get you down, I'm not that blue. If you can get the Escort from Jo go on ahead and sell it. I told Mom about it and she said she didn't care as long as the money was for the kids. And just remember this, all's I've ever wanted was to be with you, that's all I've ever wanted, and you know it, too…

JOANN

Every time I think about Long Beach I get hot flashes. I know you're feeling sorry for yelling at me and I accept your apology. Anyway, sitting on this bed I can still think of more things like you and me and...!!! Do you still have your Guns 'N Roses CD? Every time I hear it, it makes me think of Long Beach. You certainly remember that, don't you? Cheryl has got herself a real good man in Anthony. He gives her money and takes her everywhere. Buys her anything to keep her happy and satisfied. They go down to L.A. and he buys her shoes and shorts and tops. He also bought her a slit bra, one where the nipples can stick out........? And slit panties! I miss your love so bad!! And I am sorry about what I said. Cheryl got an engagement ring. If you want you can go ahead and tell me to pick one out, too, because I really want a big ring with both pearls and diamonds. But I don't want us to go into debt so maybe a nice sized ring with a diamond and maybe a pearl would be nice. I saw one ring with a black and a white pearl and three diamonds on each side, right and left! Do you think that's too flashy? Cheryl says she really is going to have a kid! And she's only been living with Anthony two weeks! I bet that happens to us! SMILE! Would you be real happy? What if I'm already pregnant and the kid was striped, you know. Yellow and black? Tiger! FUNNY? But it wouldn't be so bad if it takes after its Mommy. I can't wait to have your baby but at the same time I'm scared to death. I wish you were here where you could touch and hold me. Like in Long Beach. It was a beautiful four days. I remember everything that happened. First we went to that club with your sister and her husband but I got carded so you stayed outside with me. That was just so neat. And you never left me alone by myself in the motel, not at night. The nights were fab, all that kissing and touching! We would crawl under the covers and play, then the undies would come off and you would get on top of me. Then we would kiss and you would do little suckees on my boob and then we would start pushing and, God, did that feel good! Then we would come to the climax and both let go our juices, then rest and wipe the sweat off our faces and catch our breaths. Each night was like that and it was so beautiful. But soon we'll be doing it again, and it will be as beautiful or even more beautiful, I hope...

JOHNNY

'Three packs for a young cocksuck, I wanna young cocksuck,' this ol' barebacker down the row was screamin'. So Rube yells, 'Just spits on it, Baby, 'n goes back to sleep!' Rube cracks me up. Nothing bothers the guy. I thought that was just great!

IRENE

But that's not all. The Bluebook on an '81 Escort wagon is nearly $2200 and that's a lot of money to just burn up. I thought JoAnn was very generous to make amends for you, and for you to ask Jackie to take the car from her before she's even had a chance to get it fixed is not fair. Are you planning on paying JoAnn back?

She said her uncle is a mechanic and can get it fixed for free. It is certainly something we should consider. By the way, Sandy told me she saw your Dad driving toward work out at Vintage last week so he must be feeling better. She was on her way home from the hospital when she saw him. Did you know he's been trying to call me here at the house this past week? I know it's him but I'm afraid to answer because I don't want Earle getting upset. Maybe you could ask Bud if he's been calling? Or maybe not. Maybe it's best not. What are your thoughts?

CARSON

There's this big bar there, right offa Colorado 'n the Five, 'n one time there was real fox sitting with this older guy there, and she's looking at me. 'N the next thing we're playing a coupla games of eight-ball and she takes me back to the table to meet the guy an' have a few drinks, he buys the drinks, okay? Then she asks would I like to go over to the hotel with 'em, so I go, 'n the next thing after we walk into their room is she starts grabbing me, an' the guy, he's not doing nothin', just standin' there watching, 'n I say, 'What's happening', man?' And he just shrugs, you know, 'n she's just great, like really great, gets me onto the bed 'n away we go, 'n every time I pop, well, she goes right back down on it; off we go again, an' alla the time the guy is just sitting back, not getting excited none at all, just watching, so I say, 'What's your deal, man? Don't this interest you none?' And he says, 'No more 'n eating a good piece of steak does.' So that's Glendale, okay, kinda people they got down there. And you know some a' 'em, too, like that little buzzhead, that Armenian scammer that sniffed around here, L'il Paul, that cat, 'member him? Yeah, like that. He's got some peeps into the car salvage biz that run a lot of scams, fake vin numbers 'n car titles for cars that've been in a wreck, shit like that. Deals with 'em all the time, says they want both flake *and* crystal. Has some biker connects, too. Now I could get some phone numbers, do something real there. There's a lot of AA's there, too, not just them Armenians assholes. No, no. Not alcoholics: African-Americans – AA's, man, Crips, Bloods, them kinda bangers.

There's even some black bikers out there. I don't know what the fuck their names are, or what colors they fly, but I could find out. They move a lotta crank...

JOHNNY

Okay, jus' say you're in a fight. They've put you on the 'crete and you don't wanna get up, okay? So maybe what you do is just lay there, 'n jus' look at the faces that're looking at you. I mean the kinda faces people show then. Now that can be a trip, see, 'cause if you're really tripping, you can see that every one of 'em's thinking something real different than what you're thinking, like, *'The son of a bitch can't get up – he's afraid to;'* or, *'Fuck, I didn't hit the fucker that hard;'* or, *'I'm gonna make this shitbag puke,'* right, 'n like that? You follow my thinking here? While you're thinking, *'Well, maybe I should grow my mustache back,'* like ol' Rube here, lookin' gnarly as shit with that ol' Pancho Villa bushing up under his busted-up, ol' twisted to the side snot-locker, ha, ha, ha...'

JOANN

Cheryl caught me crying in the laundromat this morning (our washing machine is broke). Why is it you don't want to be with me and me alone? Your EX-wife came by the school today and said what was I doing with your Mom's car? I didn't know what to tell her except you gave it to me. Was that wrong? She was nasty and said she'd see about that. Cheryl said she believes you love me but if you really did you'd tell me something about our baby and this business. Even tho I love you I don't need this. How did EX know I had the car? How does she even know who I am? Would all this go on if we were married? Everything you do until we get married will mean how the rest of our lives will be! Understand, you big dummy? She was on her way to talk to you, she said, with another woman that looked like her, but smaller, and a tall, real black, smoky black, black guy with a curly goatee and yellowy teeth and real curly, perfumy hair. You know how I am about smelling things. I thought you said you don't have visitor's rights right now?

CARSON

Where am I going with this? Listening to this don't excite you none? Oh, yeah? Then tell me something like maybe you *would* do. 'Cause maybe it'll give me something, get me outa my rut. *My* rut, not yours. Well, like thinking 'bout you doing it with someone else, maybe. Like watching that. Hey, I was *never* watching you with Eddie! The hell I was! No, no, okay? That's 'cause I know Eddie and I don't like him, okay? And it's gotta be with someone we *both* don't know, like a stranger, right? Yeah, a stranger! You know that! I see that there little grin... com'mere... no, now you tell *me* somethin'...

JOHNNY

I know one thing. I must stop this feeling sorry for myself. Regret can kill you as sure as cancer. Remorse weakens your body. Sorrow over things that are too late to be prevented. If I feel a feeling I just push it, convincing myself it's a huge feeling, which pushes out hard against the fact that not only can I not do anything about anything, but I really don't know what is going on. All I know is what other people tell me. And what other people've been telling me isn't what I want to hear. Like people're saying you're back seeing someone. Or that there's another bozo, this one's a spade. I mean shit like that. Do you know what that kinda talk does to me? Is that what you want me to feel? All fucked-up and pissed and so goddamn mad I can't even see straight? I know I shouldn't be jealous. I know I shouldn't be pissed. I know I should learn to trust people. I know, I know, but fuck it all to fucking hell, I am pissed! I am so pissed all I can think is I'm just gonna have to go out and just hurt someone, either in here or out there! Now, god-damn it, if that isn't a fucked way to think I don't know what is. I certainly know that...

JACKIE

So someone saw me with someone else. What's that mean? I'm free to talk to a lot of people. And who did I just hear about? Your cute little girlfriend. And I know it's true because Teri saw her riding around with Anthony G. Scott. Yeah, Anthony Gregory Scott. That guy! There's quite a little reputation going on there, too! You're not the only older man she's been with either, believe you me...

JOHNNY

Yeah, 'n that's not all. Another time me 'n this buddy of mine Eddie Hughes 'n this other dude was up in Bakersfield trying to sell some crystal to some local bikers there, 'n this other dude was into country-western, not them old dudes like Merle Haggard or Buck Owens and them, but Clint Black an' Dwight Yoakum, rockabilly cats like that, so he took us out somewheres to this little strip mall and a biker bar there and got us all fucked-up and wanted us to start a country-western band of our own, with him playing steel pedal 'n me keyboards and Eddie bass. You didn't know I could piano, did you? Right, 'n another thing, you know a lot of them country-western stars are little dudes? Most of them are. Black and Yoakum are. On his tiptoes Black 'bout comes up to my belt buckle. I'm not kidding. Well, anyways, we got so shit-faced Eddie traded the whole load of crystal to this real fucked-up dentist for a complete set of used dental tools, an' that's how I got this bridge cracked, this one here. See this? Eddie was gonna straighten it for me, see. I'd been having trouble with it after I'd gotten into some kinda beef with some different biker guys, 'n he cracked it right here trying to fix it. See up here? Now I'd like to get that fixed, if I could. Do you think that's possible? Anybody been giving you a hard time that I can help with?

JACKIE

...off the pole, stride, stride, Shorty George forward, Shorty George back, slow cat glide into the spot, 'n scissor, scissor... beyond platform's edge, rising out of the dark, old man's face...booty slap, strut forward, booty slap, strut back, 'n drop...'n scissor, scissor...*on the B pole, Ter-Ter pointing*... high tone Donna Summer *"Oh, Love To Love You, Baby,"* rising, bass line pounding... bend body backward, hair brushing the shag...arching toes, curve belly upward...raising head, look across belly over the G...framing that face...*off sequins along the G, sparkles bounce red dots across the face*... 'n grind, 'n grind, Sure...*he's still right there...her really ugly shoes*...'n shiver... *hasn't shaved her legs*... an' shiver again... *doesn't get it*... start to open thighs... *coloring book colors*... slowly scooting close, closer... toes arching... *get Dawnie colored pencils... John-John, too*...tap fingers close to the mound...'n grind, 'n grind again, moving fingers to the G...*that drunken face...fifty if a day... yes... looking straight at me... somebody's daddy*...'n slow grind again... *letting him look...Count One, not my daddy... 'n Two, Jesus, no soap in dispenser...tell Gary...Count Three, no hand towels for make-up neither...'n Four, 'I'll never let you down.' Right, who hasn't said that? What'd Mom call it: 'What diaper drek? "'Diaper drek!'" Ha, ha, she's funny sometimes*...hook now under the string...*his eyes right there...yes* ...'n grind... 'n grind again...*eyes going big now... yes ...'N... PULL...NOW... PULL...ALL...ASIDE... SHOWING HIM RIGHT INSIDE ME...'n HOLD, HOLD...'n suddenly he LAUGHS, closing his eyes, and his head drops...* 'n quickly I move, flipping over to my knees, my face down to his face, my fingers touching his chin, lifting it up, saying, *'HEY, HEY!'* into the now startled, re-opening eyes, watching them close again in quick embarrassment, dropping himself back away into the dark, a sudden burst of laughing, clapping, whistling from the other unseen men out in the darkness breaking across me now, the rain of dirty papers beginning, *"Oh, Love To Love You, Baby,"* windin', all that green fluttering up 'n up into the bright cone of cottony light about the pole, what Ter-Ter calls, *'All them dirty green birds of happiness,'* flutterlng 'n fluttering 'round 'n 'round 'n down: fives, tens, twenties, as I rise to V-invert pole strut 'n start swinging around, 'n some gold wedding-grease-grooved hand laying a single dollar bill down as I'm bending for all the others, waiting to cop a swipe at my boobs if I'll

JAMAL

'...the emotion in the motion gets the satisfaction outa the action 'n the treasure outa the pleasure...' 'You down with that, Girlfriend?' *"Love To Love You, Baby,"* 'You knows what I'm sayin'?' Donna Summer booming...'*YOU* gots to feel it like *YOU* loves it!' Oh, yeah! 'You gots to feels it like you knows *THEY* loves it!' Oh, yeah, oh, Hell, yeah. You gots... *bearclaws 'n brownies... they simple mutha-fuckas,* '... it now, Baby Girl!.. *the cinnamon roll, the apple fritter...* ''them motions of the emotion,'... *they sugar glazed cherry jellies... all them weak-minded ofay ballers,*

lean out that way to pick it up, 'n there's good ol' M.O.B. Jamal sittin' out there somewheres, thinking now for sure that he is the one to be tellin' me how to do my own thing, an'll be wanting twenty percent of all this for that – *like no fuckin' way* – there must a coupla hundred down here, but it's not the goddamn money; he can have the dumb forty of that, it's the insult...forty-five, sixty, eighty-five, ninety-five *...takes care of the phone...* one hundred 'n five *...a new pair a' shoes...* one twenty-five*...bathmat, too...* hundred 'n thirty, forty... *let's see Ter-Ter top that*...slow funk chorus goin', purpled 'n pink, pin spot shafts, slitting the air... *they chicken 'n waffled belled, big bubbas, too, all sittin' 'n smilin', iced chocolate long johns in they hands, the coconut french 'n cream filled raisin cups now inta they minds, all commencin', '...in the emotions of the motion,' 'ta' begins the whoopin' 'n the hollerin', to make it rain,* no li'l white lady gal never done it no better! Ever! *All that cha-ching flyin'...* Booya! 'N twenty percent a' that shits all comin' back to *...but... NO! God-damns FOOL... You gots to tells her,* 'No, hell, no, no, Girlfriend, I don't even wants NO piece a' that...you gets it all... that was sooo fuckin' fine, sooo fuck-in' fine... Lady G a' mine'... now looks my way, Lady Girl...

CHAPTER 16

WEST SEPULVEDA BLVD., SAN PEDRO

JACKIE

What would you think if I did? Maybe with some drinks or something I can do it with no remorse or have Teri do it with me. Some of the other girls are and make $400 to $600 a week on their tokes alone in addition to their checks. You'll love our new place. It's a beautiful three bedroom, two bath, lots of closets, shag carpets, dishwasher, patio with a locked storage room outside, locked storage area in the carport, our own burglar alarm system, paddle tennis and volleyball court, swimming pool and Jacuzzi. And $950 a month. We're really crazy, huh! But I've paid the back rent off and since I'm feeling real generous I sent the board the rest of the Work-Furlough advance. So don't say I've never done anything for you, Boy. The whole complex is still under construction but our apartment (I say "our" as Ter is here half the time and half other other places) is the one already completed, and by moving in early we got a hundred bucks off the rent for three months. About going "Combination" again. "Combination" means topless and bottomless. Ter is doing it, and says what a person feels inside is what really counts. Her and me are starting to be friends again. We've been having long talks together and understand each other much better. We're just lying on our butts today. The police were here today and scared the hell out of us. There's about five of them going around showing everyone how to burglar-proof their doors and windows and

Hands on hips, jut hips to side, 'n turn four push-outs, scissor, scissor, eight stomp steps up, kick-ball-change, top off, Shorty George back, slither, slither, eight steps round, bump, bump, using top, grind, Shorty George up, grind, grind; break muscle control, tackomie, tackomie, turn left, turn right, shimmy, shimmy, hit ass once, cross over turn, 'n bend... freeze...

what kind of windows and what kind of locks to buy. We took the kids downtown to the pet shop. They bought a little mouse, a wire cage, and plastic water bottle. John-John decided the mouse's name should be John-John even though he's a she. Other than that everything is very laid back. Since Ter and me are on nights with afternoons off except Sunday there's nothing to do all day but lay around out here by the pool. And listen, I'm not even go-ing to comment again about what some unnamed someone told you, other than consider the source, okay?

JOHNNY

No, I don't want you moving in with Cheryl and Anthony and, no, Jackie won't get the wagon. And don't be thinking everyone has more than you. No one has more than anyone else when it comes to handling their own minds and thinking. Your Mom and Grandma say they don't care if you're seeing me or not but they think drugs and you should take time to get to know other people. Great, do it if you want, but whose life are we talking about here? You know what I think. What I already said before your Mom grabbed the phone away from you and you started bawling. Stop listening to them, goddamn it, and just listen to yourself. I have some money coming from that guy Eddie. I'll send some for the phone and some for a down payment on a ring or to buy a ring. Things here have moved pretty fast since Wednesday. I've picked up a little slack by clearing their books of a couple of burglaries (which you know I didn't do – I don't do burglaries) which got a couple of people in here off the hook as well, and maybe a few fa vors coming my way, including definitely a new, earlier date. This means no new charges will be pressed against me for that, but now I'm a co-operative person and not designated a combative felon or hardened criminal or any other good shit like that.

IRENE

I was looking through your Dad's old medical records and guess even the U.S. Navy didn't want to admit his disease. It wasn't un-til my cancer that I finally admitted to myself that I was the one making it possible for him to keep on with the drinking. Now I don't know how many times I've heard that suicide bit from him. So you telling me he's real bad sick only makes me wonder. Now I've always had to be everyone's mother, his, as well as Jill's and yours. And everyone else always brought their problems to me, too, and I'd take them to heart. Well, that was just vanity on my part. Sheer vanity. Now I tell people if it's once, I'll help. If it's twice, forget it. And then when I told your Dad I wasn't going to keep on working if he kept on drinking I became the bad woman who didn't understand him and threw him out. And all he did was go right out and get some other woman to do what I did all those years, fix it so he could keep on drinking. Boy, was I dumb. I would've been better off marrying some old tire kicker. You haven't found out if that's him that's been calling, have you? I think it is…

JACKIE

Hey, boner alert, okay? Hey, good ol' Jamal hasn't hit you with that yet – M. O. B.? Yeah, *Money Over Bitches*, that he'll always choose money over bitches 'cause if he's got the money he'll always have the bitches? Ha! Yeah; that's just his trip, 'kay? 'N for him it sorta makes sense, right? So just know what you're getting into. And Carson? So lemme lay it out for you… you know what he said? Said – 'n this is him thinkin' he's only being funny – he said, 'I may not go down in history but I will go down on your sister'… so how funny was that, Babes…?

JOHNNY

No, now listen, I'll tell you! That San Pedro deal alone was a goddamn nickel on everything they did, for both me and mine, even if I *got* popped! So who knows how much that is by now? Them pricks're still in business, so it's probably thousands by now. 'N Eds 'd just love it if I let that go, wouldn't he? And he has to come into where you're working and start hassling you about a few honks of reconstituted nigger coke. What a punk thing to do! Even if you had taken it, what's that amount to? Now I told him of course you didn't. 'Think closer to home,' is what I told him, 'like maybe your ol' main man there, Mister C. C., for one, okay?' And what the fuck is paddle tennis? You don't play paddle tennis!

CARSON

It was really far out. The dude had one a' them electric hand machines, a sorta real small one, 'n me an' Ter smoked some DMT and snorted coke with him, real good coke, too, and he outlined this just incredible flower on the inside of her thigh, our secret flower. She's tough, man. I can't stand wimpy chicks. I like chicks with tattoos. I like women that can stand a little pain. One of the songs I'm gonna write is, *A Little Pain Can't Hurt*, ha, ha, ha. Then we sorta got into a little hassle, too, though, which, well... ah, fuck it, man...

TERI

How come you never have anything good to say? Don't you ever get tired of that? And quit saying you know something *'bad'* is gonna happen, something *'real bad.'* You're always saying that. You don't know that. An' talking like that? It makes it happen. Don't you know that? You start talking to a guy you get all serious on him, 'n then start bad mouthing yourself, so of course it all turns to shit. What? What? It does! Absolutely!

JACKIE

Well, then maybe It's got nothing to do with you, okay? She's my sister, man. And she doesn't even like your ass! She doesn't. Jesus, don't do that! Just cover yourself up. For Christ sakes! I don't wanna see that ugly thing. Of course I'm gonna look out for her. You don't even know what I'm talking about, do you? You ever think about that? 'Cause maybe if a person is stuck with someone it might cause them to overlook someone else, man, someone they could *really love*. Do I have to explain that? Hey, just keep messin' her around, man. Just do it! Just let your little ol' conscience be your guide. That's right. *Your little ol' conscience!* I'm sure you got one. You do got one, right?

RUBEN

What I do, Ese', es try to catch 'em sleepin', hokay? Tha's the best way. Like they partyin' down, hokay, 'n it's the night before – so's jus' go crash the party, walks in, scopes it out, 'n split. And make sure yus leaves right away, like say: 'Wrong house, man, sorrys 'bout that,' hokay? Now maybes they'll think about yus, maybes they won't, but if yus don't come back they'll probably forgets, all right? Now 'bout six es right, six in the morning. In summer tha's bes'. That way yus 've got the light so's when you leave, peoples on the street'll think yus just some homies leavin' for work, hokay? Now flip it over, hokay? Say it's yus. Say yus es holding, 'n something like that happens; some strange vatos come in 'n split. Now it don't matter their age, like they mights even be ninos, hokay, li'l ninos? Well, stops the music, kicks out the bitches, grabs the shit 'n split. Even if its yus own house, 'cause chances es yus been made. They've seen yus place, Ese'. They knows where all the bedrooms are, they knows where yus are. Now flip it over again; say it's yus's scene again; now it's not a bad idea to use ninos either, see... li'l ninos, 'specially...

JOANN

Dear Mr. Panda, you know I love you and won't do anything to hurt you but only feel like your dog. You never tell me I'm foxy or that you love me but only to see you when you need me but where are you when I need to be held and hugged, Johnny? Are you still mad at me for taking "Pain-Killer" off the wagon? I know you don't love me. How come I always have to say I love you before you say it to me? Sometimes you act like you hate me. Sometimes I wish I was dead. Cheryl wants to set me up with one of her friends. She says you won't find out, but I know you would, but even if you don't I would know and I'm not that kind of person. At one time I thought I wanted to be with either Robert or Leonard. They were not what I thought and were always telling me what to do. I get enough of that at home, plus they would get mad whenever I would talk about what was on my mind. And now I don't know if I'll ever see you again, no matter what you say. Where is the money for the phone bill? I'm not going to even mention what you said about the ring, remember?

RUBEN

Chingado, Juanito, not tha' theys can't fight! They can, but glass jaws es they problema! I don't care how mean she es; yus hit the puta's jaw... Boombala, Baby, it's over, tha' bitch *es* down...

JOHNNY

What to do? Young man in chains, looking at his confinement. Not enough time for the spiritual. All it seems I do is desire in one way or another. Does a man attach himself to others in order to hide the nakedness of his soul? What am I when I have no one? I have no one. The last few days I have entered into a sorrowful period. I feel sad and going nowhere. I'm without anyone to give my feelings to. What to do? What are my beliefs? Do I have any? Am I just lazy and weak? I am lazy and can't get over my bad habits. A man keeps his weaknesses to himself. Never give away a woman's love. Don't surrender the high ground. Every encounter is a fight to the death. Don't get strung out on a woman's love. Pussy is as common as dirt. I want to go back to my dreams where I am free, and given clean toys to play with...

JACKIE

A Sunday visit is definitely out as I'm on my way to Reno today. The management got me an engagement for two weeks at the El Rio Club there six nights a week at eighty a night plus tokes and all expenses paid. Four of us are going. This sure is going to help with the financial bit. My job is three shows nightly and in-between a hostess. The bad news here is that something else on the Chevy is broken, the u-joints are cracked or something. It won't run but just clanks. Now I really would like to get that car from your friend. If you would tell her to let me have it that would help. Which reminds me, I have to tell you about your Dad. He came into the club night before last and wanted to buy me a drink. He stayed and stayed and I had to drive him home in his van. Anyway, I got him home and he really scared me. He was standing on a chair to get a bottle and fell full weight, hit head first on the table, and I couldn't get him awake. I turned him over real careful and got the two guys from next door to call 911 while I called the doctor and he said give him coffee and rest. Then the ambulance said he was okay, just knocked himself cold. I was afraid he'd hurt his neck. Anyways, they had ammonia and we finally got him awake. He said he was okay and the Para's felt that your Dad didn't know where he was. He said his head hurt terrible. So I called the doc again and he said give him an aspirin. I said, 'He's incoherent and can't see, maybe he's fractured his head or something.' He said he's better off staying there until morning. He seemed all right when I finally left, just sort of dazed and apologizing for causing such a fuss and some other things. I didn't know what he was talking about. Then he called this morning and apologized all over again. This experience with your Dad shook me up. Things are going by so fast. You remember the summer when we went out to Lake Casitas? Remember those dragonflies skimming over the water and all those baby minnows swarming around our legs? Big blue dragonflies with those big double see-through wings? It was so hot out and after we came out of the water I wandered off into the grass and you got me and dried me off and then my hair?

CLINICAL SUMMATION:

Distraught over the difficulties besetting him due to the personal circumstances of his return to civilian life, and reverting to patterns established in his past, it appears that Mr. Dalton tried to find comfort in his favorite narcotic and misjudged its strength. This near brush with death, resulting in an emergency room hospitalization, led Mr. Dalton to understand the severity of his personal depression for which he is now seeking help. Mr. Dalton displays an unusual degree of self-understanding, and the continuing counseling sessions have been very promising in the re-establishment of Mr. Dalton's sense of self-esteem. Please note in the 02/10 session, after being visited by his sister-in-law and told that his wife and two children were in need of his help, both financially and emotionally, Mr. Dalton then said the one thing he was trying to learn was that, no matter what, life was always going to give one a beating, and that a real man had to accept without letting it make him feel sorry for himself. He added that was now his basic philosophy and, quote: "No longer a convict philosophy which applies a bucket of shit to everyone else for things that go wrong, which is my former way of thought and thinking and way of handling situations."

CHAPTER 17
NORTH VENTURA AVE.

JOHNNY

No, sir, I hate fighting, swear to God. Anyone who says different doesn't know shit. No way am I 'prone to violence.' No, I'm not. Fuck that noise. When my wife says we're always on the warpath, that's because she really doesn't listen to me, to what I'm really saying. I gotta get a handle on that. I do know I can't keep coming on to her so fast. And the next time I definitely won't. My old man always used to say kick ass if you want to reach the top. And then look at him. First thing I did last time was go to see him and it was the same old con, always feeling sorry for himself, then asking you to feel sorry for him, too. He's got a story, all right, but who doesn't? The only person I ever saw him kick was my mom. Not that I really blame him for that. With all the stupid shit she was always doing, it would drive anyone crazy. There's always two sides to a story, right? Maybe even three sides, right? You writing all this down, or just part of it? Can I see it?

RUBEN

No, no, Juanito, no, no, no, you don't wanna get into tha' one, Ese'. Tha's for vatos whus got no hope. Tha' not you. I'll tell yus what, lemme tell yus, with tha' hayna you still gots a shot, but yus go th' way you're talkin' you got none, no ways. You disappears yourself. You be gone. Yus won't be anywheres. You wants ta' know how I knows? I wus drunk, see, an' thes' churros, they jump me, jumps me bad, but I lets it go, see, 'cause I *wus* fucked-up, an' maybe deserves it, hokay? But the next day they catch me out again, hokay? An' when they finish, thes' time I tells 'em, I say, 'Hokay, I see all yus vatos later.' Ans the next day I go into this bar where I knew they wus, an' I wus scared, man, but I had me a fine filero, an' I took it to the bone, yo, got the first one rights here, right in the middle a' the chest, right into the spine, now that vato's paralyzed for life right nows, then the other two in the back, 'n the fourth one up here, 'cross the neck. 'N lemme tell you somethin,' after I done the first one I never felts *nothin'*, yus understands, I mean *nothing!* Now that's a fucked place to be, Ese'; tha's a load yus don't want, Ese'; jus' don't go there. Like I say, jus' break the bitch's arm, or leaves it all the fuck alone, hokay? Tha's the only move, the right move; es correcto, Ese', hokay?

JOHNNY

The worst thing here is all the complaining, so what's new? The fag who issues the clothing and I got into a beef so now my coveralls would look better on Dumbo the Elephant. On the plus side, I'm gonna have my tattoos scraped, all the homemade ones. I've been rubbing salt into them and a lot of the ink is gone. Having a tattoo just to prove you've been here is a hell of a way to have to prove something. Big deal, you know, so you've been clanked. So who the fuck cares? Now that guy I told you about – the guy who did the tattoo of Bette Midler on his belly, he borrowed this mirror I had and ended up losing the son of a bitch? Gone down the chocolate highway. Now I could never diddle a guy. That just don't appeal to me. I don't care if it's the prettiest motherfucker you ever saw. People or places, though, it's all the same, where your head's at. What you feel is what you see. If it's evil, then you'll see it, even in church, or Sunday School. And my last thought for the day is there's only one place you can always find sympathy – that's in the dictionary between shit and syphilis, ha, ha, ha. Oh, yeah, I guess I always figured you would go ahead and take the Escort away from her, so if that's what you gotta do, go on ahead and do it.

JOANN

Dear Di, I'm going crazy. I told Johnny he had to tell Mom he was going to marry me, as the man was supposed to do the asking. He said he would, but later. So this morning I decided to show him what I could do and said Johnny wants to marry me and she about had a heart attack. So tonight when he called she lit into him before I even got to the phone. I'm scared I've really messed it up. I told Grandma and she said I'd get over it. I can't tell Mom the money I gave her for the phone is what she gave me for the school pictures, so I told her the pictures haven't come yet. So now I have to ask Johnny for it and he won't even call.

JAMAL

I'm not tryin' to be bitchy, Jac, but what you gots is what they can't have, right, but we can't be hatin' on them for that, okay? Now, I ain't *never* seen no three moves together, right, so jus' do that in threes, right? Okay? Oh, yeah! Yeah! Fuckin'- A! Y'awl jus' make that shit up? Man-o-man, that was jus' beautiful. Yeah, y'awl adds that in now, 'n hits it again, 'n lean forward, *forward!* Yeah, *yeah;* now tha' stepback kick. Oh, yeah! Hell, yeah! That's it! That's the one, and... shee-it, Baby! Oh, yeah! Tha's it! That *is* it! Hey, Car, man! How you doin', Boy? Yeah, jus' gettin' some work in. Pull up a stool there; watch a little a' that hips-talkin', skanky-leggin', bustin'-it-open, cockrockin' ol' titty club magic at work, Baby Buddy...

MARGARET

I don't know what to say to you. If you were an adult it would be easy but since you don't behave like an adult I doubt if anything I say will have any meaning at all to you. Concerning JoAnn's marrying you, as I said before, all I want is her happiness. The main reason she is not ready for marriage is she lacks responsibility and cannot even take care of herself. I feel by the time she has worked for her keep and stops asking for help she will know more about herself and what she wants and needs time to find herself. All this talk of marriage is just so she won't have to finish school. She doesn't know anything about other people or how to decide for herself if you're really what she wants. She talks about being with you and marrying you and being happy with you but I don't think she is giving herself much of a chance to be sure. You've put her through a lot of changes and unwanted heartache for some reason, at least as I understand it, that are not at all fair to her or to anyone else. When you love someone all you want is their happiness and do all you can to make this so. You don't do things you know will hurt them. And when you are kids and just going together there is no reason for lies and deceit for there should be nothing to hide. JoAnn is a good girl and only means to do what is right. She is all I have and I only wish the best for her. I want her to be sure of her future and her happiness. I want to give her a nice wedding, as does the rest of her family. I don't want her to rush into marriage because she doesn't know anyone or anything else. She never really had a father and doesn't really know what a man is really like. If you really love her and she loves you and you do really want each other, then you will take care of your other problems without inflicting them on her. And I don't want any more angry phone calls. I don't want you to think I am against you marrying my daughter when she is eighteen and out of school, I'm only for giving her a chance to decide for herself and to be as sure as she can be. One thing is for sure, you cannot start a marriage on lies. I have said to her that until there is a big change she will not only be marrying you but your ex-wife, too – you see, I know all about that – and will continue to have the unhappiness she has now. These are my feelings and I cannot change them. If Jo wants you and is willing to share you with someone else, when she is eighteen it is her life, but she'll be making the biggest mistake of it. I do believe you mean well by her, and appreciate your honesty about being in jail, but if you can take this with a mature attitude then you're better than I give you credit for, and I'll be the first to admit it. I've told Jo she is to accept no more of your phone calls and please don't ask her to try and get me to drive her up there to see you again.

CARSON

Right with that, Jamal; I'm glad you asked me, Bro. So don't even think about *not* getting all hung up on her, 'kay, 'cause I see you *are,* man – workin' with her 'n all, right? Hey, that's no surprise, J-man. Whatta you think was gonna happen? She's a fuckin' fox for real. Take you on a *real* run through the woods. Hey, I see your look. Can't hide that. You've got the look, man. It don't bother me none, see. She's the one runs her own game, got nothin' to do with me. I wanna ask you somethin'. Didn't you work that big gentlemen's club down in Glendale? Ran it, or somethin'? Had that parking lot cat that'd go over 'n key a bro's car if he parked it out on the street to avoid having to pay the tariff to go into your lot? No, no, I thought that was funny. Had loads of bad bitches in there, too, right? I think I saw you in there a couple a' times, doing the same thing you're doing here, working with the dancers. Still know any of the brothers down there? Or any a' them Armenian?

JOANN

Johnny, who is Bette Midler? Isn't she a singer? Why would he get a tattoo of someone like that on his belly instead a' someone like Julia Roberts? Cheryl and Anthony and I just saw Pretty Woman. When you get out can we go down to L.A. to see that big hotel where it was filmed?

BUD

Dear Son, received your letter today. So glad you're well and taking care of yourself. Today wasn't too bad, not too much pain, but still there. Go back on Monday to find out what it is for sure. Like I said, I'm not dealing with the pain very well. Gets me down, kind of like my own dad was at the end. I wish you had known him a little better. I know you did as a kid, but that was him at his worst. He was pretty old then and, like I said, hard to be around. But when he was younger, I recall one time when I was a boy we was walking along, Dad and me, and I had my head down. I was tired, see, and he said, 'Bud, if you walk with your head down all you'll see is dirt.' Well, just then I looked up and we was walking along the damnedest field of flowers you ever saw in your life: blue ones, orange ones, red ones, yellow and purple ones, and he could name every one of them, too. And he was a real gentleman and took his time with things. He was never in a hurry, no matter what. Well, enough about that. I don't think I'll be up to making the drive again this weekend. I'm still under doctor's orders to stay down for a spell. The good news: Marge's come back and been a real trooper. I must of done a few good things in this life to deserve this kind of treatment. I understand Jackie told you about my fall. I don't know what you two are doing with each other right now, and it's none of my business, but for what it's worth you could've done worse. I understand she took care of me for nearly six hours until they got hold of Marge. If something should happen to me, I hope you'll still treat Marge like one of the family. She's a good woman, Johnny.

EDDIE

Okay, okay, John, I hear ya, but listen, okay? Now my little brother, how much money you think he makes? Yeah, the lawyer, him. Over ninety K a year, okay, an' you think he gives our mom any help? Huh-uh. Not fuckin' penny one. But me, I'm the big outlaw criminal loser that not only pays her goddamn mortgage 'n groceries 'n land taxes 'n health insurance 'n medical overages 'n for her sister's food who lives at the house rent free and for her idiot daughter to go to school out at the J.C., too, okay, okay? So don't, *do not*, tell me I let people down, not even my most fucked-up, oldest friends who've been with me through all kinds a' twisted shit, 'n should know me real better, see. So's all I want from you now is...did you or did you not take my goddamn coke?

JACKIE

I like hands. I like man hands. Not clean hands. Just strong hands. I like hands that do work. Strong hands. A lot of guys work and get their hands dirty. I like those hands. I don't look at eyes first. It's hands. That's first. And I don't like guys that bite their nails. And I can't stand women who do that either. And, no, I would never do camming. 'Camming?' When you do live video. No way! Never! Come shots on the tits 'n all that *sluck?* The chick looks into the camera and says, 'Oh, oh, my pussy is so wet!' Well, forget it! No way! What I am is a dancer. A *real* dancer. That's *absolutely* right! And not just physically, but astrally. What you see from me can only be seen once – it's just there, and then it's not, okay? But it's still there, you follow? Like somewhere in the air?

JOHNNY

You hear Eddie with that, 'I', 'I', 'I', alla time? When you're talkin' that, 'I', 'I', 'I', you're talking about a third person; you're not talking about yourself. You're talking about what you'd *like* to happen, not what *is* happening. 'Specially when it comes to money. You ever hear people laugh about money? Like when you go into a bank? Ever hear laughter in a bank? You don't, not when people're talkin' about money, Darling. I'll tell you, Eddie sure don't. 'N I never told him diddly-squat. 'Cause there was nothin' to tell. Specially about you. 'N he knows it, too. He *knows* it wasn't you! So don't even fuckin' worry about it...

TERI

Yeah, but I'd never had a three-fifty-seven Magnum stuck in my ear before neither! And you know what was so weird about it? Eddie thought how I did it was to pull Carson out, see, by telling them to meet me at the club. Yeah, so that's when I must snuck over and took it. Eddie's got a real devious mind, very paranoid. I mean I was impressed with as much as he thought, like he's actually thought about me, about the kind of kinked-up mind he thinks *I* have. Now lemme tell you about this new guy of his – some kinda enforcer guy. Now he has this Melvin guy call me about five in the morning when Carson's there, right? So Car leaves, talks to Eddie, 'n comes back to get me, comes in, says he's got to take me somewheres, but can't tell me nothing. 'Listen,' I tell him, 'you know I ain't going nowhere; I can't leave the kids.' 'You got to,' he says, 'your life depends on it.' Like *unbelievable,* right? And Car's not kidding, he's so scared. So when I walk in and they close the door and I'm standing there, I say, 'Now what is this, Eds?' And of course, Eds, he tells this Melvin asshole to do his thing, so he does, puts the gun into my ear and says, 'You've got ten seconds.' What an A-hole, right? 'So do it,' I say, 'there ain't nothing real I can tell you that I know; do me now so I don't have to sit here and worry. You know, shoot me. Get it over with. You shoot me, I'm dead. What am I gonna do?' I didn't know what to tell them. So I went through about the next twenty-four hours trying to help. Now there are several people I suspect, which I'm pretty sure I know who did the burn at this point, okay? It got real strange 'cause there are a coupla people I could've nailed on, and I didn't know what to do. I didn't know if they'd done it or not, but at first I pretty well suspected they did, but just by mentioning their names would be putting my life in their hands. Who? Well, like those stupid tweekers in Saticoy you used to sell speedballs to. The Penasco brothers, right? Isn't that who came back and ripped you off the night you got junked out? Yeah, those two. You know they'd come back on me for sure if I opened my mouth, right? Remember warning me about them? Anyways, Eds sent Car back to watch the kids and that's when Mom musta come 'n got them. Yeah, but I did get Dawnie's roller skates from the apartment. Yeah, Mom knows that. I told her to only let her skate in the driveway, 'n make sure she doesn't go out in the street, and don't cross the sidewalk at all. No, they're all right. Yeah, they look good. Mom's real good to 'em. Yeah, then he asked did I think *you* had taken it then? And I told him no way, absolutely not...

JOHNNY

Now what I've always figured is the other guy always knows what he's doing. If someone got to where he was using too much, I'd ask him about it. I mean, put it right to him. 'N never deal in anything you don't use yourself. That's the real key, that, and never increase your dosages. Now, not many people can do the last one, see. They think they can, but they can't. You gotta have a strong kinda mentality, see, 'n belief in yourself...

JILL

Marge was talking to Dad and he answered he felt better and she said she said something, she looked at him, and he was staring at the wall. Then she looked at him again. He said his stomach was tight and he burped and then was dead.

CHAPTER 18
KIT KAT DRIVE, RENO, NEVADA

JACKIE

The club is right downtown and there's nothing to do. There are no nice people to show you around. All we do is dance, talk on the phone, sit around, then dance again. All we are is mush in a rotten town. The Mother here is a complete and total bitch. She thinks giant boobs are all you need, and knows nothing about dancing. There's one bitch here that has one arm. So guess who has the biggest boobs? So guess who's treated like she's the Star? There's at least three other bitches I can't stand either. It's pretty bad if you go some place new and can't make at least one new friend. Candi is the only girl that's sorta together. I'll tell you what kind of place this is. This one guy took out a dollar bill and started rubbing it on her. 'Would it turn you on if I was doing this with a ten?' he goes. Or guys see me coming out of the club and start tomahawking on me on the walk across the parking lot. Well, that's your letter from Reno. Also, Reno cockroaches have to be the biggest and slimiest in the universe. I'm not exaggerating none either. They come out late at night cause of all the beer spilled all over the floors so they can lap it up. Then when you come in to work you find them all drunk weaving all around under the makeup tables and touching on your legs which freaks everyone out.

RUBEN

She's gots yus two kids, don't she? Man, I don't care if she's gots a concha that squeezes yus dick likes a velvet glove, Ese', no vato's gonna take on two kids tha' ain't his. Yus got nothin' to worry about. Yus'll be out there bumpin' yus head 'gainst the same old post, Ese'; you will. Hey, ya' Gava Mofucker, jus' fuckin' chills with tha' stupido shit... starts thinkin' 'bout wha's real out there, 'n what's yus gonna be doin' yus own self yus gets out there thes' next times...

IRENE

I'm sorry your Dad is ill again but that's always how he's been and drinking over the years. I read yesterday that a 21 year old boy hung himself in the city jail here by tearing strips out of his pants. An awful thing. You're not thinking anything like that, are you? I hope not. Earle is feeling better now but still has days when he's feeling poorly. Still taking that L-Dopa. He's taking it in pill form as he couldn't take any more injections. His buttocks were just black and blue on both sides from them. Anyway, the clinic in Camarillo has increased his daily intake and that helped. He now takes ten daily, plus two of some other kind......
...........Johnny, I'm back at my desk now finishing this. We just heard the sad news. Just got off the phone with Jill. I can't tell you what I feel. It brings up so many things. It leaves the ones left with such an empty feeling but somehow manage to go on. The Good Lord doesn't give us more than we can bear, Honey, but I feel real bad and know you do, too. On the positive side your dad was real sick for only a few years and always did what he wanted to do. Being an only son is hard, but don't forget to call your sister. I understand you and Jackie might reconcile. I'm certain this would be best for Dawnie and Little John, at least for the immediate future. You are a very special person and so important to me. I miss you terribly, and think about living near us when you get out. Earle agrees with me. He doubts he can get you a job at the Parcel Service. When I collect my thoughts I'll write more. Have you thought about getting Our Lord Jesus Christ into your life? He can help. Your Mommy loves you, John, and God Bless You. I'm going to be praying for both you and your Dad...

JACKIE

Oh, and Dawnie said, 'Is Daddy going to grow some new front teeth just like me?' Isn't that funny? Ter told me that when she got here. It really helps having Ter here. Yes, Mom does have the kids and they're okay, okay? We'll be back in Ventura like the day after tomorrow...

JOANN

Oh, Baby, I am so sorry. I found out the bad news yesterday and told Mom that's why you were so mean on the phone. I never went out on you, Johnny. Johnny, please call me. Before you do, though, you have to tell Mom you're sorry for hanging up in her face. You said you didn't want to hurt me. If you and me are through for something as dumb as me being at Cheryl's you will be hurting not just me but yourself as well. Now you haven't called or anything. You know that's not right. If you love me as much as you say you wouldn't be doing like this. Mom says you can call again, you just have to say you're sorry. And Cheryl is so a good friend! She is because she talks honestly to me so I won't be hurt. Everyone here is talking about her. I told you she's been having pains since Friday so I think Jr. will soon be on his way. I bet it's gonna be chubby looking, knowing Anthony, but she'll be happy with it no matter what. Everyone buzzed around her at first to see if she was pregnant, now they are to see what it's going to be. I told her I was going to stay with her to help with it and that's what I'm gonna do. People who talked about her like a dog are now kissing her feet like it's normal. Anthony is being real good to her and waits on her hand and foot. I wonder if you and me could be like that? They're happy and I know we could be too. Sometimes I wonder if you want to marry me just so you can see how happy I can make you or is it how happy you can make me? In all your letters you say you love me but I really want you to love me when you come back. It's gonna be rough because your **EX**-wife will know you're back and she might do something. Especially if she doesn't get you. Anyway I hope it's all over for good with her, and I think she knows it. Cheryl's old boyfriend Robert was at school the other day, the one with the red Honda. He said your **EX**-wife was known to be selling drugs with that friend of yours. He also said I looked like death warmed over and hurt my feelings. He used to tell me I looked boss all the time. Maybe I'm not PG but I don't know for sure yet. It would be nice if all marriages stayed like they are in the beginning, but they all change maybe after a year when the first thrills are gone. Do you think that would happen to us? I wish you had taken me to Planned Parenthood before you got arrested. Saw this neat old Trans-Am, all maroon and black with a white license plate that said **ONE-LUV**. Made me think of us.

JACKIE

I'm back and just now heard the news and wonder if it wasn't when he hurt his head, and not lung cancer. Your Mom called and asked if I would go to the service with her. I wanted to tell you how sorry I am. I know death doesn't make someone go away. It makes the person even more alive. You'll have to start treating your Mom nice now. I have to go to Welfare tomorrow and I'm going to the service with her as Earle won't go and she doesn't want to go alone. Jill is coming up from Playa Del Rey. I still won't be able to visit for awhile. In my absence Welfare came and took the kids. Teri wasn't with them and Mom seems to be at fault, even though I called her each and every day. She told me they're all right and in a good Foster Home. I hope when you get out that we can attack these crazy insane people and get our trip together. It was really a downer going into their room and finding it empty. Their little mouse was running back and forth in her cage and that made me cry. Even though I knew they wouldn't be there I kept hoping I was wrong. I returned home as soon as Ter called and told me and just can't believe Mom let it happen. I don't know what's behind this but I'm certainly going to find out. We're short on money now as I lost almost a week's pay, plus there's no AFDC now, and now there might be a lawsuit against me for backmonies, claiming I was working when I wasn't. The phone has been shut off again, thanks to Teri not paying the bill, but I'll write what happens or use a pay phone or borrow someone's or maybe I'll get some money tonight. Or I may have to think about trying Reno again. I certainly don't hope so, but I don't know.

RUBEN

'Kay, hokay, let's say yus' find yus gonna has to go tha' way, here, lemme show yus'… No, no, Juanito, tha's not the way to do it.

Com' mere. Gets down here. Lemme show yus...here. Now stands like this, hokay? And say thes' es the cuete. Yus think yus jus' walk up, point it, 'n do it, right? Well, yus don't. Not if it's a handgun. Now, if yus can walk up to them yus don't holds it like that. Yus holds it like thes'. Sideways, see. Not straight up. Yus holds it like thes', see? Sideways like thes', 'n puts it right in the middle of their chest, here, right here, 'n make sure it stays turned. Yus keeps it turned, hokay? Tha' way when yus pulls the trigger the recoil won't kick the barrel up so's yus miss. The worst it'll do is kick it out somewheres sideways on the body. Also, yus don't... com' mere. Look. See thes'? Try thes'. Hol' tha' arm straigh' out. Likes thes'. Likes yus holding it out all the way, hokay? Now tha' arm, tha' arm, Ese', can be pushed aside. Like thes'. See that? How easy tha' wus? So turns it like thes', right? Sideways. Tha's right. There. Now see how hard that wus to push aside? 'Kay, now tha's how yus do it. Tha' way you sure to get your shot in even even if he tries to knock yus arm away...

JOHNNY

Now there's a guy here who's retarded, see. He's an actual retard who gets real mad if he thinks you don't like him. By himself he's all right, but gets real upset when he's around other folks. He does pig and chicken imitations, real pig and chicken imitations. 'Ziggy,' you tell him, 'do a pig.' First he'll stare at you to see if you're putting him on, then if you keep a straight face he'll crack one off, do a pig, then a chicken. I'm not kidding. And they're just terrible. They don't sound nothing like a chicken or a pig. It's really pathetic. And what's worse he's even called Disneyland and talked to some guy about being a chicken or a pig voice for cartoons. They said get a tape made and sent to them. So all the time he's practicing. Jesus Christ, you get to thinking you're bad off'n you see a guy like that. He never had a mom or dad, see, and sorta trails after me. He'll do anything I ask. I asked him if he wanted to get a mom and a dad when he gets out. Just as a joke, you know, and you know what he said? He said, 'I do if you do.' Made me feel sorta bad. Now what would you think if you had one like him for a kid?

JOANN

Have you written or called her yet? Because she came and stole the car. It was parked by the gym and I had the keys and now it's gone. Cheryl said this skinny old bitch with long dyed ratty blonde hair took it. She said she saw her get in it and drive off. Mom wanted to report it stolen but I told her it was your Mom's car and that's who came and took it. Johnny, what would you do if I was going to have another guy's baby? Don't think I'm going to have a baby by anyone else because I'm not. I just want to know what you would do? Yesterday I didn't go to school. My bod was killing me. I'm kinda at a loss for words. What would happen to me if you found out I had gotten over with another guy? I wonder what is going through your mind right now? Let me tell you something, if I had I wouldn't talk about it, now would I? There are these two Afro guys that like me. Every time I walk down the hall they call, 'What's happening, Momma?' And walk me to the car every day. When I had the car! One day one of them asked me to kiss him. I just looked at him like he was crazy. Sometimes I wonder if you think I'm doing something because I never seem to be home when you call. Most of the time you call just before I come in the door. And I am at home with Mom and Grandma. And the next time you call yelling and carrying on I'm going to hang up. You can get as mad as you want, but that's what will happen. And don't think it's me on the phone when it's busy because mostly it's not me on the phone but Mom. And I know it was your **EX**-wife that took the car. And, furthermore, if you are still involved with her you're wrong. I think she is very ugly and I guess all ugly people belong together. I don't mean you're ugly because you're not and don't belong with her. Johnny, I have grown up since you've been gone. I still love you, **ME**. XO XO XO XO XO XXXXXXOOOOOOOOXO

MARGE

You know what your Daddy said? The last thing he said? He said, 'You always want just one more day....'

JOHNNY

Jesus Christ, it shocked the shit outa me! I mean it! I've got enough problems without you moving into Cheryl's place! All of a sudden you move out, just like that! I wasn't gonna even talk to you because I'm so goddamned mad! You said your mom's been hassling you ever since you moved back in! BACK IN? I never even knew you'd moved out! No wonder I couldn't get you on the phone! And this is what really burns my ass: YOU FUCKING HAD IT MADE! Jumping Jesus Christ if you didn't! Rent paid, food paid, gas paid, plus new boom box and own computer. Just because you say you can't take the bitching! How fucked is that! You said you've been at Cheryl's. If you still are and intend to stay there I'm against it one hundred percent. I'm not going to ask you to move back home, that's your decision, but I don't know what to believe. If you're at Cheryl's old place you're only a few blocks from school and there's no reason for you to have the wagon back. You don't need it. Sure, it might be cold out, but you can walk. I just don't see why you did it. You have to realize what this puts your Mom and Grandma through. I hate it when I hear things from you that piss me off. Now I'll be all fucked-up until I hear from you. You said you were afraid I'd get mad. Well, you should be afraid. I'm goddamned mad! I have something else to say, but this isn't the time or the place. The good news is I'm outa here real soon, but I don't even feel like telling you this cause what for?

GRAMS

I'm going to miss your Dad so much. When your Uncle Bill died knowing your Dad was still here helped keep me going. I'll tell you a little secret I've not told anyone. Two years ago when I knew I was really sick and the chances were pretty slim that I'd recover I really didn't much care. In a way it was a relief. Soon I would see my dear Bill again, see his dear smile, and put my arms around him. I used to pretend he was away on a trip, or over to Vegas where he often went, and it made the waiting seem short. Of course while I was laid up I prayed and wanted God's will to be done and it seemed he had a few more chores for me to see through before taking me home to see my loved ones again, including now your dear sweet dad. The only ones who still need me here are Jill and you. And even though Jill's married to a dear man, she still clings to me in some small way. As long as you and her are here I'll do my best to stay here, too, even though right now I'm taking so many medicines I need a computer to keep track of it all. I want you to know I'm always thinking of you. Did you know I was one of the few people in the family who never had a cross word with Bud? Because we respected one another and learned to never take unnecessary privileges with each other. And of course you can stay here when you return and don't even have to ask. I always have room for you. I sent you a box of goodies yesterday. The pillow is for your head in watching the late shows as you said Ruben has a TV. The rest of the box is for sharing with him. I know you don't eat much candy because of your teeth so any you don't want is for him.

JOHNNY

Jo starts crying on the phone! Then her mom gets on, givin' me a buncha shit talking about my life! Right on! Lay it on me, sayin' she can take better care of Jo than me. I said, 'Oh, yeah? How come she wants to leave so goddamn bad then...?'

JILL

Mom said Dad left all his clothes in the apartment and wanted us to look them over in case you wanted any, but Marge didn't want us to go there and I made the decision not to. Mom got kind of mad. One thing they did we all thought was lovely. They had the casket put in the huge all-glass part of the church overlooking the ocean and Ventura Pier with the blanket of chrysanthemums and roses over the casket and padded folding chairs for the people. It was a closed casket and I think that was best as I know I didn't want to see him. They gave the last prayer there and that was it. No graveyard, no shoveling of dirt, just a lovely goodbye. They gave each of us a rose from the casket. Of course it rained. The service was at the funeral home. The minister was wonderful.

He talked of God is Boss and a loving and forgiving God and we mustn't forget that. He talked as if he knew Dad. Knew his good points. The Church gave all the food. Everyone was upset and ate like pigs. Mom was very upset. Since Earle wouldn't come with her I had to support her as much as possible. Marge didn't seem upset at all. Jackie didn't come. I called and it seems something is wrong there. Her phone was out of service and Mom said the kids are in a foster home somewhere and Jackie hasn't been seen. Mom says Jackie can't be blamed entirely, that it's just as much you getting yourself all messed up again. Anyway, I'm just glad you missed that bit of conversation, and it was just a sad day for all concerned. Gene and I will try and come see you but he has to be back at work tomorrow so it'll have to wait. He said for you to know there's a couple of hundred dollars here for you when you get out. He appreciated how soon you paid back the money he gave you the last time. I'm writing this from Lama's. She's baking you oatmeal cookies right now. It seems a shame that something like this has to happen to bring everyone together again.

JOHNNY

You think you've done some dumb things?! I used to think I was tough, but you know Flaco, the big weightlifter guy? I intro'd you, 'member, the one in for G.T.A.? Ran a chop-shop out in Pacoima? Had a bottle of shampoo, see. 'Thes' es mescal, homemades mescal, Homes,' he goes. 'Right on,' I go; 'give me a drink.' Now I thought I could handle anything, but, damn, it *was* shampoo! 'N I can't handle shampoo at all, man, I'll tell you that!

RUBEN

Be cool, Ese'. Yus don't know nothin' – yus don't know where she gots her head. Your *corazon*, Juanito, jes' use yus heart, 'n looks out for Numero Uno, hokay, 'n don't do tha', *'What yus gotta do'* bullshit. Forgets that shit, understands? Whenever tha' peche shit comes up jes' walk away, walk off, yus understands, 'cause walkin', tha's the hard way, 'n only the hard way's the right way, hokay? Yus hear me? 'N com' mere, man, I wants a hug...

JOHNNY

Got the good word today, and, first, after talking about shipping me off for Work-Furlough in Palmdale or some shitbird hole like that, changed their minds like always. If I don't go around shooting my mouth off. Tonight Rube said, 'Damn near every dude in here here's because of some woman.' I said, 'You sure know a lot for a Mex.' We kid each other around a lot like that. He's a real good dude. I'll miss him. For about ten seconds, ha, ha, ha...

JOANN

Johnny, Johnny, Johnny, I guess you do love me the way you've been getting so mad at me. Yes, I did get loaded with Cheryl and some of her friends and Anthony. I never got over with him at all and even if I had, all it was was maybe I've been afraid you're just taking me for a ride. Maybe I sort of know it anyway. Is that true? Maybe this time you'll beat up your wife for taking the car from me. Will you really be out in two weeks? What is Work-Furlough? You said you got the Good Word. Does this mean we can get a place? If I had the car could I drive up and pick you up? Maybe you'll beat me up because the car is gone. All sorts of things have been going through my mind. Friends who are close to me can see this. Did you know I was PG once, before I met you? This bothers me a lot. Anthony has been talking to me about this guy Bobby Russell, a guy that's been saved and plans to be a minister. Anthony said Bobby told Randy that I had sucked him off and that I used to beg him to let me do it. Nothing like that ever happened. Bobby told Randy to stay away from me because a woman like me would ruin his chances of being closer to God. I'm just now beginning to see people as they really are. And in all truth I'm scared it isn't really love that I feel for you. I think it is, but what if it isn't? It scares me because I do want to sleep with you every night and to wake up to your warmth every morning. But it seems like every time you call or write it changes my mind. I know I have a baby inside me, which I guess by your actions you don't want to keep. I haven't said anything about the baby before because I wanted to be sure but I'm sure. My bod is going through a lot of changes now. Please don't tell nobody about the baby, Johnny. Just let you and me and Cheryl be the only ones that know, O.K.? You haven't said, but you're certain that the 17th is your date? Do they send you home by bus like you said they did the last time? Can I meet you when the bus arrives? I know where the bus station is. I wish we could get married right this minute and move out of the State of California where you could learn to love our child. I know we would have to rough it at first but I don't care. It's almost 9:30 and I'm still waiting for you to call. I'm wondering if you will. I heard that your **EX**-wife left town. I know she's not really your **EX**-wife, but since you don't love her or want to be with her that's how I think of her. I went over to your friend Eddie's house to see if he'd heard from you but saw the car there. I didn't want to go in because she might be there and also what if I was there and he got busted? Well, I'm tired of all this thinking I've done, so – till then. P.S. I don't know if this all makes sense. It might not, but I don't want to read my thoughts over. XXXXXOOOOO,

Your Panda, **ME**!

P.P.S. Big Puppy, You Better Call!!!

JACKIE

They don't like all these homeboy guys coming in here, but there are sets of 'em all the time coming 'n going. Ter is getting down with 'em on purpose, you know, getting over any way she can, doing real cheese, like jabbing them on the shoulders as she struts by, putting her hands up on the mirrors, looking back at 'em, tucking their money under her G and pulling it back out, flashing her stuff, looking back over at them again, a real stand up 'n smack me to heaven look, but, like Dad always said, 'In Heaven there is no beer,' so you gotta do what you gotta do. She is the little sister. I'm the big sister. It's the big sister who's supposed to lead, isn't that right? The thing about her, though, she's really smart. Back when we first started, when I was having a very hard go, as I am a very modest and shy person, she knew I was in trouble, and she said, 'Look, you don't have to keep getting stoned to do this. Just keep moving, keep smiling, under your breath keep saying, "Fuck you, fuck you," as you step your routines. I mean it's only a dumb job, okay?' And she helps out with the kids, too, believe it or not. She's the one that took them to get their flu shots when Mom wouldn't do it. Oh, you know what I just realized? She really uses the word dumb a lot, like 'This is dumb', and 'That is dumb.' Maybe that's why I think she's so smart. But then she thinks I don't know she's still got a little thing for Car, that it's still there and I don't see it...

BOOK THREE **SPRING**

JACKIE

It is now my plan to return to school and get a job that will provide a decent living and finally attract a man to have a permanent relationship with but only if I can attract a man as real as my son's real father. My husband is still a possibility in this plan. Or perhaps it is quite possible I might not succeed in my hopes. However, I don't think lacking sex and a real partner means anything other than I am missing out, and not that I'm not still an okay person in an occupation that is useful to people and a good mother. I hurt a lot because Welfare considers me an unfit mother and won't tell me why. As a result distrust and discord surround my family as I am now forced to suspect my own mother, for one, to be a person who called in and requested I be investigated as she still takes charge like a mother, not as a grandmother whose oldest daughter doesn't live at home and has been married with her own life for over nine years.

CHAPTER 19

BELL'S LIQUOR

JOHNNY

Eddie's coming outside of Bell's. He's drinking beer out of a quart bottle in a paper bag. 'Is that beer?' I say. 'You're getting weird, man. You been doing a lotta base, or smoking those chips, man?' Well, he is weird, that's just obvious, but at least you can count on it. You know where he's coming from. He doesn't hide nothing. Not like a chick. Chicks are worse 'n dudes. They are. You never know where they're coming from. A dude is always direct, but not a chick. Like I remember this one time, we'd hit a lick down in L. A. and this fat chick picked up on it and took us home. Two kids asleep in the bedroom 'n all that. Now I didn't dig on her, but Eddie did, so they take it up and I sleep on the couch, and in the middle of the night she comes out and starts messing around. 'Where's Eddie?' I say, 'n she says, 'Asleep.' So we do the deed and then she gets up and says, 'You shouldn't sleep out here; there's a bed in the back,' and she leaves. So I go in the back bedroom, 'n lay there 'n wait for her to come in and go to sleep with, but it doesn't happen. I keep laying there and laying there and it finally dawns on me: it's been slimy seconds! What's happened is slimy seconds! 'N I'm all fucked-up, and still drunk, and I lay on this little kid's bed and get sick, real bad sick, and go in the head and get rid of as much as I can and then go back out on the couch to sleep. So in the morning Eds says, 'Not bad, huh? I sent her out to you.' He sent her out to me! I really like that, right? But, hell, he was being a friend. So just as we're leaving she slips me a note with her phone number on it. Now that doesn't mean shit 'cause, one: she's just trying to hold on to anything she can hold on to 'cause she's been had, right, 'cause Eds probably made it clear he's not gonna see her again, an' two, 'cause two: all's she's got left is to try with me. Well, fuck, you can't expect anything different from people 'cause people are selfish, an' if I'd a' been turned off by her I'd a' probably done the same for him, sent her out to him, but now that makes me think 'bout another time. Now this time Eddie and me were fucking around with these two chicks, and like I didn't give a fuck, right, but he was hot for the better-looking one so he started talking to the doggy one. Well, the good looking one started hitting on me, 'cause I really wasn't interested and, as we have nothing else to do, we go to this bar with them, an' this good-looking one and I hit it off and Eds doesn't get anywhere with the homely one so he uses up a lot of his snort on her and I didn't have to use any of mine! So I know it bothers him, 'cause like later he says, 'I really wanted the other one, man,' and I said, 'Well, you should a' had her then, 'cause it really didn't make no difference to me.' And it didn't! So I ask him has he seen Jackie and he says he hasn't. 'She's still outa town,' he says, but tells me he's seen Carson, though...

JACKIE

So Car wanted me to make it with this other guy, but I said, 'No, I don't wanna do anything uncommon to me,' but Car wanted to, so for me it was real nice, I had these two nice-looking guys, and it just worked, which really surprised me 'cause I was pretty well set it wasn't gonna, but for Car it turned out just awful 'cause when we started all he did was watch, and then when he started in he couldn't get more 'n half hard and kept trying 'n trying and was practically in tears when he finally stopped, he was so embarrassed, and finally he just left and I had to tell this other guy, 'Hey, I gotta go, my relationship is breaking up.'

JACKIE

Red Fred was the guy's name, Hon, 'n, God, was he stupid. He was *so* stupid. Jamal told him to keep an eye on me. And that's exactly what he'd do. He'd go like this, put his head on his hand, and just watch me. If I went to the can he'd stand outside the door. Once I was in there washing my hands 'n face an' this biker, chick was in there, dyed

JOHNNY

Well, Babes, coming into Oxnard when that sun started

banging up I was so jacked to see you and the kids. Everyone on the bus was asleep and I was sorta depressed but that had to be the most beautiful sunrise I ever saw or ever could see, that tangerine orange on a white baked-out look that's like a three-layer Urethane Pearl paint job shot over a Traffic Signal Orange on all them low-story, plaster-sided Mex buildings with their blue and pink neons still on. It lifted my spirits so high. That's when I pretty well knew things'd turn out all right.

TERI

Where's she at? I'll tell you where she's at. She's all fucked-up is where she's at. I told her, 'I'm not gonna be responsible for you at all. You can lie in here and drink and pop pills or smoke weed or do whatever, man,' an' closed the door on her. I said, 'The kids are your responsibility, too.' Then the other day, I was over to Mom's and there she was, the hate just pouring off of her! Really! I just sat there and maintained! And you know what she's doing? Pamelor. Yeah, Pamelor. Ever heard of it? It's some kind of an anti-depressant, appetite stimulant, she says, but all I ever see it do is nod her out. She can't even get it here, no doctor'll script it for her no more, so she's hitchhiking to all these different doctors 'n pharmacies like out to Santa Paula and Fillmore or wherever. Yeah, hitchhiking! And Dad, man! Yeah, Dad, 'cause no one gave him a stupid birthday card so he calls. 'Well,' he says, 'I hear your sister is in trouble. Are you helping her?' 'Me,' I say, 'am I helping her?' I mean if he's so damn worried about her he should do something

black hair, black leather pants, silver chains around her waist, this sharpened screwdriver in her boot, and I've pissed her off 'cause she wants to use the crappy sink and I'm in her way or something, okay? So she pulls the screwdriver out and is coming at me. That's when I screamed, 'Fred!' He broke the door down, tore it right off the hinges, grabbed her by the hair and said, 'You want me to curb her?' 'No, Fred, I don't want you to curb her,' but he did. Drug her outside and came back in with blood on his boots. Ugh! Just the kinda guy you wanna have secretly in love with you, right?

about it himself. God, what a shit! And the other news here is Mom's getting married again. Yeah. Absolutely true! Absolutely! Like she met some fucked-up loser guy named Warren something or other out at the V. A. in rehab there and got with him somehow for about a month or so, I guess, and is sorta happy. What'cha think about that? Not much, right?

EDDIE

Yeah, yeah, I saw him. The dude's just the same. No patience, you know, none. You wanna know what he's like? I mean, like no patience. Like this one time we got hit by these L.A. guys, two guys, they came in with nickel-plated forty-fives, no fucking around, a little blonde dude and a Mex. I thought the fucking things were plastic until they put a shot into the refrigerator! Well, me, I quit! 'Hey, you dudes just take it all,' I'm outa business, I'm going back into selling used cars!' Well, you know, when even guys you don't know a fucking thing about know all about you, you better start thinking about it, that's for damn sure, but not John! No! He wants to skin 'em! They split, and I have to actually tackle him to keep him from running out the door and getting wasted!

JACKIE

Yeah! While I was out a' town. You bet she did! She lay right down on the floor and said, 'Take me.' Car didn't start it up again – not that he wouldn't; he's a male creature, isn't he – but her! 'Was it worth it to you?' I said. 'You weren't just a sister but a friend, but now you're just a slut!' I wasn't worried about him! Not one little teensie bit! I can make that man walk on nails without so much as raising a finger – no one can make him suffer like I can. An' then her? Man, I was so pissed at her I was gonna take her out into the desert, tie her to a cactus, shave her from head to toe, spray the word bitch across her tits, then call the CHP after two days just so she wouldn't croak!

JOHNNY

Hey, Ter, it's pitiful. It's just pitiful what life does to you, but, hey, everybody that's living is living right now! That's it! Everyone that's here is living right here right now! That's why right now is right now, ha, ha. I mean, forgive 'n forget, right? I mean, hey, I loves ya. Uh- mmm, it's just a great fuckin' pleasure to see ya, but you gotta tell me where she is. Yeah, you do, Ter. You think I'm bullshitting here? Either you tell me or your windows get kicked in, or your tires slashed or, hey, maybe I'll just do fuckin' both, whatever's the easiest. Sister-in law's got nothing to do with it. That's just the way it is...

I would've done it to her, too, 'cause I know some people who'd do it for me, too, several of them, in fact, but I didn't want that kinda karma around me, okay, so that's where that's at...

CARSON

But then with Jackie, man, I gotta admit it, I got a little wound-up, you know, watching it go down, but then I was really pissed off, too. I mean it got to me. She'd said she was doing it for me, but then when she was getting into it, like when I saw her body get into it, like when she started to quiver? Jesus! I mean, 'Hey, this is just fucked,' right? 'N pulled the dude off. Then he gets up really pissed, so I had to toss his funky ass, 'n then she up 'n takes off on me, just bolts out the door crying. So I go get her. 'Okay, I say, 'I'll do it; I'll marry your ass! 'You don't mean it,' she says. 'Oh, yes, I do,' I say, 'I will. There'll be no more of this kinds a' shit!'

JACKIE

My sister has taken up with my ex-boyfriend again and thinks she has triumphed over me. She has all these other men she is seeing, too, and is lying to each one. I told her Carson would just use her just like he used me, but she just laughed in my face. When she asked who brought me home from Reno I said, 'Well, wouldn't you like to know, you little twat? I smoked a joint, chugged a sixer, did some skunk, met this guy, or whatever he was, on the bus, brought him here, and screwed him to death. He's all finished now, and you can have him.' God, I loved it! 'N she actually went into the bedroom to see who it was!

JOHNNY

When I found out what she'd done to the kids it tore my guts out! I went fuckin' nuts! I searched everywhere for her, every goddamn place I knew, and I had some real heavy shit going for me. Every place I went into, guys I didn't know would swing around 'n say, 'Hey, Dude, how you doin'? How's it goin', man?' 'N give me five. And the women, man, each one of 'em, all of 'em, would actually try to hook into me, ones I never even knew, 'cause they wanted it, see, they could feel it, they wanted some of my righteous wrath 'cause I was gonna lay it on her, 'n they knew it, 'cause that night was mine, I owned it!

JACKIE

We'd done this sorta thing before, but only with chicks, Car and me, with this other chick we both knew, but this time it was like with him 'n me 'n this other guy, right? An' Car, he couldn't handle it at all, 'n that's when he asked me to marry him, I mean, like right there! Like immediately after! Like I didn't even have time to get up and put my robe on. 'Huh-uh, no way;' I told him, 'that's way too messed up.'

JACKIE

On the other hand, now with John I've always felt like I was the only one that could understand him, who could help him. I'd always felt that I could reform him, that we were a team, that he could be rehabbed. So when I saw him I said if he'd totally get out of the trades, totally disassociate himself from Eddie and all them people, that maybe there was a chance. 'Cause he has so much potential, too, and it's all being wasted. He lowers himself in his own eyes. Not that he rips people off. Nobody, and I mean nobody, I don't know a soul in this world that can say Johnny did them dirty, he's done good business, is all, and I'm hoping me getting my kids back and leading a normal life and quit-

JOHNNY

Then I walk by the school and see Jo coming out looking really tight, and say, 'All right!' She gives me forty bucks and we go over to Anthony's and Cheryl's and I tell her, 'Babes, I can't believe it, you look so good!' And she's just crazy, we can't wait an' just leave Anthony and Cheryl's, 'n get it on. She can't stop laughing, she's so blown away, an' she says, 'They told me you were out but I didn't believe it, but that's how you are; you're sneaky is how you are,' and she knows she's been acting bad, but she can't let me control her, that I've talked her into things she's not sure of. 'Well,' I tell her, 'you know I've had a lotta time to think about a lotta things, and it seems every time something's gone bad it's 'cause other people've told me what to do.' 'I know,' she says, isn't that the truth,' and then I have to ask her about other guys. 'What'd you expect?' she says. 'Expect?' I go, 'I'll kill you, you little bitch,' 'n she says, 'No, you won't, 'cause I only like *big* men, like someone very sweet I know,' and we both laugh, it was so great. 'Well,' she says, 'maybe we really can get married; it depends on how we still feel about each other,' and then we hear things from out in the living room and Anthony's yelling, 'I can't even get in my own bedroom, man!' which cracks us up. 'Baby,' Jo says, 'I'm so glad you're getting yourself together, but what'll Jackie do when she finds you're really back?' And then Anthony comes in and wakes us up and I say, 'We'll go out on the couch, man; sorry about that,' and he says, 'Hey, it's morning time, Mr. Johnny,' and asks Jo if she's going to school.

ting all drugs, with being able to disassociate from all that, it'll make him see he can do it, too. And that's gonna freak out some people we know, I mean like really freak them out.

JACKIE

I didn't know what to expect so I got myself looking really good, and they pulled up in this limo, you know, swear to God, like ol' Eds had pulled off a whole 'nother level of business, you know, taken it up the chain, and took us all on up to Tahoe on the South Shore, and we did some drinking and dancing, and some Keno 'n Blackjack, and this other real rad Vegas guy had all this money coming down, too, an' we all got on the pipe 'n drinking Cuervo Gold with Bud backs, and both Ter and I got absolutely whacked, even the base wasn't straightening us out, an' going back to Reno I got really sick and had to throw up and kept throwing up, and each time I did they'd have to stop and I'd have to get out of the limo by myself, they were all sitting in there firing up more base, you know, and the last time I thought, 'To hell with this, I might as well start walking... I can't do this no more,' and no one got out 'n came after me, not one of 'em, not even Ter or Jamal or even Fred, all of 'em just sittin' inside back there, all this snow coming down all around everywhere, the headlights going out into the dark in front of me, it was so goddamn cold out, 'n all I could think was I miss my kids. I kept seeing their little faces...

CHAPTER 20

SAVIORS ROAD

JOHNNY

Jac and I had not been together. When I first went over there she wasn't home. Not the next night neither. When I finally did see her she said, 'You can't come rushing back into my life.' 'Hey,' I told her, I said, 'fuck that noise! It's my life, too!'

JOHNNY

I was that close to putting it in! That close! I was up over her, see! 'No,' she, says, 'you can't! I have an infection, okay, and you'll get it!' An *infection*! That's when she picked to say it! *Right then! Not before!*

TERI

Well, the way I finally figured it was Johnny musta done the rip on Eddie 'n put the blame our way. Either told Eddie or someone in the can who'd talk to Eddie, okay? Now John'll say he didn't, but what he figured was either Jac or me'd have to go back to him for protection or Eddie would make Car give Jac up to prove he wasn't involved, John's real devious like that, but what he didn't figure was that Jac would be gone and Eddie would force me to leave the kids so's he could scare me half outa my mind. And I told John he could say anything he wanted, but I *knew* he did it, 'cause it wasn't me, and I knew Car didn't, and that Jac didn't, but I wasn't gonna say anything else about it, 'cause losing the kids was bad enough for him, 'n I didn't even have to say anything at all about how ignorantly stupid it was.

EDDIE

What I did I rented a car, loaded it with everything I owned, and split. You know all the crap a guy collects, so I thought, Fuck this, and somewhere outside Boulder I just did it, drove up to a big snow bank, opened the doors, and pushed it all out,

JOANN

See how firm they are? No! No one has squeezed them but me!

shirts, shoes, ties, books, suits, CD's, photo albums, all that shit, right into this huge white snow bank, a million stars over my head. Had a thousand hits of Windowpane, my black leather jacket, my boots, a tote bag full of lids, Levis cowboy shirt, forty-two bucks worth of food stamps, pair of jeans, carton of Chesterfield Kings, that was it. Was I hip? Bag of Delicious apples, two grams of traveling toot, too. That, my wallet, my toothbrush and hairbrush, leather work gloves, plus six pairs of red and green-topped Norwegian wool socks. I really loved those socks, man, and four hundred bucks. Now that was it, nothing else. Didn't stop in Denver neither, 'cause that was where she was originally from. You cut it, cut it to the bone; it's done, is how I was thinking, But maybe it's me, maybe this whole thing is wrong, maybe I should turn back around, maybe the whole problem is me, I should get some help, that woman was born with a smile on her heart; whatta my doin'? Or maybe jus' 'yadadee-yadadee-yada' and get on through there as fast as I can, right, straight on through to New Orleans. Now that's some town. Man, all those peach and magnolia trees. Walking around in the evening, the wind comes up, the whole town smells sweet. Knew I'd made the right move. Checked into the Holiday Inn, got myself a room on the top

Now, can I tell you something? No matter what I say you can't move, okay? 'Cause I said so. 'Cause you have to. 'Cause I said. Now watch this. You like this? If I do this? Remember the first time we both climaxed face to face, 'n I didn't know what to say to you?

TERI

Oh, good God, Jac! Please! Hell, I was probably just horny, or was ovulating or something, and Car was like there, okay? It wasn't no big, whoop-de-do life-changer or nothin', okay? Yes, but I never answered back. I don't think he gets it. Or else tries to get his way around it. 'Cause he doesn't know what he wants. Hell, I usually like a guy like that. It's like some switch for stupid that I can keep flippin' on or off, that'll keep the whole gumbo of it going...

floor, took a shower, changed my socks, went downstairs, bought some mirrored shades, hit the street, bam, unloaded my whole kit in four hours. Unbelievable, right? On a roll. So I bop on back to the Holiday, call United, get a reservation back to L.A. for Friday. This is a Wednesday, see, 'n I'm stoked. Now I can set up something that'll be terrific, right? So I go back downstairs, go into the bar to kick back, and there are these guys, introduce themselves, now two guys, and are they smooth motherfuckers. I mean, like short hair, sharp suits, both tall, good-looking dudes, twenty-six, twenty-seven, maybe early thirties, but young, you know, young sharp guys. Buy me a drink, have the bartender put me on their tab, buy me a steak, have it brought right to the bar, tell me they understand I've been enjoying their city, they admire me for doing so well in a new town, 'specially since I'm working alone, right, which takes a lot of balls, right, like big, man-sized balls. Tell me to stick around for a few days, take time to enjoy myself, give me the names of a couple of great restaurants with unbelievable food, just give them their names and I'll be treated like a king. 'Fine,' I say, 'great, great, that's just great.' We shake hands. 'Nice to meet you guys,' I say. They leave and, man, I like book it, I'm flat out gone; go upstairs, grab my bag, toss my shit in, call a cab, don't even turn in the car, just leave it in the lot. Catch a flight to S.F., then one back to L.A., okay? And to this day I still don't know who or what they were. And that's what I'm saying here, see. You got to look at the facts, John, just the plain motherfuckin' facts. Look, you're outa the can now. I'm not pissed off. You got a new squeeze. So maybe it's best that way, you know. Look, didn't I tell you not to marry Jac? Didn't I? You got married three weeks after I told you. I told you she'd dust you good, didn't I? Well, why is that?

JACKIE

My heart was absolutely pounding. I ran in the bathroom and just stood in there. I didn't even think to call the cops. It was really nutso. I don't know what my head does when I get like that. I just get crazy. I was spitting on my hands and rubbing the spit on my arms so if John grabbed me I'd be able to slip away. Isn't that nuts? Then I told him I wasn't coming out until I knew he was sitting down. He was sitting down, he said. I came out and said, 'Things are not gonna go on like they were before; something better is gonna happen, I know that.' Then he said what I thought was happening wasn't happening and he got up and left.

JOHNNY

Sure, there was a problem. When Jac was young she was raped, you know, and didn't get it checked out, being ashamed 'n all, an' by the time the docs caught it it'd closed her up, scar tissue blocked her tubes, okay? The fuckers gave her the fuckin' clap, see, and then when I got her pregnant she was the happiest woman on earth. She called Dawnie her miracle baby. That was just a great time in our lives, and, you know, you always know when you're fucking up, but unless someone calls you on it you just keep fuckin' up 'n fuckin' up and then something bad happens. Now that's nothing to be proud of. It'd be much better to say I could stop it myself without no one's help, and I think I'm starting to get a handle on that, I mean what I shoulda done was just tell Jac the good 'n the good only, right? 'Cause one time I remember when she was crying, there was something she'd wanted, and I asked her to tell me about it, an' she said not to worry about it, it was something she could handle, she was only crying 'cause girls were supposed to cry. And that's what I was thinking about. How tough she was. Like her face would float up to the window of the bus, or something, 'cept it wouldn't, it was just my face reflectin' in the glass, and

JOANN

Baby, I am so sore! My legs from my thighs down to my ankles and in my left leg, even my foot hurts! You sure proved everything you said you were gonna prove. My thighs have, here, look at this. See these bruises here? Don't do that! You like my hair like this? Or like this? Cheryl likes it this way. Your mom wears a wig, doesn't she? Yeah, she does...

JACKIE

And John's still got that stupid little girlfriend, too. I've been

then I had trouble finding the cemetery 'cause the bus didn't go but halfway out there, and the fucking wind was blowing off the strawberry fields and I hate the wind, man, all that dust and fertilizer flying around and I drank the whole pint before I got there and I couldn't get any kind of feeling. I thought somehow that there'd be some kinda special feeling there, like maybe Dad would be there, and I could feel it, could feel him, but there was nothing, no nothing, only a scratched-up, dirted-over, plastic strip with his name 'n dates on it which I cleaned up and then the ground, all the dried and dead grass that they'd used too much Roundup on. It really is a shitty cemetery; you ever been out there?

CARSON

No, I don't need Eddie. Who needs to work for anyone else? Top people don't work for other people, right? Beautiful, you know. Listen, I was talking to this guy. You know what he's doing? Selling inflatables out of an office in Hollywood, right on Hollywood Boulevard. Hollywood Boulevard, that's right. thinking a lot about him, but it's just so obvious that all his talk is just talk, though I do miss the warmth and security of knowing I'm to share the rest of my life with someone, being in a marriage, I mean. I think the last days are coming, man, I do. I think they're gonna be here real soon. And no more drugging or drinking either. I'm tired of waking up sick and disgusted with myself. Coming back on the bus I was still so sick, like that told me something. It told me if I ever got myself into trouble again the only person that would get me out of it was me. 'N, as for relationships, I've pretty much decided to just shrug off the feelings, you know, so the relationship can't come down on me. Like with Car saying he wants to marry me, not because he really wanted to, but 'cause someone else was getting the best of him. How can you want anyone like that? An' right now, 'n especially right now, I don't want *any* kinda relationship…

JACKIE

That's the way he's always talked. He needs that. He gets his energy from that. But all I see

All telephone sales. He has this bitchin' little office with a telephone and sells people an inflatable boat for sixteen hundred bucks. All done by credit card. They don't know it's an inflatable, see. They think a UPS truck is gonna drive up to the house pulling this trailer with their twenty-foot fiberglass boat on it looking good. He says he can get me into that right now, all I gotta do is give him a call. You get fifty percent of each sale. The only hassle is the FBI, 'cause it's an interstate scam, see, but they change offices and phones alla the time...

EDDIE

For sure I believe she'd do it, John, but for Car, not you. He's had her twisting, man, so of course she would. So whatta you wanna do, blow him away, for Chris' sakes? But, listen, B.J., at the end a' the day, for me, personally, who gives a shit who took it? 'Cause in all truth I just don't think about what any a' you assholes do that much, 'n that's the whole of it. What you guys do, or don't do is just not on my mother-fuckin mind, okay? But what *is*, is knowing if my thinking *is* right; now it *was* you, right?

JOHNNY

No, Babes, I've been false to many things in myself 'n said

is how's it gonna be any different than it's always been, a man who wants me because he can't have me?

MILLY

I just wish you wouldn't complain so much and would make a start on something. And I don't mean doing that dancing or whatever it is you two are doing so that I can't even tell my fiancé or friends where you and Teri Ann are working. You think you can just go out there and flaunt yourself sexually and there is no price. Well, Missy, you are so wrong. And I did not turn you in to Welfare. If you have no respect for yourself, then no one else will either. And don't say money. If you had stayed home while I was sick and couldn't babysit you would still have the kids and the Welfare money, too. I am sick to death of you blaming me for all your troubles. Maybe your father did leave us, but I never left you or Teri, and

shit where I didn't even know what I was saying, being full of deceit and lying to myself, yet acting like I was right on to the facts of the situation. Knowing my dad is no longer here makes it completely clear to me to be completely honest and straight with everyone is the only way to go, okay? I think you could be civil to Warren, too, if he should ever want to meet you again after what you said to him about him being just another old, dried-out drunk.

JACKIE

We shared a joint, and he was sitting there just looking at me. 'So, listen,' I told him, 'I'll be here, I'll be understanding to you, I won't turn my back on you, if you need money, or a place to stay, if I can help I will. If you want someone to talk to you can talk to me.' And he listened, he did, he saw I meant it, which really freaked me out, him looking at me like that. He wasn't even reaching for the joint, jus' lookin'...

JOHNNY

I'll tell you, you know what she said to me? 'I don't like you as much as you like me.' That's what she said, and that there were: '*Psychological problems.*' '"Psychological problems?!" Fuck that,' I said, 'there are no psychological problems, there's just other dudes! That's what it is! You tell me you love and care,' I said, 'and then put a "but" on the end! "I love you, but,"' I said. 'You don't know how to communicate,' she said. 'Well, fuck that, too!' I said. 'I know how to communicate! I communicate just like the Beaners in East L.A. The way I communicate is out the end of a thirty-eight! You keep on fucking around with me and I'll fucking-A do it, too!' Well, that went in. You could see it. It really did. She just took it in, and then got real upset and real quiet and real silent, and then I looked at her and saw she was liking me again, and I just got caught out, man, I mean I did, I just started pukin' my cookies up, man, kissing her, hugging her, telling

JACKIE

'Yeah,' I said, 'that's right. I am seeing other people, but no one important, no one serious, okay? But remember when you her I loved her, 'till death do us part,' I was truly hers 'for-ever,' all that good shit. 'Cause the next thing was: 'We can't,' right? 'There's this bladder infection, see, so, no, we can't, but later maybe, later in the week,' that as a matter a' fact she felt so bad she wasn't into seeing anyone. 'So,' I said, 'what the fuck does that mean?' 'It means I'm sick, is all,' she said, and then she said something that sorta hit home. 'You just push and push all the time,' she said, 'and make me say things you don't wanna hear,' and I don't know, I don't know, I don't know why that hit, but it did, so I said, 'You mean I can't stay here? Not even tonight?'

asked me did I want another baby and I said I did and you said nothing?'

LAURENCE H. GOLDBERG, M.D.

This is a twenty-three year old white female, one prior birth, gravida 2, para 0 abortal who was admitted at 36 weeks gestation with a history of ruptured waters and spontaneous onset of labor. During this pregnancy the hematocrit has remained in the 25-29% range and the platelets in the 25,000-30,000 range. Blood pressure 110 over 74, temperature 36.9, fetal heart tones 144, pulse 80. Abdominal exam: uterine fundus measured 27cm; estimated fetal weight was 2200 grams. Lab data: hematocrit 28, platelet count 16,000. Hematology Service was consulted. They suggested platelet transfusion to cover the delivery and immediate post partum period. This was performed. Platelet count immediately after transfusion was 57,000. Patient went on to have a normal spontaneous vaginal delivery of a 2600 gram male infant over a midline episiotomy. Patient incurred a 4th degree vaginal laceration which was repaired with some difficulty. Frequent episodes of abdominal cramps and diarrhea. Platelet count the day following delivery was 42,000, dropping somewhat steadily thereafter to a level of 28,000 on 3/21 when last enumerated.

CHAPTER 21

"THE RED PINK MOTEL"

JOHNNY

Eddie is so fucked. Even if I sell a quarter of blow I'll only get four bills. And what's that? I can't even get my own place with that. All I can do is give it to you to pay for the kids, so, okay, I'll do it, but as for me not being as smart as everyone else? Listen, in some regards I know too many things! Like in just going out and doing your own thing, okay? Like the most dangerous thing there is getting to think that everything is yours, okay? 'Cause if everything is yours, then nobody else exists, okay? See what I mean? 'Cause if everything is yours then all you have to do is to go and get it: TVs, tires, computers, tools, dope, whatever, right, even cars and trucks, even other people's women. And if someone tries to stop you? Hey, they're just in your way! See what I mean? Now that's something that's dangerous. Now that's a fucked attitude. That way of thinking is real fucked, real, real fucked, and people are better off not knowing it. And that's something I'm just now figuring out without no help from no one, okay? And I want you to know that, okay?

JACKIE

Ter, I want you to know I'm really, really emotional right now. You know how I've always been afraid of Dad? Well, today I got this big flash that must've come to you as instantaneously as it did to me – the poor old man is going to die! Now I've cried and felt very emotional over strange and foolish things before, but this is just so great! He cried when I told him Mom was getting remarried. Can you believe it? And said, *'But what about me?'* I'm not kidding! He really did! Now I've often wondered who and what he is, and now I know. He has the frailty of plaster lace. Now I know you're still really pissed at me, but I just had to share this with you 'cause you're my very own sister and I love you. Probably if we would've had some earlier understanding between us we could have mellowed out in how we act with one another and none of this B.S. between us would've had to go down. Incidentally, I told Carson him and me were definitely through. So go on ahead with him if that's what you really want. I mean it. I told him not to come around here anymore. I said all he's done is hurt the both of us, you and me, and that I'd have you in my life a hell of a lot longer than him, or any other man.

CARSON

What I like to do, see, is get a woman on the dance floor, a woman who's never slow-danced. You rub up against them, your thigh between their thighs, but all legit, all in the open. They can't believe it, see, that they can feel you before they even know you, that they get wet before they've even kissed you. I just love it, watching that, watching them discovering that, watching the look of it crossing their faces…

TERI

That could be, 'cause what you really hold out for is someone who's fun, who can tease, who'll rap, who'll show you something different, 'cause most guys can't, or they won't, or they think they don't have to, you know what I mean? Now Car, he's great. In bed he'll talk to you. He'll tell you stories, just to explore things a little with you. He really will. Like he might go, 'I'm telling you, we've got about an hour here, we should make it memorable, but, what the heck, screw that, okay; we don't haf'ta do nothing, okay? It's just comfortable to be with you. I can just lay back with you and not haf'ta take things so fast that you know the future can never live up to the past.' Now that's just his opening rap, his "relax you" rap, ha, ha. You like that? Yeah, then the middle rap, the like, *"confessional"* rap, you know, here he's confessing, like how he's not really

JOHNNY

So when I saw her I said, 'Hell, we've already been through the violent stage, the black-eye 'n beating stage; we've got our kids; let's see if we can really care for each other. We can work things out. I'm definitely growing, you know, making some real good choices now.'

this slick stud type a' guy who's always trying to blow women away with all his hip-hop street jive he's learned in Afro type rap beats 'cause that's what black guys are into, learning each other's technique, see, how to just overwhelm you with technique, like how to twist it, and where, man, "Just get down there, 'n dial her ol' number, either side to side or 'round an' 'round, or straight up and down." 'Now isn't that fucked,' he'll say, then ask if you can sorta help him out, give him a clue which way it should go, like: 'Do you want that with the bowling ball grip at the same time?' 'The bowling ball grip?!' Now that's just the middle rap, ha, ha, ha, ha. Hilarious, right? And then the end rap? Hey...

JOHNNY

'Let's be straight,' I say, 'what is it?' I get back that things won't be as they have been, that most a' her behavior's been caused by her own fears which she didn't understand at the time but now does, that she's real excited about me being out, and hopes it stays that way, that if I'll just be a little more patient it'll really pay off for us. 'N lookin' at her I just believe it, so I say, 'Okay...'

JOANN

So I've been talking to Cheryl a lot and she says it's my life, but to really start thinking about it, and lately I've been thinking who's gonna live it with me? Or who's gonna live it, period? It really ain't no biggie, but she pointed out something, like what are you doing when I'm in school, and for the last two nights when I'm here alone? I hope you haven't been where I think you've been. And last night Cheryl says she and Anthony saw you driving down Thompson with your hand out the window holding a joint between your fingers with someone else in the car. She wasn't going to say who it was, but that I could guess, but I can't believe you'd do that so I told her you didn't, but did you? Also, you can't have any dope! You could get put back in jail for that! This is really freaking me out!

JACKIE

People like that, people with those thin lips? No, no way; I learned that one a long time ago! Never trust no one with a tight little mouth like that one. Like Eddie's, how sideways it is? Like it's been put in just on one side, I mean like his teeth aren't in the middle of his lips? When he talks? You notice that? Like that's what I was tripping on the whole time. Well, it just so happened that he took Car up there with him to see if I had their stupid cocaine. Like I would still have it even if I had taken it, right? All I know is they showed up. Now Eddie's real good at figuring people out. You know that, but here's what you don't know. So Eddie says, 'Let's go over to this hotel,' and we all go into the bar there and it turns out they'd been talking to this older guy, like a tanning bed kinda guy, with that burned leathery look and the silver hair and the vodka watering eyes, that kinda creep, an' this real shit cologne, too, and already had him waiting upstairs in the suite, and Eddie said, 'Okay,' he'd come back for us later, see, that this would pay him back for the stupid coke, and I said, 'For Christ sakes, Eds, I never took your goddamn bullshit coke,' and Car said, 'Well, look, you might as well – don't look at it like it's anything – just be a spirit, and if it bothers you don't be there, just leave your body, okay?' but looking at Eds as he was saying it. Right. No, really. That's what he said. Anyways, we were only in there for a few minutes. Car intro'd me to the guy, and the only thing I said to him was, 'Honestly, I don't think I'm right for this line of work, Hon, okay, but show me the goddamn money.' 'N when he got his roll out I grabbed it and tossed it to Eds, saying, 'Here; now why don't either you or Car blow him, man, 'cause I sure as hell ain't; there's his money,' and walked. Now that's when you really get to see Eddie, see, 'cause it's like, well, that it sorta flashes outa him, coming outa that lopsided face from somewheres deep inside him, okay, 'cause what he's really doing has nothing to do with any money; it's him wanting you seeing yourself bringing yourself low, okay? You follow? I mean, it's him getting you to do shit he *knows* he can make you do, okay, like he does with John, an' Car, an' Fred, an' Larry B., or whoever – everyone that's into him for something, right – 'n watching *that* is what gets him off, and then, now wait a minute, when he sees you seeing it getting him off, it gets him off even more, 'cause he knows you can't do nothing about it, and that's when I busted it, 'cause I *did* walk. Now I told you that, that I always knew he was doing that shit on John and Car and them, but I never thought he would be doing it on me, right? You don't, do you. You always think you're different, but you're not – not at all! Then with Car running after me right there with Eddie watching, me saying there was no point in my saying nothing else neither, no matter what they thought, that they both were fucked? I told you that, right? 'N so later, right after they screw the guy over, we all go casinoing, an' then I get the Observation there, the Overnight Observation, 'n the next day is when Welfare here comes and takes the kids, okay?Yeah, here! Sure! 'Cause the Reno Welfare reported it, some kind of Interstate thing, I guess, but I still think it was Mom! Yeah, Mom! Mom! Her! I guess Welfare got a report there'd been the drunk and disorderly, plus a being out of town, plus a solicitation charge! Well, it wasn't a solicitation, but only a D & D, and Jamal was righteous enough to put up bail, and's been talking to some big time lawyer he knows about it for me...

JOHNNY

Jesus H. Christ! I told you I don't want you going on about her! There's nothing to it! She just has my kids, is all. I told you her and me are friends only and I have to get Mom's Escort back from her and you don't seem to give a shit that I have kids by her and that I don't wanna hurt her none either. You know how hard it is for me to hurt anyone. And I want you to know and to realize that for everyone's sake, both yours and mine, as well as hers and the kids, that I've got to get some money together for her and help her get the kids back. That's why I'm there, and that's my main problem, but know this, you're my main thing...

JOANN

Cheryl says I shouldn't let you wrap me around your little finger. I told her it wasn't like that, it was the other way around. It is, isn't it? But I don't want it either way like that because I love you so much and want everything equal between us, You know how hard it is to be with someone you love when you know they're hurting you and can stop whenever they want. Doesn't what we have mean anything to you? People always say, 'Girl, you must be crazy to wait for him, or they say, 'Girl, you must really care for him.' Can't you see that? And some of my closer friends, ones you don't even know, just say, 'Girl, you must be nuts, especially now that he's here and is doing this!' Well, you tell me...

CARSON

No, man, not at all. What she said was, 'Look, if you can't handle it, forget it. Some dudes can, some can't. I'll just get an abortion then.' 'No way,' I said, 'I think that's flat out wrong, but, even so, even if you do keep it, how do I know it's even mine 'cause it could be ol' John's right? You slept with him again, didn't you?' Or, hey, maybe even ol' Jamal's here, right? Ha, ha, ha, the ol' brownie in the bakery, right? But then I'd know, wouldn't I?' Ha, ha...

IRENE

My cold is much better but we had to put Pepsi to sleep Friday. She vomited all night and legs paralyzed. Earle suspects poison. Took her to the Vet's and veins already collapsed. Just broke our hearts. About your dad. He always wanted to kick up his heels. And always had a lot of explanations. And in a way I thought it a relief having him out of the house 'cause he always thought he was so much smarter than anyone else, always telling people how they should behave. It drove me up a tree, and the sad thing was even if I'd done everything to suit him to a tee it wouldn't 've made no difference. I always tried to be understanding of him but he didn't want it. Even after he moved out that last time and was sick and I went over to that old red-pink motel there on Thompson and kept knocking and knocking and knocking, yelling, 'Bud, are you all right in there?' And he finally shouted, 'None of your business!' And he only stopped drinking when they finally scared him to death that he was at death's door and then he went and died anyway. Earle makes demands, too, but only because he wants the best for us both, not to lord it over me. He's been having chest pains and down his arm and went to Doctor Plattner. Had a cardiogram, which turned out okay, but blood pressure way up and sure got scared. Doctor Plattner said its sympathetic pains over poor Pepsi's death and heart was okay. In spite of the L-Dopa and other pills he's been faithful to his exercising and little by little does seem better. He's still so slow in his movements it seems a miracle he's able to get up each day.

CARSON

Yeah, Ter blew me off. Yeah, it hurt, but not that goddamn much; no more 'n a bad mosquito bite, but then, you know, you jus' get your sweet li'l ol' Momma babes to kiss it... 'n...

CARSON

No! Hell, no, John! First time I ever saw Jac was *way* before I even knew you, man! She was getting out of Ed's Corvette, okay? At the 7-Eleven, okay? The one out by The Ban-Dar? Had all them thin silver hooplets on her wrists with that cool druggy look, running her fingers through her hair, tossing it over her shoulders, looking right at me, floating her eyes 'cross mine, and then gone, like taking me right with her, 'n knowing it, too. Knew *exactly* what she was doing. You've seen that shit before. And it isn't like a dude's got any choice. An' it's just not her. Bitches can do that one alla the time. You know that. So why wouldn't I be after her? Her calling me out like that? Was I a punk or not? So what was I suppose to do? It was *never* about you! It has *nothing* to do with you! *No way!* If it was about anybody it was Eddie! Whose goddamn Vette was she getting out of anyways? You ain't never had no Vette. All's you ever had is that crappy ol' blue pickup piece a' shit you wrecked. Besides, whose piece a' junk is it that you're driving now anyways? Jac's, right? 'N she gave it to you? Sure! Like in stealin' her keys, right?

JOHNNY

Fuck, no, Car; here, lemme pour you another brew. Slide that damn glass over. Course she gave me the keys. 'Cause she's

JACKIE

You think Ter's so great? You wanna know how she got hired? She got hired in the closet. Yeah, that's right; in the closet with the brooms and mops by both the manager and the boss. She said it was a 'beautiful experience.' 'A beau-

always my wife, man, always! 'N she knows that, see. She understands that. She knows all sorts of shit about me you'll never ever begin to know, okay? That you don't even wanna know. So, here, take a chill pill, okay? Here's a lude for you, man. Go on, take it. It's all good. And lemme tell you something else. Remember my old man? Yeah, him, the one with the inhaler at Jac's, 'n offered you a hit, 'n then tried to run you off? Well, this one time him an' me was down on the pier with all them winos 'n crackheads 'n he says, 'Living's no big deal – look at them poor bastards. They're living, aren't they? What's the big deal about that?' So, Bro, whatta you think of that? No, no! Hey, you dumb fuck, jus' swallow the damn thing; don't chew on it....

tiful experience? Well,' I said, 'it might have been a beautiful experience for you, but do you think it was a beautiful experience for them?'

JACKIE

Jesus, John, you don't gotta pin everything on him. I'll take some of the blame. Besides, who was the one who told me he was this real far out dude, that he'd done hard time, 'n all that crap, right? 'N when I saw you trying to do what he'd already done, why wouldn't I be interested? I mean if you thought he was so much better than you, right? So whose fault is that? Yeah, I know I told you, and then I got that Observation there, an Overnight Observation, and a D & D, Drunk and Disorderly, the Nevada Highway Patrol. They picked me up walking along the highway. It was freezing out, too. Yes, sure, 'cause the Nevada Welfare, some Interstate thing, I guess, sent a report I'd been found on the side of the road in the snow all dazed-up and sick on myself. So the next day Social Services comes for the kids, but I still think it's Mom. Sure, 'cause she already knew I was outa town. It *was* Mom! Welfare doesn't move that fast. Who else coulda told them?

CARSON

You know what, Tweetie? You know what you remind me of? I once saw a cat trying to put a bite on a dog, man, 'n that's what you remind me of. You know what's gonna happen to you? You're gonna end up with tape 'cross the heels of your socks, man; yeah, wearin' a pair of old men's carpet slippers with gaffer's tape 'cross the heels of your socks, man, 'n standing out there in the night scufflin' on some empty street corner, headlights bouncing off the dirty silver of the tape, wavin' your arms 'round and 'round in circles, shouting out a buncha shit to no one, to a buncha cars going by, and it's embarrassing, man. I'm embarrassed by it, it's embarrassing to see you, to even admit that I know you…

CARSON

Yeah, 'n then he says, 'But hey, you know what? Fuck that noise! It could be that you're a *better* man than me. So let's just keep it friends, man, like no hard feelings, okay?' 'N, 'Whatta you want?' 'N I say, 'Life, liberty, and the pursuit of pussy.' 'N the fucker off 'n *cuffs* me! Yeah, *cuffs* me! He did! Now a cuff, that's not a slap. A cuff is with the back of the hand. It's contemptuous, right? So now I'm on the floor looking up at him, 'n then, then, now get this – he breaks out in ta' tears, and *then* attacks me!

CARSON

The big jerk was *crying!* Yeah, like a little bitch!

JACKIE

Whatta crock a' shit! John'll say he's not jealous, but he'd rather sit out there imagining things instead of coming inside and seeing for his self. And when he does come in I can't talk to anyone. If I even say, 'So and so said, "Hello,"' he about has a shit fit. You know what my mistake was? I never shoulda slept with him again. A big, big mistake. Then when I told him it'd be better if he'd start to look for a place of his own he went nuts. Absolutely! That's why he wants me to quit the club and go to work in a coffee shop. No way am I gonna go to work in some damn coffee shop…

TERI

How come it's folded in newspaper, Jac? That's really tacky. The ink gets right in the coke. Look at this. Where'd you get this crap? It's gotta be pure bunk. Who'd you get this from? Not from Eddie. Here, isn't that gross? This stuff is just a mess. Ugh. Just razor that top part off. Let's get some heavier paper for this. Tear off that People mag cover there. Did Gary tell you he wants you to use some Scotch Tape to tape your lips shut so no one can peep inside your quim, ha, ha, if your G-string slips? No, he really did! God, what a maniac! Then he said he'd personally do it for me…

JOHNNY

What I did was try to drag her out of there, but she'd collapse onto the floor an' when I'd pick her up she'd start twisting and kicking, an' I didn't wanna hurt her, so I'd let her go, an' she'd collapse back down in a heap again, so finally I said, 'Fuck it,' 'n went off to get a couple more pitchers of beer…

JACKIE

The man I love came here tonight from a fight with his ear all swollen an' half bit off and never fought back. Said he did that for me 'n he's abandoning his old kinda life for a new one with me, that I'm his higher angel and knows that higher forces are involved, that we've known each other in another time, another place, and that he'll always need me, both for the rest of this life, and in the next…

EDDIE

Car was there, all right, him 'n Gary, 'n that black dude, Jamal something, her half-assed manager, or something, all of 'em just watching her dance every dance, her and that new chick, the tall, leggy one with the fine lookin' chest, but not really paying attention, mostly just sittin' there bullshitting back 'n forth about shit like old cars 'n that, Carson about this bitchin' black 'n white CHP Mustang with a V-8 and a five speed he just picked up offa this Chicano dude that owed us, talking about how great it felt just to sit in the thing, let alone to be driving it, 'n the black dude about his ol' retro Caddy that he'd lowered 'n put custom fender skirts on, plus a gold metallic flake paint job, like some fuckin' Watts pimpmobile back in the day, right, not even noticing John when he came in the side door, none of 'em, right in front of them, and, '*Whoa, Hoss,*' – now I've seen that one before – '*just get outa the way, Bro,*' 'cause John's like on automatic, right, an' just immediately goes into all of 'em, just wailin' on 'em, tables 'n chairs flying. I really had to laugh – now hold on, hold on – 'cause then Jackie comes down off the platform, see, and starts hitting on him from behind, on John, see, slapping 'n scratching at him, and he whirls and grabs her up and tries to take her out the same ol' door, but can't get her arms or legs through, so's he just drops her right on the floor. It was a riot. 'N that's how I got it together with Rita, she was standing up there on the platform just freaking, and I got a hold of her, telling her, I said, 'Hell, calm down, Darling; it ain't happening to you. Just watch it like it's a TV show, okay; like your favorite Sit-Com or something, okay?' 'N she did. She started digging on it. Chick's got a lot of potential, man. You could see it. She's... hey... so, fuck...'

TERI
Said he didn't want no one peepin' into my little jewel box but he hisself, okay? No, no, I'm not. Go ask him yourself. Here... no, no, the bronze foundation stick... one of the ones you got for your stretch marks... the vitamin E one... one of those... that one... yeah... does this stuff work?

JOHNNY
Lifting the glasses off the dickhead's face, kissing each lens, sliding them onto her chest, nipples now like eyes behind the lenses, lets out a cry, 'n turns, kicks up her right leg, "legs clear up to her neck," Rod Stewart song, so great, swings on her left, ass bent to the light, milky boobs hanging, taking glasses off, stroking them back and forth along the G-string spangles between her bossy l'il butt cheeks, slows, turns and straightens up, legs now spread over the guy, smiling down at him, glasses suddenly up to her mouth, kissing them, dropping them slowly back into his jacket pocket, stepping back quickly, left leg up across her right, 'n pivoting, 'n striding away...

JOHNNY
Jac was really good, and coming back was laughing, asking how'd she do. 'Rockin',' I told her, 'truly.' Ter said Jac was about the

best interpretive dancer they'd ever seen in there, that when she first tried out all the other dancers stopped to watch what she did, that she never did the same moves twice. I just sat back enjoying myself, having a beer or two. We shot the shit 'bout this 'n that for a bit, then I left, deciding to go over to Cheryl 'n Anthony's to see if Jo was still pissed, wanting to see what it felt like to have someone's arms around me who wanted t' have her arms around me.

JACKIE

Rotate, rotate, slide, slide, letting out a cry, remove glasses off man's face, kissing each lens, open earpieces, half-assed slide them onto a tit, nipple behind the lens, leg kick 'n turn, bend, ass to the spot, titties hanging down, slowly spread legs, take glasses, start rubbing them up and down along thong, head upside down now, looking back at face framed between my legs, 'n suddenly spin and turn, standing up to smile down at him, glasses coming up to my mouth, kissing them, folding the earpieces, dropping them back into the coat pocket, laughter breaking from his smile, then step back, bringing left leg across front of waist, letting out another cry as I move off, wiggling my fingers a-la-ta-ta-bye-la-bye...

CLINICAL SUMMATION:

To fill the void activated, Mr. Dalton states, by his wife's abrupt withdrawal, his consequent masturbation reactivated his feelings of guilt about his childhood masturbation done in periods of loneliness and sorrow when his mother, in anger and depression, withdrew from the family, as his father was a person who frequently left the home for lengthy periods of time, although occasionally sending hamburgers back to the house by way of taxicab.

CHAPTER 22
OUT ON EAST MAIN ST.

JOHNNY

It was just so great being back, you know, sitting outside the club, watching them old farts going in there, trying to get both a hard-on an' a buzz-on all at the same time. Hell, I knew most of them assholes, too, grew up with 'em, which was sort of a downer seein' as how they all wasn't kids no more, which got me to thinking 'bout Dad, how he used to hang out in there all the time. 'Finding myself,' he'd always say, 'n I thought how are my own kids going to think about me? Thinking like that, of me being some broken down old fart sitting with my elbows up on the bar laughing at something that wasn't funny jus''cause I could name the goddamn nicknames of every dickwad sitting in there doin' all that feeling sorry for themselves B. S. Dad always did 'cause he never went after what he wanted to go after. No way were my kids ever going to think of me that way, not if I could help it, 'cause I sure as hell could help it, 'cause I absolutely was gonna go after everything I wanted, that's for damn sure...

IRENE

Incidentally, Bob Johnson's wife burned to death in January. She was smoking in bed alone and was a dear friend of your Grandpa's before she married Bob Johnson. I never told you about that. Your Grandpa carried on with her after that marriage, and almost persuaded her to run off with him, almost, but your Grandma put a stop to it. I never told you about him. He died by the heart in his sleep at night. It was just as well as he couldn't taste his food anymore. Said it all tasted like coffee grounds. Only things he would eat was bits of soft bread with cherry jam. Oh, and hot tea. He was a good man and too

JOHNNY

Well, most people think drugs are fucked, see, 'cause for most people they are, but if I'd a' been ripped when I got busted the last time I wouldn't a' been busted 'cause I would a' been too laid back to be uptight when I saw the cops so I wouldn'ta freaked and taken the fall…

good for your grandma after the things she did to him. She was seeing many other men because of working at the Ojai Springs Hotel and he never said a word or raised a finger until that one episode. This was always the family secret, but I want you to know what a good man goes through so you won't be so down on yourself. He accepted many things and was always doing for other people. And he stuck things out for the whole ride. If something happens to Earle, John, it will be up to you to help take responsibility for me should I get sick. Have you thought about that?

EDDIE

Yeah, first he blasts in here 'n demands I front him two ki's 'n some walkin' around money. I mean I already gave him an ounce, which he was supposed to sell, and then he's asking me if I'd stepped on it? Then he tells these dumb smokes that it's German pharmaceutical, or similar shit, they should see the Porsche the guy drives, that guy being me, right? So this one Smoke goes, 'Well, I don't know about that; all I know is I get a nosebleed from it. You sure this isn't some scummed-out biker shit?' And John: 'No, no way, man; the guy's no biker, he's a Mex!' 'A Mex?' this guy says. 'I never seen no Mex with a Porsche!' Whatta bunch of burnouts...

JACKIE

John was the first person who'd said 'I need you.' No one'd ever said anything like that. Like no one, you know. He was into sopers 'n speed then, an' I was really for him 'cause when he was high he could make me laugh. Those were our best times. The deal then was mechanics' tools, acetylene torches, expensive brass ones, 'n paint compressors, stuff like that. He an' his buds would go round to these gas stations 'n body shops, 'n rip off metal tool cases and sprayers and big floor jacks, 'n take them down to L. A.; sell them in swap meets. I went along with it. I wasn't very mature myself, that's for sure. We had lots a' reds, too, an' what I'd do was take enough to where

I could get up and bump and bang around in the privacy of my own home, but not get hurt, you know what I mean. It's really trashy, you know, you go into some big music store like Red Rooster Records and there's some numbed out chick in there careening herself from side to side into the bins 'n stumbling down the aisles in big wobbly curves where everyone can see her. A lot of chicks I work with are like that, come to work all barbed up 'n think what they're doing is dancing...

JOHNNY

Now look at this place. It's not like you've never seen a goddamn tittie bar before, 'n forget all that purple pussy, man, that's pussy you can't have. I mean all this is just another goddamn boring bar, pole-dancing or no. Well, it's either this place, Bro, or it's me, 'n I wouldn't put it past being me neither...

JOHNNY

'N she says, 'Let's go to bed,' see, so I say, 'Excuse me?' I'd only been knowing her ten minutes, see, 'n she says it again, 'Let's go to bed.' So I go, 'Excuse me, ma'am, I don't hardly know you, but it seems pretty obvious that we've got us a situation here where there's no one else loving you, now wouldn't I feel like a fool loving you?' Ha, ha, ha. Here; wanna buy a snort? Straight outa Bogata, man; smoother 'n a baby's butthole – What?

JOANN

After what you said last night I know you don't care for me anymore but why are you going back to her? I guess that's where you've been, isn't it, and not at your grandma's like you said. Maybe this is the way it has to be, but keep this in mind – you still have a chance with me, but you have none with her! Maybe I'll get used to it but I think it's mean of you not tell me directly. I think I deserve that, or don't you have the guts? And I now know for real that she has the car so don't say she doesn't. Here I was hoping I would be the first thing on your mind. I now know I'm the last. I'm sorry if you're getting pissed, but how else should I feel? I know you don't want me to be pregnant but I don't think you can stop it. I've already missed

JOHNNY

Fuckin'-A that's my wife up there! Yeah, her, the smooth one on the other pole, okay? So, listen; so why're camels called the ships of the desert? No? 'Cause they're full a' Arab semen, all right? Ha, ha, ha. Hey, Gare, bring that nozzle down here. Give us another splash here.

JOHNNY

Up on the sink, legs apart, her saying, 'I really can't get into this, I really can't, I can't.' 'Sure you can,' I tell her, 'just lean back and take it as it comes,' 'n against herself she tries, she does, I have to say that, but working on her is nasty, hard, cold, her juices thin and faint, piss-smelling. So's I work harder 'n harder, then round 'n 'round, 'n 'cross an' back, then slower 'n slower, really slowing it down, her beginning a little, just a little, then a little more, legs squeezing harder, tighter, smashing my nose against the bone, her going into a series of little whimpers, two, three, maybe four, but nothing worth a shit, the weakest kinda climax, an' lets go her legs, hurt-look-

two periods, and the next one is to be the thirtieth of this month which I don't think will come. What else are you going to do if I am? Tell me to get rid of our baby? Nobody in this world can make me give up this baby!

JACKIE

Well, you lie, little pink ones, ones like you don't even know you'll say until you open your mouth. Just like that volcano up in Washington, what's it called, Mount Saint Helen's? It just erupted, either for good or for bad. You know, like sayin', 'I love you,' sayin' that 'cause you want someone to like you, or that you don't want someone to be hurt, or, well, I mean, it isn't really what you thought you were gonna say, but there it goes, you've said it, either for good, or for bad. Now that's what I call a pink one. An' people do that one all the time. At least some do, know what I mean?

JACKIE

We were just standing around in the kitchen, Eds an' Ter an' Car 'n me, opening some beers, Eds telling some joke, then ing as she stands down, saying, 'Sorry, I'm sorry, but I can't do the same for you.'

Johnny was there. Man, he looked just awful, 'n Eds says, 'Hey, Dude, hey...' something like that, real friendly-like, and Johnny doesn't even look at him. He was sorta turned sideways, 'n not looking at anyone. Now I've seen that one before. He does that, an' the next thing the light in his eyes goes out, an' he just goes for it. So now I'm getting real tense, with Car saying, 'Howdy, Big John, how you doing?' Smiling at him like, then Eddie tries to hand Johnny a beer and Carson says, 'Well, good people, well…' something, 'cause I don't hear it exactly, then: 'Time for me to go,' but John turns around and walks back out into the living room. You know, we hadn't even heard him come in. He can do that, you know, walk up on you before you even know it, and I looked at Car, 'n said, 'I think I better go out there.' So I go out, an' John's sitting on the arm of the couch. He looks up at me, and I don't like it one little bit. 'Cool is still having trouble looking at me,' he says. 'Now why is that?' 'Ah, com'on, John,' I say, 'are you gonna start that up again? Didn't you already get enough of him? He's just here as a friend.' 'Friend!' he shouts, 'n jumps up! Well, I leapt back about ten feet, 'n he laughed – it really cracked him up. So I started cussing him, calling him everything I could think of, an' he grabbed my wrists and said, 'So why don't you take him in the bedroom and fuck him then?' 'Sick,' I says, 'you're just sick! Maybe I will!' 'N he raised his fist, like he was gonna clock me, then sorta spun around and started for the door. I was just shaking. He went out, then looked back, 'n said, 'You do, I'll kill you both.' That's what he said, he'd kill us both. 'Yeah,' I said, 'you'd really like to, wouldn't you?' An' yelled for Eddie to come out, which he did with Car right behind him. Now that was the worst, man, that moment, 'cause I was real sick right then, I just got sick. Here I'd planned on being happy, you know, having things work out, and Car must've said something, which I didn't hear, I was already running toward the kitchen, 'cause Johnny said something, an' I heard Car say, 'Yeah, 'n they'll be stuffing cotton up your dead ass, too, man!' What happened next I don't know. Somehow John had me in the kitchen. Him and me was at the sink, 'n he was splashing water on the back of my neck. I said, 'I'm sick.' An' him and Ter grabbed me. I don't remember nothing else 'cept how cold I was. My hands and feet were really cold. John took me and finally put me in the tub and ran warm water and that helped, then Eds said he'd take us all out. I said, 'Where's Car?' Ter said he left. John said he didn't wanna go out anywhere, but I told him he had to. So we all went out to The Ban-Dar, 'n John wouldn't say nothing. Then I wanted to dance and John said no, he didn't want to. He said, 'n this is exactly what he said: 'Fuck no, go dance with someone else.' 'All right,' I says, 'I will,' 'n got up and began dancing by myself. So of course some guy I don't know comes over and starts dancing with me, a real nice guy, and then I went back to the table 'n John says, 'Did he feel your tits? No, I take that back; your breasts; did he feel your breasts?' 'Of course not,' I say, an' he goes, 'He did; I saw him,' 'n turns to Eddie an' says, 'You saw it; the guy felt her breasts.' And Eds says, 'Jesus Christ, John, I didn't see him do nothing, but if you wanna know what I think, I think you're off your ass, man, is what I think...'

JOHNNY

I'm not real proud of this one, this guy pouring beer from a pitcher into everyone's glass. 'Hey, man,' I said, 'how you doin'?' Getting him turned to me. 'Hey,' he says, 'n held out his hand, wanting to shake hands, see. So I shook hands, then rammed my left into his gut, grabbing the pitcher with my right when he doubled over. It was real fuckin' clean. No one even saw it. They just looked surprised that all of a sudden he was sitting on the floor. I put the pitcher down on the table. His wind was gone and he couldn't talk. He was trying to say something. He tried to say it again, and finally goes, 'What'd you do that for?' 'Do what?' I says, and walked off, 'n then I was out on the dance floor, watching the dancing, 'n someone tapped me on the shoulder. So I stepped forward, 'cause someone might be about to pop me one, right, 'n then turned back around to look. Well, shit! It was Jac! 'So,' 'she goes, 'what'd you just do? I saw it,' she says. 'You just had to do it, didn't you! The guy never said nothing to me! All's he said was he'd bring us some beer!' Well, motherfucker, 'cause she had really set me up, telling me the guy'd said he wanted to eat her. Yeah, eat her, an' her face was really fucked-up, all triumphant-looking, like she'd really done something great. 'Go screw yourself,' I said, an' went back over to the guy's table. And this time all his buds are up, ready to fire on me, so I get ready, but when he sees me he goes, 'Oh, no, man! No! No! I don't believe this!' Holdin' his hands in front of himself, warding me off, see. 'No, man,' I go, 'listen; I owe you a hell of an apology, I fucked up, I really fucked up.' 'N he goes, 'This is too fuckin' crazy; just stay away from me, man! Keep away!' Keepin' his hands up, see. Now I felt real bad about that one...

JACKIE

'I'm way too spaced to be aggressive;' he says, 'all's I want is for you to suck me off.' Well, I tried, and it was awful. His come was bitter, and I told him so, too...

JOHNNY

You know me. You know every move I make. You know... hey, am I gonna surprise you? I will *not* put my hands on you! No, I will not! Just calm the fuck down! What's happened t' you? You become one a' them people that just look at people 'n don't say nothin'?

JACKIE

Where are the keys? Where are the keys, goddamn it? You did not leave them in the car! You did not, you *shithead!* You are a *shithead* and I've got the papers to prove it! Look what you did! You asshole! You fucking asshole! You threw the keys! You dope! You did! I don't believe it! Look what you did! I can't even open the door! You kicked the door in! I can't! Don't you show up at the apartment, goddamn you! You cannot have the car! I'll have the fucking cops! Oh, you asshole! *Asshole!*

JACKIE

As to my being a person who takes money for sex as some have accused me of? First of all I have not even thought of that word in connection with myself. My sexual life is no one's business but my own, but I would never take money for sex because that would cut it. That is why people are so interested in whores. Whores are cut emotionally and people are interested in people who can cut the most emotional thing there is. As for myself, I never want to lose my feelings, even if it means I have to be hurt or let myself be hurt time and time again, okay? An' that is exactly the kind of person that I am. And if you don't understand that about me, you don't understand nothing.

CHAPTER 23

THE STARLIGHT VIP ROOM

JACKIE

I feel love and joy tonight. After I finally got John to go, Car called and said he finally realizes he needs my love and protection as much as I need his. He is basically good and kind and that finally came through tonight. He said he was totally, completely, and always would be forever done with Ter and I believe him. His voice was warm and soft and full of feelings. I want to be gentle with him as much as I want him to be gentle with me. It is frightening to think about, because I recognize his pain and innocence in the fullness of my world as I recognize the fullness of my pain and innocence in his world. He was very sincere and called me three times and then once again later when I was almost asleep. Perhaps we do have the same needs, being born in the same time together, as he says. He also said predestination, it's living its own life and there's nothing we can do, some people are born to love, some to be loved, some to be lovers together forever. Well...

CARSON

Don't be telling him anything about it. Just go sit with him and let him do the talking. That's what he's gonna be doin'. He'll be doin' a lot of talking. Jus' listen, and then leave. Jus' say you have to get back to work. He'll talk, you listen, you leave, then let him sit with it. The longer the better. Then I'll go over an' have a beer with him.

CARSON

I already know what he's gonna do, okay? I already *seen* all his bullshit...

JOANN

You tell me you don't love her but twice me and Cheryl have gone by there and saw the station wagon, or one that is exactly like it, including where "Pain-Killer" was painted on the rear door. It's a brown and yellow one, so I know it's your

JOHNNY

What's all the fuckin' screaming about? The keys are on the goddamn bar! Jesus! How can I help but listen to you! Gary, you got some gauze, somethin' to muzzle the noise comin' outa her mouth? Over there! Right where you left 'em. Take a walk! Hey, gimme a dice cup down here! Can we get a dice cup here? Hey, Car, you ain't died yet? Hey, I'm not sittin' with no motherfuckers here, man. So com'on over here. I'm gonna let you knock me down 'n cut me to death, hokay? Ha, ha, ha. Ah, com'on, Car, com'on over. Have a brew. 'Now look,' I said to this guy, I asks him, 'Whatta you been doing, man?' 'Getting a piece of ass,' he says.' 'Hey, Duke,' I tells him, 'turn it over; there's pussy on the other side,' ha, ha, ha, ha, ha...

Escort and either Jac still has it or you've been there. Once I was gonna go in, but Cheryl wouldn't let me, and I think that's the first time I really broke down and let her see how really upset you've made me.

TERI

And now who knows what she really wants, but I do know what's fair and that's what I told her. 'Look,' I said, 'so I've been with him a coupla times; so what? I'm not gonna defend myself. How many guys have you slept with you don't care nothing about? 'Girl,' I told her, 'no man can make you feel bad unless you wanna feel bad. Get yourself together. Be an island unto yourself. Don't let some man tell you how you should feel. You've always said that was Dad's trip with us. So what makes this any different? Take control of your feelings. And keep your composure. Just do it.' Like the other night, she was having this real bad time, so she let Johnny come over and she said it was fun, but when he left in the morning she said she found herself feeling good he was gone. 'I liked it, you know,' she says, 'having my own space.' 'Hey,' I told her, 'you keep that up you're really gonna be something else; you'll be the hottest damn momma in this whole damn town.' It's true. She will. Hey, watch out, man. Now see how I've changed toward her? Check it out, 'cause you know what I told Car my self? 'Hey, Mister Bird 'n Bee Man,' I said, 'just buzz off; fly the fuck away from us.' 'Cause that dude's been getting it all his

JOHNNY

Jo holds me, kisses me, says she dreamt I was lying in bed with her all cuddled-up. 'Lets stop bringing up things that happen,' she says, 'an' please finish and forget about Jackie and any other women that're in your life but me,' that when she knew for certain I was getting out she sat up each and every night praying I'd need her, that when I asked her to marry me her heart just soared...

own way, right? 'So how come?' he says. He wanted to get specific, right? So, so I told him, I said, 'Hey, Car, all you are is just a player, okay? So what's the point; you're not a serious type person anyways.'

JACKIE

Okay, John, look, it's just set in my mind that I know what I need. And if I see someone sayin' they love me, if they're not easy about it, then I just wanna get away, all right?

JOANN

Baby, after breakfast a friend came over and asked me what I saw in you. I told him I was in love with you and that you were the most fabulous person in the world. He also said you were ugly. I told him ugly people are mean and bad and sometimes like to mess people over. Get it? I don't think he'll be coming back around for a while. Did you tell your Mom and Grandma about me? Do they hate me? If they do I hope their feelings change when we get married. I know my people will when they find out you want just me and me alone. All sorts of things have been going through my mind. Mom and I got into another giant fight. You don't seem to know what it's like living with her. You say try harder. I feel lost in a world of tries. I'm trying too much. My school work is tries. My Mom and my Grandma is tries. I got five D's so far at school and one C and I'm spending all my life in thinking. My mind is getting lost in thinking, but I've decided not to let things bother me, not even big things. And get myself together. Because life won't be so bad being a dummy with you. One reason I'm so messed up is everyone is so afraid I'll not be something. Everyone is talking "grow up." I don't know what to do. Every time Mom yells at me I think of the things I've done wrong she doesn't even know about.

Then I remember that first night when I made you feel really good. When you told me that. Did you know I felt really proud of myself when I did that? We should've finished what we started right then and not even waited until later. Every time I eat a lot or sleep late or get tired Mom thinks I'm gonna have somebody's baby. Yesterday I saw this bitchin' Camaro. On the back it said: "Sweet Talk." It had big red open lips and a red tongue under the writing like a Rolling Stones thing. The guy who was driving followed me more than a mile. Now don't get mad. I also had this dream where accident-like things got us into a jam and you couldn't get us any money to get out of it. I hope that's not true. I also hope you got my note I left at your Mom's. She also said you hadn't been around for two days, and hoped you weren't sick again but she wouldn't say with what. You aren't sick, are you?

JOHNNY

For some goddamn reason I said, 'Okay, Eds, you dumb fuck, let's just say I took your blow, I owe you. I'll pay it back.' 'Big-J,' he grins, like he's the goddam soul of generosity – I mean it's a fucking joke – did we talk about the Pedro gig? Did I say, 'Hey, Motherfucker;' did I just sit there 'n stare at his snake-slitty eyes while he says, 'Count on me,' that it's still: 'Best friends forever,' like I don't have any real idea of how much is still owed me, that I didn't say, 'Oh, yeah, 'n I hear that you tried to get into Jackie's panties, too,' like I don't have any fuckin' balls? It's just sick! That I can't even ask for what's mine? And just take what he wants to say? It's fuckin' disgusting! 'N all's I hear myself say is, 'Hey, I take care of my family, man,' an' I'm looking down at his money, hearing, 'John,

JACKIE

People ask me what I want for Christmas. I just want my kids to be happy. It's my kids that are keeping me sane. My stepdad always used to say all he wanted for Christmas was for his kids to be happy. I never understood that before. I guess you don't until you have kids. You don't understand nothing until you have kids.

just take it. You need it. Don't even think about it.' 'N hear myself say, 'Well, shit, I'll pay this back, too,' an' see myself reaching
for it...

JACKIE

That night this all black, black little cat came down the hall. This was earlier before anything happened, and it had these weird eyes, you know, like camera flash eyes. I'd seen it around before, too, but this time I knew it was a spirit, you know, like coming to warn me of something, so, of course, I paid no attention, right? You don't, do you? Jus' that I was already a little freaked out going into this thing...

CHAPTER 24

MILL CREEK CANYON

JOHNNY

She just flipped out on me. She does that. I told her I was leaving 'n I did. I'd hurt my arm, see, 'n she came home with this faggy, pencil-dicked, razor-scarred M. F.-er. An' her? She was all fucked-up. 'Like you can come in', I said to her, 'you live here, but you, man, like book it – you weren't invited.' So he goes, 'She invited me,' an' she chirps in with, 'I did.' So I started calling him, 'Mo-fo' this, 'n 'Mo-fo' that, an' had me one a' them kid's plastic baseball bats lying right next to me on the floor so when he grabbed me I came up with it 'n hit him right here, here, over the ear. I had these steel-toed work boots on, too, so when he hit the floor I musta got some good kicks in. She was still flipped out in the morning, askin' me if I'd called her a bitch.' I said, 'Do I ever call you a bitch?' 'No,' she said, 'you don't.' We made up, but, fuck it, you know. I just knew I shoulda stayed away, see, that if I went back it'd end up something bad. Like every time I go out there, either the Palomino or the Starlight or the Ban-Dar she just flips. She's not her real kinda self out there, know what I mean? It's like there's this vicious kinda rutting-like vibe that gets in her or somethin'. Anyways, I left before the cops came, then called from the corner and she said she hadn't called any. The asshole wasn't hurt that bad, she said, but I'd better wait till morning before coming back.

GRAMS

You know I've always said you have real good country sense, John, and you're real bright in learning things, but sometimes it takes a hard go-around before it all makes sense to people. Sometimes it isn't love that holds the marriage together, but marriage that holds the love together. God is no respecter of persons. He knows what the proper order of life is, and for us it isn't always what it seems. I know that when a sweet girl comes along to help you and love you it all works.

It did for your Granddad and me, as it has for a lot of other people. I've been calling the Probation nearly every day telling them you're at work like you asked. Did I tell you this about your Granddad? That he accepted things and always did things for others. He was always happy and laughed all the time. Do you remember his fly escape? That you used to ask me about when you would play in my sewing machine drawers? That little thimble-like thing? Have you ever watched flies and how they won't walk over a sharp edge? Well, they won't, and Daddy noticed that and made a little thing to fit in window screens. Made it of aluminum, like a thimble, but open, with the sharp edge out. Flies trapped inside would walk on outside because of the light, but flies from the outside wouldn't walk in because of the edge. He got orders for them from several hospitals here in California and a huge order from India. You know the fly problem they have over there, sacred life and all that. Then that damn war came and India cancelled. That sort of took the pep out of him. Sometimes things like that would happen. There'd be setbacks and he'd lose his enthusiasms, but he never took it out on anyone. A good man always has to go through a lot in this life, so don't get discouraged. Did you know you have the same hazel-green color of eyes as your Granddad, and smile like him, too?

JOHNNY

Hey, that's right, but listen, I don't care how fucked-up it is, it's still gotta be together, right? So maybe I don't care what's gonna happen. You ever think of that? That maybe I get my rocks off that way? What the hell do you know about it? I will tell you this, though, I will say I had more drinks than a drinking man should have.

JACKIE

Car came over and said he knew men were supposed to be strong and able to take care of things. I said, 'Is that what men were supposed to be like, 'cause that certainly didn't sound like any of the men I've ever met.' Well, he laughed, he did, he said, 'Look, I've been into thinking about this thing we've got going, and it could work out. Whatta you think?' 'Well,' I said, 'I know we've kidded a round about this,

CARSON

Other guys? There's *always* other guys. Every woman out there, she's got a dude somewheres, an' if you're a backdoor man sooner or later that shit runs out, 'n you'll be stylin' in your coffin, right? Now I hate to admit this, but Teri got me to thinking on this, okay? Yeah, Ter, her, your sis. I admit it. She put it to me 'n I've started thinking on it, okay? Now when I was a little kid I ran with some pretty bad muchachos. These guys were in some pretty bad beat-downs, and the one thing I learned is the one that gets pissed is the one that wins and I've never been afraid to fight ever since. So Big John? That don't bother me none. An' the only question is, how far do I wanna take it? Like out to the max? Waste the guy so I'll be one of the ones? Yeah, 'n then end up gettin' my pretty self sliced up 'n stabbed in Soledad for using the wrong toilet like my older brother did when he first went in, an' dint know no better?

CARSON

And speaking of that, I got me this big plastic straw, about twenty-four inches long, see, so's you don't have to lower your head when you snort a fat one. You know how ol' Eddie gives you the snort and watches when you lower your head? Well, fuck that. I don't lower my head for no one, 'n not with one a' these bad boys, right? So

about really living together, but I just might give it some real thought when we stop kidding about it.'

JACKIE

John, John, please! Do you think if I thought it was right, really right, that I wouldn't be there, one hundred percent?

JACKIE

Back there in the Starlight, right there in the VIP room. Just severed the hell out of it, plunged it right through the glass. And do you think he'd go to the hospital, get stitches? Nuh-uh, not him. He musta lost near a quart of blood. I know 'cause I ran in there and saw him like in a daze just crouching down on the floor, watching it spurt out. The guys picked him up and carried him out front, 'n Eddie gave them ten bucks for what was left of a bottle of

ol' Eds can blow me. Here, see this fucker? Isn't that jus' beautiful? You ever seen a better straw?

tequila and poured it over the gashes and Johnny wrapped it up hisself with a bandana. We tried to talk him into going to Emergency, but no, not him. Well, when he got up and started wobbling he finally had to. They re-bandaged it for him, and said, 'Check in,' but he wouldn't, an' he had that damn dressing on for over a week, even though he was supposed to go back and change it. 'At least go to a doctor,' I told him, it got to stinking so bad. Well, same old thing, it finally got to hurting so much he had to. An' when they took the bandage off it was all infected with this real bad stuff and he had to go to the hospital and almost died. Then no one came to see him either, no one, 'cept Teri once. He had to face it all by himself, which was real good for him, you know – make him face it. Not even his mom came...

JOHNNY

You think I don't know that? The first time I looked into that little goddamn wicker crib and saw him I knew! Of course he's not my kid! That's no goddamn surprise! Yeah, an' that goddamn big head of his ripped the shit outa you, too! It did! You've never felt the same to me! *Never!* Every time I slide in there that's what I get to think about! And do I get any credit for sticking around? Trying to make a go of it? Well, fuck that! I got nothing against him! He's just a baby! No, it's you! You're the one lied...

TERI

They were smashing beers on the table, is what they were doing. I don't know who started it, but I think Eddie. He smashed his, then Car, then Jamal, then Johnny dumped the pitcher over, then Car crashed his glass on the pitcher, smashing it, then Johnny stood 'n lifted the table, crashing it over, spilling everything, beer and glass flying all over the place. I didn't know what the hell they were doing, but

JOHNNY

'Confused!?!' Hey, I've been so confused before that I've painted black dots on my face! So don't tell me *'confusion!'* You

don't know *'confusion!'* That's a buncha happy horseshit. No? Are you kidding me? You got any watercolors? Dawnie? She got any? So let's paint some goddamn dots 'cross your face then. Go get her little tin box...

they all were laughing about it, like they were doing something really hilarious...

JACKIE

No, no, certainly not! I haven't even thought about it, let alone done it with anyone. Sometimes it just isn't there, no matter what, okay? Sometimes I just don't want it, okay?

JOHNNY

The last time I was sitting on the floor. We were gonna be happy together. She was talking on the phone. She'd just come in from the pool with just her thong on and was standing with her legs apart up over me. I put my good hand on her. She got hot by trying to keep her voice straight and take what I was doing to her. Her voice started tightening, 'n we both got hot. 'N when she put down the phone I went right into her an' let 'er fly, but instead of staying in there an' letting it smooth out, I pulled out 'n had her bend over, and started rubbing myself across her butt, getting cum all over it, then sideways up along her tits to jack myself up again, but she went nuts, saying that I didn't see her, that I really didn't see her, that I really didn't see her at all, 'n wouldn't let me get back in, her face all snarled up, pulling back away into the darkness, and I just sat there with my hand over myself, trying to figure out what she was so mad about...

JACKIE

Listen, Car, I know what happened has scared you, but if everything is said right out front and there are no more games, I think you'll accept what you feel for me as much as I accept what I feel for you. And if not, well, at least once in my life I'll know what it's like to be completely ready to give every part of my being to someone else, as

CARSON

A twenty-two hollow point, man, three holes in the gut. We were sitting on the couch when he came in. You know what he said? 'Another two days, man, 'n I woulda had her back.' Tha's what he said, he *'woulda had her back.'* He had it pointed right to my chest. 'Well, don't talk;' I said, 'just do it!' Now that was a big, big mistake, 'cause he cocked it, see; he pulled the action back, an' all's I had time to do was pull it down to my stomach before it went off. I kicked him back in the chest and took the gun and said, 'Okay, man, it's your fucking turn!' Holding that bitch right to his eye, but I couldn't do it! Maybe if he would've challenged me, but he didn't. He's not as dumb as me, see. His eyes went about this big! He knew, see! So I gave the gun to her and said, 'I'm going for help,' but I collapsed at the door. I told her to call for help, but to let him go. The cops kept trying to ask me about it, but I wouldn't tell them. Now that was my second and last shooting, right, you better believe. Now the first one, my first shooting, I was dealing a little scag then, making a lotta money, but I don't like using people, and that's what it was, plus, you lose all your friends. The only ones you have are the ones that're strung out to you. Now on this last one they had to operate on me twice, 'n my brothers wanted me to turn him in. They said get him sent up and we'll do him for you, but I said no, 'cause I already coulda done him, see, and he knows it. So that's what went down, but I'll never testify to it, not in no court. Besides, I've got total disability now for thirty-two months, and that's to the good, 'n plus I'm gonna start night classes at Community, you know, music theory 'n things like that, 'n plus, you know, plus, I've got some other type things to think about now, like some more serious type

well as be ready to receive another person's love, perfections and faults. Of course it's hard for me to believe your life first started when we met. Maybe, but not right away. You were too busy running your own game, right? Now if you don't want to call, or are afraid to call, I understand. In any event I do feel confident we'll always be friends. I do want to have sex with you, and don't feel confident of that at all.

JACKIE

Just before Dawnie was born Johnny was going around saying, 'Well, at least I'm mature enough to know I can't accept responsibility for this.' What things, like dealing with other orders of real life situations, an' some other sorta stuff like that…

CARSON

…this shrieking, high-pitched burning, like a bandsaw cutting into bone, smelling that burn, then – *'What? Right as it happened?'* No… no… in my mind was all scrambled eggs…

an asshole, right? And then this friend drove him out to the hospital 'cause the pickup was broke down, and halfway there just dumped him out. Told him his whole attitude toward the pregnancy was just shitty, he didn't even wanna know him, 'n pushed him right out of the car. And then at the hospital when John finally got there, the doctor told him it was a very smooth delivery, very, very smooth, an' that I was quite a remarkable woman, 'n Johnny said, 'Of course she is, I know that.' Well, that made me feel good, and he did walk all the way there. He wasn't able to hitch 'cause it was dark so he walked all the way. I mean, there are things about him…

SHERIFF'S DET. E. R. CONAHAN

Received a call from County-General. According to doctors there, learned Mr. Dalton left the hospital without checking out. Contacted the wife, Jacqueline Louise Dalton, who requested a night watch on the Wildwood Lane apartment complex off Savior's Road up Mill Creek Canyon, Apt.# 3-B, as well as at the Starlight Dance Palace & Gentlemen's Club, 16367 Telegraph Rd. during her working hours, from approximately 7:30 p.m. to approximately 3:30 a.m. or at times slightly longer depending on circumstances, but no later than 4:30 a.m.

CHAPTER 25
WILDWOOD LANE

JACKIE

Whoever knocks on this door for some evil cause, I, or whoever is inside the apartment will take ***ANY KIND OF ACTION*** *at once! Think twice before knocking!! I, J. Dalton, will do anything to anyone who tries to scare me or to scare or harm my children. SO GET LOST!!!*

JOHNNY

Yeah, I did go out to get him. That's no surprise. Everyone knows that. Everybody knows he was trying to take me down. I turned my back on it. I told my wife, I said, 'Carson is gonna get it some day, and I sure as hell hope it isn't me that does it.' Now I meant that, but a coupla bros I know, how they put it was, 'Carson's going around packin', man,' they said, 'so watch your back.' So I went down to Pacific Pawn 'n bought the gun there. The old bastard in there, he sold it to me, then hassled me 'cause I wouldn't sign the papers. 'You got my money,' I told him, 'sign the motherfuckers yourself.' And at Jac's she wouldn't open the door and I knew Car was in there. All's I said was, 'Well, I hear Cool is a good gun greaser and I want him to grease my new gun for me.' Which was real good, see, like not kicking the door down or any kinda shit like that. I mean if he wasn't gonna come out and get down to it, it was over, you know, nothing more to worry about. I mean the fucker's hid, my wife's watching, she sees that, hey, it's over. So I just walked. I never shot no one. No reason to. Now I have a pretty good idea who *did* shoot him, but it wasn't me. At least I *think* I know who...

IRENE

At the time Earle and me was asleep, but just a short time before I'd gotten up and gone outside and stood on the porch calling the cats, thinking they were hungry or something was wrong, but none of them came. Then, at the exact same moment that Johnny grabbed her, Jackie just appeared to me. I was in a dream, sleeping, and the clouds opened up and there she was in the sky calling down to me. Jackie has the prettiest hair, you know. Everyone's always commented on how pretty her hair is, and she was tossing and twisting it in big swirls about her face, just calling out to me. Then Johnny appeared, and it's God's own blessing that he didn't go through with it, 'cause I saw that he did. Right there at the doorway. Had his arm around her throat and his mouth all twisted up with this terrible look on his face.

JOHNNY

Ah, I've always known how to fuckin' handle her; its no big deal. She's always had guys hanging around her, you know, guys she meets at the Starlight, 'n like that. I figured it out. All you gotta do is just go over there and hang out a while. You know, don't do anything, don't get excited, don't get pissed, just be polite, and never, never, ever try to touch her. That's the main thing. Never, never touch her. She never believes it, see, 'n she can't stand it. She really can't. You know, just stay calm, keep smiling, be polite. Now that's what it takes. It usually takes a coupla hours, but not always, an' if it don't work the first day I just go back the next and do it again, keep smilin', keep calm. Well, she always has to find out, see, and that nails her, it does, she always clears the other guys out. It always works. It works so well that the other day, after I showed back up, I was doing that, and I just reached out and patted her on top the head. 'Ah, hell,' I said, 'I can't do this to you.'

JOANN

Dear Di, walking along this empty street I see a man. I know who he is and call to him. He turns, recognizing me, but the woman with him pushes him away. He sees me, but shrugs his shoulders, walking on without answering. I try to follow, to catch up, but I can't. No matter how fast I walk I never get any closer. Finally I stop and try to remember his name. For some reason I can't, even though I know who he is. I yell for him to stop.

JOHNNY

I got this feeling she was standing there at the door just 'cause she knew she was looking so good, and she says, 'Oh, I really do love you, you know that, but it's not that kind of love now, it's a different kind.' Then she said if you stay with a person because you don't want to hurt them you'll only end up hurting them more. 'Well,' I said, 'fuck that noise; you're not thinking about not hurting me, you're thinking about *me* not hurting *you!* And that's just fucked...'

JACKIE

'Nuh-uh,' I said, 'no way, Cowboy, just forget it. 'Cause I don't want to. I just don't.' He wanted to reclaim me, see, to get amorous about it...

JOHNNY

You can't believe what other people say! They don't take responsibility for what they say! They even talk about their own feelings like they're visitors from another planet! You noticed that? You know, like, '*This feeling came on me! That feeling came on me! And the next thing I knew I had his head down and was banging it on the ground, or some kinda shit like that!*'

JACKIE

Hiding from oneself? How foolish. Not even convenient. Most people are really strange. If they had their way I would've been completely drowned by now. Things are completely uprooted around me, and what's weird, I seem to thrive off it in some perverted kind of way. It's all quite alienating. No one can really do anything for anyone else. We're all here for ourselves. Such mixed emotional trips. Johnny is now completely desperate. Carson wants me back and tries to be quite persuasive, but says the pregnancy isn't entirely on him, that I should think about it. The male ego is really strange. No one's around unless they want a screw, or to screw you up. What'd Johnny say, that by the time I was ready to

JOHNNY

I tell Jo to get her best clothes out of the closet 'cause we're gonna go shopping for a ring after we see my Mom first, and then we'll come back and see my Lama. Jo says she knows that's supposed to mean something, but why should she trust me? She has to drive 'cause my arm's hurting so bad, which is really a trip, she's such a terrible driver. Jerks the car all over the place. Says she wishes me and Jackie the best of luck, then completely flips over, saying, 'I believe you when you say you'll always love me,' that she's just upset right now, to disregard some of the things she's been saying, that she's counting the days till we move in together, and for me not to be scared of her mom, or her grandma, that neither one will go to the police for her being underage. Says she guesses she shouldn't talk so much, and says she can help me get stronger and stronger each day, and then says, 'I'll shut up.' Then says she knows she belongs to me, and me alone, because we've almost not made it so many times but I always come back to her and she never completely leaves me. She's asked herself why is it that I don't leave her and why, whenever I've left mad, I always return later and we make up. 'Making up is good,' she says, and knows I love her as I don't tell her things she doesn't believe. My being silent, she says, doesn't mean I can control what she's thinking and if I don't like what she's thinking why don't I just come out and say so? I say, 'I'm not trying to control anything, 'cause everything is already laid out for you long before you're born, Panda, so it doesn't matter what a person might try to do,' which is sorta the way I'm thinking right then. I tell her she'll like my Lama a lot, that Lama is a real warmhearted, very down-to-earth and plain friendly person, but would she mind not talking for a while and to not be looking over at me so much since we're getting into rush hour traffic? She says she's never been in real and true love before, just puppy love, and already likes my mom. She asks if I think I'm too old for her, and I tell her that's not for me to say, but something

give it away I'd be paying some guy twenty bucks to take it? Why is it I never meet anyone who's concerned about being happy with someone else, and that's all they really want? I just have to believe that if my kids ever see me happy, no matter how many men I have to go through, they'll see things can work out for them, too, in their own lives.

no one can tell her but herself, though plenty of other people will sure give her an opinion if she wants one. Then I have to grab the wheel and swerve to keep her from sideswiping a Greyhound bus that goes by, or maybe it was a Trailways.

CARSON

Don't look at it that way. If you talk to it, tell it you feel really good about it, explain that to bring it into the world wouldn't really be fair, ask it to forgive you, that even though it won't be here this time, that you know when things are right you'll have it again, that you'll recognize it when it finally comes, 'n you'll feel pretty good, least till the suction starts, ha, ha, ha. No, you don't haf'ta do it! No, I mean it! You don't wanna do it, I don't wanna. Swear to God! I mean it! Swear on a stack of Bibles. You got a Bible here? Go on, go get it, I'll swear...

JACKIE

Pregnant for sure. Just got the result of yesterday's test. Don't yet know my true feelings, but burst into tears. Raced back from Planned Parenthood and called Car. He said he loves me. Somehow hearing that made everything worse. I went to work, but instead of changing into my outfit, got stoned and lay on the couch staring hopelessly at my heels and robe. Finally got up and made some attempt to change, then decided I was in too terrible a shape to be dancing...

JACKIE

Then I told Car if he really did want me like he was actually now saying, he'd have to accept them, too, 'cause the kids *were* me, that I was not one of those bitches who didn't want her own kids and would use the excuse of loving some man who didn't want kids as a way of justifying herself, that I may have said I'd *do* something like that myself, you know, choose the man over the child, but that was just 'cause I musta been partying 'n throwing that out there to see how a certain person might respond, that maybe he'd have enough guts to say, 'I'd never ask that of you.' Also, that I'd made a decision about Johnny, too. 'A real decision,' I said, telling him I knew Johnny didn't want a real life with a real family and a real job at something that was steady, that he didn't wanna a life at all, all's he wanted was to get back in the trades again and live off a' whatever kinda snaps he could put in his body, and he wasn't even into Fenty or K-pin or even 512's yet, that he didn't know how addictive all that dazzle was. An' I told Car, I said, 'Listen, I'm all done with that kinda life; that anyone in that kinda life is not for me, not even someone as good as you...

CARSON

First he beats me up at the Starlight, then shows at the apartment 'n she tosses him out, then feels bad when he calls, saying she knows how he feels. I tell her, 'Can that crap, give him his walking papers, and let it go.' Well, so she does. And then he shows back up, 'n says he's gonna kill me. I say, 'That won't get her back; you kill me, you're going right back in the joint again, and she won't wait, you've already got proof of that. You left once, 'n you leave, you lose, Turkey, that's the name of the game.' So he comes back with, 'I'm still gonna kill you.' *'Kill me?'* 'All right, man; do what you haf'ta do, but get this: if you're gonna get crazy then I'm gonna get crazy, too.' I didn't see no gun.

JOHNNY

Now I've been loved by many women, more than my share, and I don't care, a woman's different than a man, they think different. Like maybe you're after one, and she don't want diddly-squat with you, then alla' sudden, for no good reason at all, wants to tie her whole goddamn life to you. Now the thing I did was marry a woman I didn't love. Dad always said,

TERI

We were watching this old black and white movie where the woman is torn between two men and trying to decide And one of them, the one the woman thinks she loves, catches her in bed with the other one, and she loses them both. I thought it was a shame. Jackie said it wasn't. I said, 'Why do you hate men?' 'I don't,' she says, 'I just hate people.'

IRENE

Oh, in the old days we used to go dancing out at Ban-Dar's. I know that ol' place, all right.

'When you're young , love is a stiff cock, 'n sayin' "I love you," 'cause you've never said it before.' Well, that's so true, 'cause I knocked her up right away, then she got knocked up again. An' I love them two kids, that's just the way it is, but my problem with her has nothing to do with them at all. My problem here is she's the vengeful type, jus' like her whole family. Her family got the kids away from me. Her mom and sister did. You wouldn't believe the amount of trouble this's caused me.

Lord, it's been there over forty years now at least, you know that? My first husband Bud 'n me would go. It wasn't too far from where we was back then. You wanna talk about shooting rats, or raccoons? 'Cause as far as I'm concerned that's all them darn things are good for. No one 'round here should have one for any other reason. Yes, Earle has one. You wanna see it, go ahead, but don't 'spect me to get it for you. In the back cabinet over there, the drawer right under the vase of roses and chrysanthemums. Yeah, that one. They are lovely, aren't they. No, Sir, my Earle did not, no matter what Johnny's told you. John's always been the one to stretch the truth of a thing. It's over there. Go ahead. You'll see. No, Sir, I don't know what kind of pistol it is. I believe a Star something. I'm sure it's there. Well, John's always had a home with me, but I'm just sick about this. I told him he'd just have to leave and make it on his own. 'You're old enough,' I told him. It's over there, you'll see. Go ahead...

EDDIE

Ah, John's fuckin' harmless. The money he's had coming wasn't never enough to pay off the debts. I never hassled him about it – I've let it slide. I know how he thinks, I know he's got it all worked around and twisted in his head that I owe him, so I let him take a little. What's the diff? That don't hurt me none. If it mellows him out

JACKIE

I don't know, Car. I only know I can love you because you said your dream was always to be with the woman you love, and when I said, 'How do you know when you're in love?' You said, 'You know when you dream of the other person, and I dream of you.'

a little, why not? He's been wound up pretty tight since he got out. I've been there myself. I can use him maybe in a couple of the sets I'm runnin', some new people maybe, he gets himself straightened out.

JACKIE

When Jamal and Car got into it Car wasn't scared at all, 'n Jamal's real big. Now I've seen plenty of men get into it, so I know when someone is scared or not, and Car wasn't. They were both staring at each other, and Jamal had brought over this box of doughnuts, pink and vanilla glazes and, right in front of Car, goes, 'That's what she's like – frosty on the outside, but, oh, so softs on the inside...' like saying this right into his face. 'N Car didn't even react. He just got up 'n went to the fridge an' said, 'Let's get some milk then to go with 'em; sounds pretty damn good to me.' I thought he was gonna be really pissed, but he wasn't at all, 'n that was really impressive, you know, 'n walking back all's he said was, 'You know, I like to see black guys drinking white milk,' 'n Jamal, he goes, 'Yeah, is that so? How 'bout seein' 'em eatin' white pussy then? You goes for that, too?' 'N Car, he goes, 'No, man, never seen it, never will; all the pussy I ever seen was all pink through and through,' I mean, you had to laugh. You gotta give him that....

JOHNNY

Lama looks at Jo 'n says, 'You look pregnant, and if you are that's just crazy!' She tells Jo at her age she's got no business having a family, that kids are nothing but a worry, each and every one of them, and it's getting worse every generation, that it'd be different if I had a job where I could make a living. Well, I had to laugh, Jo's sitting there about in tears. 'And you're the kind that'll probably have a dozen, too, to your own sorrow,' Lama says, that if she had it to do over again she wouldn't 've had any. 'Absolutely not, I just didn't have no better sense then. Look at them people in Africa and India and people like that, they everyone have two or three little kids hanging on them and they don't do anything about it, the poor little things, it's an absolute tragedy, starving, getting sick and killed. Now I come from a big family,' she says, 'but times was different then, you have more grief with one now, than you did with a dozen then.'

JOHNNY

The butthole was moving in; she'd had to choose so's to get it over with for the both of us. 'I know you're hurting,' she goes, 'but I'm the one that's hurting, too.'

JOHNNY

I went there to see my wife. Carson Cool was there with her. He started running his mouth. Like he owned her. Like I wasn't even there. I left and came back to the car and picked up my pistol. Went back, carrying it in my hand. Going down the hall a woman coming out of an apartment saw me with it. Called the Pigs. The Pigs called the Paramedics. The Pigs and Paras were there moments after I shot the person, A.K.A. victim. I'd kicked the door open. My wife was sitting on the couch. She was naked except for her babydoll nightie. The babydoll was baby blue, and one I had given her. The asshole was dressed, but no shoes, no socks. When I fired he turned his body to the side. He did this just as I shot. I don't know where he was hit. The Paras were coming as I left. I walked past them in the hall. I knew one of them. He used to buy lids from me. He

JACKIE

Told Car I'd been convinced I'd never be ready for any sort of long term commitment again, that it scared me to see such a sudden change in all my plans, but since it felt so good to be thinking about joining our life forces and energies together, that I now thought that maybe I could begin to face all my fears about it.

JOANN

Wash clothes, wash dishes, wash floors, wash TV. Ha, ha, ha! Funny?!!! What a life! Call me, call me…

JACKIE

I mean I'm just starting to feel good about my life and I just don't think I'm ready to be part of another person again. Can't we just be friends? Well, for one thing, it has to be someone who's easy to be with, not the kinda person who always has to get involved, okay?

wasn't looking at me as I walked by. No one recognized me. It was quiet outside. The streetlights were on. I saw two cop cars V-ing up, cock-blocking the driveway, but I'd parked around back in the alley. They never saw me. I walked around the corner.

JACKIE

John had that green T-shirt on, the pine green one all ripped, what I was seeing, all that ringing, flashing, the metallic burn off the gun and electrical cuts into my teeth and gums, his back big going out the door, his face flashes, looking around. I stopped screaming and gave Car a sponge from the sink and held it to his stomach. Car said he'd be all right. 'Are you insane?' I said, him saying something I couldn't hear, what I was seeing, me shuddering yet again, suddenly gone all wet, turning, with dry cotton mouth gag and electric jag cuts deep in teeth and tongue and groin inside all gone weak, stinging, yellow sponge now red, still smelling the burn off the gun, shivering, ringing, John had that pine green Isky Super Cam Tee all smeared red, 'cause Car was talking all I could hear was someone screaming and that stopped, everything stopped, the sponge from the sink, the whirling whining in my ears, pressed it on Car and he said, 'Take this fucking gun,' and I said, 'Are you nuts?' He said, 'Why are you screaming?' And said, 'Call 911; call 911,' and I said, 'Let me get a dish towel; you need a dish towel...'

CHAPTER 26

NORTH GARDEN ST.

JACKIE

Car was so shy. It took him a week 'n a half to call. 'Well?' I said. 'Yes,' he said, he really did, he knew what he wanted. 'Well,' I said, 'we'll see, won't we?' And then he said, 'No, I, really think it'd be cool, you know,' and then, well, there we were, and I told him, I said, 'Yeah, I am pregnant; isn't that a blast, but why not just call it off? That's still an option.' 'N he said he'd think it over. 'All right,' I said, and he said: 'Okay, I've thought it over; let's just do it, but first I wanna see the little blue stick, or the dead rabbit, or whatever, ha, ha, ha…'

JOHNNY

I got a cold sixer and Jo and I drove up the hill and parked under the Cross and she wanted to know what was the matter. I told her I didn't wanna worry her none with any personal problems, but something bad might a' happened depending on how things worked out, and asked her what did she think about love anyways? I said, 'What is it?' 'N she said, 'How do I know what it is? Don't you love me? I love you.' I told her I was working on it, and I needed to borrow the car.

IRENE

Telling him he couldn't count on me anymore didn't make him feel good, but it did me, 'cause while it's always wonderful to talk to him, I'm usually at a loss in saying what I really want to, as to how he's doing and what he's doing. I always know what I want to say after he's gone, but this time I was able to, not that it'll make much difference. There's not much you can say to a person once they've got their mind made up they pretty much know it all, but maybe I got through a little, 'cause after we talked I thought, *'Well, it don't seem like what he's*

JOHNNY

Ramon's got these two black and chromed-out choppers, big

750's, in the living room plus gasoline spilled somewheres, plus rubbing this chemical flea and tic killer on his dog's back so's the whole place stinks. He's got a long enclosed glass box there by his chair, two skinny, dusty rattlesnakes in it, baby ones, like long angleworms, crawling over each other on the sand, flicking their little forked tongues out, black ones, 'Red Desert Rattlesnakes,' he says. 'I just bought 'em; endangered ones,' he says, 'paid over five hundred bucks each for 'em,' an' says, 'Okay, Big John, let's fuckin' pretend we just met, 'kay, 'n start this whole conversation all over.' 'N I say, 'So, okay, what's the difference between then or now; it's still gonna be twenty-two bills.' 'Well,' he says, 'you've got your head up your ass 'cause it's the wrong house to be talkin' shit like that,' 'n yells at his dog, this pug ugly pit bull to go get him a goddamn stick so's he can use it to beat someone to death. Then says, 'That's good snort; it's got that dry, dusty taste.' An' I tell him, 'Yeah,' I say, 'so go get the goddamn stick, Bro, 'cause it's still twenty-two, period.' 'Buster,' he yells, 'vete al diablo!' An' that big-headed fucker is trained, man, 'cause it splits, 'n someone puts a towel 'round my face 'n pulls me over backwards, 'n this older Mex is looking down at me with this ol' blue Aztec warrior tatted 'cross the side of his neck, 'n this vato, he goes, 'Should I put some leather to 'em?'

done is bothering him so much, but more like what I might think of what he's done.'

JOHNNY

I'd busted the door open, see, and she said, 'What'd you go and do that for? All you had to do was knock. When have I ever not opened the door for you?'

JACKIE

'Cause we think alike, 'cause maybe he was here, 'cause maybe you were gone, 'cause what else can I tell you – that he's good at going down on me, and you're not? Is that what you wanna hear? No, I don't think so. No! Goddamn it... will... you... listen...?

JOANN

You remember that time we were getting down and you

JOHNNY

Excuse me, but whatta you know about blackouts anyway? You know anything at all? How drunk've you ever been? 'Cause you don't look like the kinda person that even thinks about a drink, let alone takes a drink. You ever gone to the window 'n looked out to see if your car was there 'cause you didn't know where it was parked, let alone if you'd even driven it home? No, I don't mean where you've passed out. I mean where you've blacked out. A blackout's different. You can do things, you just don't know you're doing them. That's what I'm talking about.

JOHNNY

So this time we start it again. Ramon says, 'So where'd you you get this shit? This the fly you ripped offa Eddie?' 'N pushes another line an' the cakes at me, and I laugh 'n say, 'Ramon, man, now I know you, right? I know your kinda moves. It's still twenty-two bounces for the bindle, flat take it or leave it,' 'n slide the mirror back. He grins at me, an' I say, 'Ramon, man, you fuckin' taco-munchin' pendejo, I didn't come here for called me Mommy and I was shocked and said, 'I'm not your Mommy?' Remember? Well, can I be your Mommy now?

JACKIE

I'm truly sorry, I truly am, I don't like seeing you like this, please don't be like this. I just don't think we have any purpose anymore. I know I've always had this romantic fantasy that we'd be a family for always, but I just don't see it. I think we've just had our kids, and that's it…

JACKIE

No, no, I absolutely, completely 'n totally didn't think he'd come back at all. I knew he was all messed up, but I didn't really get behind it, act on it. I just thought he'd get hold of himself, and that's sad, too, 'cause now I don't know what to say to either Dawnie or John-John. They still don't know where he's at, and think at their Lama's. 'N he had this sick-inside-himself look, like he knew what he was doing but he just couldn't help himself, 'n he looked really bad, 'n all I could think was, *'Just get out of here; go!'* I kept on talking to him, but nothing no old times, new times, or good times, 'kay, jus' the full pack a' rubber-banded slam-cakes there, so's you can go on ahead an' *call* Sir Edward, tell his royal red ass what I said, 'n what you really wanna do.'

CARSON

Yeah, he came and saw me in the hospital, asked if I needed any money or anything. I said, 'No,' but I dug him for it. It showed a lotta class. If I saw him on the street I'd shake hands. When I saw him he thanked me. I said, 'For what?' He said, 'For not dusting me.' 'Listen,' I told his P. O. 'He's an all-right dude; you send him up there he's rat food, so don't do it.' And another thing, if there's even any hope of the least kinda chance I'll get back together with Jac, which is something I'm not even saying I care about, you understand, I sure don't wanna have to look her, or her stupid kids, or even her little sister in the eye, knowing I got the big guy dead.

JOHNNY

I'd started to cry. I didn't even know I was. It wasn't like I felt it. I just was. She said I didn't have to do that. She kissed me, but there was nothing in it. I said seemed to go in. His eyes wouldn't hold. He sort of hurt me too, but what was strange was somehow I knew nothing was gonna happen. He wasn't gonna do anything to me. I'd said, 'John, look, I do love you, you know, but not like this, it can't be like this. You gotta get out of here.'

JACKIE

'Serious?' Car said. 'If it's serious then I'm not in it!' Wow! Isn't that great? Which made me really determined not to let him know how I felt. So then I asked him about other women. 'Well,' he said, 'now that's a sorta hard one to answer, but if you really wanna know there's really only been one woman for me.' 'And who's that?' I ask, and he says, 'You.' 'And why's that?' I ask, and he goes, 'Well, now that we're talking about it, that you're sorta tender with me, okay?' *Well...*

JACKIE

I do not want to hurt you, or make you feel bad, or discouraged, or to think bad of your-

I said, 'How can some li'l monkey ass piece a' shit steal my old lady? I can't believe it! Fuck this!' I said, 'I'm leaving!' 'Oh, no,' she said. She was blocking the door and she laughed. Isn't that a bitch? I laughed with her, even though I was crying. We were looking at each other, an' I remember saying, 'My blue eyes into your brown,' and she said, 'Yeah, and together we get gold.' And that was it – the old thing we used to say – but that was all. 'So,' I said, 'so, okay, Sweetheart.' We just understood one another, you know, and it was done. She had this sorta sad-like look on her face, you know, an' that was all there was. I just stepped by and walked...

self, but the very first time you said you were gonna leave me was something I never forgot. You never should've threatened me. As far as I was concerned it was over with right then and there, and I shoulda said so, kids or no kids…

JACKIE

Would you please lower your voice? Jesus Christ, your voice! You really don't get it, do you! No, you don't! Do you really like being like this? Do you? What's the point? There isn't any point! There is not! I don't wanna hear it! *'Custody of the kids?'.* Are you fucking *nuts?* Are you fuckin' crazy?

JOHNNY

Mom and Jo hit it right off. Mom says she had a funny dream about Jackie an' me, an' that Jackie never came to see her but once, and never after we were first married, but Jo has, and all on her own. Earle doesn't say nothing, just goes into the other room, taking the portable TV with him while Mom and Jo talk. Mom says she should've been someone's cook or housekeeper and done it for money, not for love. Jo says 'That's awful.' Mom says it's not. Mom says she's depressed, though, she's been thinking about Dad so please ignore her. She starts in yapping about her dead cats. Jo takes Mom's hand and puts it on 'Our baby.' That's the way Jo says it, *'Our baby.'* 'Look,' I say, 'we gotta go; we gotta get back. I've been working.' I say to Mom, 'I'm on nights.' Mom walks us out to the car and says, 'You know, John, I don't want you to think your dad was so bad 'cause he wasn't; he always cared for you kids. And I have to tell you, I still think about him from time to time.' I ask if Earle is treating her okay. She tells Jo she'll get her a real nice dress for Easter, and that I'd better take real good care of her if I know what's good for me, Jo, that is, and then says for me to drive real careful. I tell her we're on our way to see Grams, 'n Grams'll say the same thing, about me driving real careful. 'Well, you just do it then,' Mom says. Then she says Earle says he wants the car back, that even if Jackie still has it and needs it for the kids, that I have to go get it and bring it back there and right away. 'And I mean it,' she says. Then she kisses Jo. And starts bawling. And Jo gives her a hug. Then Jo starts crying, too...

JOHNNY

'Where's he at?' I said, ''cause I'm not done with him.' 'Well, shoot me then,' Jac says, 'cause he's still at the hospital. That's what you'd really like, isn't it? Wouldn't that be better for you, me dead, or completely fucked-up? Isn't that what you're really here to do? You can still do it! You're still lucky. You'll get away with it.'

JOHNNY

It's still not resolved. We could still get together, or I could tell her I don't even know her. Then, on the other hand, if we do get together, I'm afraid I'll blow it again, I'll let her down...

TERI

What he says is true. Jamal went over there around midnight to score some of the weed Jac was fronting for Eddie, and Johnny came in in the middle

JACKIE

John! John! He's already said he'd leave so's you and I could talk! Haven't you learned nothing? He's leaving, for Christ sakes! He is *so* just here as a friend! Go! Get out of here, Jamal! Go! Go! Goddamn it, John, stop waving *that stupid gun* around. John, you fuckin' idiot! Get outa here, Jamal! He's gonna let you go! *Go!* John, stop waving that stupid gun around. John, you fuckin' idiot! Jamal, just get outa here! He's gonna let you go! Go!

of it. I don't think he had any intention of harming her, but just was all fucked up from being out on the street for so many days with nothing going right. I do not believe he was on drugs of any kind. No, Ma'am, I'm certain he wasn't.

JOHNNY

I'd looked into her eyes, see, 'n said, 'How come your eyes are so dead?' 'N she says, she goes, 'Cause I've already decided...'

JACKIE

Ter told you I was acting nutty, too, didn't she; that I'd flipped out on angel dust or somethin' heavy, right? I don't do heavy. MDA? I never took MDA! I see where somethin' funky is gonna happen to her she keeps this kinda garbage up...

DEPUTY SHERIFF MUNOZ

Get on your face! Get down on your goddamn face or I'll blow your goddamn head off! GET ON YOUR FACE!

JOANN

You have to bring the car right back. You have to promise me. Say you promise. Do you promise? You have to! Because you do! Stop it! I can't stand it when you gets all mad on me. It hurts me. And you know it does. And I know that's not what you want.

JOHNNY

'Cause she'd seen I coulda killed the motherfucker, see. She saw that. I knew that. It'd been right there in his eyes. I'm talking about ol' Carson. He was kacked if I wanted it that way, see, and he knew it. He was kacked, see, and Jackie saw it, too, man. She'd seen the look on his face. He knew, 'n she knew. There was no fuckin' doubt about it. That's why I never had to shoot nobody, you understand? There was no reason to. She knew the look on his face. I'd already done all right, see...

JACKIE

Of course I can handle myself. You know what life is? Life is daily living: a good job, a good screw at night, get up and cook

JOHNNY

She said, 'You just can't go around threatening people.

What is wrong with you?' I said, 'Nothing is fuckin' wrong with me.' 'N told her I'd just leave; that I wasn't gonna do anything to anybody, that I was done with doing things to people, I was finished with all that, from now on all I was gonna do was to do things *for* people, and if she had any problem with that I would just leave. I saw her step out of the doorway. I was tight. She said it again, that I couldn't just go around threatening people. I said, 'Oh, yeah? Who the hell am I threatening?' I knew I wasn't gonna hurt her. I had to shift position so's I wouldn't lose control of myself,

a good breakfast. That's what life is. That's how I handle myself with just daily living. *Just daily living!* Goddamn it, John! Are you fuckin' listening to me? With daily fucking living! How can I explain it to you when I just explained it to you? Oh, shit, John, don't wave that money at me! I know where you got that money…

then I saw myself step toward her, but I knew I wasn't gonna hurt her. My arm went back, but I held it. I knew she was just as unhappy as I was. So's I just turned and left. I knew she was watching. I went on down the steps and outside. What happened next I don't remember. Drinking coffee in Denny's was next. Holding a napkin to my mouth. My lip was bleeding from a cut inside my mouth and I was swallowing the blood. Drinking the coffee with the blood started making me nauseous. I left Denny's and drove around. I drove back to the apartment.

JOANN

I don't want to say this, Baby, but she's just old, and don't remember what real love is.

SGT. DET. PHYLLIS STUBBLEFIELD

Mrs. Dalton never thought he was going to kill her. Not even when the pistol was pressed to her head. Further stated was certain he never meant to shoot her, the pistol discharged by accident, clearly missing her, and that she will not press charges. When asked to clarify this point, Mrs. Dalton added Mr. Dalton declared that death didn't matter – if she wanted he would prove it by shooting himself right in front of her. When told that Mr. Dalton, taken to the Sheriff's Substation, had subsequently punched a hole in the wall of the Interrogation Room while stating: "I should have killed her when I had the chance," reiterated her position of accidental shooting. Ballistics was called in, verifying the firing of one gunshot only by retrieval of a single slug from the southwest bedroom wall above the TV. Prior to the arrest, Mr. Dalton had gone to the family apartment and was greeted at the door by one Mr. Jamal K. Rice, a black male, age 27, later identified by Mrs. Dalton as a family friend. First holding the pistol on Mr. Rice, Mr. Dalton subsequently let him leave the apartment unharmed. When Deputies Pollard and Munoz arrived, Mr. Dalton was holding Mrs. Dalton with his left arm around her neck and the Star automatic's barrel pressed into her right temple.

SGT. DET. STUBBLEFIELD

Regarding the prior shooting incident at Mrs. Dalton's residence on 6-16, Mrs. Dalton stated she knew nothing: "I don't know who it was." Mrs. Dalton said her husband was not the assailant. "It could be anybody. Men often try to follow me and my sis home because of our work, often they are belligerent and drunk. Sometimes they get real angry. We do have a bodyguard, but sometimes he is not available." The bodyguard, Frederick Rogers, 32, AKA "Red Fred", a known Hells Angels Motorcycle Club Associate, escorted Mrs. Dalton home that night, but stated he never entered the apartment. Currently traveling on a cross-country run to the annual Sturgis motorcycle rally in Sturgis, South Dakota, he will be returning in mid-to-late August for a follow-up interview. Remains a possible suspect. When questioned about the relationship between Mr. Dalton and the victim, Mr. Carson E. Cool, 25, identified as a transient living on the streets of Ventura, and described by Mrs. Dalton as "My sister's boyfriend only," Rogers said, "I'm not thinking about any of that shit, man. I'm only thinking about getting my bike ready. I don't know beans nor bullshit about them two. Whatever they're into is none of my business." When asked about his relationship with Mrs. Dalton, Mr. Rogers said, "I love her, man," and refused any further clarification..

BOOK FOUR **SUMMER**

BLUE SHEET: DALTON, JOHN RANDOLPH

HT: 6' 3-1/2 WT: 236 SEX: M HAIR: BRN EYES: BLU

DOB: 08-06-59 CAL: R0442402

COMMENTS

4th incarceration in past 4 years. Knows routines, regulations. Approved for general population, exercise yards. Requested online Community College studies, expressing an interest in Animal Husbandry and Veterinary Medicine, said working with animals calms him down. States wants to do his time as quietly and as quickly as possible. Also requested immediate work assignment, stating preference with any of the following positions: (1) working with the training of K-9 Police and/or Fire Department Rescue dogs, citing that growing up in a dog person's family – his mother currently has 6 or 7 dogs, mostly toys/miniatures at this time – has given him insight into how a dog needs to be trained, and cites personal experience working with professional and commercial business patrol dogs such as German Police Dogs used in junkyards, and private patrol dogs such as Large Standard-Bred Dobermans; (2) office work, for air-conditioning and coffee rolls; (3) or Food Services, specifically the 3 am to 8 am shift when everyone is sleeping to avoid, as he put it: "...any possible personal hassles." Follow-up procedures for Food Services to be initiated after completion of placement and psychological testing.

CHAPTER 27

SALINAS YARDS

JOANN

I did know you were supposed to go to court again because I did go to the City-County Bldg. Friday and when I asked the man in front he said they had taken everyone away in the morning. That couldn't be, I said, but he said it was. I stood there and tears just came down. He said he was sorry but you were gone. I want you to know that. I saw a picture of you today when you were about one and 1/2 yrs. old and I hope the baby looks like you. Your mom says she wants it to look the way you did, black curly hair, but my eyes. She said it would be the most beautiful baby you've made yet. I don't want to put you on the cross but what is it you meant when you said are we still two persons or are we one? I just hope it isn't more bullshit because I don't want to be hurt anymore. I lost once. I don't want to lose again. I can say I had you once and hope to have you now and for always. But also don't think that just because of the baby you have to be obligated to me because if you feel that way I'll just get rid of it. And also don't think I'm playing a game because Cheryl said you would think that. I think you should know me a little bit better because I love you – YOU! Maybe everything you have told me is the truth about how you do really feel about me. You know how I feel about you, Johnny. Johnny, what did it mean in the newspaper when it said you put your arm through a glass door and the police came and took a gun from you and you said, 'Okay, let's go home?' Oh, I also want to tell you I really have been losing more weight, even though the baby is beginning to show more and more…

JOHNNY

Well, if that isn't the shits! Goddamn, Rube, I can't believe you've got another King under there! Are you motherfuckin' me? Lemme see. You *are* motherfuckin' me! Look at that shit! Fuckin' King a'

Hearts! If that don't drive ya outa the yard. Here, lemme shuffle. Gimme that deck. Winners ain't whiners. Lemme shuffle. Thank you, thank you. Whiners ain't winners. New hand a' cards, new start in life. Here we go, here we... Jack a' Diamonds to the man in blue, Seven a' Clubs to the man with the tattoo...

JOHNNY

You, Babes, in mind as I sit here listening to the radio trying to let you know how much you really mean to me. I told you I would always have you in my mind. You know me by now that while I keep getting busted, that what we have for each other will always be between the two of us. That's why I've always said that nobody knows how I feel toward you but me. Why you've put up with me is what gets me mad because I know better than anyone that what I do is wrong. You know me, you know how hard it is for me to say that love talk but I will say this, it's times like these that tells me who it is that really cares. You know that. It sure would be sweet to be out there tooling down Main, a cool brew between my legs, my Babes at my side – Dr. Pepper her drink. Mom said you were moving back into Anthony and Cheryl's. That's okay, that's okay, but I don't trust Cheryl. I just hope everything works out for you as I know if I was out there now I'd just start acting crazy again and be no help so maybe this is for the best. I know I have a hard road to go but, hey, I'm getting started on it. This is the thought I had last night waiting for sleep after lights out – I'm glad I'm a man and going to die before you because then when I go I'll know the feeling of me will still be going on and I'll never know it when it isn't, which, I guess, goes to show you it is you, you that is in my mind and not any other. For right now, you know, I'll be needing some money so whatever you can send I can sure use. The best way is by Postal Money Order. That way I am the only one that can cash it. I do believe you came to see me. Mom said you did. She said you came to the City-County Building but too late. I gave her a visiting slip for you so if you and her decide to come we can talk things over. I know you having my kid will bring us closer together as time goes by...

CORRECTIONS OFFICER GOMES

That big bastard there, the one not barking, the one just watching you? That's ol' Vex. He's a DDR, same kind of Shepherd casinos in Vegas use for their casino yards and personal homes, what we call a perimeter guard dog. East Germans breed them. You never wanna turn your back on him. Weighs almost a hundred pounds 'n his jaws close at two hundred and seventy pounds per square inch. Standing up, he can put his paws on your shoulders and look down at you. Well, maybe not you, but almost everyone else. Crunch your cannon bone in just one bite. Vex! Vex! Vexter! Get your ass over here! Just wait out here, right here, till I get him leashed up. Gorgeous bastard, ain't he? Put that apron on and these gloves and keep your hands real wide on that stick. This guy's the real deal. You don't want your car stole, or your pickup, whatever, just put him in it. It's liable to be jus' him and someone's arm lying on the front seat when you come back an' get in. I'm not kidding. That dog'll eat anything: napkins, lettuce, tinfoil, beer cans; anything you wanna toss him:... fingers... hands...

JACKIE

I bet you're sorta surprised to hear from me this soon considering how messed up you and me were and how everything went down but, believe this, I did not say anything to anyone, like rat you out, especially not to that woman detective that came over here twice asking me to flip. All I said was I didn't know when you were going to grow up and not always bust up our lives like some old nightmare out of the past but that was just the way you were for now, okay, and so what, but as to any of the rest of it that might've happened, I said to her I can't say nothing, it's all too private, personal and, frankly, just none of your goddamn business, that even if I did know what to tell you I didn't know anything because everything that happened was just so oh my god crazy that to even try to talk about it would made me feel guilty and mad and happy and upset all over again, so, in short, I told her not one damn thing about what she was asking me about, not even when she tried to get in there with the, 'Happy? You said happy? How was that?'

her face all pouncy looking, but I said I.... oh, shit, John, this is just too confusing to even go on with so just forget it, okay? Who really cares? In short I told her nothing. And the second time she came I just closed the door on her. Now you asked about the kids. Well, Dawnie's been yelling at me a lot and spanking her doesn't work but just makes me feel bad after, and she's been giving Mom a real hard time, too. John-John is missing you. For his birthday he wants to go to Disneyland, but doesn't want his sister to go, so we've been talking about it a lot. Ter is now crushed out on some older jerk she's met, saying things like, 'Moving towards a greater commitment is just a reality to me,' and, 'Cause I can't live without him.' Her and me have been talking about going up to Alaska cause Gary knows some people up there that have clubs and manage talent. She's talking to the booker tomorrow so we'll see. They'll pay a lot of money. You asked about Carson. That isn't even worth discussing. Him and me were never really together and, truthfully, I can't talk about this anymore and, incidentally, there's a bunch of new girls at the club here, all of them younger than me, so the money is low, but I've been busting out some new moves and getting them in my performances, and that's been keeping me in business, but I think it could be I'm knocked up again for real this time and now what to do? I mean it could be real. Babies cost money so Alaska could be good. Tell me what is up with you and maybe I can get up there sometime and we can discuss whatever. I don't know what will happen, though, and right now it's one day at a time and get rid of your watch and live in the moment, and all that blah, blah, blah, so tell me what you think. If Ter and I do go up north Mom won't take the kids this time so they will go with us. Never again will we leave them alone. So you don't have to worry about that. Not much else is going on, just the same ol' same ol'. On your end just keep your spirits up and write if you want to. Please let me know when your next hearing is and anything else...

JOHNNY

If you can clean and jerk two hundred pounds you oughta be able to bench three, three-fifty easy. Gimme the fuckin' bar. Here.

Put them two other fifties and twenty-fives on, 'n lock 'em down tight. Now don't drop it. I don't want the fucker coming down 'n crushing my windpipe. That's how they did Richie Lobato, right? Good ol' Lobo. Got him right here in the yard. That next bench over. Here, lemme slide in here…

JACKIE

'Cause I thought all boys just died if they didn't, but I didn't want to get pregnant either so I wouldn't cooch with 'em, I'd just blow 'em instead. The only one that was nice to me was Johnny, an' this was before him and me ever got together, an' one night out at Valentino's some guy said something really shitty about me 'n Johnny followed the guy out to his car and punched him right through the window, shattering the glass, 'n everything, cutting his hand all up, an' he wasn't even my boyfriend then. Then he told me he was going down to L. A. for the weekend with this other girl, and I said, 'Well, I'm not going to be sitting home while you're doing that,' 'n he said he didn't want me to do that, and I said, 'What have you got to say about it?' 'N he said, 'Listen, I'm still going, but I don't want to take a chance on losing you,' 'n I said, 'Can't lose something you never had,'' n he said, 'Okay, I'll take you then,' and I said, 'No, you won't; it doesn't work that way.' An' he went ahead and went, but called me from somewhere each night he was there, like real late, like when the other girl was asleep, see, and…

JOHNNY

No, Doc, I'm gaining weight like a motherfucker. You know what I love? I love my flip-flops, man. *My flip-flops.* They're the only goddamn things I have that always makes me feel good, know what I mean? That don't fit no *other* motherfucker, right? 'N my old lady? Her? She's either being the worst bitch, or the sweetest, rockin' down to it ol' lady in the whole goddamn fucked-up world... who the fuck knows, right? So whatta you think...?

TERI

How can you say that to me? I never *ever* got after Johnny! Not once, and you know it! There's no way! I never even thought it! What the hell are you thinking? That is crazy! You've got some food there, corner of your mouth. That side; the chocolate bit, okay? And Car? Please; you keep talking an' talking about him yourself, so what's up with that? 'N I didn't need your goddamn permission anyways. So why not say Jamal then? Yeah, throw him in there. You're really outa your tree now. I can really see that, me with Jamal. That is so completely paranoid. Where did you get that? I absolutely am not going around with him. Jamal Rice? Your Jamal? Is that what Gary said? That's such a lie. Hey, wait a minute. Let me finish. 'Cause Car was messing up both you *and* the kids, okay? Yeah, the *kids*. And that's a fact. Okay; so there you go…

JOANN

Cut pineapple. Cut veggies for turkey. Decide turkey time. Open pickles. Serving plates. Cranberry sauce. Salad utensils. Stuffing spoon. Forks. Pumpkin pie crust. Talk to Mom about car. Write to Johnny about Cheryl Beth getting the "A" tatted around her ring finger. Write: "Did I tell you Cheryl tried to get an "A" for Anthony tattooed around her ring finger? Cheryl said they went to get a pizza and stopped at the tattoo parlor and Anthony went in the chair first and got a "C. B." tattooed around his ring finger. Then it was her turn and Anthony said the way she was yelling you'd of thought she was having open heart surgery, jerking and thrashing, and telling the guy to quit because the needle hurt so darn bad, went right into the bone behind the knuckle. Cheryl says when she's braver she's going to go through it." What would you say if I got a "J" tattooed around my ring finger to go with the little stars on my ankle? I could get the "J" blocked in pink and outlined in blue. Didn't your Daddy have open heart surgery?

JOHNNY

...excuse me? *'That I couldn't keep away from her?'* Yeah, well you might be able to say that, I suppose, but can I have one of those? American Spirits, no shit. Them're new, right? No, I'll smoke it out in the yard. What else ya wanna know? How can they be healthier? You're still inhaling the smoke, aren't you? Smoke will fuckin' kill you, Doc. The carbon monoxide in the smoke calcifies your capillaries, right? Didn't think I knew that, did ya, 'n your heart is crisscrossed with zillions a' little capillaries, right? Plugs 'em right up. Makes a guy real hard-hearted, ha, ha, ha...how about two? Can you spare two? Great... thanks...

TERI

Maybe the blue 'n white polka dot sundress then. No, I'm just kidding about Jamal. He's actually a sweet guy, and's decent, too, okay, but, hey, you 'n John 've been banging it since early high school so why would you even wanna change that? Besides, I'm used to seeing you with that big boob. Well, he is a boob 'n everyone knows it, with all those stupid deals he's always trying to pull. They always go wrong, don't they. Yeah, they do. Here, look at this. Here's a little bracelet I bought you. I actually bought two. They're Rasta bracelets. Whichever one you want. Either one'll go good with that dress. This green one's friendship, the red one's for around your ankle, for you know what. No; I don't care. Whichever one you want. Or take both of 'em. The red'd go good with that dress, right? Why'n't you try it?

JOANN

There's no way I can hitch a ride up there, and I have no car now plus I got a parking ticket which I have to pay for so I don't have any money for gas. Then Mom is still really mad about you taking her car so I'm not allowed to drive it anymore and she definitely won't bring me up there. I will just have to wait to see you when I can. Don't worry about anything. I don't want you to do that. How long will you be in there and what is it like? Forget what I said about the baby. My Mom is talking with me about what

to do and she thinks I'm too young but I'm not. I know I could take care of a baby. How long will you really be in there? That will help me make a decision. Cheryl Beth says she knows whatever I decide will be the right thing and it really helps to have a good friend like that to talk things over with. She has had the same situation as us and knows what to do and has been telling me about it except Anthony has never been in jail so I guess that's different. By the way, her and Anthony have just split up, and she says she's going to have to give the baby up for adoption. I am not living with them as Cheryl had to move back home but her mom wouldn't take her back so now she's living with me at my Mom's house. Cheryl says for herself she wouldn't go through with having a baby again. Mom thinks I shouldn't. I'm now starting to think that way. She wants me to go back to school, too. Cheryl and I saw Batman. It was really great. I wish I could have seen it with you. Mom and Grandma got me some new pink fluffy slippers with white fur inside. They also gave me a locket in the shape of a heart and I put a gold star inside it from the packets of red and gold and silver stars you bought me in Seal Beach, remember? The slippers are really comfortable. I think you would really like me in them, especially if all I was wearing was them, and the LOCKET, ha, ha, ha, ha! ! ! ! !
Loving You Always, Your

ANDA PANDA, ME-----

CHERYL BETH

There isn't any way I'd loan her my car for her to drive all the way up there. I told her I'd drive her to Planned Parenthood and end the whole stupid thing. She said she loved him. I said, 'That's like loving your dad, but you don't have to fuck your dad, do you?' She said I was just mean and maybe she and I weren't good friends at all and never had been if that's the way I was thinking. Then she tried to take my keys out of my purse and almost got them and Anthony had to take them from her and she asked him to take her and he said, 'Why would I do that?' and she started crying and he went over and put his arms around her and I got up and pulled him back and he said, 'I wasn't doing anything,' and she looked at me and said, 'That's what you think!' and left.

CHAPTER 28

LOS CABOS LANE

GRAMS

I'm not saying anything about that young girl you brought down here, but I won't be here much longer, Johnny, and I know you know that. Did you know that that gun you got from Earle was another fellow's gun who'd done the same thing, tried to shoot his wife, but succeeded? I told your mother about it and she said she'd had a dream that you had succeeded, but for some reason it didn't come true and said she knew God had been the one who kept you from pulling the trigger. And I think that's true. And when you close your eyes, Johnny, God is always there. Then trust on him to keep on showing you the way…

JOANN

Well, I kind of lied about how I've been. I've been afraid to tell you this, but I got a chance to go to Vegas with some friends of Cheryl's, and no, they weren't either Leo or Robert or Anthony but Cheryl Beth's big sister and her new boyfriend, Miles, and it was really great. Las Vegas was fab! I'd never flown on an airplane before. It was so neat! I also got to go on the New York, New York roller coaster. That was the best ride I've ever been on. The funniest thing happened when I rode the ride. When we came to the end I was glad it was over because it was so scary and then got so embarrassed because when I looked down a boob had popped out of my top when the coaster hit the platform stop. Could you imagine how I felt? ME… XO… XO… XO…

RUBEN

But a *bitch*, Ese'? No, no, any O.G. will call one a'them young ones a *jayna* or *hyna*. 'N thes' new ones a' mine? *Es* a *hyna*, hokay? Sixteen years younger, hokay, 'n tha's cool, tha's… hokay, like I'm at the bar 'n I's had two drinks, *dos*, 'n she's tuggin' my sleeve sayin', 'Yus already had two,' 'n I ses, 'Yeah?' 'N tells the bartender, 'Hey, *dos mas* here, 'n *dos mas* afters that, hokay?' Yus gotta stop tha' li'l *hyna* shit rights there, hokay? But hey, no shit, even me, I hadda take a paternity test 'n guess wha', it *wus* my kid! So tha's good, right? I mean, I tolds her I'd do the right thing I gets outa here, so that's wha' I'm gonna do, evens though the nino'll be maybe seven or eight by then, but no way, Homes, I gonna tell *yus* wha' to do. Tha' nino might not even be yours, yus thoughts of that? So she said she'd get rid of it, hokay? 'N maybe tha's tha' li'l *hyna* shit again, hokay? So's yus gots some wiggle room, Ese', 'n gots two choices: one, she gets rid of it; 'n two, lets it be; 'n then gets a DNA done, hokay? Lots a' pendejos don't know nothin' 'bout DNA, hokay? 'N yus gets her t' do one, hokay? Yus hearin' me', Ese'? Hokay, then...

IRENE

Hold on; hold on now, John. Here's what the rest of it says:

'...the balance is $412.51. His payments are $80.00 each 23rd. We haven't received a payment since September 23rd. We have written many letters trying to help, but he still hasn't contacted us. I have offered reduced payments or a sell-down or return of the merchandise or anything at all to be helpful. I am in no way asking you to act as a collection agent in our behalf. However, I am asking you to discuss the matter with him and have him contact me and let me know what the problem is concerning his account. Mr. Dalton seemed a responsible person when he opened the account, so there must now be some problem. I realize Mr. Dalton comes from a decent family, and under normal conditions would never just ignore his obligations. I would appreciate any suggestions you might have on this matter. Thank you very much. GENSLER LEE DIAMONDS, A. L. Diaz, Credit Manager.'

What the heck is this about, John? Did you buy a diamond ring for someone, as if I didn't know who, and are you going to ask her to take it back? Or to pay for it herself, because I know you certainly can't. I'll tell you this, I do not want to get any more letters like this.

JOHNNY

Dear Jac, just as I don't know whether you'll read this or not, or even if this'll reach you, I don't know where you are in your head right now, you didn't say, but I've been going over things in my poor messed-up brain trying to find out exactly where you are. All I can come up with is that somehow, while I was still standing right there in front of you, you had already moved on without me even knowing it. And while I'm not saying that's not fair, I thought at least I would've seen it coming, but I sure as hell didn't. Certainly not with that cross-eyed, motherless, clown-dicked Carson asswipe anyways. Well, I sure sound like RIDICULOUS, don't I? But one thing is for sure, I have always been there for you, NO MATTER WHAT!!!!! AND I STILL AM, so I know this may be asking too much, but more than anything I want to see the kids at Christmas. Or can you bring them up for an afternoon? Any afternoon? Now in a few days there's gonna be a MAIN EVENT here, and five snitches in Protective Custody are not gonna be around for the Christmas Party. At least five. At least that's the word. So with that kinda shit flying around, it's hard to get my thinking cap on and be able to sit down and concentrate on where things are at. But I'm trying...

RUBEN

Hey, Earp, why's yus mouth all squinched up? Yus been sucking on tha' li'l filero? *Say what?* Yus supposed to carry it everywheres, man! *Everywheres!* Even's in the office! Yus don't know where they're gonna jumps yus again. Some place where yus donna 'spect it, Ese'. Yus knows that. I mean get on top of yus thinkings, hokay? 'N keep yus head up, 'n watch yus back at *all* times, Ese'; at all times. Head on' a swivel, Ese'. Whatcha want, Ese', a Tums? I gots some... in tha' drawer there...

JOHNNY

...and what I've been thinking is maybe you need to really look at this thing we've got yourself. I don't know no one else who's gone through what we've gone through and not really made it in the end. There will come a day when everything else around you will stop and you'll be all by yourself, but will I be there like I've always been? Can you really look in your heart, let everything just quiet down, and see who is really there? Now the big news here is they bumped me and Ruben apart over some bullshit kitchen cafeteria stuff from my first bit, accusing him of getting apple and grapefruit juice, orange slices and Wonder Bread to make pruno with, batshit stuff like that. You remember him, the big guy who lost his eye in a barroom fight and didn't even know it? Got a beer bottle broke off into his face and his brother took him outside an' said, 'Are you all right?' and he said, 'I'm fine; I just can't see outa my right eye.' And his brother, 'Well, you ain't got no right eye no more.' So I've got a new cellie now who's this old grandpa dude in for some state income tax fraud beef. They've got him in the wrong lockup for some reason, but it's real good as he's telling me lots of good dope about owning your own business, which is the only way to go. Like Chevelle restorations. Like you buy the old ones cheap, fix them up, make a coupla K on the turnaround. Especially the SS ones you get from auto dispersal auctions for around 5 K, rebuild the engines and trannys for a coupla K, and sell them for as much as 11. There's a good market for that so I'm hatching a few plans to get this started. You know how I've always wanted a Z28 of my own, too, a ZedSled, right? I've got some cool ideas about teaching guys bodywork, blocking and surface refinement painting techniques on something like that, maybe start a school or something. But back to you, while I know this may be asking too much, more than anything I do want to see the kids at Christmas. I already asked you this, but can you bring them up least once before the holidays? Now here's something I didn't tell you. That last night just before that accident happened to Car, Eddie had gotten us some primo which I was bringing over to you, okay? 'N here's what happened, just so's you know. He laid it out on the mirror. I scooped up the first hit and immediately went back to suck up the last dirty grains and went slack-bam onto my knees, grope dropping out of my mouth, and that's when I thought of you! Instead of chains of love whipping around me, I was trying to take it in me! You hear what I'm saying?! Instead of exploding inside you I was trying to explode inside me! And that's when I saw it! I've got it all BACK ASS WARDS, HON! ALL OF IT!!! It's the big insight of my life, and you, JAC-JAC, are the core of it all! How can I deny that? Drugs are not you! YOU are YOU!!

JACKIE

I got your letter and thought I'd tell you that there's a new girl who works with me at the club who gave me a psychic reading to put me in touch with myself and said there were two lights coming off me, two main ones, but one was green, which means growth, and the other aura was white, that's the spiritual, and that I shouldn't even try to attach myself to any man at this time with my spiritual side now starting to open itself up, and when she asked me about you and me, and what had really happened cause everyone was still talking about it, I told her there was so much confusion going on what with both this Jamal person and Carson going at each other first, then you with the both of them, then you and Carson getting into all that weird gun stuff, that I didn't really know what'd happened, but again after the shooting when the cops were there and you had me around the neck, I thought I knew what had happened between us, like to the both of us, that, I don't know, I can't describe it, but during the shooting I felt something burning inside, like climaxing or something, but even more crazier than that, I mean, well, I couldn't tell what it was, that, well, maybe I don't know, cause maybe all it was, was just some stupid climax, that I'd come, see, I think I did, okay, but maybe I hadn't, I don't really know, 'n all she did was look at me and then say, 'Wow!' And, 'Really!' And, 'When are you going to see him again?' Like real envious, or something. Then, in talking about it with Ter, Ter said I was probably just having some kind of a seizure, and I told her, 'No, I don't get seizures like you do, I'm no epileptic.' 'N Ter said, 'Let me get this straight. This happened when Car got shot, or when Johnny came back 'n grabbed you, or which?' And I said, 'I don't know, maybe even both times, but what difference does it make? It was just awesome, right?'

TERI

Right after you split and I went down to Huntington to get that cash Car owed us? Well, he had that Francie chick with him. Yeah, Francie-what's-her-face, her, the one we met in Nevada. Right! The one from Huntington selling everyone the dust an' percs, 'n could never get the money straight, remember, like her brain was all sunburned or something. Yeah, her, so then we all go out onto the pier to grab some crab legs and beers, an' with her sitting right there he starts telling me that getting shot wasn't the only thing that messed him up, that it was you! Yeah, you! That you wanted it all to happen exactly like that, that you set the whole thing up, he knows you did, that you wanted him to get shot, and then, get this, he tells me to tell you, 'Hello...'

JOHNNY

I am glad to hear you and Carson have broken up. Like it says in the Bible, Judgment Day is coming for us all, and I think I know Carson, he's okay, he handled himself good, but he's a mean little fuck who's just out for himself cause no doubt he got the shit kicked outa hisself when he was just a baby but he's not no baby no more. And neither are you or me. And thinking about that it's real clear to me you've always been the kinda person who has to fuck the leader of the band, and that is not the behavior of a full grown woman. I can wait for you to grow up, but I don't know how much longer it will take. We've had some real good times together and who knows we could have some more, but when that'll be is just as much up to you as it is up to me so that's something we can talk about. The new squeezer here says one of my problems is not taking some responsibility for the choices I make, including the kind of women I choose, so in thinking about it I know I love you, cause I do, and I did choose you, but the question is, is the choice any good? It may not be anymore. And it may not be for you, too. You see what I'm thinking? So I'm real glad to hear you and Carson have broken up, which is no surprise to me, but thinking like this really gets me down, bums the shit outa me. That's on the one hand, but when you flip the cards over, what no one sees is you've always come back to me, always, and that's something I've never been able to say no to, not even in my worst moments. Do you hear what I'm saying? Do you? That I'm just goddamn stuck! Goddamned if I'm not! Son of a bitch! Jesus fucking Christ! I can't think of anything that makes me madder than that! When you see the kids I want you to kiss them for me, tell them I think of the both of them all the time, and am really looking forward to seeing them, and I guess I'm saying I wouldn't mind seeing you either... I wouldn't...

IRENE

I don't know when this heat wave is going to end. It's been 107 to 111 all week and the air conditioner's condenser burned out and only the tiny unit in the bedroom works and I'm worried sick about the animals because of the heat so they have to stay locked in the bedroom all day except for when we take them out to do their business. It's been so hard on everyone. Did I tell you Lejo's left eye was popped out and we took her to the vet and it was a massive infection in her mouth and we had all her teeth except four extracted which relieved the infection and her eye went back in her socket but now she won't eat as she can't chew so we have to feed her with a syringe. I cook hamburger for her and mix it with chicken broth and water and squirt it in her mouth. Right now it's too hot to write any more. I'll finish this later...

JACKIE

The other day Ter told me she thought her and me were both on the same kind of trip with men, 'n I said, 'You know what? I used to have to get stoned to make it through the day. Now I don't as I'm returning to being a quiet, shy person who gets easily hurt by others, the way I was before I met certain people, certain specific people we both know.' And Ter said, 'I believe it,' and took hold of my arm, 'n took me over to the kitchen sink and said, 'You better wash that rinse out of your hair now. Here, I'll do it. Just close your eyes.' She turned the water on, and had her arm around my shoulders and was actually hugging me, but hiding it, see, while she was shampooing, so she knows what I'm talking about. Told me I didn't have to color my hair no more, which made me laugh. 'Hey,' I told her, 'I don't have to go that fucking far, right? Which made her laugh, too, see, which was real good...

JOANN

My Mom and me are going to Planned Parenthood next week, I thought I'd let you know. That way when you come back you won't have to worry about me trying to pin you down, like you said. I just thought you should know... or maybe I won't go. Cheryl Beth says I shouldn't. Mom says I can go to Community College if I want to put all this behind me. I'm thinking about it. I don't want to tell you what else happened. But, no, I am not seeing Robert or Leo or anyone else at all. Why would you think that? And Cheryl Beth IS back with Anthony and she IS keeping her baby. Sometimes things just don't work out and sometimes they do. Right now I haven't a clue, but time will tell. And I will take the ring back if that's what you think I should do. Why do you want me to do that? Do you still feel that way? Cheryl said if she was as sentimental as me she would carry all the letters Anthony wrote her in a purse, too, but she would look pretty stupid with two real big giant yellow manila envelopes sticking out. Anthony gave her two milk chocolate hearts as big as balloons for her birthday. I'm really sorry for what happened on the phone Saturday. My Mom has been on my back all weekend and now. Loves Ya, Loves Ya, ME...

JOHNNY

Fuck no, Rube, I've got some other connections down there. You must know some a' them people. Like Rayo Flores, for one. You know him? Was in for Ag. Assault? The San Pedro dude they call Flipper? We got good history. Make a few calls. Check it out. You could ramrod the thing from in here, and I'd crew everything out, out there...

JACKIE

Now I have to tell you about this dream I had. You were just coming in and we were at this circus and I was trying to find the kids but all these people were acting weird and wouldn't let me. They kept trying to make me part of the circus, like painting my face and making me a clown. I got real upset and this one clown I think was you saw that and came over and helped me find the kids and I got them but everyone kept acting silly. I'd made all these little clay figures for the kids and dropped them in the sawdust and all these people were trampling around and we couldn't find them and I was getting frantic and then when I woke up I remembered what they spelled, they spelled out the word TOGETHER!

TERI

Sitting in that awful heat in that yellow and blue painted taqueria drinking brown bottled Tecates with Jac and eating refried beans and green peppers and them kids drinking cokes and making a mess of everything I started getting sick and had to leave and go out and lay down in the car and it was even hotter there and I was all sweaty and my stomach was all seasicky and I looked up at the headliner with those flies walking upside down on it and thought I'd better go back in and throw up there 'cause we had to drive back in the car in this heat and I went back in and into the toilet and couldn't make myself do it, even bent over the toilet with its yellow stain ring right at the water line and the smell, and I came back out and sat there and looked at Jac and the kids and thought, *'Not me, man; I'll never do it,'* and then knew that wasn't true, 'cause I'd already missed three periods and I knew right then that I would, 'cause those kids were really sweet, so what the hell was I thinking 'cause maybe it had already started.

CHAPTER 29

SOLEDAD PRISON ROAD

JOHNNY

Could you get me a TV? I've got earphones for my little radio but a TV would be a big help. The photos are a big help but are sorta a downer. I never realized this before but it's distance that fucks you up. You can only look so far and that's it. You can look all the way down the corridor and then you see a wall. Then in the yard when you look across it you see a wall. There's no place to go unless you mind travel. That's why the TV. You watch TV and if you don't watch the story you can see a long ways. You can get out into some country. Westerns, hunting and fishing and car shows are best. I've also been thinking up my own movies, and I have one where this girl rides a horse out in the country and is happy. Remember when we lived out by the oil fields and there were those horses across the street? You'd go over and give them sugar cubes? And those bikers that had them five dollar seams of PCP wrapped in tinfoil? The first time we ever saw that? They lived out there in the back of the barn? The ones that got ripped by them La Colonia bangers outa Oxnard and got their arms and legs broke?

JACKIE

It's been a good day. The kids are running crazy and me with them. We've been playing volleyball and swimming. Everyone has been so nice to me and everything. Gary has been great about giving Ter and me extra shifts. He has been keeping everything easy at work and teaching us so much, like how to buy nice clothes and have easy feelings with people. It'll be so different for sure when you come back. I'll be able to do so much more for us. No more living in a sleeping bag in the park for you, ha, ha. Or at the Salvation Army transitional barracks. Ever since I've started getting my own money again my mental attitudes are so much better. I'm not scared of half the things I'm usually scared of. Well, I am really pooped. My shoulders, neck, legs and arms all hurt from all the carrying of drinks, walking, then dancing every fifteen minutes or twice an hour plus taking customer hassling. The biggest change is I no longer let anyone change me. We've been real happy here. A really cool apt., pool, etc.; the thought that money is not too much to spend to have a good time. Which is about time. More later... no, Gary just called and wants me to take the early shift so I have to get the kids over to Mom's. I have to try to get as much money as I can now before I have to stop working again. I figure I have about another month or so left. Oh, almost forgot this. Jamal has gone down to L. A. and is working in Glendale again for this chain of clubs, so that's a possibility for more work later and gave me two hundred bucks as a going away present to get the car fixed, which was real great of him, and Gary has a friend who comes in here who owns a Conoco station that's going to do the brakes and fix the driveshaft or U-joint or whatever it is on Wednesday so we'll be able get up there to see you. I will bring the kids. Also, I got a second nosebleed yesterday, which scared me, but it turned out to be nothing. All it needed was a sliver of an ice cube and it stopped like right away. Also, and, no, I have not brought anyone home with me, and haven't even thought about it, and plenty of people have asked me out to breakfast and that I've done, but that's all. And I haven't gone to anyone else's place either...

JOANN

I hope you don't get all mad about this one but your stupid **EX**-wife came into Shakey's where me and Cheryl and Anthony were and she was with this other old bitch who looked like her and she started grabbing my hair and was twisting it and tried to get my ring off and started hitting at me on the side of my face and this other bitch was yelling, 'Fuck her up! Fuck her up!' and Anthony had to grab her off me, and then chased them both out so I went outside and called her an ugly old dirty cunt bitch and she gave me the finger and I gave it back and she does have your car so what is going on? And what I really want to know is how did she even know you had given me my ring? Now don't get all mad at me that I am keeping the ring and not just selling it like you said she told you, so don't believe anything she tells you, and why are you even talking with her about this? And if you do get mad about it you are wrong but I don't want you getting mad at me at all. Maybe I will call you to see what you think. But maybe I won't. What do you think about that and when is the best time to call? Sometimes I think about that night when we drove up under the Cross. When I jumped out and went over there and sat down with those two old women, the ones that were looking up at the Cross, and I started looking up at all the stars and you got out of the car and came over and said, 'What the hell are you doing?' And one of them said, 'Spotting flying saucers; we've just saw two, right over there,' and she was pointing, but I didn't see anything, and you said, 'Jesus Christ, Panda, get back in the car.' That was the first time you'd called me Panda that whole week! What if a flying saucer had come down then and we had got on it and went somewhere far away where nothing bad could've ever happened? Wouldn't that have been neat? I still don't know if I will call. You better tell me, or forget it, and I am not selling the ring, but keeping it, period! Or maybe I will call. You have to tell me when. You can do it, can't you, and if you can't, why can't you?

IRENE

Have to have cataract surgery on Tuesday and am worried about who is going to feed the dogs. Can I call Jackie and see if she will come over? She was here the other day and let John-John and Dawnie play with them in the backyard. Lejo nipped Dawnie and she got real mad and who can blame her? Jackie said she heard that the food industry is now considering cutting back on the production of all pet food. That can't really be true. As if there isn't already enough to be worried about without worrying about that. I'm going to ask her to buy some fifty pound bags of kibble, as many as she can get, just in case. You can keep kibble for a really long time. I saw your other girlfriend the other day in Safeway but she didn't say anything but just ignored me like I wasn't there so I thought you should know. I should of bought the kibble then but didn't want to have to carry it out to the car by myself. Those bags are too heavy for me to lift. Earle wasn't with me as his legs and back are hurting him again. Did you contact that Hispanic manager fellow at the jewelry store yet? Don't think I will make those payments for you because I won't. Earle said absolutely not, so don't even bother asking…

JACKIE

Red Fred, uh-huh… remember that big dope I told you about that used to follow me around? Did I tell you he showed up at this party at Eddie's and went outside and threw up on Eddie's truck and passed out so they pushed him up into the back, into the bed. He's real big, too, just like you. It took about three guys to get him up in there. You know who I'm talking about, don't you, the Ban-Dar bouncer, the one that used to just pick me up under one arm and carry me off the floor if he thought I shouldn't be dancing for someone? It wasn't jealousy. He was just protecting me. He was the bouncer, right? You remember me talking about him, right? Well, anyways, Eddie took him to a robo-wash, the kind where you drive up on the tracks, and I was saying, 'Eddie, you'll kill him,''n Eds said,'He threw up on my truck,'and drove us through. The windows were all sudsy and Fred got blasted. He didn't even move, though. It wasn't funny neither. I remember looking at him, barely able to see him in all the spray. This was the guy that I'd see taking cigarette butts out of my ashtray and putting them in his mouth just because they'd been between my lips. Then we drove him home, and Eddie tossed him out on the lawn. Fred didn't even remember it. The next night he came around thanking everyone for taking him home and I thought what am I doing, spending my time with these kinds of people? If that'd happened to you, if Eddie had thrown you into the back of his truck you woulda clocked him so hard his teeth would've ended up in his stomach. It was something for me. I mean I didn't think it right then.

It wasn't until I got home I thought it. So there it is, okay? There's no X in my pencil for you. Pretty cool phrase, huh? I thought it up myself, too. Well, it's true. I am c ming up to see you (SP). This damn pen is run ing ou o nk

Lo e Y u, J kie

JOHNNY

I heard what you said about Carson going back to Long Beach and it really was a slap alongside the head, know what I mean? Something lit up about that piece of shit cause I know how that little frog fucker's mind works, like a rear-ended car wreck, all whiplashed 'n twisted into an enjoying-fuckin-people-over kinda brain, 'specially if they're friends, know what I'm saying, because remember when I got whacked off in that Nardo Suarez deal, remember, when even you didn't believe me, an told me Eddie wouldn't believe me either? That was down in Long Beach, too, right? And talking it over with Rube, an' listening to what he had to say, and now you reminding me who it is that is from there, and like could of known where and when I was gonna be down there, and with how much! Specially, Rube says, with how much! You ever think about that, Carson being from Long Beach originally, and knowing all kinds of peoples from there to set the rip up with, get hisself a big ol' finder's fee, right, and then like move me completely outa the game as the fuckin loser so's he could take over my set? I told you the guy had no quality. Remember me telling you that? And neither does Eddie. He didn't say jackshit when I ran that by him, just fucking blew me off, saying that was all just paranoid bullshit having to do with Car 'n you, but I told him to think about it, that I'd always been able to keep my love business and my money business separate, and that he knows it, but if he thought I couldn't, then he could get hosed. So fuck the both of them. I'm just really glad all that's over, and I don't have to think about it anymore, but it sure as hell makes sense, don't it...

JACKIE

'Cause I did, I did! I was soaking wet, like *squirting* wet, okay? Don't tell me that's *crazy!* Of course it's *crazy.* Everything was *crazy!* No, no way! Haven't you ever *climaxed* without being *touched?* Yes, you *can!* You *absolutely can!* Don't tell me it's not *possible!* It's *possible!* I didn't even know I'd come until I touched myself! Like afterward, okay? When that lady cop had me out to the patrol car and was telling me to calm down. *No, absolutely not!* 'Cause I *had!* I *did! Jesus Christ,* Ter, I am not always trying to do you one better! For *fuck sakes,* can you just listen? No, no, she was really nice. She was. She was saying, 'Okay, now just take a breath 'n swallow it, an' then another, then let them both out, feel them both going out. You're going to be better, okay? 'N do it again - feel that? And here, here - take my hand. You're going to be okay, right?' Like squeezing my hand, see! *No, no,* listen to me. This is the part that makes it really interesting. No, *goddamn it,* he *didn't!* No one *did!* I already told you that! And her, this is when she says, *'Who was it?' "Who was it?"* I go, and that's when I realized *they didn*'t *know! They didn't have a clue!* 'Who was *what?*' I say. 'The *shooter?*' she says. 'N I tell her, I say, 'How do I know *who it was?* I couldn't tell *who it was!*' 'N that's when I felt myself, and I was *just soakers*, Sis, I mean *soakers!*

TERI

You told him that? Why am I not surprised? Of course he'd believe that! Every man I know would like to think that! Really! An' better than Car's? What you mean is you told him you *like his* better than Car's, right? *'Like,'* right? No, no, I definitely do not wanna know what Johnny's is – of course he loved being told that! Of course! That was really smart. Who cares if it's true or not? Ha, ha, ha, ha. Hey, you've slobbered all over this thing. What'd you do, lick on it before you inhaled? This's disgusting. I'm not putting that in my mouth. When're you gonna learn how to roll these things? Here, take it back. Don't look at me like that. Whatta you gonna wear? No, no; not that top! It's too damn tight. You're already starting to show. You wanna show? I don't think so. Here, take the light blue one. It's got more of a flair. You look great in that. Here, put it on…

JOANN

Johnny, tell me what to do. I'm supposed to go to Planned Parenthood next Wednesday but I haven't heard from you and since I can't see you I don't know what to do. Sometimes I think I won't go. Is that good? Today out at the Swap Meet I saw this bitchin girl with WILD tatted across the back of one knee, CHILD tatted across the back of the other. She had really nice legs. A lot of guys were cruising her. Right now I'm thinking I'm going to go. Please tell me...Kiss U, Panda. Did you get the money I sent you? I pigged out and ate a whole chocolate cake last night. Guess why.

JOHNNY

Ziggy, man, Jesus Christ! Look at you! You put on all that muscle, man! Lookin' like ol' Arnold! You still doin' them calls? Yeah? Give me a call, man! One a' them rooster ones, them cock a doddle do ones. Yeah, that's it! That's fuckin' bitchin', man! Wow! Gimme another...

JACKIE

That big roach coach over there alongside the fence. Over by the buses? The one that says Dogtown Dogs on it? Get me and your aunt ginger ales, your brother a Coke, 'n one for yourself. We'll be right here in line. Here's three dollars. Here, lemme brush your hair, ...there... okay... now hurry up... and be careful of the cars, okay? Some of them are coming in way too fast. John-John, no, no, you're staying right here. No, Dawnie, wait. Here... once more... there...you look real pretty now. Go on, an' hurry yourself up. We'll be right up there in the shade under the walkway. No, wait a minute, John-John. What did I say? Dawnie, wait a sec! Aunt Ter will do it. She's not going in with us. If we get called we'll have to go in and if you're not here they won't let us in. Dawnie Gwen? Did you hear me? Dawnie! God damn it, Dawnie; come back here right this very instant!... Dawnie!... Oh, shit... Ter, here, here; take John-John. I've gotta go get her...

JACKIE

I'm just remembering this. We were riding in his truck and he was going real fast and I was stoned and thinking about us going head on into other cars and told him to slow down and he said, 'Bullshit,' he wasn't going to let my fears control his behavior. No one had ever talked to me like that. It really made sense. I was just ready for him. And the funny thing was I'd made this date with this other guy for the same night, some guy I didn't even know that I'd seen in the arcade that had stared and stared and stared at me before he even said anything to me, which scared the crap outa me, but really excited me, too, and only at the very last minute did I decide to not go, and keep my date with John. That was that afternoon in Venice where we rented roller skates and had that good Peruvian flake and got high sitting on the trash cans and talking with all the alkies and the guys spearing trash that were doing community service and John said the only good thing he saw in that was that you got to work outside. The ocean was real sparkly that day, and we held hands skating along...

CHAPTER 30

8 BLOCK, LEVEL 4

JOHNNY

Jesus Christ, Jac, I'm feeling fine now. My mind is perfectly clear and I still love you more than ever. When I got out of the lock and up into the walls I was thinking about how much Dawnie looks like Dad. It stunned me, knowing with him no longer here it makes it clear to be completely honest and straight ahead with everyone is the only way to go, especially with the kids. I remember once not going home just so I wouldn't have to answer him about where I'd been. But I got hungry so I went home and had to lie so I wouldn't get a beating. Then I got a beating anyway for lying. The point is, that's what I've been realizing here, not to do things I shouldn't do, and let anger control my thinking when I don't get my way when I do do them. You know me, how things happen cause it's myself I'm angry at, and not anyone else. Like Rube says – when I said, 'Shit happens,' – he says, 'Right, specially when yus got shitheads running it.' That's what I'm just now realizing. And I'm gonna turn all that sorry shit around. If I ever start hassling you and carrying on again, all you'll ever have to do is show me this goddamn letter right here, with my personal promise of NEVER AGAIN.

JACKIE

John-John, put your seat belt back on. Dawnie, help him with his belt. I don't know why your Daddy said that. He doesn't know that yet. Leave the cigarette lighter alone! John-John, stop it! Yes, but maybe not real soon. I'll tell you as soon as I know. John-John, get back in your seat. I've got a Sugar Daddy lolly here. Get back in your seat so I can give it to you. You want me to stop the car? I'll stop it. Okay, good; here. That's it. Now help him get the wrapper off. No, Dawnie, you do it. Yeah, I've got one for you, too.

I don't know why the wrapper's yellow. That's just the way it is. No, I didn't leave him one. We'll just have to send him some. Maybe even a whole box, okay? You think he'd like that?

JOHNNY

Chingado; gimme a break! How many of them cans of prunes did you get? Three? They count those, man. Sure they do. It'll come back on you. 'Cause I used to work in the kitchen. It sure as hell will. You can't talk yourself outa that. Just don't say nothing. Or tell 'em I took 'em 'n ate 'em. Yeah, that'd be better. Lay it on me. They already think I'm crazy, so that'd make sense. 'Cause they saw me back in there. Sittin' on the crapper, okay? Where else? How many of 'em you got left? You take 'em all. Yeah, all of 'em. 'Cause I'm not gonna need 'em, amigo, all right? You know they moved me outa here, right? Down into laundry. So don't tell 'em until I clear, right? Now don't say I never done nothing for you, okay? Right? Okay, then...

RUBEN

Two stabs back here, 'n one throughs the palm of my hand, sliced this flap of skin here; see thes'? No, like a toothbrush handle. Yo, sharpened plastic ones. Left 'em on the floor. Three vatos, man; not jus' two. Gots me right through both blankets...naw... naw... 'Then what happened?' Yus means 'fore I gots busted back here? That? Hokay. Wha' happens, Ese', wus I wus comin' outa my room and thes' two peegs saw me eatin' in Babita an' starts followin' me. When they comes after me I threw the room key down the street. They spread me 'n called a backup, 'n they searched the street but didn't find it. Alls they could book me for wus intoxication. All the cargo wus in the room. They didn't know wha' hotel. That wus cool. Then them pinche veteranos from up north, yo, Julio, he wants it all, man, you know those mo'fuckers, 'n this vato, he gets me in the car, *my* car, an' pulls thes' cuete on me, 'n I ses, 'Hokay, man, go aheads 'n do it, but if I go I'm not letting go of thes' wheel, cus the first thing I'm gonna do es jerk thes' whole cocksuck ta the left, 'n firing that fucker won't change that ans yus 'n me es both gonna go.' We wus doin' about eighty, eighty-five, see, 'n I ses, 'As a matter a' facts I'm gonna do it anyways so yus mights as well pull the trigger,' 'n I rips the wheel reals hard 'n hits into the divider 'n he lost his shit when we slammed 'n I gots the gun…toss me down tha' Motrin, Ese'. I don't wanna get outa bed right now… yus wanna use my hype, it's in the drawer there…

JOHN-JOHN

What's a PlayStation? Daddy said he would get me a PlayStation. He said he'd make a phone call and someone would bring it to me. Can I have one?

JOANN

Dear Di, I wrote this to Johnny but can't decide whether to send it or not. Dear Johnny, I think you are being mean to me. The phone doesn't ring. When it does it isn't you. In a way I'm glad. I don't like ending up crying all the time. Cheryl Beth is back with Anthony. He came back on his knees. He told her theirs was a love that was forever. He got a red and blue bracelet of baby hearts tatted around his wrist for her. When they left we all were glad because the baby was so miserable all the time and wouldn't stop crying no matter what anyone would do. And it wasn't just crying, but screaming these really shrill, razory shrieks, like something was cutting into it all the time. Nothing would comfort it. This was night after night. Cheryl Beth took it to her Pedie, but that didn't help. Mom and my Grandma said, Well, it was just a bad baby. I'm not so sure I want a baby. Maybe you aren't coming back for a long time. Tell me that isn't so. And you are being mean to me. Right now I feel like a bag of dirt...

JACKIE

You're sayin' that Jamal hasn't hit on you yet? Gare… yes... but you don't expect me to believe that? 'Cause I already know! Of course he has! Well, he does own a piece of the club, too, so why wouldn't he? 'N he's got that certain thing, too. Well, that he can get right down into it. Not just the dirty, okay, but like if you're not living down into your real life, that's all I'm saying, then maybe you do need someone like that for a while, okay? It's no big thing. You think he's the daddy?

RUBEN

Dos? Dos? Marries both of 'em, 'Ese. Sees which ones sticks when yus riding out yus bit, hokay? Tha's the one... like doubling downs in Blackjack, 'Ese. You draws dos Queens, but you don't knows whats the flop cards'll be yets. That's alls I'm sayin'. Havin' dos'll makes it claro which ones es *the* one, when everythings been dealt, hokay?

JACKIE

Jeeeeez, Ter-Ter, you don't look so good. Oh, my God... hold on ... hold on... I'm pulling the car over... Dawnie, keep your belt on... here, Ter, here...

JOHNNY

It's these goddamn dryers. You ever notice how frickin' depressing it is working around these? I think it's all the electricity bouncing off the glass 'n metal 'n concrete, 'n shit. All that ringing inside your ears? Makes your fuckin' head hurt, right? Isn't that right? Well, try tellin' that to the squeezer – what's he say? Something about negative ions, positive ions, the electrical charge that comes off the dryers. Don't know what the fuck he's talkin' about, the core spinning in there behind the glass; just like his fuckin' brain inside his ol' brain pan, right? Ha, ha, ha. Man, phew; you know what you don't know? How heavy wet laundry is the first time you lift it out. You get strong as shit working down here. Just leave the rest 'a them sheets and towels in the trolleys. The morning crew 'll get 'em. Hand me that clipboard; I'll fill the totals out...No, no, I've got a hearing coming up in a coupl'a months...fuck...hey, you gotta get the dude on your side. Like jus' really listen to him, Bro.

Say things like, 'Right, right, I never thought of that; that really makes sense; explain that to me again, okay?' No, it works. It does. That's the only way...

JACKIE

Heartman, Heartman, it's so damn hot right now, like that night, remember, when it was so hot, 98 degrees at nine o'clock, the air like insects crawling all over your skin, and we were coming down from San Marcos Pass in our old truck and you said I had the best ears in the world cause you said they were so small and only heard the good in what people were saying? Well, it's a night like that. The air is so heavy it feels like it's smothering you. I don't know why, but this kind of weather always makes me real horny. There are these real big dark and full clouds coming in so it might rain. All I want to do is not to go to sleep but slip my nightie off, which I am doing, remember that in the truck? See what I mean? My hand going down there? I'll bet you do. Dawnie was in for some real heartbreak yesterday and it really pisses me off. Why is it the only people that can hurt you are people you like? We met some new people here and yesterday their little boy had a birthday party and I thought the boy liked Dawnie but she wasn't invited to his party and today she is still very hurt and upset and I don't blame her. I've been very open to these people and was really starting to like them. From what we'd been talking about I thought we had a lot in common and that they liked us, but I guess not. John-John didn't care, so that was good. Doctor Garland took a look at the baby today on a sonogram and I don't know if I should tell you now or let it be a surprise, but Ter was there and we both were looking, and she said, He looks exactly like Johnny, and I said, You can't tell that, he's way too tiny, and she said, Oh, yes I can, and Garland said, It's a little too early to tell anything except that he's a he, but everything looks right on schedule, and Ter said, I'm not talking about his little thing-ee, (which we could see) but the shape of his little head, that it's exactly the same size to the body that Johnny's head is. Ter always surprises me with how she thinks, so I wasn't that surprised either. So there you are – I've gone and said it. We are having another kid, one that looks exactly like you. What do you think about that? Maybe it won't look exactly like you, but maybe it will. I think it will. I'm just lying on the bed now with all the windows open and I'm outside the sheets, running my hands all over the bump, and I'm burning up and wish the rain would start. Oh, I forgot to tell you this. Mom said she would get us a new stove and dishwasher when she gets better. Her leg is numb from the knee down, veins plugged up again, has a large aneuryism (I don't know how to spell it) and her doctor wants to cut it out before it bursts. She said she'd rather die than have her leg cut off, so we came home while she decides what to do, even though her doctor said he wasn't talking about cutting her leg off. But you know how she is when she gets something in her head. Said this Warren guy won't marry her if she only has one leg. Well, what can you say to that? We really had to laugh. Ter said in that case she'd amputate it for her. That made her even madder. Mom's doctor is real nice to her just like mine is to me. Wish you were here. I am turning the light out now. I'll finish this later, I will, I... I... I... you...

JOHNNY

Jackie, Jac, Jac, Jac, I'm still feeling pretty damn good right now and want you to be, too. Ol' Rube is snoring like a freight going off a' the tracks, trying to get enough air into his honker. I'm waking him up all the time to keep him breathing. It really pisses him off. He always says he's not snoring. Also, to cut the noise way down. It's another real hot night here, too, and while I'm cutting down on my smoking, right now I'm tapping the tobacco down tight, sitting back on my bunk striking these matches, and when one flares, just before I bring it up to my lips, I see your eyes in the flame and that sweet little upper curl of your lips. There are so many things I'd like to do to you and with you and you know what I mean, Flower, you do, cause we always have and always will, like that one time I was getting started and was whipping on it and you walked in and said, "Hey, wait for me! Wait for me!" Remember that? "Hey, wait for me!" When you was pregnant with Dawnie and your boobs were so damn great? I can still taste that coppery taste. All's I've ever wanted was to be inside you, and not just bumping uglies, and you know it, too, something that's always stayed with me, something I'm always telling you, along with other things we do I shouldn't even be thinking about, but all that's what keeps me going, and you know why it does, you really do, and that's what will keep me going out there, too. On that front I'm already working on a few things, including bringing charges against the Ventura Sheriff's Department. The legal aid worker I was telling you about? The trip with her is not to promise to do what she says, then to do it, and that gets her excited, thinking she's getting somewheres and starts working harder on your case. She thinks I have a case, too. And thanks for the new pics. I've taped them over the sink. The one of Dawnie with her two front teeth missing makes her look real fierce, like a cute li'l old bulldog pup. Two things that bother me, though. You said you didn't know exactly when you could return again in that you were working two shifts at the club and hardly had any time because we needed the money. You know I'm trying to get things turned around here. The other thing is I don't want to think of you in bed with anyone else. Thinking that makes me sick. Thinking about any of that makes me sick. Remember me finding those torn up panties of yours, the black ones, all wadded up and buried in the bottom of the kitchen trashcan with them dried white crusts in the crotch when I got back from L. A. that time, and all that trouble started, and I guess that's all I got to say for right now except to tell Eddie to get fucked if you see him, which I hope you don't. Stay the hell away from him – he's bad news. And don't accept no money or product from him. We'll figure something else out. I hate for you to have to go back on AFDC, too, but if you have to with a new kid coming you'll have more money until I get back out. So that's okay, I'm okay with all that, 'n I've been pondering on it, and another boy is good, but if either Teri or the Doc is wrong, I'm okay with that, too, cause it is what it's gonna be, and I'm okay with all of it, cause it all just goes along how it wants to and either you go along or you don't, but if you don't, it doesn't care about that at all and goes on without you, so you might as well go along so you won't be the fool lying alone in your empty bed saying, "What the fuck, man?" 'N hear yourself answering, "Hey, fool, it's way past that, man. You just totally blew it." You know that's not me no more, not how I am no more, so I'm totally looking forward to this one and will be on my best behavior, 'n make everything absolutely correcto this time, you can count on that. As for money, I'm working on a few things in here to help with that. I told John-John I'd get him a PlayStation. Rube's got a crew that's got a truckload full. One of them'll bring about ten of 'em to you. They'll be coming the week after next. Also give Dawnie one if she wants, and take the others and sell them for yourself, 'n just remember what I'm saying to you, it's totally true, I love you, I do, and always will, cross my heart a hundred times and a hundred times more and hope to die if that's a lie. I'll be able to call on Thurs to find out when you are coming back up. Want you to know I'm just not blowing smoke rings. Someone's up running water somewheres down in the block. You can hear it trickling like a stuck toilet somewheres. Time to wrap this up for now...

Love You,

Love You,

Love You,

JOHNNY

BIOGRAPHY

The author of four books of short stories, Dale Herd's experience as an itinerant laborer working out of casual labor halls across America has informed his writing. He currently lives in Los Angeles with his wife. They have three sons.

COLOPHON

Design Hans van der Kooi (8-13.nl)

Text is set in Caslon Pro and The Sun

Photo cover Dale Herd

Photo author Deborah Blum